THE ONLY GENUI[

Alex Roddie is a writer of historical and studying Computing Science at the Universi[escaped to the hills and worked at the Clach. and 2011. He climbed extensively and never stopped writing about his adventures. After founding the popular winter climbing blog, *Glencoe Mountaineer*, he began working on this novel—a process aided by his practical research into Victorian winter climbing equipment and techniques. He now lives in Lincolnshire with his partner Hannah.

Praise for *The Only Genuine Jones:*

"This is extraordinarily accomplished storytelling - tense, taut and deeply atmospheric ... The thrill of climbing is tangible, as is the sense of human frailty. This is an adventure story, a love story, a historical fantasy—but above all, this is a book in praise of the awesomeness of Nature and the men who risked their lives to be amongst it. Their astonishing feats are worthy of such a novel as *The Only Genuine Jones.* I am not a climber, yet the writing is such that I felt like I was with Jones, as he climbed into the snowy heights ... A must-read for anyone who for whom the great outdoors—and great writing—has a strong allure."

Susan Fletcher, award-winning author
of *Corrag, The Silver Dark Sea*, and others

"... very well crafted with a plot that hung together well and strong characters that pulled things along nicely ... The whole alternative reality idea worked well for me."

Chris Highcock, author of *Hillfit:
Fitness training for hiking, backpacking and hillwalking*

"The book has a number of strengths and I particularly enjoyed the brisk plot, the cast of historical characters and the fascinating, flawed hero, O.G. Jones. Anyone with even a passing interest in the history of British mountaineering will recognise the names Collie, Raeburn and Crowley to name but three. The settings too will be familiar to anyone with a love of the mountains: the Clachaig in Glencoe and Wastdale Head in the Lake District being popular places in mountain lore then and now."

Nick Bramhall, outdoor blogger

BY THE SAME AUTHOR

CROWLEY'S RIVAL

To David

from

Alex Roddie.

THE ONLY GENUINE JONES

ALEX RODDIE

www.alexroddie.com

Published in 2013 by FeedARead Publishing
www.feedaread.com

Paperback Edition

Cover design and montage by John Amy, www.ebookdesigner.co.uk
Ice axe original photo courtesy of Monte Dodge

British Library CIP

A CIP catalogue record for this title is available from the British Library

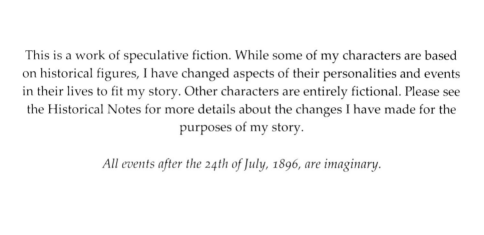

This is a work of speculative fiction. While some of my characters are based on historical figures, I have changed aspects of their personalities and events in their lives to fit my story. Other characters are entirely fictional. Please see the Historical Notes for more details about the changes I have made for the purposes of my story.

All events after the 24th of July, 1896, are imaginary.

Contents

"The Birth of a New Age"

How to Survive an Avalanche

24th of July, 1896

SIMON BARKIS KNEW that he could not climb for much longer. He had not eaten or slept for over a day, and his body, although young and fit, wanted to give up. Dry clothes, warmth, rest: these things had been sacrificed, left at the foot of the north face, and not for the first time he wondered if the prize would be worth the pain.

Mountaineering had become warfare. The Matterhorn launched volley after volley of artillery to defend its upper citadel. The beautiful sport had been reduced to a game of chance in which the winner gained nothing tangible, and the loser would never climb again. What sane man would play such a game?

A rope's length above on melting ice, Holdstock battled for the summit. Barkis paid out the rope over his shoulder although he knew that if his partner fell they would both die. Looking down, the Matterhorn's north wall fell away between his legs: six thousand feet of ice and rock, a meaningless chunk of Swiss geography that a few men would die to conquer.

Stones bounced past, released from deep freeze by the heat of the sun. Barkis imagined what might happen if one hit him. He would fall from the ice where he clung, supported only by a few strands of cord and some metal spikes. He might even enjoy his plunge through sunlight until the first bounce. Would it hurt? Would he survive the impact, or would he burst in a red spray on the snow?

He shook himself and tried not to indulge these morbid fantasies. Their rival, Aleister Crowley, couldn't be far behind. It would be a shame for him to beat them so close to the top. Risking a look to his right, Barkis glimpsed a solitary figure climbing rapidly with a single ice axe, unfettered by ropes and equipment, blessed with more skill and confidence than either of his rivals.

A shout from Holdstock: 'I can see the cornice! We're almost at the top!'

Then the sky exploded.

Holdstock vanished in a wave of snow. At first Barkis felt disoriented by the scale of the avalanche, until he felt the blast of air and realised what had happened. The full width of the face had gone! With only seconds left, Barkis took in the rope and made it fast. He tried to calculate whether he had enough time to place his ice axes more securely. As he wriggled his right axe free and slammed it into the ice, his mind permitted only one emotion: panic. He could feel every heartbeat, every exquisite sensation of fatigue and cold and pain, as if his body strove to experience as much as possible in those final moments before destruction.

The wall of snow hit. He felt his claw points blow out of the ice under the pressure, and his feet cut loose. All he could do was hold on until the torture became too great to bear. Already he could imagine the long plunge to oblivion, and an icy grave in a crevasse far below.

Finally the pain came to an end. Tongues of spindrift hissed down the scoured cliffs. Below, the destruction swept the wall until it spent its fury on the distant glacier. He was alive, and after receiving an answering call from Holdstock, Barkis realised how lucky they had been. The Matterhorn had played its last card and failed to kill them.

Aleister Crowley had not been so fortunate. No sign of him remained. Barkis felt elated for a second when he realised that nothing could now prevent their victory, then guilt took over. Had the mountain made him this callous, he wondered, or was it a consequence of the game they played? Could he really be so unfeeling about the death of someone he had once called a friend—someone who had sat with him in lectures at Trinity, scrambled with him over the rooftops of the college to escape from the Proctors? Crowley was only twenty-one.

Barkis took off his hat and gazed into the void. You were the best of all of us, Crowley, even though you took a different path in the end.

'Crowley's gone,' he shouted up at Holdstock.

'There's nothing we can do. We're a rope's length from the top! I'm climbing on.'

A rope's length from victory, and the birth of a new age for their noble sport. Everything would be different from today.

PART ONE

THE NEW MOUNTAINEER

"JONES FELT VERY SMALL"

CHAPTER ONE

Hogmanay Hoolie

31st of December, 1896

'JONES? I HEARD he got thrown out of the Wastwater Hotel at Christmas.' The coach rumbled over a pothole in the road, and Owen Glynne Jones woke with a start, wondering who had mentioned his name. He did not know his travelling companions. They were Scottish mountaineers, hard men who took their climbing seriously. He had not introduced himself; the days when the name of O.G. Jones inspired respect and admiration were long past.

A gust of wind battered the side of the carriage. The driver cursed the road and the weather, and the occupants of the Glen Coe coach grinned nervously to each other in the darkness. Jones remained slouched in his corner, pretending to be asleep. He felt exhausted after ten hours of travel up from the Lake District.

'Aye well, Jones may be a good climber, but he causes trouble.'

'I hope he never brings his unsportsmanlike practices to our mountains. I heard he practised a hard climb fifteen times with a safety rope before claiming the first ascent!'

Jones had heard it all before. Why were some climbers so conservative? He believed in challenging the tired old traditions, striving for something better, yet he had been rewarded with disgrace.

'I'd like to see him try that trick on Tower Ridge,' the first Scot said with a chuckle, and his companions laughed.

Jones sat upright and opened his eyes, no longer able to ignore the insult.

'May I have your name, sir?'

The four other occupants of the carriage looked at him in surprise. They all wore tweed jackets, too shabby for polite company but perfectly acceptable for the mountain inn at the end of their journey. A plating of driven snow over every window made the twilight seem even darker; Jones could not make out their faces.

'Harold Raeburn of Edinburgh,' the first man said in a gruff Scottish accent. 'Who might you be, laddie?'

'Owen Glynne Jones, of London.'

Awkward silence.

'Well, well,' the second gossip said. 'We are in exalted company!'

Jones did not like his sarcasm, but he resisted the urge to retaliate; he would be spending New Year with these gentlemen. His unhappy Christmas at Wastdale Head proved that disharmony in a gathering of climbers had a way of poisoning everything. Perhaps it was time he started building bridges instead of burning them.

'Mr Raeburn, it is a great honour to meet you. I've heard a great deal about your exploits.'

'Likewise.'

The second man laughed at that remark, and Jones felt his heart sink. After the unpleasantness last summer, he no longer felt welcome climbing in Snowdonia. Even a lot of his old friends in the Lake District disapproved of his methods. Surely he would not find the same attitude in Scotland?

Raeburn stared at him for a moment, as if trying to make up his mind whether to accept the offer of friendship. Then he smiled.

'Sassenach you may be, but I'll not have any visitor to Glen Coe feel unwelcome. We're all climbers here.'

'Thank you. Perhaps we'll share a rope tomorrow.'

Raeburn didn't reply to that, and Jones thought maybe the famous Scottish ice climber felt uncomfortable accepting the offer in the present company. Jones had heard about him through the pages of the Scottish Mountaineering Club's journal: he had a reputation as a progressive man, not unlike Jones himself, and relished difficult climbing.

He peered through the window but could make out little through the ice. Presently, beyond a curve in the road and an uphill stretch, the carriage finally creaked to a halt. Nobody ventured to open the door and let in the weather. So much for the tough Scottish climbers, Jones thought.

The coachman opened the door himself. Snow blasted in, and in the gale Jones caught the heady scents of moor and mountain, peat and wood smoke, and the freshest air he had ever breathed. The Clachaig Inn stood isolated in the western reaches of Glen Coe, a lonely hostelry beloved of poets and mountaineers. In the darkness, Jones could see little of this famous place. The coach lamps cast twin cones of light upon a megalithic wall, drifted deep in snow, and windows glowed with the warmth of fire and companionship. He looked up into the sky and could see nothing but whirling snowflakes. The cold thrilled him, and all at once he felt a rush of gratitude that he was able to escape his dull routine in London and come to places like this, where life felt more real and legends were made.

Snow was already drifting over the pile of luggage that the coachman had dumped in the yard. Jones found his knapsack and ice axe, and, without waiting for the others, made for the front door of the hotel. He pulled it open. Heat, laughter, tobacco smoke, the malty smell of beer: all of these familiar things burst through the doorway, raising his spirits. His spectacles fogged up with the sudden warmth.

After leaving his axe in the lobby with a dozen others, he stepped into the public bar. Bare floorboards bore the marks of decades of nailed boots; no carpet would last long in this room. A cheerful fire crackled away in the grate, belching out both heat and soot in equal measure. Damp boots basked in the glow. The bar consisted merely of an open hatch next to the pantry doorway, where the barman topped up glasses from an ale jug; looking into the pantry, Jones could see iron-hooped beer barrels and the glassy sheen of bottled whisky. The Clachaig felt spartan compared to the mountain inns of England and Wales.

Conversation flowed in the bar, and the main subject seemed to be the passion that united them all: mountaineering.

'I believe the central buttress might go.'

'With this snowfall? I doubt it.'

'How about a jaunt over to Stob Ban?'

Jones noticed a gentleman leaning against the wall near the pantry doorway. Dressed in grey tweeds, pipe clenched between his teeth and whisky glass in hand, the thin man looked utterly relaxed and happy with the world, beaming at nothing in particular. Jones recognised his old friend Professor Norman Collie, and at once strode over to greet him. They clasped hands.

'It's good to see you again, Professor!'

'You made it! I confess I had my doubts whether the coach would ever get here in this blizzard. Welcome to our promised land!'

Jones was happy to see his old friend. They had been through a lot together, and although he had never told the older man, he admired Collie more than anyone. He guessed that the two of them were the only Englishmen present.

The door banged, and the Scottish climbers stomped in out of the storm. A cheer rose from the customers already in the bar. It seemed an SMC meet was in progress; the barman soon found himself confronted with a mob of thirsty men demanding drinks. Raeburn nodded at Jones and Collie.

'I'm not sure Raeburn approves of my presence here,' Jones remarked. 'The others certainly don't.'

Collie gave a patient smile. 'My dear friend, nobody holds you in higher esteem than I, but you must learn to swallow your pride every once in a while. If you want your reputation to recover, you must nurture it.'

Jones meditated on that advice for a moment, and reflected that his own gusto in countering the attacks on his character had contributed to his downfall. His impetuous streak had got him in trouble yet again.

'I feel like I have ruined things, and all because I choose to climb in ways others consider cheating. I wish I was more like you.'

'I'm better at listening than you are,' Collie said drily. 'No, perhaps that is unfair. Look here, you need a dram.'

Collie stood by the side of the queue and chatted with Raeburn for a few moments. The barman passed a jug of ale to Raeburn, then ignored the next man and served Collie first, pouring a generous measure of whisky into a new tumbler. Collie passed the glass to Jones. Just how did the Professor make everyone love him, he wondered? He was a Londoner like Jones, yet he climbed all over Britain—and the rest of the world, for that matter—and found a home wherever he went. Snowdonia, Wastdale Head, and Glen Coe all regarded him as one of their special patrons.

They stood in companionable silence for a moment. Jones took a sip of his dram. The flavour of the local malt, a mouthful of smouldering peat, evoked memories of long days and hard climbs. He felt his worries begin to fade.

'Sorry for bringing my troubles on holiday with me,' Jones said after a minute or two.

'Feeling better?' Collie clapped him on the back. 'Let's mingle a little. Have you met Simon Barkis?'

The hero of the Matterhorn appeared to be well on the way towards drunkenness. Huddled next to the fire and nursing a pint glass, the young man was singing to himself and leaning dangerously far back on his chair. Jones had known him for about a year. They first met in the Lake District and had climbed together several times. Despite being only twenty and a rather inexperienced climber, Barkis had talent and together with Thomas Holdstock had made the controversial first ascent of the Matterhorn's north face last summer. Jones admired his progressive ideas and the contraptions he and his friends invented to make climbing easier. In addition, Barkis had defended Jones in the unpleasantness over the summer, and for that he would always regard the lad as a friend.

'Hopkinson, get me another drink!' he shouted at them, then looked surprised to see that the newcomers were not, in fact, Hopkinson.

'Jones! Good heavens, how do you do?'

Jones sat down opposite him and raised his hands to the fire. 'All the better for being here! I don't think I ever congratulated you on the Matterhorn business. You've inspired a lot of climbers, even if you put a few noses out of joint in the process.'

Barkis smiled awkwardly, and glanced at Professor Collie. 'You ought to congratulate Holdstock. He did most of the work.'

'Don't be modest, my boy,' Collie said, laying a hand on his shoulder. 'This is Barkis' first visit to Scotland. We are all expecting great things from him.'

'I for one intend to be utterly hungover tomorrow morning,' Barkis declared, then downed his pint. 'An easy walk in the snow will be about the most I can manage.'

A bell sounded. Heads turned, and the barman coughed to ensure he had everyone's attention.

In the excitement of re-introductions, Jones had forgotten that the birth of a new year was fast approaching. He raised his tumbler to propose a toast.

'My friends—a toast to the old year, and to eighteen ninety-seven! May it bring peace and happiness for us all.'

Even though many of the men present had no reason to like Jones, and indeed many probably mistrusted him, everyone stood and raised their glasses with a cheer. Their voices, as one, rang with friendship and hope for the future.

The lobby door banged again, wind gusted into the bar, and a newcomer walked in without removing his coat. Jones turned to greet him, face flushed with warmth.

'Friend, will you join us in toasting the new year? I'll buy you a drink.'

It took only a moment to sense that something was wrong.

The stranger removed his hood and turned to look at the group. Intense blue eyes studied them with an expression of cynical disregard. His face was youthful, beautiful; Jones recognised him instantly. He had seen that arresting gaze before, knew that mop of black hair, that petulant set of jaw.

Without uttering a word, Aleister Crowley turned on his heel and left the bar at speed.

*

Jones sat back down, feeling shocked. Nobody spoke. Could it really have been Crowley himself?

He glanced at Simon Barkis, who had far more reason to be afraid of Crowley than Jones did. The enmity ran deep there. Between Jones and

Crowley there had been a respectful rivalry, but between Crowley and Barkis there had been a struggle for life itself.

'Crowley is dead,' Barkis said in a low voice, face suddenly pale. 'I saw the avalanche take him. I recovered his broken axe from the glacier four thousand feet below the summit. Damn it, I attended his funeral!'

Raeburn walked over, pint in hand, and leaned against the wall next to the fire. 'People do survive avalanches. I have seen a huge avalanche on Ben Nevis take a roped team of five, all of whom survived.'

Barkis shook his head. 'There is a great difference between a slide on the Ben and the catastrophe that shook the entire Matterhorn that day.'

Raeburn seemed taken aback by his tone of authority. Perhaps he had not expected to be challenged by a youth. Barkis remained full of energy and enthusiasm, a little innocent at times perhaps, but he had grown up over the course of the last summer; he carried himself with greater maturity and confidence, and at times a haunted look crossed his face, as if reliving the moment when the avalanche hit. Jones had never spoken to him about it. The moment when a climber comes to within an inch of his death is a profoundly personal thing.

As if sensing the uncomfortable atmosphere, Collie cleared his throat. 'We are all tired after our journeys, and if we are to climb tomorrow we had better get some sleep. Shall we meet at half past five, gentlemen?'

Barkis groaned, and Raeburn laughed.

'Aye, half past five will be grand. I would like to climb with Jones, and Barkis too, if he is sober enough.'

Collie looked pleased. 'You shall make a strong team, perhaps the strongest that has ever met in this valley. I don't think I could keep up with you. I'll go for a wander along the Aonach Eagach instead.'

They said good night and tramped up to their rooms, but Jones felt that 1897 had already been blighted by an unhappy omen.

*

The blizzard exhausted itself long before dawn. Jones awoke to find the moon smiling down upon a landscape of breathtaking beauty and stillness. After breakfasting with the others, he set out in the company of Harold Raeburn and Simon Barkis, who lagged some distance behind, complaining of a headache. Raeburn set a brutal pace despite the lad's suffering.

After the flat approach along the road, they spent an hour toiling uphill through deep snow. Raeburn took the lead, forcing a trench through the drifts, and finally they broke out into the upper bowl of Coire nan Lochan — a place of such silence that Jones could hear his own heart beating. The sky blushed pink in the east, over the shoulder of Gearr Aonach. Stars burned steady out of the cold depths. This felt like a primal place where humans were not welcome; it belonged to atoms and frost, the slow turn of the heavens, and the ravages of geological time. These mountains could remember volcanoes and glaciers. Jones felt very small, and although he preferred to look on mountains as gymnastic challenges to be overcome, he understood why some chose to make a religion out of climbing. All his earthly concerns were insignificant compared to this timeless landscape.

They paused to let their breath catch up with them, and to contemplate the beauty of their surroundings.

Jones looked down the deep glen up which they had climbed. A V-groove between two ridges framed one of the peaks of the Aonach Eagach, where Collie was climbing up to the ridge at this moment. As they watched, a spark of dawn fire danced on the summit. It blazed there, hovering, for one magical second; then the fire grew and flashed out like a lighthouse across the glen. Behind, the cliffs of Stob Coire nan Lochan changed in an instant, from a dark place to one of delicate radiance: a watercolour painted with one massive brushstroke. Hard cascades glinted within the gullies that seamed the cliffs.

Raeburn nodded in satisfaction. 'It is almost always worth it.'

Barkis seemed overcome by the beauty all around them, his hangover temporarily forgotten. 'We are in the Alps, surely? But when were the Alps as beautiful as this?'

Jones felt impatient to be climbing. 'Raeburn, you're the native. What shall we do?'

Raeburn pointed with his axe. 'That broad gully over there is the usual steep way up, but it's hardly worthy of our attention. Little real climbing has been done here.'

Jones thought the gully looked straightforward enough, but dangerous with its load of soft snow. His attention wandered to the other couloirs. Two of them caught his attention, narrow clefts dividing the impossible buttresses. Lips of overhanging snow capped each one: cornices which must have built up overnight in the strong winds.

Raeburn followed his gaze. 'Good man. Those two central gullies have never been climbed, but plenty of folk have looked. I call them South-Central and North-Central. South-Central is rather the steeper and icier.'

'Then let us prospect that,' Barkis interrupted. 'I don't want to be climbing on accumulated fresh stuff. One avalanche is quite enough for me.'

'What about the cornice?' Jones asked.

Raeburn shrugged. 'There ought to be a way around. I say we go for it. Someone else will only come along and claim the first ascent if we leave it for another day.'

His competitive attitude appealed to Jones, who had fought vicious arguments over the rights to a first ascent before. As they kicked up the steep snow in the direction of their gully, Jones noticed a fresh track traversing the cliffs some distance to the left. He feared he knew who had made those tracks, but did not mention his concern to the others.

*

'Safe, Jones! Climb when you are ready!'

At Raeburn's signal, Jones moved quickly. His tiny stance, hacked from ice the colour and texture of white marble, cramped his feet and chilled his fingers where they clung to a notch above his head to maintain balance.

Beside him, Barkis grinned through the narrow opening of his balaclava. The blades of his axes were buried deep in the ice, and Barkis had tied himself to them with lengths of rope, from which he rested in comfort. In addition to negating the need to chop steps, those novel ice axes had the fortuitous effect of forming the perfect anchor for the whole party.

Holdstock and Barkis had used this revolutionary equipment to conquer their north face. The tools were, in fact, unlike anything Jones had ever used. No longer than a man's forearm, they sported deeply curved, serrated picks that bit into the ice instead of hacking chunks away like the tools commonly used by mountaineers. Jones wondered if his detractors would consider the use of such axes cheating; most probably, he guessed. Well, the winds of progress were strengthening.

The pitch of ice ahead appeared to be the steepest on the climb. A traverse out right led to a daunting bulge some twelve feet high. Raeburn's lead up this obstacle, cutting steps with two-handed swings from his heavy axe, had been inspiring to behold. He balanced on the steep ice with nothing but the nails in his soles for grip. Barkis, with his new equipment, enjoyed the extra security of metal ice claws specially made for climbing this sort of terrain.

Jones climbed a few feet of soft snow before reaching scoured ice once more. Behind, Barkis paid the rope out over his shoulder. The steps provided by Raeburn were nicely angled and well-spaced, and Jones climbed with ease to the traverse. He looked out across the line of steps with relish. The moves would be highly exposed, with the full drop of the gully beneath, and the prospect of a hard swing into the far wall should a slip occur. The rope pulled him onward. He set the edge of a boot onto the ice and transferred his weight onto it.

His mind thrilled with the joy of difficult climbing. Spindrift blasted down from above, a roaring waterfall of fine snow that ran down his sleeves and collar, robbing him of warmth. Instantly, the steps vanished. He hugged the ice until the slide had stopped. Looking down, he could not see his boots, buried in a shifting pile of fine powder.

'Is all well?' Barkis called from below.

'All's well,' Jones shouted back, and after a moment, Raeburn replied likewise.

The traverse, daunting even when swept clean, would be twice as hard now that it lay under a drift. Jones retrieved his ice axe from its sling and excavated a little way ahead until he had located the first hold, then slowly stepped onto it. With his left hand he felt blindly above his head for the lip of the first handhold. There it was, at the perfect height. Raeburn, although the taller man, had thoughtfully cut his steps at just the right level for Jones.

He took a step, and another. There could be no retreat now; turning around would be difficult, even with his practiced sense of balance. Protruding rocks forced him outwards, testing his balance yet further. After more clearing, he stepped off the traverse and onto the bulge of rounded ice.

The rope from above hung straight down, and he felt happier about his situation despite the possibility that Raeburn's belay might be poor.

He couldn't see any holds. The strain built up in his calf muscles as he struggled to remain upright while he scrabbled, with increasing frustration, for the handholds. Powder sprayed down onto his face, coating his spectacles. His right leg began to shake from the exertion. At the last moment, Jones brought his axe up and swung it into the ice, where the pick held, anchoring fast. He gripped the slippery shaft but it offered little security. The rope above him suddenly fell slack.

'Raeburn, take me in tight!'

No response. 'Raeburn! Do you hear me?'

Still nothing. 'Blast,' he muttered, then looked back down towards Barkis. 'Barkis, give me some slack. And be ready; Raeburn cannot hear me.'

'Take your time, old boy.'

He grunted. Tiredness was setting in, deep within his muscles, and he did not have time to loiter on this confounded overhang. He tensed, squinted upwards, and jumped.

Both hands clutched at the ice, searching for something to grab onto. He felt a sickening lurch as he slid back and came fast against Raeburn's rope— but nothing checked the fall. Jones cried out as he fell into the chasm below.

The noise was incredible. Snow, chunks of ice, rocks, span past him everywhere; a confusion of tangled ropes and debris. Then he stopped falling with such force that the impact winded him.

He found himself upside-down, one lens of his glasses smashed, ice axe nowhere to be seen, both gloves gone. Barkis' rope held him, anchored to those novel ice axes thirty feet above; Raeburn's rope hung straight down into a cone of snow at the bottom of the gully.

'Is all well?' Barkis shouted anxiously.

'Yes,' he tried to cry, but it came out as a whisper. The rope crushed his chest like a python. He grabbed the hemp line and hauled himself upright, but it did not diminish the pain.

Barkis started to lower him in jerks and stops. After about ten feet his boots landed in the top of the avalanche-drift, and Jones was able to take pressure off the rope. He gulped down lungfuls of freezing air, thankful he could breathe again.

Then an awful thought struck him. What had become of Raeburn?

Digging furiously with hands that had begun to stiffen from cold, Jones located the second half of the rope. He pulled it through, noting the damage it had sustained during the avalanche. After shifting what seemed like a tonne of unstable snow, he finally found the end, which looked like it had been cleanly cut, no doubt by a sharp rock during the fall.

'Where is Raeburn?' he called out.

'He didn't fall past me,' Barkis replied. 'Must be still up there somewhere.'

'Damn it! See if you can make him hear you. I need to find my axe.'

While Barkis shouted, Jones dug deeper into the drift. He found a glove, frozen stiff and useless. Then, after some minutes, his fingers touched the splintered end of an axe shaft.

After pulling it free from the snow, Jones noticed with dismay that he had not discovered the remains of his own axe, but rather Raeburn's, who used a different model. The shaft had snapped cleanly into two halves. Luckily, Jones had recovered the fragment equipped with pick and adze, which he could use to climb with. Things now looked bad, but he forced himself to be positive. He had suffered no injury, other than bruising; and neither had Barkis, who rested in comfort at an anchor that had proven its security. They had at least sixty feet of undamaged rope. Speed would now be critical if they were to save their companion.

Within minutes of climbing, Jones reached Barkis' level. Snow from the avalanche coated the lad, and he breathed hard through a heavily iced moustache.

'Are you all right?' Barkis asked him.

'I was going to ask you the same. I'm fine. Thank God for those axes of yours.'

Barkis nodded. 'I think I ought to remain here while you climb up to Raeburn.'

'Do you have any spare mittens? I could only find one of mine, and it's thawing out under my coat.'

Barkis produced a pair of leather gloves from a pocket. They would not provide much protection, but would be better than nothing.

'Wish me luck.' They shared a tense smile.

*

This time, Jones took no chances with the traverse. He cut new steps across it as quickly as he could, afraid that another avalanche might come sweeping down. Determined to get over the bulge quickly, he hacked at the ice with force, gouging out wedge-shaped holds that he grabbed and hauled on, thrusting over those steep few feet.

More steps had to be cut up the next section of ice. Jones kept his eyes open for any sign of their missing friend. The upper gully had a scoured appearance; a channel swept down the centre of the snow bowl a little way above where the avalanche had begun. Blue sky peeked over the crown-wall at the top. The cornice, which Jones had noticed from the bottom of the gully, must have collapsed. So much for Raeburn's claim that the cornice would be nothing to worry about.

Now that he had reached a less exposed place, Jones searched about for somewhere he could make himself secure. There seemed to be no anchors, so he started to dig in the hope of finding something. After a minute or so he found a buried spike of rock, and hitched his rope around it; but as he turned to excavate a seat in the snow beneath, the spike moved. Jones feared he had dislodged a loose boulder until he realised that the spike was in fact a boot.

Digging as fast as he could, with the assistance of the buried Raeburn who now struggled with all his strength, Jones swiftly uncovered both legs and an arm. In no time at all, Raeburn was free of the drift and slumped weakly in the snow, gasping. Snow stuck to every inch of his clothing.

Jones found himself smiling broadly. 'By God, Raeburn, I am happy to see you!'

'Aye,' Raeburn wheezed. 'I may have broken my arm—hurts like the devil.'

Jones reached into his pocket and took out a hip flask. Raeburn took it without comment and took a hearty slug of brandy, then handed it back.

'Thank you. Is Barkis all right?'

'He's fine,' Jones reassured him. 'His quick-thinking saved my life.'

Jones looked up at the remains of the cornice. For just a moment, harsh against the morning sky, the silhouette of a hooded man gazed down upon them.

CHAPTER TWO

A Fresh Start

13th of January, 1897

J ONES FELT EXHAUSTED after a day of trying to teach physics to a class of lazy boys. He believed in his work at the City of London School, but on days like this it was easy to feel disheartened. God knows he tried his best. Colleagues often praised his lecturing style, but after five years, he wondered if he had made any real difference: the brats in his classroom never seemed to care about what he was trying to teach them, and he found his supplies of enthusiasm running low.

Sometimes he caught himself thinking that his life in London was an insult to his own character. He had been born here, grown up here, been educated here, but it never felt like home. Must be my Welsh blood, he thought: I was made for adventure under an open sky, not stultifying boredom in a classroom full of savage little beasts who would rather be doing anything than listening to me.

Even his rooms felt unwelcoming this evening. After fumbling with his keys in the hall, he pushed open the door. Years of residence had not driven away the bookish odour that seeped from the walls. He struck a match and lit his lamps, tapping the one that always guttered. That's better, he thought; the place looks a little cosier now.

After dropping his keys onto the corner of his desk as he did every night, and changing out of his robes into a smoking jacket, Jones sat in his armchair and stared out of the window across the Thames. Lights danced on the water, but behind that artificial beauty loomed a forest of chimneys.

Jones sighed. His life and work was here, and yet his imagination painted mountains behind those columns of smoke, glittering in the light of a moon that rarely shone in London. At times like this, recently back from a trip and faced with the ugliness of town, he felt haunted.

Then he noticed the calling card left on his desk, no doubt placed there by the housemaid. On it was printed the name "S. BARKIS, ESQ." and on the other side Barkis had written, in perfect business hand: *"I find myself in town tonight & will be at the Alpine Club. Do come. S.B."*

*

The rain began as he turned the corner into Queen Victoria Street. Foolishly, he had left his umbrella at home. Soon the rain had soaked through his overcoat, and at the earliest opportunity he hailed a cab and jumped in with relief.

'Where to, mister?' shouted the cabbie from his seat.

Jones hesitated, unsure of the exact address. He was not a member of the Alpine Club, although he had applied to join several years ago; the climbing establishment didn't like him.

'The Alpine Club, please,' he said hopefully.

'Sevile Row?'

'That's the place.'

After fifteen minutes they turned away from the squalid Thames, making towards the Strand. The City came to life as electric lights pushed back the winter gloom. Congestion slowed the traffic, and for some while the cab languished in a jam of snorting horses, carriages, and even the odd motor-car. Cabbies shouted greetings to each other, horns honked, and the rain got heavier, which only seemed to make the stink of the street even worse.

Eventually the cab broke out into Piccadilly Circus. Jones happened to notice a familiar figure walking amongst the evening shoppers.

'I say, I'll get down here after all.'

He paid his shilling for the two mile journey, and hopped down straight into a pile of steaming manure. Cursing, he crossed the road at a dash, careful to avoid the worst of the slurry that sprayed up from the wheels of passing vehicles.

'Barkis!' he cried out, not expecting his voice to carry over the din.

To his surprise, Simon Barkis turned and waved. Jones reached him quickly, and drew him into a shop doorway out of the rain.

They shook hands. Barkis wore evening dress, with black frock coat and top hat, and carried an umbrella. Spots of street muck stained the hems of his coat and legs of his trousers. Jones realised that he had never seen him in this context before; they only ever met at remote mountain inns, where the conventions of society were suspended and people lounged about in their shabbiest, most comfortable country wear. For the first time in their acquaintance, Jones felt conscious of the social divide between them: Barkis was, and always would be, of a higher standing than a mere schoolteacher. Climbing friendships, however, transcended the gulf of class.

'How do you do, Jones? You must have received my card.'

'I was on the way to the Alpine Club just now.' Jones laughed. 'I'm ashamed to say I had to ask the cabbie where it was.'

Barkis looked embarrassed. 'Awfully sorry—I assumed you would be a member. I have an item of business to attend to first, with Mr Beale, but you may as well accompany me. In fact, meeting you here is rather a stroke of luck.'

'Oh? Why do you say that?'

'In good time!'

*

Every mountaineer in Britain knew the name of Arthur Beale. For many years, Mr Buckingham had manufactured the only safe and tested rope for Alpine mountaineering. After the death of the old man, Beale and his partner took over the business. Climbers respected Beale & Cloves as the best Alpine outfitter in London.

Barkis strode along Shaftesbury Avenue as if he owned it, clearly enjoying his visit to London tremendously. When pressed further, he refused to divulge any information about the visit.

'Come now, you are being awfully mysterious,' Jones protested.

'Nonsense! I shall say simply that I am going to put a business proposition to you, and I believe that your presence at my meeting with Beale will help inform your decision.'

'I thought you had gone into business with Thomas Holdstock?'

'That is true, as it happens.'

That stirred Jones' interest. Everyone knew that a company had been formed to manufacture Holdstock's new ice gear. Jones often thought about their gully climb on New Year's Day, and the more he thought, the more he realised that the new system, with its speed and safety, would inevitably supplant the old ways of laboriously hacking steps out of the ice.

They reached the shop. The window display mostly featured rope by the yard, but also some large prints of Alpine views, and several ice axes. As they entered, Arthur Beale strode forwards to greet them. A large man, Jones thought he looked like a walrus in a waistcoat. They followed his lead up a staircase and along a corridor to offices on the first floor. After exchanging pleasantries, Barkis brought up the business of the evening.

'Mr Beale, as I promised in my letter, I have a proposal that I believe will make you a lot of money.'

Beale nodded, but he looked sceptical. 'I've heard of you boys and your new ice gear. Shall I call for the package you sent me?'

'That would be perfect timing.'

Beale shouted down the stairs. Presently, an assistant brought a wooden box up into the room. Jones rushed to help him, and together they placed the heavy box on the desk. The assistant cut the string binding with a knife and made his leave. All three peered into the open container. Barkis reached into the newsprint packing and lifted out a pair of the new ice axes; they gleamed in the gaslight, more works of art than engineering. After the axes followed a pair of specially made boots and their ice claws.

Beale took one of the axes, holding it with reverence in his big hand. 'It's surprisingly light! Are these the axes you used to climb the north face of the Matterhorn?'

'No, I used prototypes that day. These are the finished products, ready for sale.'

'Trade price? Pardon my directness.'

'The cost to you is one pound per axe.'

Beale's eyes widened. 'I could have a Swiss axe imported for a fraction of that cost.'

'No Swiss axe is as capable as my design.'

Beale placed the axe carefully to one side and asked to inspect the other items.

Barkis handed over one of the boots, with its claw already strapped in place. Jones picked up the other and turned it over in his hand. The leather felt waxy. He noticed that the sole was only sparsely nailed, and appeared to be quite rigid. Despite the weight of the boots, the claws looked surprisingly light; he guessed that great skill had gone into their forging. Beale poked and prodded the boot, pulling back the tongue, tugging on the claw straps. He seemed determined not to show that he was impressed.

'Who is going to buy this equipment?'

'I would buy it,' Jones said at once.

Beale ignored him. 'What will the Alpine Club say?'

Barkis, who had maintained his polite reserve until this moment, now came to life. Passion animated him; he rose and marched about the room, waving his arms as he spoke.

'Hang the Alpine Club! They are opposed to any disturbance of the status quo. They exist only to promote their own interest, which is mostly to prevent serious climbing. The future of exploration is in hard routes by extraordinary men.' He turned suddenly to face Jones. 'You're the kind of man I'm talking about. Tell him what this gear is capable of.'

He had begun to wonder exactly why Barkis had brought him here, but was only too pleased to give an endorsement. Jones briefly outlined the incident in the South-Central Gully, explaining how the ice axes had saved his life. When he had finished, Beale nodded and thanked him for the story.

Barkis now stood, leaning with both arms on the desk in front of Beale. 'We have already sold fifteen complete sets. The exploits of their owners are being praised from the Caucasus to the Pyrenees. Mr Beale, I fought and almost died on the Matterhorn so that ordinary climbers can participate in this new age of exploration and adventure. The golden age of Alpinism may belong to our fathers and grandfathers, but I say it is time for us to make our own mark! There is nothing I believe in more passionately.'

He sat back down again, face flushed. Beale paused to consider the lad's words. After a few seconds had passed, punctuated by the ticking of the desk clock and the noise of traffic in the street, the tradesman finally cleared his throat.

'You believe in your products, young man, and that'll take you far. Look here, I'm a bit of a traditionalist. I'll make no apologies about that, for the traditions of mountaineering are old and grand.'

Barkis merely nodded. He seemed to have burnt out his extraordinary energy.

'You make bold claims, but I can see your way might be the future—for the truly barmy, anyway.' Beale grinned. 'All right. I'd be delighted to do business with you.'

They shook hands, and after discussing a few more details they left with a promise that Beale would contact the company very soon to make an order.

Barkis danced along in his own world of celebration as they walked towards Piccadilly Circus, and even Jones felt that a victory had been scored for progress.

'Do you see what we're up against, Jones? Old Beale gave in easily in the end. He's not nearly as conservative as he claims, not when he smells money coming his way. Opposition is going to be a lot fiercer than that if we're to make any difference. You'd better get used to shoving this idea down tradesmen's throats.'

'Hold on, what do you mean by that?'

Barkis chuckled. 'I'll come out with it. I want you to join the company as an adviser.'

Jones felt a surge of excitement. 'Go on.'

'You will be the man coming up with the ideas, determining where they fit into our modern climbing culture, and ultimately testing the products. We need someone to liaise with the mountaineering clubs as well. Everyone knows you, Jones.'

The proposal did not come as a complete surprise, but nevertheless Jones did not know how to respond. He saw both reward and risk in what Barkis offered to him. It would be a radical change in life, an abandonment of his career with no way back, should things go ill—and that prospect excited him. Perhaps he needed to act boldly. He had always been the type to jump for a chance with both hands and count the cost afterwards.

Only one thing held back his reckless impulse to accept on the spot. 'I hate to raise the subject of pay, but I have been doing tolerably well on a schoolmaster's salary …'

Embarrassed by his mention of money, Jones fell silent.

Barkis ignored the faux pas. 'Don't worry about that. Holdstock is propping up the business until it becomes financially sufficient. We can afford to pay you a reasonable salary.'

'In that case, I accept!'

*

22nd of January, 1897

The move from London to Cambridge happened quickly and with little fuss. His fellow teachers professed their sorrow at his departure, and the kindly headmaster in particular tried to persuade him to stay, but Jones did not believe his insistence that the school would not be the same without him. A career in teaching meant nothing to him now. Another decade of chalk dust and shabby books would finish him off, he knew it, and the rising sense of futility would drive him to drink in the end.

The door had opened and the exit to freedom beckoned. With a little guilt, but not much surprise, Jones found that he felt no regret at the thought of leaving the school. Before he knew it he had left London behind forever, and trembled at the intoxicating freedom ahead.

Barkis had arranged a pleasant flat just off Trumpington Street for him to occupy, and the place felt welcoming at once. The first floor of number twenty-three Fitzwilliam Street would be his new home. Compact terraced houses, three storeys high, marched along both sides of the street. The distinctive yellow brick exterior had long since been blackened by soot.

His possessions fitted into just a few cases and bags. Jones had never been the sort of man to collect rubbish in his home, and other than his clothes, mountaineering equipment, and a few books, he owned little. Unpacking did not take long: his wardrobe and drawers full, a line of books marching half-way across a single shelf, and a corner piled with knapsack, boots and rope, and his work was done.

He had just begun to think about making a cup of tea when a smart double-knock sounded at the door. Certain that the visitor must be Simon Barkis, come to check he had arrived safely, he opened up without delay.

To his surprise, a young lady stood on the landing. She wore a blue dress that enhanced her slender figure and confident poise. Jones could not help noticing traces of wear or repair, indicative of a second-hand garment; similarly, her hat was also not of the latest fashion, but it was tastefully adorned with a blue ribbon and balanced on her brown curls at an angle. Jones judged her to be about twenty-five years old. She had the harassed expression of a woman who had a long list of things to do and not enough time to do them.

'Good day to you, miss,' Jones managed to say, temporarily bewitched by her green eyes.

'Never mind that,' the young lady said shortly, albeit with a smile. 'My name is Miss Elliot.'

Jones felt flustered and off his guard. He thought that he ought to make some formal effort at introduction, although she did not strike him as the kind of girl who would offer him a hand to kiss. He briefly considered offering his own hand for her to shake before thinking better of it.

'How do you do?' he said with all the composure he could muster. 'I'm Mr Jones.'

'I know who you are. Please follow me directly.'

She turned on her heel and trotted down the stairs at a brisk pace, skirts sweeping the floorboards. Jones pulled his shoes back on and jogged to catch up.

A two-wheeler waited in the street, the horse snorting clouds of steam into the freezing air. Traces of snow lay here and there on the cab's roof, evidence of the snowfall that had affected East Anglia overnight, but of course none had fallen in London; the newspapers warned of travel disruption in Scotland.

He offered the young lady a hand up into the cab, which she accepted. He climbed in after her and closed the door. As the vehicle began to move, Jones felt it safe to speak to the attractive but rather frightening creature who had brought him here.

She sat demurely by his side, staring pointedly ahead, ignoring him.

'I must confess,' he began, 'that I don't know what I'm doing here or where we're going.'

She turned to face him. 'I am taking you to the office of the Holdstock Company. Did you not receive my telegram?'

Jones told her truthfully that he had not.

She seemed taken aback. 'Oh! Well, no matter. Perhaps in that case you deserve a little more explanation. I am Mr Barkis' secretary, and I arranged a meeting with the directors for noon. It is meant to be my break time,' she added.

'In that case, I apologise for being the cause of your inconvenience.'

'It isn't your fault, although I see nothing wrong with taking the tram.' She gave him a look. 'I have enough to do as it is without having to escort you to the office.'

It occurred to Jones that he was about to attend what amounted to an interview with Thomas Holdstock, a man he had met but did not know well. Barkis had assured him the job was already his, but Jones had not attended an interview for several years and he could not help feeling nervous. Miss Elliot's startling arrival also demonstrated that he knew almost nothing about the other people with whom he would be working.

Optimistic as always, Jones forced all these minor concerns out of his mind, determined to make the best of his opportunity.

*

The reality of the company office fell short of his expectations. Trinity Lane, a claustrophobic alley near Trinity College, was mostly occupied by undergraduates, but the office squeezed in between a shop on the corner and the university lodgings. The property had a mean and dilapidated appearance, like an old-fashioned prison or a cheap boarding house. Rusting spikes guarded the windows. Three doorbells lurked amongst the peeling paint of the doorframe; the top one bore a tiny brass sign reading "HOLDSTOCK EQUIPMENT LTD, 2ND FLOOR."

Miss Elliot unlocked the door and led Jones into the hallway, which proved to be as dark and unwelcoming as he had expected. She lit the lamps and invited Jones to follow her up the staircase. At the landing on the top floor, a door opposite a filthy skylight led into the office itself.

Miss Elliot offered him a chair and left to make a pot of tea, leaving Jones to contemplate his surroundings. The room felt decidedly cramped. Three desks jostled for space along one wall, not leaving much room for a filing cabinet. Naked floorboards creaked as he shifted in his chair. Looking out of the window to his right, which had been clumsily washed, he could see the ornate stonework of the Queen's Gate at the end of the lane, and beyond it a courtyard surrounded by university buildings. Everything looked very grey. I seem to have moved from one dismal educational establishment to another, he thought.

The girl returned with a tea tray, which she set down on the tidiest desk, rather more firmly than was necessary. He watched her as she poured two cups of tea. Lips pressed together in a hard edge of disapproval, or irritation;

when a curl of hair strayed across her face, she flicked it behind her ear with an impatient sound in the back of her throat. Jones wondered if she resented performing servant duties. No working girl wore clothes of that quality or style.

Jones thanked her for the tea. The girl sat a little way apart with her own cup, watching him. After some minutes, she put it down and broke the awkward silence.

'Why are you here?' she asked. 'It took me weeks to get this job, yet you appear out of nowhere. The famous O.G. Jones …'

Jones shrugged. 'Barkis is an old friend.'

'Ah, nepotism.' Miss Elliot made a dismissive click of the tongue. 'Barkis may be your friend, but you'll find he's a terrible employer.'

'Sorry to hear that.' Her bitterness made him feel uncomfortable. 'At least the work you're doing is valuable.'

'That's the sort of thing Barkis says all the time. Do you really believe it, or are you just regurgitating what he has told you?'

Her bold gaze never left his own. He found himself angered by her lack of social grace, her interrogatory attitude, her petulance. His first instinct as an Englishman was to be polite at all costs, but he could only take so much.

He set his teacup down, the loudest noise in that tense room.

'Excuse me, miss, but I think your questions have become impertinent, considering we do not know each other and have only just met.'

'Ha! You don't remember me.'

He didn't like the grim amusement in her tone. Could he have met her before and forgotten? Where? Certainly not in the mountains. Not many women climbed, and he would not have forgotten a face—or figure—like hers.

'Please remind me.'

'Three years ago, I went climbing by myself on Tryfaen,' she continued. 'You insisted on rescuing me and escorting me back to Pen-y-Gwryd. I didn't take kindly to the intrusion, and you behaved like an absolute pig. I don't think it occurred to you that I had no need of any assistance.'

Now he recalled the incident with shame. It highlighted the difference between the person he had been a few years ago and the person he was trying to become. The arrogant Jones, who boasted about his achievements and refused to be bested, was a ghost he needed to shed. Many of the best climbers passed through that phase, before finding humility—or so he told himself.

At last he understood why Miss Elliot seemed so hostile to him. No wonder she hated him after such a disastrous first impression.

PLEASE LEAVE A REVIEW
They really help new authors!

If you enjoy my book, I'd appreciate a review on Goodreads.

Simply visit
http://www.goodreads.com/book/
show/15992566-the-only-genuine-jones
Or scan:

Don't forget to follow me on Twitter
@alex_roddie

www.alexroddie.com

'I am most terribly sorry about that shameful incident,' he said quickly, anxious to recover what dignity he could. 'I only regret I could not find it within me to apologise on the day.'

His contrition seemed to satisfy her. Professor Collie would be proud of me, Jones thought: another bridge built, or at least shored up with fresh timber.

Just then, the office door opened and in strolled Simon Barkis, wrapped up in a woollen overcoat and scarf. He extinguished his pipe and set it down on his desk.

'Ah, Jones! Have you moved in? I apologise for stealing you away so soon after your arrival. I have examinations coming up, so my time is not entirely my own.'

'No apology necessary, I assure you.'

The sudden change in their relationship felt a little odd, and it struck Jones just then that this was an unusually youthful business: both directors about twenty, and a secretary not much older. At twenty nine, Jones would be the oldest person present by a number of years.

Meanwhile, Miss Elliot drained her cup of tea and left the room without acknowledging Barkis with so much as a nod. Thomas Holdstock entered shortly after. The owner of Holdstock Equipment had never been a frequent visitor to the mountain inns of Britain, but Jones had met him occasionally at Wastdale Head. Sandy hair flowed over an honest face that had smiled out of every newspaper front page last summer. He wore motoring goggles pulled up over his forehead and an old shirt and breeches, waistcoat unbuttoned.

'Dreadfully sorry for my tardiness,' Holdstock said as he strode over to shake Jones' hand. 'The bloody Phaeton broke down again, and then of course the press wanted a few lines for the local rag. You know how it is!'

Ah, the hard life of the wealthy *bon vivant*, Jones thought cynically.

'How do you do, Mr Holdstock. Allow me to congratulate—'

Holdstock cut him short with an easy laugh. 'Please, the Matterhorn affair was, honestly, nothing.'

Jones tried to hold back a smile. 'Actually I meant your business here. It's just what climbing in this country needs.'

Holdstock's smile faded a fraction. 'Well, quite. That's why you're here, after all.' He slouched behind his desk and lit a cigar. 'So, welcome to Holdstock Equipment! How much do you know about us?'

'Only what Barkis has told me.'

'He's given you the talk about the future of climbing? Despite the newspaper frenzy surrounding the Matterhorn affair, most climbers seem to be bumbling fools these days. Our market is therefore speculative at best.'

Barkis frowned. 'I say, that's a little pessimistic.'

Holdstock took a long drag from his cigar. 'No, it's realistic. Have a smoke, for God's sake. We have no financial worries, but to make the venture a success we need expert help. Barkis here thinks that man is you.'

Holdstock gave him a searching look. Jones lit his pipe as ordered. He found his new boss a little intimidating, despite his youth; something about his exaggerated air of ease and confidence seemed inappropriate. Jones did not think a businessman in such an uncertain market could afford to be complacent.

'May I ask what my duties will be?'

Barkis cut in before Holdstock could reply. 'The fact is that we both have other commitments. I'm an undergraduate, and Holdstock is both an author of some repute and the director of an automobile company. Miss Elliot is our only other employee.'

Holdstock waved his hand. 'The girl is perfectly capable of handling all the menial work. Your task will be more creative. I want you to be the man selling our cause to the climbers of Britain. If we want to create a market for our products, we must inspire climbers and make them realise they are capable of so much more. It's time people stopped looking back to the golden age forty years ago and started looking forward to the new century.'

Jones blinked in surprise that Holdstock's views so exactly matched his own. 'It's about time people started talking this way. Given the exploits of Mummery and the growing trend of guideless climbing in the Alps, I'm surprised it hasn't happened sooner.'

A knock announced Miss Elliot's reappearance. She handed a slip of paper to Barkis and left quietly.

'It's a telegram from Aleister Crowley.' Barkis' face turned white. 'He wants revenge. My God, he wants revenge for the Matterhorn.' He passed the slip to Jones.

"YOU HAVE STOLEN MY IDEA AND I WILL EXPOSE YOU STOP ECKENSTEIN KNOWS STOP FROM CROWLEY"

*

24th of January, 1897

Two days later, Barkis sent Jones to Snowdonia in the company of Miss Elliot, with basic expenses paid but not enough funds to provide for a servant. Miss Elliot had sneered at his enquiry regarding the whereabouts of her maid. Although a middle class woman would usually be expected to travel with a servant, Jones had formed the impression that Miss Elliot was not as well-to-do as she would like. He wondered to what extent her disdain of social convention was genuine—perhaps in anticipation of Pen-y-Gwryd's bohemian atmosphere—and how much of it was a mask to cover her financial worries.

When the train finally reached its terminus at Betws-y-Coed, Jones felt more cheerful. The native Snowdonian climbers may have turned their backs on him, but he had been climbing here for nine years and this part of the world felt like a second home. Welsh blood ran in his veins, after all, despite his English birth. Good Welsh rain on his face made him feel glad to be alive.

A coach took them through the forest and moorland uphill to Pen-y-Gwryd: a little collection of slate roofs gleaming in a sunbeam, a haven amongst the mountains, white upon windswept tan. Four gnarled trees guarded it, bending with the prevailing wind. This was a harsh place to eke out a living, but the proprietors of Pen-y-Gwryd had always given a warm welcome to all who stayed there.

Miss Elliot smiled to herself as they approached the inn. 'All of the best moments of my life happened in this place.'

Jones agreed with her, and found himself cheered by a rare moment of warmth from his travelling companion. Something about mountain inns made them special worlds. So many remarkable stories, so much excitement, passion, and bravery all stuffed into one building, left a lifelong impression on all who visited. In these places, people were judged by more honest means than in everyday life, and only the things that really mattered won respect: climbing ability, storytelling, musical talent, kindness, comradeship.

'It's good to be back,' Jones said. 'If only we knew why we have been sent here.'

'Don't ask me; Barkis never tells me anything. In fact, I'm amazed he let me out of the office at all.'

Jones shrugged. He disliked the way Miss Elliot's tone had gone from happy to resentful in less than a minute.

'He likes being mysterious. I gather we are to meet my friend George Abraham, who is likely causing some mischief on our behalf. I'm afraid I won't have much heart for the smoking-room company; too many unfriendly faces these days.'

'You have enemies? Surely not!'

Jones couldn't think how to defend his reputation without insulting her in the process. The coach pulled up outside the front door of the inn before he could conjure up anything suitably witty to say.

At first glance, Pen-y-Gwryd looked remarkably ordinary; built of local stone, swamped by a cloak of ivy, like a hundred other provincial hotels.

Jones noted with dismay that the stables had suffered some decay since his last visit over a year ago. Indeed, the signs of neglect were everywhere: flaking paint around the windows, weeds in the yard, no cheering column of smoke rising from the chimney.

The coach departed, leaving a heap of luggage beside the front door. No servant emerged to help with the heavy lifting. Jones extracted Miss Elliot's trunk and his own smaller knapsack, then held the door open for her to enter the hotel.

He followed her inside. A powerful smell of damp wafted over them. Wallpaper yellowed in the corners of the entrance hall, candles had burned down and not been replaced, and spiders surveyed their kingdoms from shadowed galleries. No beaming faces and warm welcome this time. The Welsh farmhouse of song and tale seemed quite deserted.

Jones made his way through to the bar, which felt neglected, like a favourite pair of boots packed away damp, and found again years later destroyed by mould. He wondered what had happened to the happy place of his memory. Everything seemed to be conspiring to push him away from the old sanctuaries he had once loved.

Miss Elliot looked about her in distress. 'I don't understand. What has happened to the place? Where are the crowds? Where is Mrs Owen?'

'Ann's dead.'

A figure walked into view, polishing a wine glass with a cloth. Jones recognised a lad he knew only as Williams, who had once been a kitchen boy.

Jones dumped his bag. 'Look here, Williams isn't it? What has happened to the inn?'

'Mrs Owen died last year. It's just me running the hotel now, Mr Jones sir. Mr Morgan pays me, but he lives in Llanberis.'

Jones and Miss Elliot exchanged a look. He was prepared to stay, but he didn't know how his colleague would feel about the prospect.

She shrugged. 'I suppose it will be fine. May I assume you have rooms?' This she said to the boy, with deep sarcasm.

Williams looked hurt. 'We have only one other guest staying here tonight, miss. Two, if you count Mr Eckenstein sleeping in the coal shed.'

Jones grinned. Some things never changed.

*

Jones found his room to be dirty and cold, but considerably more accommodating than many Alpine huts he had endured, so he counted himself fortunate in the circumstances. After breakfasting he suggested to Miss Elliot that they took a walk up Snowdon.

She had changed into practical country dress. Her skirts only just hovered above the level of the road, and Jones reflected, not for the first time, how absurd it was that propriety still expected women to wear such ridiculous costumes in the mountains. She carried a lightweight ice axe which she used as a walking-stick as they strode uphill. A leather knapsack sat between her shoulders, and she wore freshly waxed climbing boots which struck sparks on loose rocks in the dust.

Her spirits seemed to have recovered well from the shock of seeing her beloved Pen-y-Gwryd in such a sorry state, but she strolled in silence. Jones realised in that moment that Miss Elliot was a woman of some resilience, despite her aloofness and sarcasm—but then only remarkable women became climbers, even in these modern times.

'You are staring at me, Mr Jones.'

He protested that he was not, and hastily changed the subject. 'Where shall we walk? We have at least eight hours of daylight. We could go over Crib Goch, perhaps.'

She smiled teasingly. 'Do you not think that a little easy? I have done it seven times already. Please don't make the mistake of underestimating me. I am probably as capable a climber as you are.'

Jones doubted that, but did not say so out loud.

Presently they reached the top of the pass between Capel Curig and Llanberis. At this high col, or bwlch in Welsh, nestled a little whitewashed building called Pen-y-Pass: a far smaller hotel than the Pen-y-Gwryd, but offering accommodation to mountaineers wishing to be that little bit closer to Snowdon. Jones had never visited Pen-y-Pass, but he noticed an automobile and several carriages parked outside. Perhaps the usual Pen-y-Gwryd crowd had defected to the newer, more luxurious lodgings. In the circumstances, he could not blame them.

Above and left, the peaks of Crib Goch and Snowdon brushed the clouds, their precipices dashed with snow. Now the walkers turned left along the mining road into the heart of the mountains. Just a little way ahead, a solitary figure sat on a boulder, staring into the mirror of Llyn Llydaw. As they drew near, Jones recognised his friend George Abraham: photographer, mountaineer, and without a doubt the most energetic of Jones' younger friends. A pile of bulky photographic equipment lay on the ground by the side of the lake.

Abraham jumped up and waved as they approached. 'Jones! It's about time you showed up. How are you?'

'I'm well—but how is Ashley? Is he here?'

'Alas, my brother is climbing with Robinson in Wastdale.' Abraham smiled at Miss Elliot, who waited to be introduced. 'Jones, where are your manners?'

'This is my colleague, Miss Elliot.'

'A delight, madam.' He kissed her hand; always the charmer, Jones thought. 'I'm George Abraham. You may hear me referred to as "that cursed photographer" tonight, but my friends call me "that clumsy fool George." I answer to both.'

Miss Elliot smiled. 'Jones claims you are a loveable trouble-maker.'

'Well, I'm not so sure about being loveable,' Abraham replied with a laugh, 'but I do like to stir things up, as does Jones of course!'

Jones put his arm around his friend's shoulder. 'Speaking of which, do you know why we have been sent here? I gather something is to happen tonight in the hotel. Barkis told us nothing at all.'

'Reading between the lines of his telegram, I think he hopes a new mountaineering club is going to be formed. Barkis wants you at this meeting to ensure the interests of the company are spoken for. You had better be ready for a stiff argument.'

'Another one?' Jones said with a sinking heart. 'I've been trying to put the rows behind me.'

'I think you'll find the others are slower to forget, my friend.'

Abraham hoisted his tripod and camera over a shoulder, and together they climbed the steepening track towards Glaslyn, the upper lake cradled by the precipices of Snowdon and Crib Goch. Hard snow filled the hollows in the ground, resisting prods from axes. Jones found his attention turning to the cliffs of Y Lliwedd over to the left. This double tombstone of crag, a wandering place of complex routes and loose rock, had been the focus of several expeditions from Pen-y-Gwryd—some with fatal consequences. Ice laced the gullies and a line of cornices guarded the summit ridge.

'Has the Slantendicular been climbed yet?' Jones thought out loud.

Abraham looked at him, seriously for once. 'You cannot seriously be thinking of climbing Slanting Gully? It's choked with ice!'

Still unclimbed, then. Jones felt the buzz of excitement before a first ascent. He pulled out a pair of Holdstock axes from their resting-place between his back and knapsack.

'That, my friend, will not be a problem.'

CHAPTER THREE

ELSPETH

24th of January, 1897

MISS ELLIOT ACCOMPANIED Abraham on an ascent of Slanting Buttress, an established route both of them would find well within their powers. Jones wondered how Abraham would be able to drag his enormous camera and tripod up the climb with him, but he had taken his photographic gear on far harder routes before; his zeal in recording notable climbs had done much good in bringing climbing to the attention of the public. They parted on a cone of frozen scree at the base of the climb, and from this point Jones proceeded alone.

Snow soon appeared here and there, and to his surprise Jones noted a fresh boot-print in one of the patches, the imprint of every nail crisp. Above, the lure of the Slantendicular drew Jones onwards, as if the gully emitted a magnetic force that specifically attracted insane climbers. Jones paused for a moment to commit the scene to his memory. Black walls, overhanging in places, gripped a ribbon of ice that led straight up to victory. Many had attempted Slanting Gully but none had succeeded. So far it had claimed the life of one man, a Mr Mitchell, who had attempted to climb it solo. Local quarrymen recovered his corpse from the cave where (according to legend) King Arthur and his knights slept through the aeons. Jones wondered if the knights of the round table would object if he climbed into their cave and woke them up. He tried not to dwell on the fate of poor Mr Mitchell.

Upon reaching the hard snow at the foot of the gully, Jones stopped to put his claws on. This was the first time he had used them in anger, although Barkis had shown him how to attach them. A system of straps and buckles secured the framework to the boot.

He started to climb, and immediately found the new technique a joy. With a merest flick of the wrist, he buried the pick of an axe deep in the ice, providing a secure hand-hold. Kicking his boot into the ice engaged the twin front-points, which were shaped like miniature chisels. He found that he could walk up steep ice with little effort. How remarkable, he thought, that only a year ago ice like this would have taken hours longer to climb.

In what seemed like no time at all he came up against the fearsome Crack Pitch, the highest point of all previous attempts. Mr Mitchell had fallen into the cave from this point three years previously. Another unsuccessful party had described this obstacle as a narrowing crack, eighty feet in height, overhanging at the top. In summer conditions, smothered in mud and slime, it would doubtless be very severe; today, however, Jones found the feared Crack Pitch completely banked out in blue ice of the finest quality.

He set to work, heartened to find conditions close to perfect. After some distance of this steep climbing he began to feel the strain on his calf muscles, but he had climbed steeper ice than this without claws and special tools; in comparison this felt easy, almost unsporting. He smiled at the memory of cutting steps up the Devil's Kitchen with a stolen farmer's hatchet.

Before long he had conquered the pitch, and arrived at the snow shelf above. To his enormous surprise, he found himself face to face with a young woman sat in a scooped-out seat in the snow. A curl of smoke rose from the cigarette in her hand. She wore a black woollen jacket, grey scarf and a pair of men's breeches. Jones found this so surprising that he almost fell back down the gully again; then his surprise gave way to annoyance that his first ascent had been taken from him.

'Good morning,' the woman said mildly. 'It's a pleasant day for a climb, is it not?'

Her accent was strongly Scottish, from the Highlands, Jones thought.

'How the devil did you get up here?'

The woman did not seem to be moved by his bad language. She reached into the snow beside her and lifted up a pair of short ice axes, not unlike his own. She also wriggled her feet in the air, and Jones noticed the ice claws attached to her boots.

'The same way that you did, Mr Jones.'

'How do you know my name?' he demanded. 'Who are you?'

The woman stood and shook the snow from her jacket. Although quite small and slight of build, she seemed to possess a coiled power, like a tiny clockwork machine. Her face, angular and uncommonly clever, was not pretty in the classic sense but nevertheless possessed a certain grace.

'My name is Elspeth, and of course everybody knows who you are. May I call you Owen?'

'Certainly not.'

Jones thought she looked offended. He realised he must have sounded quite rude; perhaps the Crowley scares had made him twitchy.

'I didn't expect to find anyone else up here,' Jones said in what he hoped was a conciliatory tone. 'Do you realise you have just made the very first successful ascent of the Crack Pitch?'

Elspeth smiled and shrugged, as if the conquest of a feared climb was nothing much at all. As someone who felt entitled to boast a little about his exploits—tastefully, of course—Jones felt affronted by her casual attitude to the whole business. If she was going to take his first ascent from him, she could at least savour her victory, he thought.

'Would you care to accompany me to the top?' she asked. 'From this point up, the gully is a mystery. I would not say no to a rope and a companion.'

Jones considered. His initial distrust of the young woman had not faded, but on the other hand refusing to rope up with her would be rude. He had to grudgingly admit that she must be a talented climber.

He withdrew the rope from his knapsack. After uncoiling it and checking it for kinks, he passed an end to Elspeth and tied on himself with a bowline knot around the waist. Elspeth remained in her snow-seat and paid the rope out over a shoulder.

Jones climbed onwards, still not entirely certain he could trust his new companion. As he climbed he passed a slab on the left, below a ledge, deeply scratched by clinker-nails. Jones realised with dismay that these marks must be evidence of Mitchell's final struggle as he slid to his death. Comforting himself with the knowledge that he was a better and safer climber than poor Mitchell, Jones increased his pace and within a few more minutes reached the cornice at the top of the gully. He looked down: sufficient rope remained. He set to work hacking through the overhang of snow with his axes.

When Elspeth had joined him on the ridge of the mountain, her dark hair flecked with snow, they sat together on a boulder and contemplated the view. Cloud drifted in from the Irish sea. The intricate coastline of Snowdonia faded under a bank of mist. Jones smiled to himself as he admired the familiar pyramid of Snowdon above them.

Elspeth lit another cigarette. 'So, that was the fearsome Slanting Gully. Times must be changing.'

'How do you mean?'

'Who was it who said that all climbs go through three stages: an impossible prospect, the most difficult climb in the world, and an easy day for a lady? Well, Slanting Gully has been through all of these stages in a single morning.'

Jones could not help but laugh. 'You misquote Mummery, but the point is a good one. Miss, you are quite the most talented female climber I have ever met.'

'Please, call me Elspeth.'

He found a grudging respect for this stranger who had proven herself his equal, yet he still felt uneasy. Perhaps it was her startling familiarity, manly dress and casual attitude, or perhaps it was simply that he had never met anyone else who was a better climber than him—except Aleister Crowley.

They sat in silence until a jubilant cry broke the calm of the morning. It came from the rocks a little way away along the ridge. Up popped a brown lady's hat adorned with blue ribbon, sat upon a tumble of tawny hair. Miss Elliot planted her ice axe firmly in the bank of snow a little way back from the ridge and hitched her rope around it, then with expert speed took the rope in as Abraham climbed.

'Another woman in the hills,' Elspeth remarked. 'Times truly are changing.'

'They are in my party. I should go and meet them.' Jones stood to leave.

Elspeth touched his shoulder as he stood. 'Mr Jones, it has been a pleasure climbing with you. I am staying at Pen-y-Pass tonight; will you be joining the company later?'

She seemed so polite and sincere that Jones decided to ignore his first impressions of the girl. 'I'm staying at Pen-y-Gwryd, but I'm sure we shall meet again.' He raised his hat. 'Good day to you, Elspeth.'

He strode away in the direction of Slanting Buttress, where Abraham was dusting snow from his tweeds. Miss Elliot stood serenely on a rock, gazing over to the shark's fin of Crib Goch on the other side of the cwm. Her slim figure cut an elegant silhouette against the horizon. Abraham asked her to remain still while he set up his camera and tripod to record the occasion.

He waved, overcome with excitement, as Jones approached. 'Jones! You made the first ascent of Slanting Gully!'

'Alas, that honour did not go to me,' Jones said with some regret.

Miss Elliot regarded him calmly, hands on hips. Her pretty face revealed only the hint of a smile. 'It looks to me like you were beaten to it by a lady. How deliciously ironic.'

'Who is she, Jones?' Abraham insisted. 'I must congratulate the woman who bested you!'

Jones looked back, but Elspeth was already running down the ridge at a competent pace, skipping from rock to rock and glissading the patches of snow.

'She gave only her first name: Elspeth. Apparently she is staying at Pen-y-Pass tonight. You shall have to write if you want to gloat.'

'Nonsense!' the younger man cried. 'It is at the Pass that we must dine this evening. The only reason the three of us are sleeping at that miserable farmhouse further down the valley is that the new hotel is utterly full.'

Despite the high spirits of his companion, Jones felt a sense of foreboding at the prospect of an evening at Pen-y-Pass. There would be old friends there, but also new enemies and possibly bitter quarrelling—not to mention the embarrassment of a young woman announcing to the entire company that she had beaten Jones to the first ascent of Slanting Gully's Crack Pitch by a mere five minutes.

As Elspeth had said, times were indeed changing.

*

The new hotel at Pen-y-Pass turned out to be just as full as Abraham had foretold. Many of the visitors, unable to find a room, had resorted to pitching tents in the yard; from the hillside above it looked like a prisoner of war camp. Maybe in a way that's what it is, Jones mused: exiles from the real world.

Abraham struggled with his photographic gear as they walked down the path from the Crib Goch ridge, although he had already halved the load with Jones, giving instructions to treat the delicate plates with care.

'We ought to hurry,' Abraham said. 'It would be poor form to be late for dinner.'

'Will they be able to accommodate us?' Miss Elliot said anxiously. 'It seems to me that they are already over-crowded.'

'Don't worry—Eckenstein says that the dining room is very large. The staff have been advised that extras will turn up for dinner, so all is in hand. Professor Collie is in charge as usual.'

As they approached the hotel, Jones noticed a small party walking in from the other direction. A solitary figure remained clinging to a boulder a little way away from the road. Despite his size, the man climbed gracefully, like a woman. The bushy beard, long pipe, and knee-length socks identified him at once. Eckenstein was enjoying one last problem on his boulder, a place where he often went at the end of the day to teach climbing techniques to his friends.

The approaching climbers drew near, all wrapped up in woollen coats against the wind, hands in pockets. Jones recognised Archer Thomson, the man who had perhaps done more than any other to progress the sport of climbing in North Wales. His companions were strangers.

The groups drew level, and Thomson gave Jones a terse nod. As always, he seemed haggard, as if his zeal for climbing had caused his health to suffer.

Thomson ignored Jones, instead smiling at Miss Elliot. 'How wonderful it is to see you again. You look radiant.'

She smiled, and to Jones's surprise, flushed with pleasure. 'Thank you, Mr Thomson. It's good to be back.'

Thomson's smile faded as he turned to Jones. 'I'm surprised you have returned, Jones. I do not wish to be rude, but I have to tell you that you are not welcome at Pen-y-Pass. Mr Abraham, the same goes for you too.'

Thomson spoke with authority; only natural, Jones supposed, now that he was a Headmaster. He felt the old frustration well up again. Some arguments, it seemed, refused to die quietly; but he remembered his promise that he would try to build bridges from now on.

'Mr Thomson, we may have quarrelled last summer, but I have always extended a hand of friendship towards you. Will you not take it?'

Thomson looked at him for a long moment. 'I wish you well with your exploits in the Lake District, but you are a source of friction and you will never be welcome here. Good day to you.' He raised his hat to Miss Elliot. 'Madam.'

The group continued towards the hotel. Jones stood still, fists clenched. 'Ignorant old fool,' he muttered to himself.

Miss Elliot turned on him with a critical look. 'Archer Thomson is one of the kindest men I have ever known. He taught my brother and I how to climb. He's far more of a gentleman than you are, Jones.'

He had to admit that she made a good point. 'He's a fine man, which makes our quarrel all the more pitiful. Yet I believe that the fault lies with him.'

'What was the argument over, anyway?'

'The unpleasantness, what else?'

They started to walk towards the hotel once again. Abraham took over from Jones, who had lapsed into brooding silence. 'Last summer, my brother and I helped Jones make the first ascent of Kern Knotts Crack in Wastdale. It's a severe climb. We held a rope from above so that Jones could make the moves in safety.'

'I kept trying at the damned thing,' Jones said, kicking a stone out of his way. 'In the end I worked out the sequence of moves. I was so happy I had solved the climb I invited some of my friends to watch me make the ascent without ropes.'

'But of course that's not ethical, is it old boy? Not according to Archer Thomson, and half of the other climbers in Britain. A thing is to be climbed on-sight, or not at all. Crowley did his best to stir it up into a proper row.'

'Naturally I defended my position,' Jones went on, 'and shortly afterwards Thomson objected to my plans for a guidebook of the Welsh climbs. He is against publicity in the strongest possible terms. I see nothing wrong in improving my position through climbing. I'm no good at anything else.'

Miss Elliot stopped and stared at them both. 'I despair at how childish men can be! A friendship ruined over a question as petty as this?'

Jones felt hurt. 'It's not a petty question. There are important considerations …'

Miss Elliot stormed off before he could finish.

'I think she likes you, Jones.' Abraham fell silent for a moment, then laughed out loud. 'But she's right. You are a lovely man, everyone says so, but you can be a stubborn ass at times.'

They walked in awkward silence. After a minute or two Jones realised that Oscar Eckenstein was following a little way behind. He felt nervous at this meeting after Crowley's telegram, but he could not just ignore his friend, so he stopped to allow Eckenstein to catch up.

Eckenstein was large, hairy, and dressed in an old smock covered in burn marks. His nailed boots struck sparks from the road as he walked, and a stream of smoke wafted from his pipe, which usually contained the most pungent Navy shag he could find. Jones thought he looked like the offspring of a coal miner and a great ape, possibly with a little viking thrown in for good measure.

'Jones!' he shouted. 'What are you doing here, you oaf? Don't you know all of Wales is screaming for your blood?'

'Eckenstein, it's good to see you …'

'Never mind that—you're in trouble this time. I have heard some unsettling rumours about you.' He frowned after Miss Elliot, who slammed the hotel door shut behind her moments later. 'Who's the girl? I see you've managed to offend her as well. You always were an idiot when it came to women.'

Jones cringed. Tonight would be a struggle.

*

A telegram waited for him at Pen-y-Pass. After giving the runner a penny—he complained bitterly about the extra uphill slog from Pen-y-Gwryd—Jones opened the envelope.

"GET ECKENSTEIN ON OUR SIDE STOP HELP THE NEW CLUB GET GOING STOP GOOD LUCK FROM BARKIS"

Abraham read it over his shoulder. 'Orders from the office? If you want to get Eckenstein on board you're going to need all the luck you can get.'

Jones felt grumpy. 'Let's just find something to eat.'

Boots, ice axes, drying coats, scarves, and mittens crammed the entrance hall of the hotel. Damp clothing spilled into the lounge, a cosy little room tucked beneath the staircase leading to the rooms upstairs. A book-case in one corner mostly contained volumes on Alpine climbing. People sat or crouched everywhere: on the sofa beside the fire, cross-legged on the floor, leaning against the newly papered walls. Conversation and laughter filled the air. Jones greeted people he knew, most of whom responded cordially enough, but a few rewarded his efforts with stony silence. He seemed to move through this happy place in his own bubble of poor humour.

Abraham pointed into the spacious dining room. 'There she is.'

A long table had been set for dinner, gleaming with silverware and china. Some of the chairs were already occupied. Miss Elliot sat at the far end of the table, opposite Archer Thomson.

She looked up with a forced smile as the two men approached. 'Gentlemen.'

'I apologise if I offended you,' Jones said at once.

'I think it is Mr Thomson you ought to apologise to.'

Thomson had changed out of his climbing clothes, but still had a windswept appearance. He seemed annoyed at the interruption.

'My dear, the time for apologies has passed. Much as it injures me to say it, I simply cannot countenance the thought of Mr Jones intruding on our community any longer.'

Jones took a seat to Miss Elliot's left, while George sat to her right. 'Nevertheless, I wish to make amends. It was never my wish to offend anybody.'

'Yet you persist with your unsportsmanlike practice of top-roping difficult climbs. You presume to pry for details of our routes for your guidebooks. You have photographers following you around like puppies. In short, you are a vain man who seeks thrills and publicity, and in the process you will destroy everything we hold dear.'

'I see nothing wrong in the pursuit of publicity!' Jones began, his patience fraying.

'When our beloved mountains are crawling with every Tom, Dick and Harry eager for the next vulgar sensation, will your stance still be as liberal, I wonder?'

'Gentlemen, please!' Miss Elliot cried. 'This argument is hardly a fit topic of conversation for the table. Can we not be at peace here, at least until after dinner?'

While they had been arguing, the dining room had filled to capacity. For the first time Jones saw the extent of the party that had descended on Pen-y-Pass. He picked out many familiar faces, including, to his delight, Professor Collie.

Collie stood and cleared his throat. The excited chatter of the company quietened down, and heads turned in his direction. The Professor beamed happily at his audience, face rosy from the wind, or perhaps a glass or two of port. Jones reflected that were it not for his sour humour, he ought to be utterly content. He felt ashamed for bringing the undertone of discord with him.

'Ladies and gentlemen, good evening to you all! It is a pleasure to see so many of you here, old friends and strangers alike. I hope everyone has had a rewarding day in the hills. For the regular frequenters of Pen-y-Gwryd, a word of apology. It will not have gone unobserved that, since the sad passing of Mrs Owen, our most beloved Welsh farmhouse has suffered some decline. The new hotel where we now find ourselves may not be quite as spacious as our palace of old, but I hope everyone will agree that what it lacks in space it makes up for in convenience.'

Eckenstein, seated at the distant end of the table, grunted loudly. 'Nothing wrong with the coal shed in the yard at Pen-y-Gwryd. Keeps the rain off my back.'

Laughter rose from the company. Collie's smile broadened. 'It would take severe circumstances indeed to change your habits of such long standing, Mr Eckenstein. Before dinner is served, I would like to raise a subject that might benefit us all. It has long been suggested that we ought to form a sort of Pen-y-Gwryd club. My proposal is broader: I want to form a society to promote all aspects of British climbing.'

Mutters of approval sounded throughout the room. Elspeth stood. She now wore a simple yet elegant black dress, matching exactly the colour of her hair. Once again, Jones was struck by the sharpness of her gaze, the determination in her pose.

'Do you have a question, Elspeth?'

'Aye, Professor. I want to know if your new society will represent the needs of the progressive mountaineer, or if it will be just another club for plodding fuddy-duddies?'

Half of the folk present shot to their feet immediately in protest. Jones found himself applauding, along with a few others.

The Professor raised his hands. 'Friends, please! Elspeth, as always your comment is insightful, even if you lack tact.' He considered the point. 'The so-called progressive movement is such a new phenomenon that we cannot even be certain what it is yet.'

'Simon Barkis, Thomas Holdstock, O.G. Jones, and Aleister Crowley and A.F. Mummery before their untimely demise: to name but a few, these are the men who are shaping our future. We need to adapt to the times.' Elspeth fired a wink across the table at Jones.

Collie, who belonged to every mountaineering club in the country and had contacts everywhere, including among the most stalwart traditionalists, looked troubled.

'Since you are clearly referring to the ascent of the north face of the Matterhorn, it would be pointless to step around the issue any further. I agree that major ascents such as this, and that of the South-Central Gully in Glen Coe, are indicators of the way the tide is turning. It would be foolish for us to ignore this, but at the same time, we must cater for the needs of the majority.'

'Slanting Gully was climbed today!' someone shouted out, uninvited. 'Surely you cannot ignore that?'

Uproar once again, until Collie calmed everybody down.

Eckenstein rose, removed the pipe from his mouth, and waited for permission to speak.

'If the Slantendicular was climbed, let the man who did it speak for himself.'

Elspeth, who had remained standing, gave a little shrug of her shoulders. 'Jones and I climbed it. With the new Holdstock axes and claws, it really is not a difficult climb by any standards.'

Heads turned in Jones' direction. He stood. 'I agree with Elspeth's appraisal of the route. The fearsome reputation of Slanting Gully is ridiculous, given a modern approach to the climb. It is this modern approach that we must cultivate.'

George Abraham, Jones noticed, was looking at Elspeth with unconcealed admiration.

Collie nodded slowly. 'Well done, Jones—and Elspeth too, of course.'

A man Jones did not know jumped to his feet. 'I submit that any technique that renders such a route easy is wholly unsporting in character.'

Again, murmurs of agreement. 'Surely we cannot endorse cheating?' someone else cried out. 'Or is that all Jones is good for?'

'Please remember that a mere ten years ago, many of the men in this room denounced the use of a rope as unsporting,' Collie pointed out. 'I believe in our traditions and institutions, but only a fool resists progress. Let us put it to the vote. All those in favour of a new club inclusive of progressive mountaineers, raise your hands!'

In the end those for the motion won the argument, despite a close vote. By the time dinner was served, it had been agreed that a progressive mountaineering club would be formed immediately, for the exploration of all British mountains and cliffs.

Jones felt that the first victory of the evening had been easily won.

*

The company dispersed shortly after dinner, and Jones withdrew with his friends to the lounge. A heavy hand fell on his shoulder as he passed through the doorway.

'I want a word with you, boy,' Eckenstein growled in his ear.

Jones cleared his throat. 'Abraham, would you accompany Miss Elliot to the lounge? I will join you presently.'

Abraham nodded, giving Jones a worried look.

Jones followed Eckenstein out into the yard. Snowflakes drifted down on the crisp breeze, settling on the paving stones.

'I know why you're upset,' Jones began.

'The ice claw is my idea,' Eckenstein said, his eyes flashing in anger. 'I drew up the blueprints two years ago. The claws being sold by Barkis and Holdstock are remarkably similar. I hear you have thrown in your lot with those scoundrels?'

'Please calm yourself, my friend. In truth, I thought your idea had already been stolen by Crowley.'

'You thought entirely wrong. Friends don't steal from each other.'

'Please enlighten me.' Afraid of Eckenstein's temper, Jones took pains to keep his tone reasonable.

'Crowley and I planned to go into business together. We built prototypes, which he climbed with extensively. I believe he also designed a short ice axe.'

Jones nodded. 'He used this equipment on the Matterhorn. From what I gather, he had shared his ideas with Barkis and Holdstock months before. Nothing was ever patented before the company was formed.'

'So you admit to stealing my idea?'

'The short ice axes were not your idea! Crowley invented them, and never patented them. Everyone thought he was dead.'

Eckenstein gave a short laugh. 'And dead he is, the fool.'

Jones paused. He had assumed that Eckenstein knew of Crowley's survival. 'We have reason to believe that Crowley is still alive.'

'I don't believe you. Crowley's number was up. Only an idiot would attempt to climb on a face like that. It's a miracle the other two survived.'

'I agree, but the point is that there has been no malicious behaviour here. Ice claws have been around forever. The new design is merely a slight tweak on an old idea, to enable direct climbing on steep ice. I do not believe you filed a patent on the design, Oscar.'

Eckenstein took a long drag on his pipe. 'I made an oversight. Nevertheless, I see this as an unfriendly act.'

'Will you not correspond with my employers? You know Simon Barkis well; he's a reasonable man. He would like to have you on our team. You are the authority on technical matters, when it comes to climbing gear.'

'You ought to know that it is impossible to flatter me. We will climb together in future, as we always have, but you will never mention this matter to me again.'

Eckenstein sounded calm enough, but Jones decided not to press the matter any further; once he had made up his mind on a subject, it could not be changed.

'Good job on Slanting Gully,' Eckenstein said before stomping back inside, leaving Jones alone.

He smiled. Coming from Eckenstein, that was a sincere apology for any offence he may have caused.

*

Jones walked back to Pen-y-Gwryd alone. He had left the party at the Pass in high spirits: some bizarre game involving a chair and a tobacco tin had been in progress, with scores recorded in chalk on a bit of slate. Such unusual methods of entertainment seemed to characterise mountain meets. He remembered once entertaining twenty friends for half an hour with no more than a handful of spoons.

He felt unable to face Miss Elliot's criticism after the quarrel with Eckenstein, although he trusted Abraham to take good care of her. Eckenstein's accusations made him feel strangely guilty. For all his bluntness and love of confrontation, Eckenstein had been a true friend to Jones for years. He wondered if he had been wise in abandoning his teaching career so rashly. What if the Holdstock Company really had dishonestly copied the ideas of others?

Footsteps pattered behind him. Jones looked back, but in the darkness could not tell who it was.

'Good evening, Mr Jones!'

He recognised that accent.

'You are not going to join the company this evening?' Elspeth said breathlessly as she drew opposite.

'Alas, there is too much on my mind presently. I must thank you for your kind words before dinner.'

'I told the truth, and nothing more.'

'Yet you modestly declined to mention that you climbed the crux pitch unaided. You did not have to mention my name at all. I must admit, I expected to be humiliated.'

She chuckled. 'In the circumstances I saw no reason to further tarnish your reputation. Besides, it suits me to remain in obscurity. When people speak of Slanting Gully, it is you who will be remembered, not I.'

'That seems unfair.'

'Yet it is you who has made your name through climbing feats. I wish for no such recognition.'

They reached the dismal buildings of Pen-y-Gwryd, lit only by a few candles inside the shadowed windows. Jones doubted the sole custodian of the building would still be awake at this hour.

'I ought to escort you back to Pen-y-Pass,' Jones said.

Elspeth laughed. 'I am perfectly capable of walking back alone! Good night to you, Mr Jones. I may call upon you at your flat in Cambridge in the coming months, to discuss future mountaineering plans.'

'Good night, Elspeth.'

Jones entered the hotel and tramped upstairs to his room. It was only after he had got into bed and blown out his candle that he wondered when, exactly, he had told Elspeth he lived in Cambridge.

CHAPTER FOUR

CRACKS

26th of January, 1897

JONES FOUND HIMSELF alone and restless after returning from Wales. Despite the minor victories of the trip, he judged the mission a failure. The first ascent of Slanting Gully had been taken from him, he had completely failed to win over Eckenstein, and his happy memories of Pen-y-Gwryd had all been destroyed. Unhappy omens seemed to have soured his new opportunity.

Without really knowing why, he took out the manuscript of his book, entitled "Rock and Ice Climbing in North Wales". The handful of typed pages had languished in a drawer for months now, untouched. Sometimes he thought the project scared him a little, as if he worried that the completion of the book might destroy his reputation forever. Nobody had complained when he published a similar volume on climbing in the Lakes, but the Lakeland mountaineers thought of him as one of their own, despite his Welsh blood.

He looked at the sheaf of paper and felt tempted to throw it on the fire. It had brought him nothing but trouble, and nobody in Wales seemed to want a guidebook anyway; perhaps the climbing world wasn't ready for the idea that all men would be better off with access to the mountains. Climbers wanted to keep people away from their crags, not draw in the crowds. At its best, when striding along an arête in the sky with the glories of nature all around and a firm friend on the end of your rope, mountaineering could feel like the greatest of all human endeavours; but at his low moments Jones sometimes thought the sport lurked in a dark age of superstition and elitism. He believed in a future free from all that clutter.

The cost of publishing this book would be high, but despite his doubts, Jones didn't throw the manuscript on the fire. He had left his career to help bring progress to the world of climbing, and to lose heart now would leave him with nothing at all. Instead, he picked up his pen.

*

He felt more cheerful the next morning, and he whistled to himself as he strolled through Cambridge on the way to work. After crossing the road and joining Trumpington Street, he passed the neat lawns and classical architecture of the Fitzwilliam Museum. A carriage rattled down the street, but the tramline was silent, and Jones felt more like walking than waiting for the next tram. He felt an expansive sense of freedom he rarely experienced in the confines of town.

As he walked past King's College, Jones could not help but spy out potential climbing routes on those intricate spires. He had often climbed church steeples while he lived in London, pining for the mountains. Now he wondered if undergraduates ever got up to similar pranks, and resolved to ask Barkis about it at the earliest opportunity.

A light touch to his elbow disturbed the daydream. Miss Elliot stood there, alluring as always, dressed in a green coat and one of the most ridiculous hats he had ever seen. She touched her hair with a hand, as if she could feel his gaze.

'What are you looking at?'

He couldn't help smiling. 'Nothing. How do you do this morning, Miss Elliot?'

'I'm well, thank you. Are you going to walk me to the office?'

He couldn't decide if he could hear sarcasm in her voice or not, but he was in such a good mood this morning he decided he did not care; besides, he was becoming accustomed to her sarcastic remarks. In fact, he had almost grown to like them.

They strolled side by side, a pace apart.

'I suppose Barkis will want to ask us about what happened in Wales,' she began. 'Have you heard from him since we returned?'

'No—I think he is sitting a Classics exam today, and is frightfully busy with revision.' Jones shook his head. 'Isn't it odd that the young and inexperienced are in charge while we do most of the work, just because they are of higher social standing?'

She looked at him thoughtfully. 'That's the way the world works. Take Holdstock, for example. He would rather gad around in his motor-car than do any real work. You and I will have to do everything just because our fathers aren't gentry. And before you start, Barkis is almost as bad. I don't care if he's your friend.'

Although he had begun to agree with her complaints, Jones felt he had to defend Barkis. 'Nobody is forcing you to work here.'

'Do you have any idea how difficult it is for a woman to earn what I need to support my family? My father is sick and needs constant attention.'

That bitterness again, that disappointment. Jones felt sorry for his careless remark. 'Perhaps you ought to speak to Barkis if you have grievances. I'm sure he will take your circumstances into account.'

'Believe me, he knows all about my circumstances. My father knew Sir George Barkis in the '60s when he climbed his new route on the Jungfrau. Although he's never said it directly, I gather Barkis only employed me out of a sense of duty to my father, now that his health is in a bad state.'

'I never knew Simon's father did a new route on the Jungfrau,' Jones said.

She stared at him. 'I sometimes wonder if you know that boy as well as you claim to.'

Maybe she had a point. Real life, with its subtleties of behaviour and social conventions, could not be more different from the unconventional atmosphere of a mountain inn—the context in which he mostly knew Barkis. Away from the mountains, their relationship felt very different.

'Perhaps you're right.'

'Of course I'm right.' She turned her eyes on him, sincere for once. 'He may not listen to me, but he'll listen to you. Please would you speak to him on my behalf? It's only a matter of time before I lose my temper with the spoilt little boy.'

'Who's a spoilt little boy?'

Jones turned to see who had said those words, and there, of course, stood Simon Barkis. He looked amused.

'I'll see you inside,' Miss Elliot said, her tone icy, before turning the key and letting herself in.

'Put the kettle on, will you?' Barkis said as he followed her in.

*

Miss Elliot spent a few minutes coaxing the fire to life before she could make the tea. The fire didn't give out much heat, but the office was so small the room warmed up quickly enough, and as she bustled around with kettle and teapot Barkis sat down at his desk and invited Jones to sit with him.

'Must apologise again about this rather squalid place,' he said as he lit his pipe. 'We're trying to get a better office on Trinity Street, perhaps with a servant or two.'

'I'll believe that when I see it,' Miss Elliot muttered.

Barkis frowned. 'I've told you before, this situation is only temporary. Holdstock says there is a small complication with the accounts.'

'I wish he would keep me informed,' she said, hands on hips. 'Perhaps he has forgotten that I am supposed to be the treasurer as well as the scullery maid.'

Barkis ignored that remark. 'Tell me about what happened in Wales,' he said to Jones, turning his back on Miss Elliot.

Jones recounted a summary of events, making light of the Slanting Gully embarrassment and focusing on the progressive mountaineering club and his conversation with Eckenstein. To his surprise, Barkis didn't seem to be concerned by Eckenstein's hostility.

'We don't need him, Jones! I expect you're just as good at thinking up new designs for climbing equipment.'

'Actually, I don't think that's true. Eckenstein is the expert. He has far more practical experience than I do. All I've ever done is teach physics to boys at school.'

Barkis waved a hand vaguely. 'It's all the same sort of thing, though, isn't it?'

'Not at all. I wouldn't know what to do with a forge if you put one in front of me.'

'Well, no gentleman would! That's the sort of thing working men concern themselves with.'

Miss Elliot seemed to be enjoying watching this conversation, as if she knew it would be confirming her theories about Barkis. The boy couldn't help it: he had grown up in an environment of privilege and ease, and the only reason he spent his spare time trying to sell climbing gear was because he believed in the progressive ideals that Jones shared. He certainly didn't need to make money, but Jones did not have that luxury. Suddenly he found himself wondering what would happen when Holdstock lost interest—as he inevitably would in the end—and withdrew his funding. The company would never be financially sufficient until a serious man took control. Despite what Barkis thought, they needed Eckenstein.

'I think you ought to be more concerned,' Jones insisted. 'Eckenstein has the power to either cripple or save us.'

'It really is not as important as all that. All I care about is that he isn't going take us to court.'

Miss Elliot put the kettle on its hook over the fire, and straightened. 'Mr Barkis, since Jones seems unwilling to do so, I must ask if any ideas have been dishonourably copied.'

Barkis' eyes widened. 'That is none of your business! If Holdstock were here he'd damn you for the impertinence.'

'Aren't we lucky that you don't have Holdstock's backbone, then?'

47

She walked over to the desk and leaned on it with both hands, glaring at her boss. Jones admired this determined woman all the more. He had known Barkis far longer, and felt inclined to side with his friend on many issues, but for once he found himself cheering Miss Elliot—and very keen to hear the answer to her question. The matter had been troubling him ever since Eckenstein planted the doubt in his mind.

'I have a right to know just as much as Jones has!' she pressed. 'You and Holdstock may treat me like a servant and pay me half the wages of a man, but I am both secretary and treasurer of this company and I want to know the truth.'

Barkis looked nervous, conscious of how naive and inexperienced he must seem to them. He had absolutely no authority over Miss Elliot, and he knew it.

'I'm sorry if you feel mistreated. It's no secret that Eckenstein originally designed similar ice claws. Crowley had a pair built, but when he died without having patented the idea, Holdstock decided it would be best for everyone if we made use of them. Once we discovered what this equipment could do, it would have been tragic not to act. We're guilty of no crime!'

Jones thought that sounded like a pathetic excuse for stealing someone else's ideas. It might not legally be theft, but it felt dishonest.

Miss Elliot shook her head. 'Crowley is going to be very angry with you.'

'I still think someone is playing a prank on us. He can't have survived.' Barkis smiled at Jones, but it seemed forced. 'The important thing is that we are making progress, thanks to you!'

Jones did not, at that moment, share his friend's enthusiasm.

*

The work of the day began after they had drunk their tea. Barkis seemed to be engrossed in his revision and took no notice of business, instead muttering phrases in Greek while pacing up and down the office, much to Miss Elliot's annoyance. Jones considered asking Barkis what he ought to be doing, but after their argument he felt a stubborn desire to prove himself resourceful and experienced. If they could not benefit from Eckenstein's skills, Jones would have to do his best to compensate. To that end he wrote a letter to Professor Collie asking when the new climbing club would meet, and started work drafting an article on progressive mountaineering.

The office felt even more cramped now that he had to work in it. As a lecturer he had enjoyed a private room with antique furniture and a small library; here he had to share a desk with Miss Elliot, and his writing slope battled for space with her typewriter.

A package arrived for him late morning. Miss Elliot seemed curious, but Barkis did not even notice the delivery. When Jones opened the envelope, he discovered a handful of photographic prints, together with a letter from George Abraham, promising him full rights to the images within the terms of their usual agreement.

'It must be handy to have your very own private photographer,' Miss Elliot said, craning her head over the typewriter to see what Jones had in his hands.

'Abraham is hardly that. He runs a studio in Keswick, and I often employ him to document my adventures.'

'And you wonder why people label you a self-publicist?'

Her playful tone halted the indignant reply already forming on his lips. Jones was gradually learning that sometimes she didn't mean any harm by her cutting observations.

'May I see the photographs?'

He rose and walked round to her side of the desk so they could look at them together. All five images depicted the same scene: a broad slash of ice between black walls. From the angle Abraham had taken the picture, the ice seemed to be vertical or overhanging. Jones noticed his own figure climbing up the gully, poised easily in that improbable location with a smoking pipe sticking out of his mouth. Could that really be him? He often found it difficult to imagine the exposed situations he got himself into until Abraham produced the photographic evidence, but on this occasion the effect was even more striking.

Jones felt his enthusiasm flutter back to life. After all the disappointments and quarrels, he still believed in what they were trying to do, and he knew that pictures like this would help to spread progressive ideas. If this didn't inspire climbers to challenge the old traditions, nothing would.

A knock to the office door disturbed his thoughts. Jones rose to answer it, and was greeted by a young police sergeant, carrying his helmet under one arm. Jones felt in his gut that something must be wrong.

'Good day, sir. Do I have the pleasure of addressing Mr Barkis or Mr Holdstock?'

The sergeant spoke with the local accent. He seemed friendly enough, Jones thought.

'Actually, I'm Mr Jones. Would you like to come in?'

The policeman's smile did not waver. 'If you would be so kind.'

He pushed past into the office and added his coat to the rack with the others. Miss Elliot looked surprised at the intrusion, and Barkis rose to shake hands. Nobody spoke for a second.

'May I offer you a cup of tea, sergeant?' Barkis said when the silence became uncomfortable. 'The maid would be only too happy to brew another kettle.'

'No, thank you—this will be a very brief visit.' He pulled a notebook out of his pocket. 'For the official record, are you Simon Barkis, currently an undergraduate of Trinity College?'

Barkis looked pale. He hadn't committed any crime—Jones still believed that, despite everything—but this morning's argument must have tested his conscience, and perhaps uncertainty about Crowley added to his worries.

'Yes,' he said quietly.

'And where is your partner, Thomas Holdstock?'

'He's gone to London.' Barkis glanced at the clock on the wall. 'Actually, if I don't leave now I will be late for my Classics examination.'

The policeman seemed amused. 'Sorry sir, but you will leave this room when I advise you to, and not before. We are investigating allegations of fraud and patent breach. Consider yourself lucky the Proctors haven't caught wind of this yet.'

Barkis opened his mouth to speak, but no sound came out. Jones sympathised; the Proctors and their constables were responsible for enforcing University law, and in Cambridge they had a reputation for acting swiftly and viciously. Armed with truncheons and pistols, they had powers to arrest pupils and deal out summary justice. More serious offences usually resulted in the undergraduate being sent down in disgrace. For a man like Barkis, expected by family tradition to excel during his time at Trinity, expulsion probably meant more to him than the threat of prison.

The sergeant did not seem to notice Barkis' discomfort. 'When we have concluded our investigation, we shall present our findings to the Proctors. Perhaps if you help us I'll have a word with my friend Professor Mason, and he may be more lenient when it comes to the tribunal.'

'I think you ought to tell us who made these allegations,' Miss Elliot said.

Jones caught her looking at him. He could tell what she was thinking: it must have been Crowley!

'Obviously I am not able to divulge the gentleman's name, but his information is being taken very seriously indeed.'

The sergeant put his coat back on and made for the door. 'This is just a warning not to leave Cambridge without notifying us. We shall pay a more formal visit within three days, and may summon any one of you to the police station for questioning. Good morning to you.'

*

At five o'clock, Jones and Miss Elliot left the office. The afternoon had been an unsatisfactory one, and after the policeman's visit Jones didn't get much work done. It all seemed rather pointless now.

Miss Elliot locked the premises behind her as they stepped out into the dark lane. Jones stood on the pavement for a moment, breathing slowly, trying to imagine that he could smell clean mountain air instead of smoke, oil, manure and soot. A tiny flake of snow drifted down and landed on Miss Elliot's hat.

'Snow,' he said with satisfaction. He wondered if this winter would prove to be as good as the last one.

His colleague shivered and rubbed her gloved hands together. 'Come, let us be away. My father will be angry if I'm late for supper.'

Suddenly she seemed melancholy, and Jones felt an unexpected surge of affection for her.

'Will you allow me to walk you back?'

'Perhaps we will walk together for a while, until we reach your road, at least.'

She took his arm and they walked in silence until they reached the junction with Trinity Street. A medley of grand architecture jostled for space wherever the eye wandered: towers, crenulations, gargoyles, tall windows and carved stone. In the darkness, the effect conspired to oppress, like a Gothic prison. The shops remained open along with the taverns, and a few pedestrians hurried past, hands in pockets, scarves flapping in the wind. A pair of horses drew a tram clattering away in the opposite direction.

'Tell me something,' Jones said as they strolled past King's College. 'Why do you dislike me? I know our acquaintance did not begin on the best terms, that day on Tryfaen, but surely you know me a little better now. I'm trying.'

She sighed. 'I don't dislike you. If we are talking frankly, I shall simply say that there are things about you that drive me to despair on occasion, but perhaps that says more about me than about you.'

'Well, we have only known each other for a few days. In the interest of harmony, may I call you Rachel?'

She laughed. 'As you said yourself, we hardly know each other. I don't think that would be at all proper.'

After a while, she mentioned the subject that was foremost on both of their minds.

51

'What do you suppose will become of this investigation?'

Jones felt even less cheerful. 'The whole affair stinks to high heaven.' He fell silent.

'Tell me what you're thinking,' she pressed.

'I'm thinking poor Barkis is scared to death of what his father will say if he gets sent down.' He hesitated before continuing. 'Instinct tells me that something is wrong, and I am convinced that Holdstock is behind it. I think he's hiding something.'

She looked sharply at him. 'May I remind you that I am the treasurer? No fraud has been committed on my watch, Jones!'

'But you said yourself that Holdstock often ignores you and does what he pleases. Anyway, I'm talking about the patents. I think Crowley's original ideas may have been copied, and he is going to be furious.'

Miss Elliot sighed. 'Men and their feuds. You don't like Crowley, do you?'

'Of course I don't like him. He can do us a lot of harm if he wants to.'

She tightened her grip on his arm as they walked through the falling snow. For a moment Jones realised that, despite his troubles, things could be a lot worse: he had a home to go to, a regular wage, and a pretty girl at his arm.

'I don't like it one bit, Jones,' she said after a few silent moments.

Neither did he. Jones hated the taste of a beautiful opportunity gone sour. Now that he had closed the door on his teaching career for good, he had to make the best of it.

CHAPTER FIVE

THE CRASH

1st of February, 1897

S PURRED ON BY the threat of a further visit from the police, work at the office increased in pace. Miss Elliot set to work processing the paperwork that their few sales produced, and Jones spent most of his time sending and receiving telegrams in the hope of contacting every climber currently using the new ice tools. Sometimes he wondered if there was any point to it. If the police shut the company down, it would all be for nothing.

His other task was to get his article into circulation. He had named it "The Progressive Ice-Climber", and posted it to all the climbing clubs of the country together with copies of Abraham's photo. He had also sent a copy to Collie, in the hope that if the new progressive club became established, his article could be included in the first journal.

Meanwhile, Holdstock had not been seen for days and Simon Barkis, when he appeared at all, seemed to be in a frightful rush as he scurried between Cambridge and London, engrossed in a legal battle that he remained uncommunicative about, despite its importance for them all.

On Friday he burst into the office. Miss Elliot looked up in irritation, but did not move from behind her pile of paperwork; Jones suspected she preferred working without either of the directors around. Barkis dripped all over the floor, cursing the rain. He wrung out his scarf into the waste paper basket.

'Ah, Jones! Any more visits from the police?'

He thought that Barkis' friendly greeting sounded strained. 'Not yet.'

'Good, good … I have made an important discovery. Is Holdstock in?'

'I haven't seen him all day. Anything I can help you with?'

Barkis pulled off his boots, cleared his desk of junk with a sweep of an arm, and sank into the nearest chair. 'Pull up a seat, my dear fellow.'

Jones did as instructed. Meanwhile, Barkis retrieved a document case from within his coat and opened it up, spreading several sheets on the desk.

'This is a copy of a patent filed in November 1895 by Aleister Crowley.'

The design specified an ice axe twenty five inches in length with a curved pick for anchoring in ice. Compared to the axes being manufactured by the Holdstock Company, the design appeared conservative.

'Why, this looks exactly like the axe Crowley was boasting about as early as 1894. It's completely different to the modern axes we're selling.'

'Quite,' Barkis confirmed. 'A crude hooking tool, with a straight shaft and no grip for the hand, you will notice. This is the thing Crowley used on the Matterhorn.'

Jones nodded, sharing Barkis' relief. This document, at least, proved that the design of the ice axe was safe.

When Jones saw the second design, however, his heart sank. This patent bore the title "Ice Claw, or Crampon", filed by an Alexander Godwin in January 1896. In most respects it looked identical to the claws currently manufactured and sold by the Holdstock Company.

Barkis looked at him. 'I would welcome your thoughts. I have never heard of an Alexander Godwin, but I sense Crowley behind this.'

Jones didn't like to think of his friend as a crook. Instinct told him that Barkis followed Holdstock's lead in every matter, even though the company's founder hardly ever contributed his time to the business. The more he saw of things at Holdstock Equipment, the less he liked the situation.

'I'm not sure,' Jones began hesitantly, unwilling to make direct accusations. 'The basic idea of an ice claw is an old one. The only novel feature is the addition of the front points, and it's quite possible that two people could come up with the same idea independently.'

Barkis leaned back in his chair and frowned deeply. 'When Crowley lived with me at Saint John's Street, he often used to hint at his remarkable climbing contraptions, but never really went into detail. A few times, when we went climbing in Wales, he used a short axe exactly like the one in that picture, but I recall he had a pair of quite old claws he had picked up in Savoy and modified himself. He never gave any hint about patenting the idea.'

'Then how do you explain this design?'

'I can't account for it. Long before we started production, Holdstock assured me that no patents for ice claws existed. I left the legal side of things to him.' Barkis frowned once more. 'Maybe I ought to have checked myself. I'm worried, Jones.'

*

'Where can Holdstock have got to?'

54

That was the second time Barkis had asked this rhetorical question in an hour. He paced about the office, flitting between his desk and the window, which he peered through anxiously from time to time as if on the lookout for the police. The dismal view, of rain-washed streets and shades of grey and brown, only seemed to further depress his mood.

'Stop fretting,' Miss Elliot eventually snapped from behind her typewriter. 'I'm sick of watching you pace up and down like a caged animal.'

'I can hardly be blamed for worrying,' Barkis replied. 'If only Holdstock would come back—or the police, for all I care! Anything to avoid this interminable waiting.'

Jones felt the same way, but preferred to cope with it by keeping himself busy and getting on with his work. He considered mentioning this fact, but the office door opened before he had a chance to speak. In strode Thomas Holdstock. His leather overcoat streamed with water, and a suitcase bumped along behind him as he dragged it over the floorboards. Eyes wide and gaze flitting nervously from side to side, fists clenched, nostrils flared: this was a frightened man.

Barkis jumped up from his seat. 'Where have you been?'

'Never mind that.' Holdstock dumped his bags and darted over to the window, which he glanced through for a moment before pulling down the blind. 'I need to get out of here. I've come for my things.'

Miss Elliot watched the scene with interest, but Jones found himself unable to look. Every minute he spent in this office confirmed his worst fears. First the police, then the suspicious patents, now Holdstock acting like a wanted criminal … it all conspired to make his high hopes for the progressive spirit in climbing seem like a foolish dream. It would all come crashing down around them. For the first time since leaving London, Jones genuinely wished he had never accepted Barkis' offer.

Holdstock, meanwhile, stepped over to his desk and began stuffing items into his pockets, raiding the drawers for papers and making a lot of mess in his hurry. He opened the cash box with a key and helped himself to a handful of banknotes.

Miss Elliot stood up. 'What are you doing?'

'Making a small withdrawal.' Holdstock continued to rifle through his drawers.

'Not without my permission.'

Holdstock's eyes flashed with anger. 'Just who do you think you are? I own this company and pay your wages! You'll do as you're told, damn you!'

Barkis approached him, hands held out in a calming gesture. 'Wait a moment, Tom. Miss Elliot is quite right—you're acting like a fool. She's the treasurer and those are our funds.'

'This has nothing to do with you.' He turned to Barkis' desk. 'Where did you get those drawings?'

'The patent office. I've been waiting for you to come back so I could ask you about them.'

Barkis looked so earnest and trusting. Faced with the obvious truth, that Holdstock had swindled them all, Jones felt sorry for his naive young friend.

Holdstock snatched up the documents and flipped through them. 'They all seem to be here. I think I'll look after them for you.'

Miss Elliot remained standing, and now moved towards the door. 'I don't think you should take those papers out of this office, Mr Holdstock.'

'Just how do you intend to stop me?'

Jones sensed trouble. Barkis seemed paralysed by indecision, and Miss Elliot now stood between the crook and his only route of escape. Holdstock had a dangerous look about him.

Jones moved between Miss Elliot and Holdstock. 'I think you ought to put the designs back on the desk.'

Panic and anger battled for control of Holdstock's expression. What had motivated him to such haste, Jones wondered? Had he decided to cut his losses and run before the police found him?

'Please, I have to get away. The police are right behind me!'

A loud knock sounded on the door behind Jones. Holdstock froze.

'Expecting someone?' Miss Elliot said sarcastically, but she looked frightened.

'Open up! Police!'

Holdstock grabbed his suitcase and made for the window, still clutching the crumpled drawings he had stolen from Barkis' desk. He struggled to open the window.

'Wait a moment, for God's sake!' Barkis pleaded. 'What are you going to do, climb down the drainpipe? You need to calm down and talk to the police. I'm sure this must be all some mistake.'

'Crowley has stitched me up! I have to get away!'

The police knocked on the door again, louder this time.

'Don't you realise you look guilty as hell?'

Holdstock turned back and looked at them, one leg through the open window as he struggled with his suitcase. 'Sorry to leave you like this,' he said awkwardly. 'I didn't think it would end this way.'

He threw his case down into the street, stuffed the patent applications down the front of his shirt, and started to climb down the drainpipe.

*

When Miss Elliot opened the door, several policemen rushed into the office and ordered everyone present to stand at the edge of the room.

'Where's Holdstock?' the sergeant demanded. 'We know he was here!'

Barkis looked terrified. He pointed to the window. 'You just missed him.'

The sergeant cursed and ordered two officers after him. Out in the street, Holdstock's automobile chugged into life. Jones ran to the window and looked down. The open-top Phaeton moved no faster than a bicycle, but the policemen did not have bicycles and it soon outstripped them as they ran after it blowing their whistles.

Moments later, Jones heard two shots fired. A loud crash followed the shots, and everyone rushed to the window to see what had happened. The policemen continued to blow their whistles as they ran towards the crash site.

When Jones got to the window, he saw the Phaeton in a crumpled heap where it had hit the corner of a building head-on. Smoke rose from the wreckage. At first Jones thought the policemen must have fired the shots, but even from this distance it was obvious that neither carried a gun.

'We have to go down there and help him,' Miss Elliot said.

The sergeant ordered his policemen to move them away from the window. He looked himself, then ordered his remaining officers downstairs to help their colleagues apprehend Holdstock.

'You will stay here,' the sergeant ordered. 'What goes on down there is no concern of yours.'

'But he's our friend!' Barkis said.

'He's my suspect first and foremost, and you will do as I say!'

The sergeant stormed around the office, searching through loose papers, upending drawers, and making even more mess than Holdstock had. Barkis looked on helplessly, as if he had known in his heart this would happen all along.

'Where are the patents?' the sergeant demanded after some minutes. He looked at Barkis first, then Jones, finally glaring at Miss Elliot. 'I checked with the patent office. They were withdrawn today.'

'Holdstock stole them,' Barkis said quietly.

'When they are recovered, we'll establish exactly who is to blame for this. You and you,' he said, pointing at Barkis and Miss Elliot, '—you're under arrest. Jones, get out of my sight.'

Jones blinked. 'Excuse me?'

'You've only worked here for a few days. I'll need to question you, but you are under no suspicion.' When Jones didn't move, he looked exasperated. 'Get out, for God's sake!'

Jones looked at his friends. Barkis seemed to silently plead for him to stay, but Jones felt angry with him for allowing Holdstock to hoodwink them. Had Barkis been aware of the scam in any way, he wondered?

Miss Elliot just looked resigned. 'I'll see you tomorrow, Jones. This will all blow over, I'm sure of it.'

*

Bystanders crowded the corner of Trinity Lane, eager to discover what had become of Cambridge's first and only automobile. Four policemen tried to hold back the crowd while a fifth attended to the casualty. Jones elbowed through until he got to the front, where a policeman ordered him to stop.

'But he's a friend.'

The policeman wavered, then stepped aside. 'I suppose he ain't getting away now.'

Despite the fact that it couldn't have been moving at more than about fifteen miles per hour, the Phaeton had been destroyed by its encounter with the wall. Hot oil hissed and ran over splintered wood, belching out a cloud of vapour. The stonework didn't show a scratch from the impact. Holdstock groaned amongst the wreckage while a kneeling officer tried to see how badly he was hurt.

Holdstock's face had turned completely white, eyes staring and filled with terror. 'What happened?'

'Steady now, sir,' the policeman said gently. 'We had a bit of an accident.'

'Accident? Some bastard shot me! Just you wait until my father hears of this!'

Holdstock let out another moan of pain. Other than the bleeding wound in his thigh, and minor cuts and bruises over the rest of his body, he seemed to be more or less uninjured.

Jones kneeled down next to him. 'Are you going to be all right?'

'I've suffered worse in the mountains,' Holdstock said with a stoic grin. 'Don't worry about me. Sorry to get you involved in all this, old boy.'

'It's been an adventure.'

'Hasn't it just?' His grin faded. 'I think the adventure ends here for me, though.'

*

Jones returned home alone, feeling saddened by the events of the morning and trapped by his decision to abandon his teaching career. What would happen to them all now? Could he beg to go back to the City of London School? His colleagues would never respect him again, he realised; in all probability he would be turned away. There had to be something else he could do.

He still believed in the noble goal of Holdstock Equipment. Shedding the century of tradition and caution that surrounded mountaineering would free climbers to be adventurous and explore without fear of judgement. How tragic that the schemes of Crowley and Holdstock would destroy it all.

At the same time, he found himself wondering how much anyone actually cared. After all, it was only climbing. What could it matter to anyone but a few crackpots? Perhaps he was wasting his life on a cause without meaning.

He shut himself in his study and settled down at his desk, intending to immerse himself in writing for the remainder of the day. The weather had turned even more foul outside, and only a little feeble light trickled through the window. He lit his lamp. It did little to drive back the shadows, and in his depressed mood Jones found himself wondering how long he would even be allowed to live in this flat: it belonged to the company, after all.

Startled by a noise behind him, he turned and was shocked to see a figure sitting on a stool in the darkest corner of the room.

'Show yourself,' he demanded, suddenly wishing he had a weapon to hand.

The figure leaned forward into the light. Black hair, tousled and wild yet receding from the forehead; large staring eyes of extraordinary intensity; a confident smile: Jones recognised his rival Aleister Crowley at once.

'I have to speak to you,' Crowley said quietly. 'My apologies for breaking in. I thought if I approached you in the street you would avoid me.'

Jones stood and faced him, fists clenched. 'You shot at Holdstock! I knew you were against us, but I never thought you would go this far.'

'I'm not a monster. Won't you sit down? We can at least discuss this like gentlemen.'

Jones bristled at being ordered around in his own lodgings, and yet Crowley's calm manner deflated his anger a little. 'I will stand. Say what you have come to say.'

'I've always looked up to you, and yet you are so hostile to me.' Crowley sounded aggrieved. 'I don't know what I've done to deserve this treatment.'

Could he really be unaware of how he treated people, his insufferable air of superiority, the way he gave no consideration for others unless it suited his selfish needs? Did he really think that plotting the ruin of his rivals, even attempting to murder them, would make people respect him?

'You are a coward and a criminal,' Jones said. 'I think you started the avalanche that almost killed us in Glen Coe. You have sent threatening telegrams, stirred hatred against us, and now you've tried to murder Holdstock.'

'I'm doing what I must to restore my reputation and take back what is rightfully mine!'

Jones shook his head. 'You have no right to those designs. Our ice axes are completely different to yours, and the ice claws were patented by a Mr Godwin. I suppose that's one of your pseudonyms?'

'Alexander Godwin has a legal existence as a British citizen, I assure you.'

'But don't you see, you're breaking the law just as Holdstock did!'

Crowley looked angry. 'I don't care about the law. It's the principle of it. I should have been the one to take the glory of the Matterhorn's north face. My friends plotted against me and now I have nothing. I wouldn't expect someone as small-minded as you to understand.'

Jones ignored the insult. 'Then why the violence? Why not follow legal channels?'

'Barkis and Holdstock did not follow legal channels when they tried to kill me on the Matterhorn! An eye for an eye—that's what your god teaches, is it not?'

'You are a monster. I will tell the police—'

'What?' Crowley cut him off with a mocking laugh. 'You will tell the police that you are being persecuted by a man whose death was reported in every national newspaper. Dozens of witnesses in Zermatt saw me fall as they watched through their telescopes. Your stupidity disappoints me.'

The swine had a point. Not for the first time, Jones wondered how he had ever survived. In the end it didn't matter. Without proof, nobody would believe that Crowley still lived.

Jones sighed, and sat back down. Maybe he had no choice but to talk to Crowley about this and discover more.

'Very well. What do you want?'

'What is rightfully mine. I want recognition for my climbing powers, recognition for being the inventor of the progressive technique, and the dissolution of the company formed by those who have defied me.'

He never did things in small measures, Jones thought gloomily. All this talk of recognition and glory sounded like a desire for revenge dressed up in more palatable terms.

'I don't have the power to give you any of those things. Tell me what I can do.'

'You can be on my side instead of theirs,' Crowley said quietly.

The offer took Jones by surprise. He and Crowley had never been friends, although once they had been respectful rivals, each enjoying the game of trying to prove himself the better climber. That was before things turned nasty last year. Jones knew that Crowley had deliberately tried to ruin his reputation, and had largely succeeded. Now Crowley focused on destroying not only his friends, but the future of climbing he believed in; no, he could not consider for one moment throwing in his lot with Crowley.

'I will never help you. What you're doing is absurd.'

Crowley's smiled now seemed forced, as if he struggled to maintain control of his anger. 'Think about this for a moment. You don't want to be my enemy, Jones.'

'You have already made an enemy out of me. There is nothing more for us to discuss.'

'I beg you to reconsider. We could help one another!'

Jones found himself wondering if Crowley still had the gun he had used to shoot Holdstock. What would he do if things turned violent? Jones had no weapons apart from his ice axes.

He moved over to the door and opened it. 'Get out of my flat.'

Crowley rose, looking angry. 'But it isn't yours, is it? Holdstock pays for these rooms. Oh, and have you thought about what will happen to the dear Miss Elliot, supporting her sick father all by herself while her brother is playing soldiers in India? I hold so many people in my power, Jones...'

This time he didn't hold back the urge, and punched Crowley so hard his knuckles stung. The young man fell to the floor with a howl of rage, yet when he looked up at Jones, he seemed triumphant.

'Interesting reaction. Did I touch a nerve?'

Jones clenched his fist, ready for a fight. 'Get out!'

Crowley stood with a wince and brushed himself down. He looked at Jones with a pitying expression, yet Jones sensed that, for today at least, the balance of power lay with him.

'I urge you to reconsider,' Crowley said as Jones pushed him out of the door. 'Things will go badly for you if you resist me, and I won't wait forever.'

CHAPTER SIX

ORION

20th of February, 1897

"MY DEAR MR JONES,

"I hope this letter finds you well & in better spirits than last time we met. You asked me to keep you up to date on developments with the case; well, here it is, although none of it is good news.

"You will not be surprised to hear that I was summarily dismissed from the company within days of your departure. Mr Barkis, for all his faults, did his best to protect me & I was released without being charged for anything. The police ransacked the office & confiscated everything. The court hearing occurred as scheduled last Wednesday, as I am sure you have read in the newspapers. Holdstock has gone to prison & Barkis has been fined a hundred guineas. All of the company's assets have been seized & most likely will go to this Alexander Godwin character, which is of course Crowley's pseudonym.

"Barkis has been trying to convince the authorities that Crowley still lives and is playing us all for fools, but they will not believe it & his fine was increased for wasting court time.

"You expressed concern in your letter for me and my family. Please do not trouble yourself. We are getting by.

"Do let me know when you are next in town & we can arrange lunch. I miss you, scoundrel that you are, especially now that I find I have nobody to vent my frustration on.

"How go your efforts with the Professor's new mountaineering club? Do write soon.

"Yours affectionately,

"Rachel M. Elliot."

*

Jones smiled to himself as he re-read the letter, then folded it carefully and placed it back in the envelope. He was on the train to Scotland to attend the very first meeting of the Progressive Mountaineering Club. Since moving away from Cambridge and back to London, he had focused all of his energies into Collie's new club. Jones discovered that his efforts to contact all of the current owners of the new ice gear had been of tremendous benefit, and he hoped these twenty two individuals would form the core of the new society devoted to progressive mountaineering.

It would not be the sweeping revolution he had hoped for, but a pebble cast in the ocean was not a bad start. After the setbacks of recent weeks any progress at all felt like a good thing.

At the informal society dinner at the Alpine Club rooms last week, Collie had been unanimously voted the new club President, despite his continuing interests in the more traditional mountaineering clubs. Only a man like Collie could balance two contradictory philosophies, but that was the Professor's gift to the world of climbing: his wisdom and attention, shared equally between all who needed it. Jones himself had been appointed Secretary, Harold Raeburn the Treasurer. Jones felt a lot more hopeful about this venture than his last, ill-fated attempt to bring about change.

He looked out of the window: nothing but blackness and noise, the glass reflecting his tired face.

Startled out of his musings by a sound, Jones looked up to see someone entering his compartment. A young lady in a black travelling cloak, battered knapsack slung over one shoulder, closed the door behind her and gave Jones a winning smile.

He had seen that cunning face and lithe frame before.

'You are a hard man to track down, Mr Jones,' Elspeth said as she sat down opposite him and took off her hat, revealing a bun of black hair.

Jones caught himself staring in astonishment. 'Elspeth, what a surprise.'

'I did say I would try and hunt you down in Cambridge, but you seem to have moved on.'

'I had a disagreement with my employers, and was forced to move back to London.'

'Oh, I am sorry to hear that.'

Her musical Highland accent reminded him of the day they climbed the Slanting Gully, that bittersweet victory.

'No matter, I am on my way to better things. What of you? How go your fortunes?'

She shrugged. 'Variable. I am a lady of independent means, so may do what I wish with my time. Of late, climbing conditions have been poor in Wales, so I have decided to go to Fort William to discover what this new PMC is all about.'

Jones wondered why she had mentioned that she was a woman of independent means. People did not volunteer that sort of information without cause. He decided to probe a little.

'I assume your husband must give you an allowance?'

She gave him a hard look. 'I have no husband, Mr Jones. I refer to an inheritance.'

'My apologies,' Jones said, but he had found her reaction interesting.

'No bother.' She looked out of the window. 'It's snowing again. Where are we, do you suppose?'

'We passed Carlisle not long ago. I hope it does not snow too much this time. Last time we visited Glen Coe, fresh snow was nearly the death of us.'

'Ah yes, I heard of that incident. How is Mr Raeburn, by the way?'

'His arm is mended, and I've heard he is keen to climb with the new equipment. He obtained a set just before the Holdstock Company's stock was seized.'

'It's a shame that the new equipment is no longer available, but on the other hand perhaps it is better if only a few of us have the tools. What do you think?'

Jones shook his head. 'I think it would be better if everyone had access to them. Climbing has the power to improve us all. Why put limits on what is possible?'

She chuckled. 'Said like a true employee.'

'I joined that company so I could fulfil my own personal philosophy, not so I could make money.'

'Tell me about your philosophy, then.'

Jones felt sleepy. Not for the first time, he wondered just what Elspeth could want with him. Despite her severe appearance, he found her attractive and it would not be the first time Jones had suffered the attentions of an over-zealous fan. Nevertheless, something about Elspeth still worried him, despite her friendliness and willingness to please.

He closed his eyes and drifted into a light doze. 'Surely if you know as much about me as you seem to, you must already know the answer to that question.'

'But I want to know you better, Mr Jones.'

'Why?'

Before Elspeth could reply, Jones noticed a bulky figure walking along the carriage, casting a shadow through the window into their compartment. He recognised that silhouette. Unable to credit the coincidence, Jones hurried into the corridor to catch him.

'Eckenstein!'

His voice scarcely carried over the clack-clack of the tracks, but the bear-like figure turned and grunted.

'Oh, it's you. I suppose you want me to join you in your compartment.'

'My dear fellow, I have an apology to put to you.'

Elspeth greeted the newcomer with a brittle smile. 'How do you do, Mr Eckenstein?'

Jones sensed a change in the atmosphere. 'Eckenstein, I am not certain if you are acquainted with—?'

'We've met,' he said curtly, before sitting in the corner farthest from the woman. 'So Jones, what is it you have to say to me?'

'I was wrong. I know you warned me never to mention this subject again, but my conscience will not permit silence.'

'Out with it, then.'

'The company stole ideas that rightfully belonged to others. Even if you did not patent your designs, climbers do not copy the ideas of other climbers. I'm ashamed that I did not recognise that.'

'You are learning humility, Jones. Pray continue. I am enjoying this.'

'I thought it was some scheme designed to destroy us, but in truth Holdstock is a crook, and Barkis is a naive dreamer.'

'Yet you went along with their plans for some time before coming to your senses.'

Jones felt like a fool. 'I'm sorry, Eckenstein. Won't you forgive me?'

He shrugged. 'You are forgiven already. I just wanted to hear you grovel. I think I have earned that much.'

'There is something else you must know,' Jones said, relieved. 'I have the evidence of my own eyes that Crowley still lives.'

Elspeth seemed interested, but Eckenstein did not speak for some minutes. He stared out of the window into the night, puffing on his pungent pipe, apparently deep in thought.

'What do you say to that?' Jones said after the silence became intolerable.

'If Crowley is alive, he will certainly make himself known to me. To be frank, I have no quarrel with the boy. He always struck me as a talented climber, and blissfully free of the chains society shackles to most men. He was a good friend.'

'But he is a liar, a cheat, and a criminal!'

'Don't be so quick to judge. In my view, you have done more to wrong me than Crowley has.'

The look in Eckenstein's eyes discouraged him from making a heated response to that.

'You always were a man to go your own way,' Jones admitted.

'Indeed I am, and I would advise you to do the same if you have any sense.'

Jones smiled. 'Unfortunately I don't think the Alexandra Hotel in Fort William has a coal shed for you to sleep in.'

*

A whistle blast woke Jones with a start. The train was motionless, the window to his right fogged up. Clearing it with a sleeve did not improve things much, for a huge cloud of steam wafted past, obscuring the view. From the corridor to his left came sounds of chatter and the movement of heavy cases.

'Fort William station!' shouted the conductor. 'All change!'

Oscar and Elspeth stirred, Oscar scowling as he awoke. He immediately struck a match and re-lit his pipe.

'Welcome to the cesspit of the Western Highlands,' he muttered.

Elspeth yawned long and loud. 'My, it feels like I have not slept at all. Are we really in the Fort already?'

A porter opened the door to their compartment. 'Any luggage I can assist you with, ladies and gentleman?'

'Do we look like weaklings?' Eckenstein demanded.

The porter scurried away, and Elspeth looked at Eckenstein disdainfully. 'What did you say that for? I could have used some assistance with my bags.'

'Then Jones can help you. I cannot abide these scraping little twits that infest the railways like vermin.'

Jones laughed out loud. As always when they were not being aimed at him, he found Eckenstein's rants entertaining. 'You are in a fine mood today, Eckenstein!'

'I hate this place. There is no finer example of the degrading effect of the tourist upon a community. Before you point out the irony of my stance, I hasten to add that since I have as little as possible to do with the locals, I do not consider myself part of the problem.'

They disembarked with haste and fought their way through the crowds on the platform. Overhead, rain beat down on the high roof of glass and steel, but nevertheless Jones found himself cheered by the neat and tidy station. The terminus of the West Highland Railway was brand new. Opened in 1894 and equipped with every modern convenience, it even boasted electric lighting and a public telephone.

Elspeth's manner approached that of an excited child. 'It's good to be back on home soil!'

'Come, let us find a cab,' Eckenstein said. He began to carve a trench through the crowd.

'Whatever is the matter with him?' Elspeth whispered to Jones as they followed in the wake of their giant companion.

'Eckenstein is a railway engineer, but he only cares about the machines. As I'm sure you have realised, he's not the most personable of men.'

'I knew he was a scientist, but I didn't know he worked with trains.'

'The man is a technical genius. I think his work is under-appreciated.'

They emerged into the open. The air smelled of salt and seaweed and mountains. Cloud hung low and ragged over the hills, obscuring the bulk of Ben Nevis, the highest peak in Britain and the main objective for visiting climbers. Fort William glistened in the passing shower, a smudge of tall chimneys and slanting roofs in the wilderness of the Highlands.

Eckenstein appeared to be haggling with the driver of a four-wheeler parked in the yard. The horses looked miserable in the cold and damp. Jones pulled his cap down over his ears and hurried through the rain towards the carriage, a bag over each shoulder, Elspeth just behind.

The journey along the High Street took only a few minutes. The cab pulled up into the muddy yard in front of the Alexandra Hotel, and after Eckenstein had paid the fare, they jumped out and scurried for shelter.

With its stern facade and high gables, water streaming from the gutters, the hotel did not exactly look welcoming. Nevertheless, Jones felt glad to be out of the rain. The first thing he noticed upon entering the lobby was the enormous heap of ropes, climbing boots, and ice axes of all descriptions drying out underneath the coat-racks. The hallway smelt strongly of wet leather and boot-grease.

Eckenstein nodded approvingly. 'The advance guard is here. Perhaps we shall be assured of some civilised conversation after all.'

*

Jones joined the group of climbers heading for Ben Nevis. They left the hotel at a little after nine o'clock, which he thought was rather late for an assault on the Ben—although he had never climbed there, and deferred to Collie in all matters regarding the mountain. The heavy shower of an hour ago had passed. Cloud still shrouded the mountain, and Jones worried that his feeble navigational powers might be tested on unfamiliar terrain.

Professor Collie strode beside him as they left the outskirts of town and entered the boggy flats of Glen Nevis. He wore a deerstalker hat and Mackintosh cape over his climbing suit, and stuffed behind his knapsack were a pair of Holdstock axes.

He seemed in excellent spirits. 'We haven't got a huge crowd, but it isn't a bad start. After that dinner in London, attended by so few, I feared that the bad press from the SMC and Alpine Club might put people off.'

'You have done a good job of promoting this meet,' Jones said. 'I'm surprised so many people are open to the new ice climbing concept.'

'Most of them are not. Of the twenty two owners of Holdstock gear you contacted, I estimate eight have actually turned up. That makes you outnumbered three to one. Once again, I anticipate robust conversation after dinner tonight, as I suspect several individuals have turned up simply to cause trouble.'

The Professor had purchased a pair of axes and claws some weeks previously, despite his reputation as a traditionalist. Now he spoke with the zeal of the converted.

'I thought you would stay in the traditional camp, I must admit. You are a member of the mountaineering establishment, my friend.'

Collie laughed. 'You say that like it is a bad thing! It's not easy, being sympathetic to the radical camp when others look up to you to be respectable. I have the gift of being able to appreciate both sides to the argument.'

Eckenstein drew level with them. 'It's a foolish argument, Professor. Some people are willing to adapt to the times, others are not; that is all there is to it.'

'Which is one reason why I decided to invest in the equipment,' Collie said, 'but I still think your assessment of the situation is too simplistic.'

'We shall see.'

After passing through Achintee, just a handful of cottages at the end of a lane, the group began the long grind up the pony track. This path led to the observatory on the summit of the mountain, and therefore provided an excellent highway to ease the initial ascent. Presently, they passed into the cloud, which seemed to suck all conversation into it and leave them enveloped in damp silence. Jones found his spectacles fogging up with dew, leaving him even more blind than usual. When he expressed concern that winter conditions might not be forthcoming on the crags, Collie told him to be patient.

Another hour, and a crossing of an interminable bog, brought them to a track that wound right across the face of the mountain. Drifts of snow lay across the path here and there, and the rocks glistened with a patina of black ice. Looking up, Jones began to sense impressions of vast shadows stretching up into the sky, outlines of ridges and buttresses: a ghostly arena built for giants or Titans, not humans. Except for the clink of climbing nails and occasional coughs from the group, silence prevailed.

Noon passed before they reached a level strath where Collie called a halt.

'Look,' he cried. 'The mist is rising!'

As he spoke, the vapours that surrounded them wafted up and away on a breeze that sprang out of the north. The view—the finest mountain panorama that Jones had ever witnessed in Britain, or perhaps even the world—finally opened up for all to see.

Cliffs curved in a great arc, reaching round to enclose them on all sides. Battlements towered higher than anyone could have imagined. Every feature that the climber could dream of was there: ridge, buttress, ice-chimney, sheer wall, gully. The extent and complexity of the massif stunned Jones to silence. To the left, the North-East Buttress seemed a Matterhorn in its own right, casting down a veil of ice from the summit of the mountain to the shadowed depths at their toes, over two thousand perpendicular feet. Further right was Tower Ridge, Collie's favourite climb, but Jones found his attention focused on that wall of ice that seemed to forbid any prospect of ascent.

Elspeth appeared at his shoulder. She, too, stared at the ice wall as if smitten.

'Ladies and gentlemen, welcome to the grand arena,' the Professor said with pride, for his association with Ben Nevis was of long standing. 'I will be taking a party up the Tower Ridge today. Who wants to come?'

Jones felt tempted to take the offer, as he had heard many good things about Tower Ridge, but the challenge of that unclimbed face could not be ignored. In the end, of the ten people in the group, five went with Collie, Eckenstein teamed up with Oppenheimer to attempt one of the gullies, and Elspeth remained by Jones' side. The group split up, each team heading in a different direction. The crunch of boots receded into the lingering mists.

As Eckenstein walked past, he nodded at Jones and said, 'Good luck, boy.'

Elspeth turned to Jones. 'Does that wall have a name?'

He studied it. It looked continuously steep, complex, riven by gullies and with rock barriers near the top. By the standards of British ice climbing, it might as well be a journey to the moon, or a distant galaxy; nothing like that had ever been climbed before in Scotland.

'I don't know.'

'I think we should climb it.'

Jones looked at his watch: almost a quarter past twelve. 'I'm not sure, Elspeth. I don't think we have time.'

'You are still thinking about an old-fashioned ascent. I promise, we will have time to spare.'

'But what of the way down?'

'We can stay in the observatory.'

She seemed so excited by the prospect, so full of vitality and energy. Jones wondered what could be holding him back. Usually, he was the first person to throw himself at something hard, regardless of weather or time of day; but it had landed him in bad trouble more times than he cared to admit, and as he neared thirty his boldness gradually surrendered ground to caution.

She folded her arms and smiled. 'This is not the Only Genuine Jones I have heard tales about! What are you afraid of?'

He imagined himself as a speck on that wall, a spaceman on his journey to the stars, and thought about the tales that would be added to the repertoire of Jones legends. It would be a sweet prize. In that instant, he realised that Elspeth had won the argument, and he hurried to catch up with her as she ran over the slabs in the direction of the cliff.

*

Jones hacked his axes into a bulge of ice above his head, heart pounding. He felt exposed. Looking down between his legs, the ice swept down for a rope's length to Elspeth, anchored to her axes on the vertical wall.

With shaking hands, Jones retrieved a length of cord from around his shoulders and tied himself to his axes. He had never felt so insecure in his life. At first, the climb had felt easy, and they had made rapid progress. As the exposure mounted, hundreds of feet of air between him and the snow-covered screes beneath the wall, Jones started to feel a creeping horror that he had never before experienced on an ice climb. Always in his thoughts was the terrible prospect of that two hundred foot fall through space, to be brought up to a sudden, bone-cracking stop when the rope came tight. Everyone knew he had a habit of falling off. Today he could not afford to make that mistake.

He took a few minutes to compose himself, slowly tensioning his belay line and letting his axes take the strain. His calf muscles screamed for relief. His arms, always his strongest attribute, complained with a duller ache.

Elspeth began to climb. As he took in the rope and carefully laid it in coils over his axes, he started to doubt the security of the new tools. Would they really withstand the force of a fall? They had done so on New Year's Day, and saved all their lives, but this was an altogether more serious situation.

Elspeth reached his stance. Her face was white, wide-eyed, scared. She seemed to be at the last of her strength as she made herself secure.

'A bit steep, that last pitch,' she gasped.

Jones looked down. A lump of ice fell from his mitten and dropped through space, bouncing only a few times until it exploded on the rocks far below. Looking up, it seemed that the route opened out into a basin some distance above, and beyond that, a forbidding headwall of ice-laced rocks.

With difficulty, he reached into the pocket of his waistcoat. The broken shell of ice that clung to his mittens rattled whenever he moved, making any kind of dextrous movement impossible. He retrieved his watch and checked the time. It was a quarter past three.

'It will be dark before long,' he reminded her.

'Then unless you know of a quick way off to the left or right, I suggest we keep going. We are committed to it now.'

Jones climbed on. His muscles hadn't had enough time to recover since the last pitch. He had found one disadvantage of the new ice technique: since it was more efficient, there were fewer opportunities to rest. The uncompromising strain on the calf muscles would take some getting used to.

He paused after maybe forty feet, and placed both axes high above his head to secure himself. The rough wool of his gloves stuck to the ice that had accumulated around the handles of his axes, providing a good grip. Nevertheless, his fingers felt tired and he suddenly panicked at the thought of what would happen if he let go. His journey into space would end with an abrupt return to planet Earth.

There was no way to fix a running belay on this kind of ground. If he fell off, he would fall all the way to Elspeth's level and then the same distance again. No convenient spike of rock or threaded chockstone would arrest the plunge. Was this it? Was this how it felt to experience your last seconds of life?

His arms shook, his vision blurred, and Jones knew he would fall off.

'I am going to fall!' he shouted. He could hear the fear in his voice.

Elspeth said nothing, but, looking down, he could see her brace for the fall that would surely kill them both, her terrified face framed by his boots.

One last effort, then.

Releasing reserves of strength he did not know he had, Jones pulled on his axes, feeling his fingers starting to fail from the strain. He kicked in with his left boot. His body shook so much that the claws skidded off the ice, and he thought he was going to fall then and there. Somehow, the points bit, he stood up, and all of a sudden the ground seemed less steep.

He felt a little more secure. A little further, he urged his tortured limbs. Soon the angle eased right off, to normal steep snow, and Jones felt that he could at last relax. His whole body seemed to beat with the rhythm of his heart.

Then the slip occurred.

The snow gave way, crumbling beneath him, and in seconds he was shooting down the slope like a bowling-ball. He tried to dig his axes in, but they simply scraped through the snow, engaging with nothing. He felt a moment of blind despair.

Over the edge, and into the silence that wrapped around the mountain like a blanket.

He felt nothing. All efforts to save himself ceased. He watched the ice rush upwards, felt the cool blast of air over his skin, noted the surprising patterns made by strands of wool embedded in the ice around the shafts of his axes.

Elspeth passed him in slow motion, shouting silently, gripping the rope tightly around her waist. He wondered why she was belaying that way. The proper way was over the shoulder. Jones reflected, in a detached manner, that the force of his impact when the rope came tight would probably crush her to death even as it ripped her axes out of the ice. He puzzled over why he felt nothing at that thought.

Then the impact came. The rope snapped bar-tight.

It did not hurt as much as he had expected. He heard a crack, and the rope creaked as it slowly twisted. Two inches from his nose, three Manila strands of Mr Beale's finest rope kept him safe in one of the deadliest situations he had ever experienced. In truth, Jones had expected Elspeth to let go from the pain, shortly followed by the final plunge as the belay failed and both climbers tumbled to oblivion.

The loop he had tied around his waist now constricted his chest, making breathing difficult. He must have broken ribs; it was inevitable in any major fall. Both axes were still frozen to his gloves. If they were to survive, small miracles like this would count.

With the initial shock of the fall fading, Jones felt his reason return, and with it the pain that gripped his ribcage. He raised his weakened arms and struck both axes into the ice, securing himself to them to take the strain from Elspeth.

He looked up, but could not tell if she was conscious or not.

'I'm safe,' he shouted up to her—or tried to shout. His voice sounded feeble.

'You are a heavy bastard, Jones! Get back up here!'

He looked up. Far beyond Elspeth, that rocky headwall still frowned down, steeper and more inaccessible than before. He knew the wall had beaten him.

'No, we have to go down. I will belay you.'

After a few minutes, Elspeth began the difficult and dangerous climb down to his position. When she drew level, breathing heavily from the effort, she offered a weak smile.

'I thought that was the end for both of us.'

'So did I,' Jones said. He realised his arms were still shaking. 'How did you hold the fall?'

'At the last moment, I realised that if I belayed the usual way, with the rope over my shoulder, I would be crushed and the force would rip out my axes. I passed it around my waist and arm. That way, the rope came to a stop gradually and the force was dissipated.'

Jones the scientist appreciated the facts of what she had done, but Jones the man marvelled that she had been able to appraise all this in the space of an instant.

'You saved my life ...' he began.

She ignored him. Now was not the time. 'I noticed a shelf cutting left across the cliff. Perhaps we can use it to reach the North-East Buttress. What do you think?'

Jones looked down. He doubted he could climb back down that distance of vertical ice, even when fresh and uninjured. In his current condition, a mental and physical wreck, it would put both of them at risk. He decided to hand over control of the situation to Elspeth.

'I am in no fit state to lead. Do whatever you think is best.'

*

Somewhere near the end of that horribly exposed and dangerous shelf, the weather closed in once again. A bitter wind blew shreds of mist across the face of the mountain, and it seemed that every time Jones looked up, a plume of spindrift descended from the heavens to batter him. His spectacles glazed over with frost, rendering him little better than blind, and his cap was lost to the gods of the mountain. A deep chill, a killing chill, settled into the core of his body as he shivered in a miserable ice-cave, paying out the rope to Elspeth. His chest hurt, a sharp pain from his broken ribs, but at least the cold helped to take his mind off it.

Not for the first time in his climbing career, Jones reflected on the utter absurdity of his situation: tied to an icicle the width of his arm, snow whirling all around him, perched a thousand feet above the ground in a place no man had ever been before.

When Elspeth gave the signal, he climbed on. Another rope's length, and another, and they reached the ridge, a wild place of shrieking winds and perplexing rock formations. A frosted tooth reared up ahead, barring their way. This, he realised through the pain and confusion, must be the feared man-trap that had defeated several since the first winter ascent of this ridge just under a year previously.

Elspeth seemed to be having trouble with it. Her position looked grotesque, splayed against the overhanging step. After a while she surmounted it with an ungainly belly-flop, and signalled for Jones to follow. He wanted to remove his claws to make the rock-climbing easier, but gave up after minutes of fiddling with frozen straps that refused to untie.

Two more pitches, including the difficult forty-foot corner, and they reached the summit of Ben Nevis. The light had failed. The gale blasted snow and icy pellets into his face. Looking ahead, the rope curved down into the snow, leading on to the shadowy figure of Elspeth fighting her way through the storm. A persistent ringing filled his ears.

A faint shout: 'The observatory! I've found it!'

Jones struggled on. Pain stabbed him with every step. Normally such dangerous weather would inspire him to fresh efforts, but he felt destroyed in a way he had rarely experienced in his life. Now all he wanted was food, warmth, and sleep. Soon he reached Elspeth, but hardly recognised her: fog-crystals coated her entire body except her face, which was red and raw with the wind. He realised he must appear similarly macabre, and raised a glove to touch his hair. It was entirely encased in ice.

He looked around, but could see nothing of the observatory. 'I don't see it,' he yelled.

Elspeth pointed. A low mound in the snow concealed what appeared to be the top of a wooden door, heavily drifted in snow.

'That's the tower. Help me dig!'

Considering that the observation tower was nearly thirty feet high, Jones did not believe her, but had not the energy to argue. He dug, with an axe and his hands, helping her to excavate more of the door. The more they dug, the more the snow slipped back into the pit, confounding their efforts. After what seemed like an hour they had finally dug enough snow free to make an attempt at getting inside.

Elspeth turned the handle. The wind immediately caught the door and flung it inward with a bang. Snow whirled down the ladder that led into the depths of the observatory, and Jones hurried to follow his companion.

He helped her close the door against the wind. Now they stood in almost total darkness. A suggestion of light drew them on, and after descending for some distance they broke out into a subterranean office. The spacious room was stocked with comfortable desks and a roaring pot-bellied stove. Wooden walls accommodated bookcases and glass display cabinets. To the left, a stairway led down into another room. Jones felt bewildered by the abrupt change from chaos to civilisation at the highest point of the British Isles.

They stood side by side in a puddle of melting snow, utterly at a loss for words. Elspeth recovered her senses first, and after untying from the rope she dumped her equipment next to the stove and began shouting for help.

Jones staggered to a chair and sat down with relief, hardly able to keep his head high. His broken rib throbbed with pain and he could feel blisters on his heels from hours of steep climbing.

When he looked up again, two men stood in the room. One, carrying a lantern, was a stranger; the other was Eckenstein, wrapped in a blanket and smoking his long pipe as usual. Eckenstein strode forward and gave the blanket to Jones, draping it over his shoulders. He suddenly started to shiver violently. The ice covering every inch of his body was melting, trickling through to his chilled skin beneath.

'You look done in, boy. An eventful day, then?'

'I could do with something to eat,' he whispered, but in that moment exhaustion caught up with him and he slumped forward, insensible.

"THE MIST IS RISING!"

CHAPTER SEVEN

A NIGHT AT THE OBSERVATORY

21st of February, 1897

J ONES FELT DISORIENTED when he woke up. He already seemed to have spent an age in this peculiar place, but on Eckenstein's advice he had spent most of his time sleeping. His rib gave a twinge. Willing his injury to heal, he ignored the pain. When he opened his eyes, he found himself in one of the tight fold-out bunks in the visitors' quarters of the observatory. Lamplight streamed through the open doorway from the office, where muted voices disturbed the silence of the underground world.

This place fascinated him. Half wilderness outpost, half laboratory, its rooms were cluttered with a bizarre mixture of scientific instruments, books by the dozen, and the tools necessary for survival. The windows surprised Jones most of all. Most of them had been shuttered at the start of the winter, but if you opened them you could examine the packed strata of snow on the other side. Bands of darker snow, James Miller informed them, indicated soot blown in with southerly winds from Glasgow.

He dressed and walked in to join the others. His limbs still felt a little stiff, but that familiar burn in his muscles was a comforting thing. Elspeth, Eckenstein, and Miller all sat around the central table near the stove, engrossed in a game of cards. A cloud of tobacco smoke hung over the group.

Elspeth looked up with a smile. For the first time since Jones had known her, she had released her hair from that tight bun and it cascaded over her shoulders in black curls.

'Good morning. Did you sleep well?'

'I'm far from certain that it is morning,' Jones said, 'but I am feeling much restored, thank you.'

'Would you like a cup of tea?'

'Thank you, but I will get it myself.'

She was already up and away. Miller nodded to a seat, which Jones took.

He liked Miller, a quiet man who had spoken little of himself, but much of the place in which they found themselves imprisoned by circumstances.

Of a similar age to Eckenstein, approaching forty and passionate about both science and the natural world, the two men had quickly formed a bond and often spoke together on subjects of mutual interest. The storm had trapped the other observatory men in Fort William, leaving Miller the sole custodian of the summit of Britain.

Miller pushed a plate of bread and cheese in Jones' direction. 'Have a bite to eat. You must be hungry after all that sleeping.'

Jones accepted with gratitude. 'Thank you again for your hospitality. I don't know what we would have done without you.'

'Ah, but it's nice to have visitors. Not many people visit the summit of Ben Nevis. I am astonished by your tale.'

Elspeth returned with a tea tray, and passed a mug to everyone present. She resumed her seat.

'So, now that we are all here, I think we should ask Mr Miller's advice on when the storm is going to end. I for one have pressing engagements.'

Miller chewed on a slice of bread for some moments. 'Perhaps another day,' he said finally.

Eckenstein sighed and lifted his large feet to rest on the table. 'Suits me. I am growing to like this place. The question, Jones, is how soon will you be well enough to travel?'

Jones nearly choked on his tea. 'My dear fellow, I assure you I am as well as you are.'

'You've broken a rib,' Elspeth reminded him.

'I am aware of that, thank you,' Jones said with as much sarcasm as he could manage. 'It's not the first rib I have broken while climbing, and it will not be the last. There is nothing to prevent me from travelling at the earliest opportunity.'

Eckenstein, he noticed, watched him closely. 'You went through quite an ordeal. There is no shame in admitting you were afraid.'

'It was a shock at the time, but I was not afraid.'

Eckenstein laughed loudly. 'You attempted the hardest ice route in Scotland, sustained a huge fall rendering you incapable of leading, and had to be led away on an escape route by a girl, yet you claim you were not rattled by this?'

Jones felt a mounting anger at this prodding, but at the same time he wondered why he found it so difficult to admit to fear. People said he was fearless, reckless, blinded to danger by his ambition to be the best climber. They said he fell off too often. While these tales all had elements of truth, most people failed to appreciate that Jones felt fear just as deeply as any other climber—he could simply ignore it better than most. No matter how hard he tried to remain indifferent to these stories, he had grown to enjoy his reputation, until Crowley had started the unpleasantness. He had become accustomed to being held in awe.

'All right,' he said angrily, 'I admit it. I was absolutely petrified and thought I was going to die. Do you know how that feels?'

Eckenstein looked satisfied. 'Of course I do. It might do you some good to realise you are not as special as you seem to think you are.'

Elspeth frowned at Eckenstein and laid a hand protectively on Jones' arm. 'I think you are being unjust. Jones took that fall very well.'

'He should learn to take advice from his betters with the same grace, then.'

Jones stamped out of the office, down the stairs into the kitchen. A single candle lit this smaller room, sitting in a frozen puddle of wax on the shelf. The range gave off a wonderful warming glow. He raised his hands to the heat while he tried to calm himself.

Eckenstein had always been like this: abrasive and patronising up close, but in the long term, his advice always did Jones good. He had his head rooted in decency and common-sense, even if he did enjoy watching others squirm on the hook.

Elspeth trotted down the stairs and lit a cigarette. She looked worried. 'What was that about?'

'Don't fret about it. Eckenstein is very good at rooting out self-indulgence and hypocrisy.'

'But he is such an awful man! Why do you put up with him?'

'I put up with him because he is one of my truest friends.'

She held him there with her gaze.

'You can count on me as one of your truest friends. I hope I have demonstrated that.'

'To be honest, Elspeth, I am not entirely sure what I think about you. You are something of a mystery to me.'

She smiled impishly. 'Perhaps I like being mysterious.' Then she leaned forward and kissed him on the cheek. 'Come back into the office and make your peace with Eckenstein. It would be intolerable to spend so much time in this place with you two at each other's throats.'

She grabbed his hand and dragged him back up the steps into the office. Jones felt more confused than ever. He wondered if she was attracted to him, and if so, how he would feel about that. Jones often found it difficult to think of Elspeth as a woman: she was tougher than him in many ways, often unladylike in manner, and he found her baffling.

To further complicate the matter, Jones found his thoughts returning to Miss Elliot more and more frequently. He resolved to put it out of his mind for now.

Back in the office, Eckenstein and Miller sat in companionable silence, puffing at their pipes and continuing their game of cards. Eckenstein raised an eyebrow as Jones sat down.

'Sorry,' Jones said awkwardly. 'You are right, of course. I was wrong to raise my voice.'

Eckenstein threw a card down on the stack in the middle of the table in triumph, then turned to address him.

'Glad you have come to your senses. Now, the next question is, what do you intend to do about the problems you encountered on your climb?'

'I'm not sure what you mean.'

'You were forced to traverse off before the main challenge of the wall had been fairly squared up. We are all technical men here, and we're going nowhere for the time being. Perhaps now is the time to discuss possibilities.'

Without a word, Miller rose to his feet and, after rummaging in a drawer for a moment at the other side of the room, returned with a pad of plain paper and a carpenter's pencil. He gave these to Eckenstein.

'If you will permit me,' Miller said in his quiet way, 'I am not a mountaineer, but I have some ideas that may prove instructive.'

'By all means.'

'It seems to me,' Miller continued, 'that the fear of falling must weigh heavily on the mind of the leading man. When climbing ice, some way of reducing that risk would help the leader to focus on his task.'

'That is correct,' Jones said. 'The rope is mostly there as an aid to the second man. It's fairly useless when leading on ice.'

'Then what you require is some means of reducing the length of a fall, both as a real safeguard and as a moral support.'

'You mean a running belay. There is nothing we can use on ice, unless we find a rock spike to hitch the rope around.'

Eckenstein closed his eyes and drew heavily on his pipe, swirling the smoke around in his mouth as was his habit when concentrating. After some moments he opened his eyes again and began to draw on the pad in front of him.

Jones leaned over to catch a glimpse. 'What are you brewing up?'

'It's quite elementary,' Eckenstein said as he drew in brisk, broad strokes. 'In the Tyrol and the Dolomites, difficult climbs are sometimes equipped with iron stakes hammered into cracks. These pegs act as an artificial running belay; the Savoyards call them pitons. The leading man ties his rope to the device so that it can run freely.'

'How could this possibly be done on ice?' Elspeth asked.

Eckenstein turned the pad so the others could see. A man at the foot of the diagram was anchored to the wall with his axes, belaying his companion, who had run out a full rope's length. At equal intervals on the rope connecting the two men, Eckenstein had drawn attachments connecting the rope to the ice.

'Consider the scenario,' Eckenstein said, animated now he had a scientific problem to engage with. 'Our friend Jones here is ninety feet up a vertical wall of ice. If he falls, he will descend ninety feet to his friend, then another ninety feet to a nasty injury, nine times out of ten. However, if he can fix running belays on the ice, the length and impact of any fall would be reduced.'

'It would never work,' Jones said. 'How would you get the pitons to hold in hard ice?'

'Sharp points, serrated edges, quality steel: it could be done, with a bit of testing. The real trick would be getting them out again. I'll make you some, and you can test them for me by falling on them repeatedly. You are so good at falling after all.'

Elspeth laughed, but Eckenstein made the absurd notion sound plausible; if any man could get it to work, he could.

*

The three mountaineers reached Fort William at ten o'clock on Monday morning. The storm had finally calmed at some point in the night, and after taking his hourly weather measurement at five o'clock, Miller declared to his guests that the conditions would now permit a descent.

They said farewell to their host. Jones felt glad to be away from that underground prison, but it seemed to him that Eckenstein had been tempted to stay behind. The sun rose behind them as they waded through drifts of new snow. A soft radiance washed over the plateau, dancing from rock to rock, lighting up the highest point and penetrating down into the dark glens. Above and all around, the world basked in divine glory. All the mountains of the Highlands marched in an infinite spread from East to West, and for the first time in his life, Jones saw the promised land of the mountaineer laid out like a map, bigger than he would ever have dared to dream. His spirit soared free after days of imprisonment. The sun climbed, the moment of magic passed, and with the heaviest of hearts they descended from that paradise to the mundane world below.

They walked through the High Street in Fort William side by side, a ragged band of climbers. People in the street watched them as they passed, often in open amazement; some doffed their caps, others greeted them by name. Jones wondered what all the fuss could be about.

Eckenstein scowled at the locals, whom he regarded as degenerates to a man. 'What are they gawking at?' he muttered.

'Mountain climbers are still something of a rarity,' Jones reminded him.

'Have they not had their fill of them, these past two days?'

They reached the Alexandra Hotel, now emptied of climbers. The umbrella stand, previously buried beneath ropes and Mackintoshes, now actually held an umbrella.

They marched into the lobby. The clerk looked up in surprise to see a young lady dressed in such dirty old clothes. Collie, who had been talking to the clerk, turned and noticed them.

'My friends! I am so happy to find you all safe and well! We feared the worst.'

Jones noticed that the Professor wore his climbing gear, deerstalker and all; but his jacket was only halfway buttoned up, and one boot was not yet laced.

'Did you not receive our telegram?' Elspeth demanded.

'The telegraph office received a garbled communication. Raeburn and I were about to set off on a rescue mission. Your exploits are the talk of the town.'

'We were quite safe,' Jones assured him. 'James Miller at the observatory took good care of us.'

Raeburn stomped through the front door just then, carrying a large bag over one shoulder, a bundle of Holdstock ice axes under his other arm. He dumped his load on the doormat, breathing heavily.

Collie stepped forward to help him. 'Your arm is not yet fully mended, Raeburn. You ought to have made the cabbie carry it in.'

'I'm fine, I assure you,' he said irritably. 'It's good to see our wanderers safe and well, although I must confess I was looking forward to an impromptu afternoon on the mountain.'

Eckenstein laughed. 'Don't let us stop you!'

'Alas, circumstances intervene. Professor, the shipment has arrived.'

Collie looked delighted. He rubbed his hands together. 'That is excellent news. Jones, Eckenstein, perhaps you would be good enough to accompany us? I believe this is something you should both see.'

*

81

On their way to the train station, Jones gave an account of his adventures to Collie, who listened patiently to the narrative. When Jones had finished, Eckenstein added his piece.

'Oppenheimer and I had an uneventful day. We climbed the Tower Gully, but quarrelled upon reaching the cornice at the top. I elected to continue the battle, but he decided retreat would be more prudent. Off he went back down our line of steps. It took me some hours to hack through the overhang, by which time the storm had blown in and I took refuge in the observatory.'

Collie clapped his hands together in delight. 'The meet has been monumentally successful, more so than I would ever have hoped. Gentlemen, we are off to a fine start!'

'What good will it do if so few of us have the right equipment?' Jones pointed out. 'A so-called progressive club can only be progressive if it has the right tools for the job. Now that the Holdstock Company has shut down, I don't see how we can move forward.'

They arrived at the station. The first thing Jones noticed was a large crate in the centre of the yard. The lid had been prised off and several porters were busy removing the contents, which seemed to consist of heavy bundles of objects wrapped in oilcloth.

'What's all this, then?' Eckenstein asked.

Collie looked pleased. 'Supplies for the club—rather an unexpected windfall, actually.'

Something about this didn't sit right with Jones. He walked up to one of the bundles and opened it. Packed inside was a pair of Holdstock ice axes, complete with original leather covers for the picks and spikes.

'How could the club possibly afford to buy all these axes?' Jones asked.

'We purchased them at a substantial discount. A portion of subscription fees, plus a modest investment by Raeburn and myself, covered the costs quite adequately.'

'And where did you get them from?' Jones said as he opened more bundles.

'Mr Godwin, who has acquired the assets of your old company, held an auction for surplus stock to cover legal fees, as I understand it.'

Godwin! So Crowley was behind this. What could he be up to now, Jones wondered?

'Was Godwin actually at the auction?' Jones demanded. 'Did you see him?'

Collie seemed taken aback by this interrogation. 'Actually, I placed my bids over the telephone. I really don't know what you are objecting to, Jones. I thought you wanted this.'

He picked up one of the axes and inspected it carefully. There seemed to be absolutely nothing wrong with it. The oiled hickory shaft was in perfect condition, and the metalwork showed no blemish. Why would Crowley want to sell off this equipment? Certainly not as part of a hurried attempt to pay legal fees; Crowley enjoyed limitless access to his father's riches.

'My apologies,' he said as he handed the axe to Raeburn. 'I have cause to be suspicious about any stock from Mr Godwin.'

'As I understand it,' Raeburn said, 'Godwin sued the Holdstock Company for fraud and patent breach. Godwin is the man who has been wronged here. Why are you trying to protect a company that treated you so badly?'

He ignored that question. 'How many axes have you bought?'

'Twelve pairs, plus ice claws, for a bargain price. There is no great mystery.'

The Professor looked troubled. Jones felt sorry for worrying his friend needlessly; after all, Collie had seen an opportunity for the fledgling club and taken it with both hands. It was not his fault.

Jones took his leave, still feeling anxious. He hailed a cab, and as he was climbing into it Eckenstein appeared at his side.

'Room for one more?'

'Feel free. Driver, take me to the Alexandra Hotel.'

'Explain to me the meaning of that outburst,' Eckenstein said as the cab pulled out of the yard.

'It is one of Crowley's plots. Why else would he sell so much of his stock to Collie at a cheap rate?'

'There are two points to consider before you rush off on another crusade like the impetuous young fool you are. Firstly, what makes you think the axes were bought as cheaply as the Professor claims? He is a modest man, but also quite wealthy. He probably invested heavily in the equipment out of his own pocket.'

'But why would he do such a thing? Collie is a traditionalist at heart and always will be.'

'He was very taken by the article and photographs you sent him. Collie is no fool. He knows which way the wind will blow, in time, and wishes to be associated with the great deeds of the next century. Perhaps the PMC can be the nursery for the new heroes, if he fans the flame a little.'

'And your second point?'

'If Crowley really is behind this, why would he not wish to sell large quantities of the tools to customers who will make use of them? The market is limited. If Crowley sells off surplus stock of axes and claws, he can ensure future sales of other items. Alternatively, he might have no interest in resuming production at all. It could be simply a way of getting rid of goods he has no use for.'

Jones considered what Eckenstein had said. It made sense.

'You may have something there,' he admitted.

'Try to use your head instead of seeing plots everywhere you look. Now, how goes your progress with the lovely Elspeth?'

That last sentence came out in a deeply sarcastic tone. 'I'm sure I don't know what you mean.'

'Come now, you are quite the heartbreaker, aren't you? What of that beauty who accompanied you to Wales?'

'Miss Elliot? A colleague.' He wondered if Eckenstein could see his reddening face.

*

Eckenstein made his good-bye as soon as they reached the hotel. As was his habit, he had no luggage, only his mountaineering equipment: he intended to return to the Ben, he said, to spy out an ice wall right of Tower Ridge.

Jones hoped to escape Fort William as soon as possible. For the first time in a long while, a trip to the mountains had failed to invigorate him. Indeed, he felt drained and restless, left with a deep impression that something had gone wrong.

Other worries preyed on his mind. He found it more and more difficult to ignore the fact that he had no job, and rapidly dwindling savings. The draft of his climbing guidebook neared completion, but he worried that his reputation would act against him if he tried to publish it.

His mind dwelled on dreams of impossible ice faces and beautiful summits, and on the vague dread of Crowley. He thought about Collie's new club and realised that his initial enthusiasm for the venture had waned. The reality would be just the same as any other mountaineering club.

Jones felt dissatisfied and adrift.

Perhaps Eckenstein was right about Crowley. Even he was not such a dog as to continue the vendetta after he had achieved victory, surely? On the other hand, Jones could not imagine Crowley as a businessman. His endeavours tended to be motivated by a desire to avoid boredom.

He wandered into the hotel lobby, deep in thought, and nearly walked into Elspeth. She had changed out of her climbing gear and into a grey travelling cloak.

'I've been looking for you!' she said.

'I was about to leave town.'

'We shall be travelling on the same train, then.' She looked at him closely. 'You seem melancholy. What's the matter?'

He sighed and shrugged his shoulders. 'It's a long and unhappy story. You already know some of it from the discussion I had with Eckenstein on the journey up, but perhaps it is time you knew the full tale. I find myself in need of someone sympathetic to talk to.'

Elspeth slid her arm in his and walked him into the lounge. 'We have an hour before our train departs. Please tell me everything. I will help you in any way I can. You know I hold you in high regard, Mr Jones.'

Her eyes glowed as she looked at him, and Jones felt attracted to this strange creature he had befriended. Perhaps he ought to start trusting her after all.

CHAPTER EIGHT

THE RIVAL

27th of February, 1897

"MY DEAR MR JONES,

"I read the account of your latest adventure with great interest. You certainly seem to have met your match as a climber in Elspeth, although I must say I don't trust her. I do not know what it is about her that I find untrustworthy, but I have learned to listen to my instincts in these matters.

"I hope you are now down safe & well & are back in London. Your letter arrived some days after the given date.

"Simon Barkis has been in contact with me. He has gone into business with Arthur Beale of London, the ropemaker, & has established a branch of the shop here in Cambridge. I would not have believed there were enough climbers here to make the venture worthwhile, but apparently the shop will also cater for yachtsmen. Between you and me, I suspect Mr Barkis has fallen on hard times. I have heard rumours that his father has disowned him.

"He has asked me to be his secretary again & I think I shall accept the offer, against my better judgement perhaps; it has proven quite impossible for me to find a position elsewhere.

"I should also mention that a young gentleman named Peter Merrick has been asking about you. He seems to be aware of our association through the meet at Pen-y-Pass. He said he would write to you, so I gave him your address.

"If you are concerned about my safety, I believe I am capable of looking after myself. Nevertheless, I am touched by your concern & look forward to your visit. Nothing remotely exciting has happened since you left, Jones!

"Yours affectionately,

"Rachel M. Elliot."

*

"Dear Mr Owen Jones,

"Please excuse me writing to you like this. You might not remember me, but we met last year at Pen-y-Gwryd, and I believe we spoke at some length about the Matterhorn north face climb. It is on this subject that I wish to consult you, if you would be good enough to indulge me.

"I am not really a first-rate climber, but I am strong and very enthusiastic. I also have the vigour of youth, being in my twentieth year, and can afford the very best equipment. My point is that I wish to become a North Face Climber. How would you advise me I should go about doing this? I have read your article on progressive mountaineering, and it inspired me to experience it for myself.

"I live in Cambridge but travel a great deal, so unfortunately a meeting between us would be quite impossible, even though I would hold such an event a great honour. If you would be good enough to write a few lines to point me in the right direction, I would be forever indebted to you.

"Please also convey my thanks and cordial best wishes to your friend Miss Elliot, who was good enough to furnish me with your current address.

"I am, &c,

"Mr P. Merrick."

*

Jones sipped a cup of tea as he read his post. For once, the morning had dawned bright and sunny in London. His current lodgings boasted a decent enough view over the green space of Russell Square Gardens, and this place felt altogether more alive than the dwelling of silence and dust he had inhabited at the City of London School.

He didn't know quite what to make of the letters. The first had caused a flutter in his heart when he saw the handwriting on the envelope, but Rachel had dismissed his concerns almost scornfully. He believed that Crowley would not let the matter lie, despite what Eckenstein might say.

As for the second letter, Jones read it with a smile on his lips. It bore all the hallmarks of youthful enthusiasm and inexperience, two things he recognised from his own past. He had no advice to give the young man—whom he had no memory of meeting—except to build on his experience and climb with senior men who would teach him wisdom in the mountains. Jones resolved to write a brief but polite response.

After reading his correspondence, he began the day's work.

He had now finished the final draft of his project, "Rock and Ice Climbing in North Wales." Although he had spent much time agonising over the question of whether he actually wanted to finish the book, in the end Elspeth had convinced him that he might as well profit from his labours, and hang what people might think; indeed, the mysterious girl apparently had family links to a major publisher, and had provided him with an introduction. She was to meet him that very morning and accompany him to the interview.

Jones had scarcely finished his breakfast when he heard a knock at the door to his apartment. He picked up his jacket and the box file containing the precious manuscript. Unable to afford a typist, he had typed out every page himself.

He opened the door. Elspeth stood in the corridor, leaning against an umbrella. She wore a ladies' suit of brown serge that would not have looked out of place on the crag, yet blended in well in the city. Jones thought she looked characteristically Scottish.

A private carriage waited in the street below: a four-wheeler, and quite a fine one, kept in beautiful order. Jones was about to offer his hand to help Elspeth up, but the driver hopped down and did the honours before Jones could act.

'Thank you, John.'

'Where to, madam?'

'My uncle's office on Ludgate Hill, please.'

Jones climbed into the carriage after her, feeling a little bewildered. Red leather trimmed the seats, and indeed everything about the vehicle felt expensive and luxurious. The carriage set forth with a rumble and creak.

Elspeth leaned back and untied her hair, shaking it free. 'My, that's better. Do you mind if I smoke?'

'Not at all. Is this your coach? I had expected to walk, or take a cab.'

'I could not permit you to walk through the streets with that valuable cargo,' Elspeth said, indicating the box file with a gloved hand, 'and I don't trust cabbies. Much better to travel in comfort, do you not agree?'

'I'm indebted to you.'

'Nonsense; we are friends.' She struck a match and lit her cigarette. 'Is it not delightfully improper to be travelling alone in a private carriage with an unmarried woman?'

An unmarried woman who smoked cigarettes, he thought. He decided to change the subject. 'Tell me about your uncle. What position does he hold in the business?'

'Firstly he is not really my uncle. He is my late father's brother-in-law. James Viney is his name, and he is a partner in the firm. You shall like him. He adores books on travel and exploration.'

Jones could not help feeling a little nervous. He had invested a great deal of himself into this book, and now he had to try and sell it to a man who probably knew better than anyone how small the market was for reference books of this kind.

Elspeth's eyes gleamed through a whirl of smoke. 'Don't worry. I believe in what you have written.'

'We shall see,' Jones said, although he knew that, with no income, his near future depended on this interview.

*

A long corridor led to James Viney's office. Out of many open doorways to either side came the din of typewriters and printing machines. Jones felt nervous as they neared that door, which bore a brass nameplate which read "J VINEY, PARTNER."

They reached the door and waited before knocking. Elspeth reached into the pocket of Jones' waistcoat and removed his pocket-watch to check the time, then frowned.

'We are just on time. Good luck, Jones.'

He knocked on the door. After a heartbeat, it opened to reveal a tall, distinguished-looking gentleman wearing a long black coat and red waistcoat.

Elspeth made the introductions. Jones sensed a distinct chilliness, almost hostility, between Elspeth and her uncle. She followed Jones into the office, which was large but utilitarian, with little to betray the character of the occupant: there was only a massive antique desk in the exact centre, upon which sat just two appliances, a writing slope and filing tray. Two windows overlooked the desk, affording an expansive view of St Paul's Cathedral.

Mr Viney sat behind his desk and asked his guests to sit down. 'Sir, let me begin by saying that I do not usually consult authors directly regarding their work. There are certain processes and channels which are being bypassed here. The reason for this is the affection with which I remember my late brother-in-law, and a debt I owe to his only child.'

Jones noted his careful choice of words. This was a transaction, a favour repaid.

'Nevertheless,' Viney continued with a genial smile, 'I find myself intrigued by the book you have written. Is that the manuscript you have there?'

Jones answered in the affirmative and handed over the file.

Viney began flipping through the pages. He did not speak for some moments, until he pulled out a sheaf of photographs.

'Who supplied these?'

'My esteemed friend Mr Abraham, who runs a photography shop in Keswick.'

'His skill with a camera does him great credit, as does yours with an ice axe.' Viney put the documents down on his desk and folded his arms. 'Explain to me the market for this book. Who will read it?'

Jones had dreaded this question. 'Mountaineers,' he replied simply and honestly. 'This is designed to be a guidebook for the climbers already visiting Wales, and to teach and guide those new to the sport.'

Viney seemed amused. 'How many mountaineers would you say there are in these islands?'

'Including Alpine tourists who might be tempted by the delights of our own hills, I would say many thousands.'

The number was pure speculation, but a vaguely educated one. Jones hoped his confident approach was enough to lend it some credibility. Viney held his gaze for moment.

'Many thousands, eh? I have a weakness for well-written travel books, and the photographs are sensational enough … but, I ask you, will it sell?'

Elspeth, who had been sitting in demure silence for some time, now looked up. 'Uncle, you told me in your letter you were looking for something new and different. To my knowledge, only one other author has ever published a book anything like this.'

'Haskett-Smith, 1894', Jones cut in. 'Although my own previous book enjoyed some modest success.'

Viney raised an eyebrow. 'Exceedingly modest, I believe. Look here, books on Alpine mountaineering are so commonplace that the market is saturated. The public is tired of mountaineering.'

'Then surely this is exactly what you require,' Jones insisted. 'The era of Alpine exploration is over, but in our own mountains, much ground is unexplored. There are unclimbed peaks, unknown cliffs, vast areas where no climber has ever been. Surely this cannot fail to inspire!'

Viney looked from Jones to Elspeth. 'Well, your friend is passionate enough about his subject. Perhaps we shall give him a chance.' He stood up, and his guests did likewise. 'Mr Jones, I would appreciate it if you left the manuscript with me. I will be in contact very soon.'

Jones felt a great flood of relief. He shook hands with Viney and thanked him gratefully.

After they had left the office, standing in the corridor outside, Jones felt that he could at last relax. He exhaled deeply.

'Well, that was stressful.'

Elspeth seemed somehow diminished in stature, as if the interview had taken a lot out of her. 'The outcome was profitable, though … oh dear, I feel a little faint.'

Jones took her arm. 'Are you well?'

'I require no assistance,' she said a little crossly. 'It must be the close air in this place. Come, let us get out onto the street.'

Upon reaching the street below, Elspeth stood for a moment to compose herself, then lit a cigarette and inhaled with her eyes closed. Jones felt concerned. He had deduced that something about the meeting had unsettled her, perhaps some memory stirred.

'Will you not tell me what has upset you?'

A pause. 'I cannot.' Elspeth gave out a sigh and leaned against Jones' shoulder. 'Will you take me out to dinner tonight? I feel I need to live a little on my own terms.'

The request came as a surprise, but Jones agreed readily. He had never seen this side of the fearless and ever-confident Elspeth, and he struggled to come to a conclusion regarding the puzzling events of the day so far.

*

That evening, at a little before five o'clock, Jones left his rooms. He had spent the afternoon catching up on correspondence and working on a new article for the first journal issue of the Progressive Mountaineering Club. Professor Collie had sent him an excited telegram announcing that the first issue would be printed at some point during the spring.

He stepped out into the cold and paused for a minute to light his pipe. All seemed quiet in Russell Square this evening. Across the street and beyond the iron railings surrounding the gardens, a couple strolled between the tall bare trees, dappled by shadows and the soft glow from the street lamps. Jones felt a speck of sleet land on his neck, and raised his collar against the chill. He felt a little self-conscious in his hired top hat and evening wear.

Even though it was a Saturday night, Jones had been able to reserve a table for two at Rules, the long-established restaurant near Covent Garden. Elspeth had business south of the Thames that afternoon, so agreed to meet him there. Happily, his new apartment lay within a short distance of the restaurant, so he decided to save the cab money and walk. The meal would be expensive enough.

A cold wind cut through his jacket as he walked: a pleasant sensation that reminded him of early mornings on high mountains, and reinforced the fact that London would never be his true home. He had nothing here, really; no living family, no job, nothing to tie him down. Why had he come back? Jones liked to think he had learned from his reckless decision to give up teaching, and now intended to live more sensibly. Perhaps in truth he simply did not know what to do after the Cambridge affair ended in such shame. The seductive dream of being paid to climb had opened a doorway just a crack, enough for him to see in and realise that he wanted the riches on the other side: freedom, the chance to make a difference, and (he had to admit) the opportunity of really making a name for himself.

Just a foolish dream, but once a mind has grown a little and tasted an opportunity, it is a harsh thing for those hopes to be dashed. Now he had returned to this bleak city where he would always feel a stranger, despite having lived here for almost his entire life. The time had come, he suddenly realised, to do something decisive and break out of this cycle. The deal with Viney felt like a victory but it would not be enough. He would be thirty soon—thirty, and without a career! The realisation stopped him like a physical blow. Why had he never looked at his life in these terms before? It could not be all about having adventures forever.

He hardly needed reminding that the University of London was mere minutes away from his lodgings. With his qualifications and experience, he would have a chance of obtaining a position there. Why did he hesitate to apply? Could he go back to being a lecturer?

Frustrated by his inability to bring his ambitions to full fruition, Jones decided that he would at least get something right in his life.

He reached Rules after about twenty minutes, tucked away in Maiden Lane, a narrow street flanked by shops and apartment buildings. Elspeth waited just outside the door, underneath the canopy—not smoking for once, he noticed. She had changed into a black evening gown, and her face was veiled. Jones wondered why she wore black so often. Black suited her figure and compact stature, but it suddenly occurred to him that she might be in mourning for someone. Her father, perhaps? Jones realised he knew very little about her personal life.

'Have you been waiting long?' he said as he approached. 'I hope I am not late.'

She smiled and took his arm. 'We are perfectly on time. I'm impressed you managed to make a reservation at this time on a Saturday evening.'

'I have a few friends who work here. Shall we go in?'

As Jones held the door open for Elspeth, he looked across the threshold into a restaurant that had changed little for most of the 19th century, and indeed many said it characterised that century, for its patrons included several figures prominent in the public eye. Rules never failed to charm.

The maitre d'Hotel greeted them at the door with a smile. 'How nice it is to see you again, sir. It has been too long.'

Jones allowed his coat to be taken. 'Good evening, Reynolds.'

'I have a table for two ready in the back room.'

The restaurant seemed extraordinarily busy, but then again Jones had never come here on a Saturday night before. A cross-section of London society could be found here on any given day: writers, musicians, artists, politicians, businessmen, aristocrats. The atmosphere of power and high class conspired to make Jones feel a little out of place, given his humble background, and he could not really afford it, but as a rare treat it was to be relished.

They passed through the main dining area. Portraits of exalted and famous patrons covered the walls. Arches, picked out in black and gold, divided the restaurant into sections. Reynolds led them to a small table in the far left corner of the back room, a large rectangular space beneath a high roof with a stained glass skylight. Electric chandeliers provided both illumination and ambiance now that darkness had fallen.

A string quartet started to tune up. After inspecting the wine list, Jones ordered the second cheapest bottle.

'I've never even heard of this place,' Elspeth remarked as she opened her menu. 'Of course, I have not been away from Scotland for long. If it does not offend you, may I ask how you come to be a patron?'

Jones laughed. 'A little upper class for the likes of me, you mean? Reynolds and I met up in the Alps a few years ago, and I dragged him up Mont Blanc. The clientele may be snobbish but the staff are not. The pheasant is very good, by the way.'

Their wine arrived, and Jones poured a glass each while the waiter took their order.

'What shall we drink to?' Elspeth said, expression mischievous.

'To progress,' Jones said without thinking.

'To progress it is!' Their glasses clinked.

Jones did not usually drink wine. At the sort of establishments he frequented, the regular tavern or unpretentious city diner, the wine for sale tended to be undrinkable. Consequently, his palate appreciated porter or stout, neither of which could be had at Rules.

Elspeth nodded her appreciation. 'A fine choice.'

'Why don't you tell me a little about yourself? You remain a mystery to me. I feel I know you hardly at all.'

'Oh, I'm sure you know more about me than you think.'

'All I know is that you are Scottish, have lived in London for a short while, and have recently come into an inheritance from your father. Presumably, therefore, you are an only child, and were treasured by your father during his life.'

'You'll have to do better than that, Watson.' Elspeth seemed to be enjoying the game. 'What else can you guess about me?'

Jones hesitated before speaking, for he knew this might be a sensitive matter, but curiosity overcame his manners. 'I have also been able to deduce that you were once engaged to an uncommonly talented mountaineer, and that you spent last summer in the Alps with this gentleman.'

All colour drained from Elspeth's face. 'How could you possibly know about that?' she whispered.

'I did not mean to distress you,' Jones said quickly. 'It is simple deduction. You are probably one of the best female climbers in the world, and had access to the Holdstock equipment before almost anyone else. I have heard rumours that you climbed the north faces of Lyskamm and Mont Blanc du Tacul with the new equipment, yet you are practically unknown as a climber, so you must not have done very much before last year. In addition, you are confident around men in a way that many women your age are not. These facts point towards one conclusion.'

'Perhaps my father was a mountaineer. I might have learned the craft from him.'

'A doting father does not introduce his only daughter to a practice as dangerous as Alpine mountaineering. No, you were involved with a climber last year.'

They looked at each other for a long moment before she responded. Her eyes, monochrome and hard like the rest of her, hinted at a sudden great depth of sadness.

'You are right. He died.'

Jones felt awkward. 'I am so sorry. I did not know that.'

'How could you have known? I thought I had hidden the rest of it.'

'Yet you cannot hide your considerable powers as a climber, powers which must have been learned on the high peaks of the Alps.'

She sighed. 'We climbed a great deal together, but he died in an avalanche and I returned home to Edinburgh to find my father passed away also.'

This revelation stunned Jones to silence. He reached across the table and took her hand. 'I'm sorry. I feel like a fool now.'

She shrugged and smiled. 'Perhaps now you see why I was compelled to leave as much of my old life behind as I could, and start again. A new city, new friends. Perhaps a new lover.'

Expectant silence fell between them. For the first time since he had known her, Jones saw Elspeth's true beauty shining through the angular lines of her face. Now he understood why someone so young could appear so lonely.

He wanted to kiss her.

She leaned forward, hope in her eyes. His heart beat faster, both in response to her closeness and the scandal of a kiss in a public place. Nobody was looking at them. As their lips met, Jones felt a shock go through him; not the kind of shock he had expected, but a jolt as he came to his senses. This was not right.

Jones sat back in his chair, still holding Elspeth's hand. He wondered if anyone had seen them. 'Dear Elspeth, I am afraid this is quite impossible. I'm sorry.'

'But why?' She seemed distressed and confused.

'I am in love with someone else.'

Before either of them could react to this revelation, which was news to them both, a commotion near the bar caught Jones' attention. It seemed that a scuffle had broken out between a young man and two of the waiters.

'Let go of me this instant! It is imperative that I find him!'

Jones turned in his chair to see what was happening. The struggling man seemed familiar.

'Jones!' the man started to call out as a doorman dragged him away. 'Jones, I'll be outside!'

He jumped to his feet, almost knocking the table over. What could Barkis be doing here, and in great distress, if appearances were to be believed?

Elspeth caught his sleeve. 'Where are you going? This is nothing to do with us!'

'Please excuse me for a few moments.' He felt embarrassed. 'I'm afraid that is a friend of mine.'

*

The intrusion caused chaos in the restaurant, but Jones did his best to smooth the situation over with the staff, and after buying Barkis a glass of whisky and soda—which he gulped in a second—he escorted his friend from the establishment. Barkis' appearance came as a shock. Always a man to care for his appearance, he now looked dishevelled: open collar, a button missing from his waistcoat, coat nowhere to be seen. A desperate look haunted his eyes.

'My dear Jones, I am so pleased to have found you.'

'Steady yourself,' Jones said, holding him by the shoulders. 'You look perfectly fagged. Whatever has happened?'

'Someone is following me.'

Jones looked up and down the dark street, but could see nobody.

'Tell me about it, quickly.'

'It's that dog Crowley. He burnt my shop to the ground and has been hunting me ever since. A tree fell on my carriage in Trumpington Street. The brakes failed on the express train to London. Just half an hour ago I was attacked by a footpad!'

He talked fast, and Jones had difficulty keeping up. It sounded like the ravings of a man under considerable stress.

'You are safe now, do you understand? You can stay at my house tonight.'

Barkis shook his head. 'I have been there already. Your housekeeper told me where I could find you. Crowley will know where it is.'

Elspeth appeared. The moment she saw Barkis, her eyes widened and she let out an 'Oh!' of surprise before darting back into the restaurant.

'It's her!' Barkis shouted. 'You must not trust that woman, Jones! I know her well.'

'Calm down, you idiot! I can vouch for Elspeth. She is a trusted friend.'

Barkis shook his head. 'She is a liar.'

He doesn't know what he's saying, Jones told himself.

'Will you wait for me here just a moment while I attend to Elspeth? I'll be back in a moment.'

Jones walked back into the restaurant and found Elspeth sat back at their table, face pale with fright.

'Who is that man?' she demanded as he sat down again.

'An old friend who needs my help. I am afraid I must cut short our evening.' He smiled ruefully. 'Perhaps it would not have gone so well after my foolish words.'

Her sharp expression softened. 'Oh Jones, you are too hard on yourself. I do love you, you know,' she whispered, pressing a calling card into his hand. 'My address and telephone number.'

'I must go. I will see you soon, I promise.'

Jones rushed back out into the street, but Simon Barkis had already gone.

CHAPTER NINE

BETRAYAL

1st of March, 1897

"DEAREST RACHEL,

"Thank you for your telegram on Sunday. I could hardly sleep with worry, but now that I am assured you were not in the shop on the night of the fire I find myself more at ease.

"On Saturday evening, I was at Rules in Covent Garden when Simon Barkis appeared, in a state of considerable distress. He recounted his story to me, one of intimidation and physical attack from our friend Crowley. Barkis vanished immediately afterwards, and fearing the worst I contacted the police. The investigation appears to have been inconclusive so far.

"However, I received a letter in Barkis' hand this morning. He is laying low for a while, but will keep in contact when he can.

"By the time you receive this letter, I hope to be on the train to Cambridge. I will not be happy until I am by your side and able to protect you in person. There is also another important matter we need to discuss, but that can wait until we are face to face once again!

"Your devoted friend,

"O.G. Jones"

*

As Jones walked the last mile from the tram stop to Rachel's house on Lensfield Road, he felt a growing nervousness. He had not seen her for a month, but he believed that their intimacy had increased through the medium of their regular letters. Now he considered her a confidante and a friend. He missed her a great deal, and aspects of her character he once found annoying now attracted him.

What about Elspeth? He liked her bravery and her Scottishness, respected her formidable climbing powers ... but he felt nothing real for her, and never could while Rachel's raised eyebrow and subtle smile played on his mind. He had come to his senses.

All this passed through his head at a frantic pace as he walked. What would he say to Rachel when they met? Would they be on first name terms, or would they revert to their previous unfamiliarity? Jones liked to think of himself as a confident man, but perhaps that was simply his attempt to live up to his reputation.

He turned a corner into an avenue of semi-detached and terraced houses, dominated by a church spire at the end of the street. Jones counted off the house numbers until he came to number 59: three storeys of sooty yellow brick, identical in most respects to its neighbours.

As he approached, the door opened and out stepped a tall man wearing a black frock coat and top hat. He looked about him for a moment, then put on his gloves and walked away at a brisk pace. At that distance Jones could not discern the identity of the visitor.

He walked up the steps to the front door. With a pounding heart he pressed the doorbell. After a few moments, a young girl Jones did not know—presumably the nurse, or a maid—answered the door.

'Would you please inform your mistress that Mr Jones is here to see her?'

The girl, who Jones noticed did not wear a servant's uniform, snorted in contempt. 'I am Rachel's cousin.'

'My apologies—' he began.

She rolled her eyes. 'I shall call her for you.' The door closed.

A minute passed. Jones felt even more nervous.

Then the door opened, and Rachel Elliot stood on the step. She looked not quite herself, a little drawn perhaps, but the fire was still in her eyes, and the corner of her mouth rose in the ghost of a smile. She looked as beautiful as ever.

He followed her into the house and hung his coat by the door. The house, he noticed, was comfortable and tastefully decorated but by no means opulent. He had grown up in the same sort of middle class home himself.

She led him into the narrow front room, furnished with a writing bureau and two sofas. The carpet, Jones could not help noticing, had seen better days. Miss Elliot sat on a chair by the fireplace and indicated for Jones to sit opposite. In the corner, a tall clock ticked away the seconds.

She smiled at him, that genuine and happy smile he had only seen her give once or twice. He found himself smiling in return at the sheer happiness of being in the same room with her.

'It has been difficult since you left,' she said.

'How is your father?'

She hesitated. 'I can no longer afford to employ the nurse who used to look after him. It's a worry, but Sarah does her best.'

He nodded sympathetically, feeling a little guilty that he had complained to Elspeth about not being able to afford a typist.

'But you are well yourself? The fire did not harm you?'

'Only financially. I accepted the position at Barkis' shop the morning before, and I don't think he is in any position to pay me, even for a single day's work. It's a miracle I was not caught in the fire. I had intended to work that evening, but in the end I asked for leave to attend a social engagement.'

'Thank heavens for that. I've been so worried for you.'

Sarah arrived with their tea. She placed the tray on the coffee table next to Rachel and left without speaking, looking grumpy. Rachel poured them each a cup.

'I still don't understand why you are so concerned about me,' Miss Elliot said as she took a sip. 'You surely cannot believe Crowley is behind this? That episode is finished. The scoundrel won, and seems quite content.'

Her words made Jones feel irritated. He knew he had no rational cause to disagree with her beyond gut feeling and the ravings of a frightened man.

'Barkis certainly believes Crowley started the fire.'

'Mr Barkis was in no condition to be making rational judgements. He has become suspicious and bitter. I think he believed somebody was trying to blackmail him.'

'You see?'

Rachel's manner changed abruptly, and when she spoke again it was with the sarcastic tone she had used to rebuke him in the past.

'Grow up, Jones! Barkis let fear of Crowley tear his life apart. Do not allow it to do the same to you. I have moved on.'

Something in her words made him frown. 'Who was that gentleman I noticed leaving your house just now?'

'That is Peter, the young man I told you about in my letter. He lives just down the road. We had lunch together today.'

'And are you involved with him?'

The words slipped out before he could stop himself. Her eyes narrowed, and Jones realised he was an inch away from making a fool of himself again.

'Pleased as I am to see you, that question does you no credit,' she said sharply.

He felt hopeless, but of course he should have foreseen this. Obviously there would be other suitors. Perhaps if he had a job things would be different, but could he provide for her family? He knew he could not. He imagined his late father looking down on him with disapproval, demanding what right he had to pursue this woman with no career or prospects.

'I see I have misjudged the situation,' Jones said at length.

She sighed and sat back in her chair.

'My dearest friend, I do appreciate the noble sentiments with which you came here to protect me, but I hope you understand that I have my own life to live. You ought not to be jealous. I know you are a better man than that.'

Jones decided that there could not possibly be a worse time to discuss the matter foremost on his mind: that he was in love with her. He felt like an utter fool, and could not face another moment in the room.

Jones replaced his teacup on the saucer and rose to leave. 'It has been a true pleasure to see you again, Miss Elliot. I regret I must be on my way.'

She looked disappointed and a little sorry, perhaps realising she had hurt him.

'Oh, will you not stay for supper? We have so much to talk about. I have not seen you in a month!'

'Nobody has felt the absence more than I, but I feel my continued presence here will do more harm than good.'

Rachel stood, and impulsively she hugged him. Jones returned the embrace, aware that it could be the last they shared as well as the first.

*

Jones could not bring himself to remain in Cambridge, a place that now held more bad memories than good. He took the first train back to London. Had the journey been wasted? Perhaps. His naive dreams of announcing his feelings to Rachel had been crushed. At another time in his life, with better prospects and a greater sense of purpose, he might not have been so easily discouraged. The meeting had proved to him how directionless he felt.

He meditated on the question of what he should do next, and decided to listen to Rachel's advice about moving on, regarding Crowley at least. After all, what evidence did he have that Crowley would continue to be a nuisance? The time had come to stand firm again and stop brooding on possibilities and vague feelings.

When he got back to his apartment and let himself in, he found two telegrams waiting for him on the doormat. The first was from Simon Barkis:

"GONE TO WASTDALE DO NOT FOLLOW ME ALL WILL BE WELL SOON FROM BARKIS"

'Puzzling,' Jones said out loud as he opened the second envelope.

"I HAVE IMPORTANT NEWS STOP TELEPHONE ME WHEN YOU GET THIS FROM ELSPETH"

Even more puzzling! Immediately he realised Elspeth's urgent news must be to do with the book deal, but would it be good or bad? Although he felt tired and cold, he decided to go and find a telephone immediately to call her. Perhaps he could find a hot meal while he was out as well.

He had to walk several miles before he found a telephone exchange. The evening was a dark one, and he could not help thinking about Barkis' tales of derailed trains and footpads as he walked along deserted back alleys, taking a shortcut to Shaftesbury Avenue. Nobody attacked him. He made directly for the nearest exchange, and after paying the operator for his call he stepped into the booth and picked up the receiver.

Various crackling noises sounded in his ear as the operator connected the call.

'Good evening. This is the Mornshaw residence,' a male voice answered after some moments.

'Is Elspeth available?'

'Miss Mornshaw is not in.'

'Please tell her Mr Jones is calling.'

A long pause, then:

'Jones! You're back?'

'Evidently. Look here, you said you had something important to say to me?'

'You sound grumpy.'

'I've had a bad day, I'm afraid.'

'Oh. You told me you were going to visit Miss Elliot.' Another pause. 'I suppose I should say I'm sorry, but that would be hypocritical of me.'

Poor Elspeth. Would she be pleased that Rachel had rejected him? Of course she would. What an awkward situation. It felt odd to be having a conversation with someone he could not see, just a crackling, tinny voice coming out of a brass earpiece.

'I think she is seeing someone else.'

'Oh, that's hard on you. I feel we ought to talk in person. I really do have some important news quite unconnected with this subject. Shall I come to your house?'

'I don't know. It's late and I'm tired.'

'Rubbish. I will be there directly.'

'No,' he said more firmly than he intended. 'No. Tell me what you have to say now or not at all. I am sick of mystery and conjecture.'

'Fair enough.' She sounded a little hurt. 'I thought you ought to know that I hired a private detective to go after Barkis.'

'What? Why would you do such a thing?'

'To help you! I want you here with me in London, not chasing after Barkis and Crowley. A kiss is a promise, Jones.'

'I told you my heart belonged to someone else.'

'Yet she has rejected you. Why will you not let me help?'

Jones sighed. 'Tell me what you have discovered.'

'Barkis is in a bad situation. He has gone to Wastdale Head to cool down.'

'I know that. He sent me a telegram warning me not to follow him.'

'Really?' Elspeth sounded surprised. 'My detective gained the impression Barkis had taken pains to be secretive.'

'Perhaps he is wrong. Look here, I appreciate your help, but don't you think sending a detective after the boy will only make him more convinced he is being hunted?'

'His family has disowned him,' Elspeth continued, ignoring the protest. 'I have the letter with me now. Sir George apparently warned his son several times to give up mountaineering and his business interests, and focus on his education instead. Needless to say Barkis refused. It seems there is some family history of relatives dying in climbing accidents.'

Jones kept silent while he digested this information. He knew about Sir George's brother, killed on Mont Blanc many years ago. Sir George had given up climbing for good and forbidden his son to ever discuss the subject or pursue it himself, which proved to be the best possible way of encouraging the boy.

'Why would he disown his son?'

'Simon has brought disgrace to the family, so the letter says. You should read it. The poor lad must feel so alone, abandoned by his family, persecuted by someone whom he once called a friend.'

Alone and in a vengeful mood, Jones thought. At least the peace of Wastdale would help to calm him.

'If I was him, I would want friends about me,' Elspeth pressed.

Jones laughed. 'Are you suggesting I go to visit him?'

'Well, why not? I could accompany you.'

'Quite impossible!'

'Give me a good reason not to go.'

Despite himself, Jones admired her stubbornness. 'Firstly, practically everyone who frequents Wastdale Head hates me after that damned argument. And secondly—'

'Forget the argument. That was last year.'

'My enemies haven't forgotten it,' he said testily. 'Secondly, to be quite frank I do not have the ready money. You may have a plentiful inheritance, but I am an unemployed writer of books hardly anyone wants to read—and I don't even have an advance for my latest volume.'

'I thought you were supposed to be famously impulsive and reckless?'

'Perhaps I grew up a bit.'

'I suppose you think me dreadfully childish,' she said playfully.

'Good lord, no! You are brave, a quality I seem to have lost recently.' He frowned.

'Then let us be brave. Let me take you up to the Lakes for a holiday! I want to climb with you again, and I want to escape from the city for a little while.'

He let himself be persuaded. Perhaps he really did need a dose of silence and mountains to make himself feel right again … not to mention Elspeth's relentless cheerfulness. Anything to lift him out of this rut of self-doubt.

'I can't really afford it,' he protested weakly.

'No more objections! I will come and visit you tomorrow and we can talk about it.'

'Very well. I'm coming up to the time limit for my call.'

'I had better let you go home and rest. You do sound rather sleepy.' She laughed. 'Fearless mountain climber laid low by journey to Cambridge.'

He could not help smiling. 'Good night, Elspeth.'

*

4th of March, 1897

Preparations for the excursion took some days to make. Elspeth organised and paid for everything as promised. Jones felt uncomfortable about his inability to pay his own way, but the matter did not trouble Elspeth in the least; indeed, she seemed to relish the opportunity to look after him.

He checked his rope for rot, sharpened his ice axes, waxed his boots, and tried to brood as little as possible. Despite this, his thoughts always returned to Rachel Elliot and he found his feelings fluctuating between acceptance of reality and a calm despair at the way things had turned out. He waited for her to write to him but no letter came; he composed several letters but sent nothing, unable to express what he really meant to say.

Sometimes he wondered if he should tell Elspeth to forget about him and never see him again, but in truth he enjoyed her company. She visited daily to take afternoon tea, and her visits never failed to cheer him up.

Meanwhile, Mr Viney had been in touch to formally announce that his publishing firm would be happy to take care of his book, and had wired him a modest advance. Despite his increasing need, Jones saved the money.

Soon the day of the holiday came. Elspeth and Jones took the long night train up from Euston to Keswick. From the town they took the coastal train to Seascale, where they hired a dogcart and proceeded to drive the final few miles into Wastdale.

Sunny weather graced their journey. Fair-weather clouds sailed across a calm sky. The low patchwork hills guarding the entrance of the dale sported the beginnings of the new spring growth, a green fuzz bursting through the faded colours of the winter. Here and there, prickly gorse bushes by the sides of the road blazed with yellow flowers, their scent of coconut bringing back old memories.

'I can see the loch!' Elspeth exclaimed after a while.

'In England they call them lakes, or tarns.'

'It is a loch,' she insisted, 'surrounded by mountains. It reminds me of Glen Nevis.'

'These fells are a good deal lower. The locals are a proud bunch, though. They boast that Wastdale lays claim to the deepest lake, the highest mountain, and the biggest liar.'

'Who is he? You?'

'I am offended,' he said with mock outrage. 'A famous storyteller called Ritson used to run the Wastwater Hotel. I think he died some years before I first came to the district, but his reputation is stronger than ever.'

'Who runs the hotel now?'

'A fellow called Tyson and his wife. I don't think they like me very much after the argument last year.'

She sighed. 'I wish you would stop mentioning it.'

'You sound like Rachel.'

They drove on in awkward silence. Beyond the lake, broken cliffs and ribbons of ice reached up to the flat plateau of Illgill Head, and as they rounded a curve in the road, the fells that featured so fondly in Jones' memory towered large at the valley head. Kirkfell, Great Gable, Scawfell: treasured favourites and old friends, capped with snow and smiling in that glorious spring morning.

Then Wastdale Head itself sprang into view, a tiny cluster of stone buildings, dwarfed by the fells hemming in the valley head on three sides. What better sanctuary could there be for a mountaineer who had lost his way?

Jones smiled with pure joy. The emotion that overwhelmed him, sudden and powerful, was that of homecoming. For a very small community, this place counted as one of the special worlds where a man could be truly at home and at peace. Wastdale Head, Pen-y-Gwryd, Clachaig, Zermatt, Chamonix: the light seemed brighter in these places, the world a simpler and more wholesome place.

A network of stone walls criss-crossed the dale's floor. After going over a bridge, the walls closed in to hug the road on either side. Soon they arrived at the inn, a large white building next to the beck that came down from the hills. Two other carriages were parked in the yard, and a column of smoke rose from the chimney.

A servant took their luggage, and Jones noticed Mr Tyson standing in the doorway to the hotel, arms crossed, leaning against the frame. He wore the same cloth cap Jones had seen him wearing for years, and indeed he never seemed to take it off. Tyson had rolled up his shirt-sleeves in concession to the mild weather.

They walked up to the entrance. Elspeth leaned into him and whispered in his ear: 'Is that Mr Tyson? He does not look altogether happy.'

'He is a dalesman. They always look like that, until you get to know them.'

Tyson gave a terse nod and opened the door to allow them to pass through. 'How do, Jones.'

The entrance hall never failed to impress, clad in dark oak panelling and illuminated by candle lamps. Framed prints of George Abraham's climbing photographs adorned the walls, together with a few paintings of local scenes, bleak visions of snow, mists, and sheep huddling behind rocks for warmth: the reality of Wastdale life for half the year. A single ice axe lurked behind the coat stand. As far as Jones knew, it belonged to some famous climber of the '50s who had left it there and gone off to the Alps, never to return.

Tyson moved behind the reception counter at the end of the hall and flicked through the ledger. 'Mr and Mrs Jones … I've put you in room four. Congratulations are in order I believe. Hadn't heard a wink of the news until your missus here made the reservation.'

For a moment Jones thought there must be a mistake. He opened his mouth, but a nudge to the ribs from Elspeth silenced him before he could comment. What had she done now? He decided to play along with the game.

'Ah, thank you, Tyson. It's still taking some time to sink in for me, too.'

Elspeth smiled winningly. 'I am sure the room will be delightful. It is my first stay at the inn.'

Tyson smiled back, in his reserved way. 'Allow me to show you to your room, Mrs Jones.'

Jones took the key from Tyson, irritated at how he had been manipulated. 'That will not be necessary. I have stayed here many times before, as you know well.'

Tyson nodded, lips pursed. 'Aye, well. You know where to find me.'

Jones took Elspeth's arm and led her down the corridor towards the staircase. 'What are you up to?'

'Don't be angry. I thought it would make my presence less suspicious if we were married.'

'If we had been staying in separate rooms, there would have been no cause for suspicion.'

Elspeth stopped and looked at him. 'You asked me to organise the trip. I did what I thought was best. People would have talked.'

Jones sighed. 'I still think you might have told me what you were planning.'

'And miss that look on your face?' She laughed. 'I think not!'

*

After unpacking, temporarily ignoring the awkward issue of who was going to sleep where, Jones took a stroll into Mosedale by himself. He loved this wild little valley, surrounded by the peaks of Red Pike, Pillar, and Kirkfell. A long time ago, Eckenstein had tried to teach him balance climbing on the Y Boulder here, but Jones never really saw the point. Why muck around balancing on tiny holds when climbing was so delightfully muscular and gymnastic? Jones saw a climb as a problem to be overcome physically, not a mathematical exercise.

He approached the boulder now. Like its Welsh counterpart, Eckenstein's boulder at Pen-y-Gwryd, it was a difficult thing to climb in nails although Jones had enjoyed some success trying it in tennis shoes. He set his foot onto the stone, remembering the sequence of moves, the grate and spark as clinkers slid on smooth rock. The widening fissure at the back made him smile: he had taught himself crack-climbing here, in preparation for his campaign on the Kern Knotts Crack.

Hearing a sound behind him, Jones turned to find Simon Barkis standing there, walking stick in hand, grinning broadly. He looked fit and healthy, and happy too.

Jones dropped back to the ground and dusted himself down. He didn't know whether to hug his friend or scold him.

'We have been terribly worried about you! What made you run off like that outside Rules?'

Barkis sat down on a rock next to the huge boulder. 'Fear, mostly. It is a singularly unpleasant sensation, being hunted.'

'Are you certain it was not just a chain of coincidence?' Jones spoke gently, well aware that Barkis believed with all his heart that he was being persecuted.

'I received two threatening telegrams shortly before the fire—you know, the sort we used to get at the office. I informed the police, but they advised me to remain in London.' He laughed. 'So here I am.'

'Do you not think Crowley will realise you have come here? This has always been your bolt hole of choice.'

'I am quite certain of it. In fact, I chose my destination carefully, knowing that Elspeth, Crowley, and your good self would follow me here.'

Jones frowned. 'But you forbade me to come after you. I thought you were trying to run and hide?'

'I knew you would want to come even more if I told you not to follow me. Anyway, I can't run from Crowley. He knows me too well, and has wealth and connections. I have nothing much at all.'

Jones felt sorry for him. 'Things aren't that bad, old chap. We'll get you back on your feet again.'

'Awfully kind of you, but there is something I have come here to do. I have had the opportunity to think hard on it and prepare. You will thank me for this when it's over, I promise you.'

Jones did not like the sound of that. He studied his friend's face carefully. Barkis stared back towards the hotel, eyebrows pursed in a slight frown, fingers clenched around the handle of his stick. He seemed to possess considerable nervous tension, but no trace of fear registered in his bearing. Barkis had regained his composure. Given his dark words, Jones found this fact unsettling.

'Simon, please; you must confide in me. I fear you are not making much sense.'

He nodded, then sprang to his feet and started walking along the faint path back to the hotel at a brisk pace. 'Follow me! You shall see exactly what I mean.'

*

They walked around the back of the hotel, next to the river and the hump-backed stone bridge. They crossed the narrow strip of garden where Jones liked to lie on the grass in the long evenings of summer and drink beer, gazing up at the fells.

'Where are we going?'

They paused before the tall windows looking into the lounge on the ground floor. The sinking sun shone over the shoulder of Red Pike, casting a ray through the trees, over the beck and through the window into the room inside.

Barkis moved to one side of the window, and motioned for Jones to take up his station opposite.

'Take a look,' he whispered.

Jones wondered why Barkis could not simply be straightforward and tell him the facts. He looked into the lounge, trying to keep low to avoid being seen. In the far corner of the otherwise vacant room, Elspeth sat by herself, flicking through a book too quickly to be reading it properly. She looked agitated, occasionally looking up and glancing nervously about the room, as if somebody might be hiding. She had changed back into that black dress and hat she often wore, Jones noticed.

Presently a tall man entered and closed the door behind him. Jones could not see his face. He wore a white shirt and vibrantly patterned red waistcoat, but no jacket. A silver watch chain glinted in the gaslight for a moment.

'Who is that? I cannot see his face.'

'I believe it is Crowley. He stayed in room two last night.'

'Then we must warn Elspeth at once!'

Barkis laid a hand on his shoulder, preventing him from moving. His expression was grim. 'Do nothing to prevent what is about to take place. It is very important that you should see this. I promise, Elspeth is in no physical danger.'

'What are you implying?'

'Just watch, if you please.'

Jones did not want to watch. He did not want to consider for a single moment that Elspeth might be betraying him. Nevertheless, now that the suspicion had been placed in his mind, he felt he had to know.

Crowley—if that was who the stranger was—now lounged in one of the leather chairs opposite Elspeth, his back still turned. Elspeth began an animated discussion with the man, her face impassioned, tears glistening in her eyes. For a moment she listened while the stranger gestured vaguely with his right hand. He must have said something objectionable, for without replying she jumped to her feet and fled the room.

The stranger remained motionless for a little while, then lit a cigar and slowly stood and turned. There could no longer be any doubt. Crowley's eyes flashed with anger, his posture radiating an aura of confidence and power. The boy who believed he could do anything had come back to Wastdale Head.

The spies ducked out of view.

'Sorry to put you through that,' Barkis said. 'I know Elspeth is very dear to you.'

Jones resented what he had been forced to see. He resented Barkis' callous plan to lure him here simply to take Elspeth away from him.

'It seemed to me that they were quarrelling,' Jones said in a low voice. 'I saw no love there. I will ask her to explain.'

'Please, for the sake of our friendship, I must ask you to act as if you have seen nothing. We must allow their plans to unfold a little further if we are to counter them.'

'No! If Crowley is here, why not have it out with him immediately?'

'Because I want to make him suffer as I have suffered!' Barkis said savagely. 'He has destroyed my business interests, put my friend Holdstock in prison, financially ruined me, and embittered my family towards me. I want justice, damn you!'

Jones had never seen this side to him before. Barkis could act carelessly at times, but that tended to be a result of innocence, not arrogance; still, who could blame the lad for being tempted by revenge? He had lost a great deal, and if the day ever came when Jones found himself in a similar situation, who knew what he would find himself compelled to do?

That did not excuse his behaviour, Jones decided. A true gentleman does not act on thoughts of revenge.

He stood up and brushed the moss from his jacket. 'I will have no part in this. Elspeth will tell me the truth. She loves me.'

'She does not love you, any more than you love her. You are both using each other. Think on that before you try to tell me what I'm doing is wrong. There is something else going on here, a bigger plot than you can see and it is going to destroy all of us. I have to stop Crowley before he brings it to fruition.'

'Rachel was right about you. Suspicion and bitterness have got the better of your senses. I do not believe a word of this.'

'Then you are a fool, because Rachel is just as ensnared as the rest of us, and it will ruin her. Crowley will take away everyone you love and who loves you.'

Jones walked away, feeling hollow inside.

CHAPTER TEN

REVELATIONS

4th of March, 1897

J ONES TRIED TO AVOID everyone for the remainder of the day, choosing to seclude himself in the smoking room adjacent to the bar, his only companions a glass of stout and a writing pad. He needed time to think, and yet something prevented him from taking his ice axe and striking out into the hills, as he had done on many occasions when he felt troubled. The source of his problems was not out there: it was in this building, and sooner or later he had to face it.

In truth, Jones did not really know what he should do. He felt a strong temptation to simply leave and forget about the whole business, yet the more he turned the problem over in his mind, the more he believed Elspeth deserved the chance to explain herself. And what of Crowley? If there really was a monstrous plan, Jones felt morally compelled to prevent it. How, he did not know; Crowley might resort to intimidation, but Jones would not.

And then his thoughts turned to Barkis, impassioned and angry, intent on revenge. He didn't think Barkis would actually kill Crowley, but he would do his best to hurt or humiliate him. Surely Jones had a duty to dissuade his friend from this course?

The door opened. Elspeth walked in, towards him, and sat down on the bench to his left. Jones did not look up. He had not expected her to come in here; ladies did not usually enter the smoking room.

'I have been looking for you. Why are you sat inside drinking by yourself?'

'I saw you talking with Crowley. '

An incredulous silence followed. Then: 'You spied on me!'

'And you have lied to me since we first met.'

She clasped his hand and shuffled closer. 'I have not lied to you. It's true that Crowley approached me.'

When he did not respond, Elspeth continued: 'I can only imagine what terrible things are going through your mind, but I promise you, until today I had not seen him since 1895 when I knew him in Edinburgh.'

He looked into her eyes, and saw nothing but sincerity and concern. She seemed desperate for him to believe her, and he wanted to—but his suspicion about her had returned stronger than before.

'How did you meet in Edinburgh?'

'He had just begun his studies at Cambridge, and came up before Christmas to see a performance of the play I happened to be singing in. We spent some time together. I suppose he charmed me with his cleverness.'

Suddenly Jones realised that he knew nothing at all about his mysterious friend.

'You are an actress?'

She blushed. 'Oh dear, I had not meant to tell you that. Actually I no longer perform, since I came into my inheritance.'

'And you spent time with Crowley two years ago. Incredible. I cannot believe you didn't tell me this before.'

'I didn't know it was him! I knew him as Edward MacGregor, not Aleister Crowley … can you not understand I had forgotten all about that boy until today?'

He no longer believed a word she said. Only one question remained.

'What did he say to you?'

Elspeth looked away. 'He wanted me to be a spy, to report on your movements. I refused to do so.'

'I think you have been a spy since we first met. Now I understand why you were so keen for me to accompany you to Wastdale. Give me one reason to trust you!'

'I would have thought our moment in Rules would have answered that question.'

He recalled the incident with shame at the thought of how he had been used. 'Tell me where Crowley is. We are going to confront him together.'

'I don't want you to confront him.'

'If you have any remorse at all, tell me where he is and I can try to stop him!'

Her gaze became anguished. 'Please,' she whispered. 'I saw him leaving the hotel about an hour ago, travelling east along the path into the hills. Barkis followed him not long afterwards.'

*

Jones strode along the track known as Moses' Trod at a furious pace. Darkness approached, and an ominous cloud hung over the fells, but Jones knew the route well and danced sure-footed over the cobbles. He left the scattered dwellings of Wastdale Head and joined the track left of the

Lingmell Beck. This boulder-scoured torrent bore the drainage from the highest hills in England, and in the last rays of the evening sun the pools took on a turquoise sheen.

All around him were the wonders he had loved for many years: the beauty of the English Lake District, that unique juxtaposition of rugged scenery and pastoral charm. Down in the dale, the first lambs of the year sheltered under boulders and gorse bushes with their mothers, surrounded by the growth of the coming spring. Yet looking up, into the craggy heights far above, ravens soared and the lingering snows sintered down to ice.

Jones slowed his pace a little after crossing the beck. Now that the heat of his anger had cooled a fraction, he realised that Crowley could be anywhere.

He stopped for a moment to catch his breath, and in that moment he perceived that it had grown much darker than he had thought. A pinprick of light winked in his direction for a second, up and to the left, on the crags of Great Gable.

A sound made him turn, and he saw Elspeth hurrying along the faint path, carrying a lantern, lifting her skirts out of the mud with her free hand. In his single-minded haste, he had forgotten about her.

She drew level, breathing hard. Jones could not see her expression, but imagined she would be angry.

'Do you even know where you are going?'

Jones pointed towards the Napes crags. 'That must be Crowley's light up there. It will not take us long to catch up with him.'

He started walking again, a bit slower this time to give Elspeth a chance to keep up.

'I believe you have gone completely mad. What will you do when you get there?'

'I shall reason with the man, urge him to give up and go away.'

'From what you have told me, Crowley is altogether beyond reason.'

Jones knew he should listen to her. Crowley had proven himself capable of harming those who stood in his way, and he had no doubt that, when the meeting finally came, Crowley would do his best to hurt him as well.

They reached the pass of Sty Head, and turned left to join the narrow path cutting across the southern flank of Great Gable. Drifts of snow lay across the path, and further up the mountain Jones could just make out the gleam of more extensive ice. Holding Elspeth's lamp close to the ground, he could make out the markings of two pairs of ice claws that must have passed this way some time ago.

A rumbling boom reached their ears from somewhere in the darkness ahead, followed by a drawn-out clatter of loose stones.

'Rockfall, at this hour?' Elspeth said.

'I thought I heard it earlier as well. Perhaps the others have disturbed some loose rocks.'

Elspeth dumped her knapsack on a rock and pulled out her ice claws. She struggled with cold fingers to strap them to her boots. Jones followed her example, and after equipping themselves with an ice axe each as an aid for the steep slopes ahead, they continued along the path. Occasionally, the lantern flickered ahead, closer now, weaving in and out of the rock towers of the Napes. Jones felt increasingly nervous at the prospect of the encounter to come.

They passed beneath Kern Knotts, the cliff where it had all begun, following Jones' controversial ascent of the Crack and the subsequent argument. The climb looked cold and uninviting tonight. It would never be a major climb. It did not terminate at a summit, and it was not even aesthetically pleasing; Jones had simply sought out the most difficult route for its own sake. What did that matter? Could it ever be worth the lost friendships, or exile from the places he loved most?

Jones looked up at the Crack and hated it, the symbol of his own vanity and pride.

He felt Elspeth slip her arm into his and clasp his hand. 'You are a different man now. You have gained maturity in the last year.'

'Have I really? I feel like a traitor to my friends. Perhaps I was the one who started Crowley off on this madness. He may have led the charge against my reputation, but the argument was my fault in the end.'

'That is nonsense, and you know it well. You had nothing to do with what happened on the Matterhorn last year.'

They started climbing over the boulders, eager to be away from that place. Huge rocks creaked and moved under their weight, threatening to up-end and throw them into the holes beneath. Soon they passed underneath the Napes. Ridges and buttresses rose high above them to the right, divided by snow-filled gullies, like the knuckles of a weather-beaten hand. Jones wished they could blow out the lantern and proceed by moonlight, but the moon hardly penetrated the cloud that now covered more than half the sky.

Ahead, the familiar outline of Napes Needle stood apart from the main cliffs, a pinnacle of frosted black against the last starry portion of the heavens. Jones thought he saw movement there. A beam of light splashed over the rocks.

'There is someone on the summit of the Needle!' Elspeth whispered.

'He will have seen us. We ought to extinguish the lamp.'

'We shall certainly fall if we do. This ledge is far too exposed to be stumbling around in the dark.'

Jones looked down. A slope of ice fell away at his heels, over a thousand feet straight down to the Lingmell Beck. Above, complex mixed terrain, snow and boulders and sheer crags, spoke of impossible difficulties if their only source of light were to be removed. He knew from experience that the scramble up to the Needle could be treacherous in the dark.

'Then there is nothing for it,' Jones muttered. 'We must continue in full view.'

They started to climb the awkward chimney that led to the base of the Needle. Jones knew the climb up the pinnacle well; as an established classic, he had done it on many occasions. But what would he do now? Two or three people could sit on the summit of the pinnacle, but he would not risk the ascent with Crowley sitting on top waiting for him.

Then a low call reached his ears from above, little more than a whisper: 'Who goes there?'

That accent, polished and clear, did not sound like Crowley.

'It is I—Jones.'

'Thank heavens! Crowley is skulking about somewhere. Climb up and join me on the top of the Needle. This is the safest place.'

As he spoke, a loud report sounded from the depths of the gully behind them. Jones watched in horror as a huge boulder bounced off the walls, gouging a trench in the snow, spinning ever closer.

Panic spurred him to action. Tugging Elspeth's hand, he leapt out of the path of the boulder, up to the narrow gap between the Needle and the ridge that connected it to the mountain. The carriage-sized rock exploded on the platform where they had stood seconds before, sending a cascade of fragments showering down the mountainside.

Elspeth cried out and clung to Jones, who struggled to balance on the sloping shelf he suddenly found himself on. His claws scraped against the rock and for a moment he thought they were both done for; then he found his balance, and stood with his claw-points lodged in a crack to keep them both secure.

He could feel Elspeth breathing heavily against his chest. He tried to calm her. 'Don't worry, we're safe here.'

'You must climb up to me!' Barkis shouted from above. 'He's been rolling rocks down the gullies for a quarter of an hour. This is the only safe perch!'

'Whatever possessed you to come up here in the first place?'

'The same thing as you—pursuit of our rival!'

Jones muttered a curse, berating himself for being so stupid. His impetuous streak had got him in trouble yet again.

'Crowley has led us into a pretty little trap, hasn't he?'

Elspeth struggled in his embrace, trying to find her own balance. 'Will you two be quiet? We must find a way out of this! If we stay here we shall slip to our deaths, falling rocks or no.'

Jones looked up. He had never found the Needle climb difficult, but a layer of ice over every rock changed everything. He wondered how Barkis had got up there alone and in the dark. Fear of Crowley's missiles may have had something to do with it.

A short scramble down a cracked chimney led to a safe location beneath the Needle itself. Jones wondered if they could find refuge there, but of course there was the issue of his friend, trapped and alone at the top.

Instantly, a plan sprang to mind.

'Elspeth, I need you to help me,' he said quietly. 'Can you reach the rope in my bag?'

She squirmed, reaching round with a hand. 'Yes. Tell me what you need me to do.'

Another rock bounced down the couloir, enveloping them in a whirlwind of stone-dust and snow.

Jones coughed. 'I want you to go down there and belay me while I climb the Needle. You ought to be safe for a few minutes. I shall reason with Crowley and try to get Barkis down. Then perhaps we can escape.'

He realised it sounded like a terrible plan, but they had to do something.

She hesitated. 'Do you trust me?'

'Not in the slightest, but unless you can talk to Crowley and stop him from chucking bits of mountain down upon us, I don't see what choice we have.'

She made the necessary manoeuvres to retrieve the rope from his bag. Tying into the rope while maintaining balance was a dangerous task, but after a minute or two they were ready. Elspeth stepped up onto a small block, then began the climb down into the darkness at the bottom of the chimney. Jones retrieved his ice axes from his bag and attached to his wrists the loops of cord he had added since their last outing. He placed the lantern on the rock where Elspeth had stood, trying to point the beam upwards to illuminate his path of ascent.

After a moment, Elspeth called up to say she was ready. Jones wasted no time in leaving his dangerous stance, using his axes to hook his way up the steep crack ahead of him. He couldn't help smiling at the irony. No doubt his critics would complain about the unsporting method used to climb yet another Great Gable route—Thomson would probably call it a mechanical contrivance—but in the circumstances Jones cared even less than usual.

A beam of light washed over him from the top of the ridge, where Crowley was surely lurking. Jones kept going. Another boulder crashed into the base of the Needle, close to where he had been standing minutes ago. The rock lurched under his claw-points. He took a loop of cord from around his shoulder and hooked it over a spike at his feet, tying it to the rope to provide a running belay, should the worst occur and he took a fall. Below, Elspeth looked up anxiously, and the thought flashed across his mind that his life was now in her untrustworthy hands.

He reached the shoulder. The route onwards was exposed, he recalled, with polished holds and a big reach up to grasp the top block. More rocks rained down as he made the required moves to establish himself on the upper portion of the climb. He twisted his ice axes into the horizontal crack in front of his face, hardly able to see what he was doing. His left axe slipped a little, and a little more; he wanted to commit all his weight to it but was afraid it would fly out and strike him in the face.

A terrible scrape of metal against rock. His right foot swung free, forcing him to take his entire weight on his arms. He pulled upwards, scraping for footholds: a smear of ice, a patch of frost, a nick in the rock; anything at all.

Without knowing how he had done it, he was on the summit of the Needle, breathing hard, glad to be alive. Simon's lantern shone in his face, and behind it the hooded figure of his friend, who was staring in surprise.

'Good work,' Barkis said, gripping Jones by the shoulders to steady him on that tiny platform suspended in space. 'It's not so easy under ice, is it?'

'My dear fellow, you are an expert at understatement. Quick, you must tie in to my rope.'

Barkis put the lantern down and deftly tied a butterfly knot, slipping it over his shoulders and adjusting it to fit his waist.

'What now?' Barkis said. 'I am afraid we might have to remain here for the night. Is Elspeth here?'

'She is at the other end of my rope. We must try to reason with Crowley.'

Barkis laughed out loud. 'I tried. He did not listen.'

'I thought you were here for revenge?'

'Well, quite—but I hardly think I am in a position of strength, do you?'

Another impact. Jones suddenly felt the exposure of their position, perched on this tiny coffee table with vast drops on all sides. He decided to sit down.

*

'Crowley!' Jones shouted into the rising wind. 'We know you're up there. Answer us!'

'I have nothing to say to you,' came back the reply, echoing amongst the rocks.

'Consider what you're doing. You regarded Barkis as a friend, once.'

'We were friends, until he destroyed my life and reputation, stole my work, drove me away.'

'Come now, that is hardly fair!' Barkis shouted. 'In Zermatt you abandoned us, to try for the greater glory of a solo ascent. You laid aside all claims to friendship when you made that choice.'

'LIES!'

The word boomed out of the darkness, followed by another boulder. The Needle rocked, and the lamp at the platform below exploded in a flash, extinguishing the macabre floodlighting that illuminated the drama.

'In the name of the friendship we once shared, I beg you to stop this madness!' Barkis cried out. 'I am telling the truth. We may have copied your idea after we thought you were dead, but we treated you with honour while you lived!'

'Even now, when under my power, you are ensnared in the lie.'

Jones looked at Barkis. The darkness concealed his face, but his eyes glinted in the glow from Crowley's distant lantern.

'What is he talking about?' Jones said. 'Is there some fact you have not told me?'

Barkis looked confused and scared. 'Don't listen to him. He is trying to manipulate us.'

'I am not the one who has spread deceit about me like a web,' Crowley shouted. 'Jones deserves to know how he has been fooled. Holdstock learned of my secret engagement to my beloved, my plans to form a company with Eckenstein to manufacture the new equipment. He was jealous. He wanted the success that I deserved.'

'You exaggerate,' Barkis pleaded. 'Holdstock never meant to hurt you.'

'He told my betrothed I had forsaken her,' Crowley continued. 'He spread the rumour about the town that I planned to sabotage the expedition on the Matterhorn for my own glory, and all the while he laid his own plans for what he would do after my death.'

'Are you suggesting Holdstock plotted to kill you?'

'Please try to keep up! He goaded me into breaking from the expedition and attempting the north face alone, knowing the measure of the risks I would face. I have a written confession from a local guide who was paid a pathetic sum to begin the avalanche from the summit.'

'That is absurd!' Barkis insisted. 'The avalanche could easily have killed Holdstock and myself.'

'Yet you were roped together and attached to the face by the equipment I designed and built. He was willing to take that risk … as were you.'

'I had nothing to do with this.' Barkis' voice shook with rage.

Crowley laughed. 'You knew of it! Of course you did! Oh, I'm sure it suited your conscience better to turn a blind eye and believe the fiction Holdstock spun you. The fact is that you were half in love with Holdstock and would have sold your own mother if he ordered it. You are a dreaming idiot, a fool who blunders along in the shadows of greater men.'

Barkis said nothing to that. Considering everything that had befallen them, the proven fraud and corruption that Holdstock had been imprisoned for, was it such a leap to believe Crowley's claims? Suddenly it all made so much sense to Jones. His heart sank.

His impression of Holdstock had been of a young man desperate to make his mark on the world, not unlike Crowley, only blessed with greater charm and sophistication. Until the trip to Zermatt last year, he had been content to strive for his goal by writing books and selling motor cars; but the public loved a brave mountaineer, and he had seized the chance of immortality when Crowley's progressive technique opened up the possibility of radical new routes.

It was no secret that Holdstock and Crowley were the experienced mountaineers in the team. Barkis had been the novice, content to follow the lead of his more seasoned friends. With his trusting nature and noble principles, no wonder he had been treated like a doormat. Well, he's learning, Jones thought bitterly: Barkis could no longer be described as trusting.

Crowley and Holdstock seemed like a natural partnership: both gifted in their own way, both desperate for immortality. How sad that neither would consider the possibility of sharing the glory. Greed had divided them in the end.

At last, Jones felt he understood why Crowley pursued them so relentlessly. Everything he had once cared about and worked for had been taken from him. Jones knew he could no longer argue against a cause like this. It was time to offer Crowley a hand, and God help them if he did not accept it.

'I understand,' Jones shouted up to him. 'I see how much you have lost, and why you feel compelled to follow this path. What can we do to help you?'

'Don't give in to him,' Barkis said in a low voice, but he sounded broken inside, now he had finally admitted the truth to himself.

'There is nothing you can do to appease me,' Crowley replied. 'I've got you exactly where I want you!'

A huge roar reverberated around the cliffs. This was not just a small boulder being pushed over the edge; this sounded much bigger, an explosion perhaps. Jones heard the clatter of smaller stones falling ahead of the main deluge, felt the tremors rise up out of the mountain, through the Needle, and into his bones.

Barkis slumped against the rock, immobile, his posture one of a man who had given up. Jones gripped his shoulders and shook him.

'Hold onto me!'

They clung together as the landslide hit Napes Needle. The mountain leapt beneath their feet, and Jones felt himself falling through space, the platform where he had crouched seconds before no longer there. Flashes of light from Crowley's lantern stabbed through the confusion of whirling snow and rock, illuminating moments of chaos: a rope snaking through a mottled canvas of black and white, a boot spinning into oblivion.

For one instant, Jones felt his mind clear and there was only one thought left: Rachel.

Through the thunder he heard a voice cry out, Elspeth's voice, strangely above him: 'Aleister, no!'

*

When Jones came to, the first thought that crossed his mind was how remarkably cold he felt. A chilly breeze stroked his skin. The ground felt lumpy beneath his back, and he thought he was lying head-first down a slope, but could not be sure. Pain crept into his limbs. His injured rib, which had been healing well these past two weeks, now throbbed once again.

He opened his eyes, and looked directly up into the stars. The moon was out now, and although thin and weak it cast a little light onto the hillside, just enough to show what was snow and what was rock. Some way up the slope he could see a cone of yellow light playing over a patch of rubble.

He remembered Elspeth's cry as the rockfall had hit them, and wondered if she had survived.

Beside him, Barkis groaned and jolted in panic as he came to. They lay on debris from the avalanche, and with the disturbance it started to slide further. Luckily, the lifeline connecting them with the mountain had survived, and they came up against the rope.

Jones tried to get to his feet. The pain in his legs intensified, but they supported his weight and he did not think anything was broken. It hurt to breathe. He marvelled at his good luck, and wondered how many lives he would have left by the end of the season.

'Barkis, are you all right?'

'My leg is hurt,' he muttered angrily.

'We'll get you down. Are you safe? I must help Elspeth.'

'By all means.'

Jones untied and began to crawl up the slope of shattered rock. Soon he realised that the lamp he could see up ahead was being held by the shadowy figure of Crowley, stooped over something on the ground. The loose material under his feet made an awful noise as he slid and stumbled up the slope, and Jones realised he had no chance of making a covert approach.

The lamp washed over him, blinding him for a moment. 'Stay back,' Crowley warned in a low voice. 'She's hurt.'

'You have that on your own conscience.'

Following the rope, Jones reached the ledge where Elspeth had been sheltering. His body tensed, waiting for an attack from Crowley, but somehow Jones sensed that the time for violence had passed. He felt disoriented; something about the surroundings seemed to have changed. It took a few moments for him to realise that to the left, beyond the cracked chimney where the bulk of Napes Needle ought to be, there was nought but starry sky.

Crowley's landslide had gouged a huge section away from the mountain, destroying the icon of British climbing in the process.

Elspeth lay on the platform's edge, a small shape in the darkness, her pale face flecked with blood. Jones thought he could see a cloud of breath rising above her open lips.

He rushed to her side, knelt, checked for a pulse. She was alive. Her eyes flickered open and found his gaze.

'Jones …'

Crowley shoved him out of the way and took Elspeth's hand. 'Elspeth my darling, it's me. I'm here.'

'Aleister? What have you done?' She tried to shift herself, and gave out a cry of pain.

'I thought you were safely in the hotel!'

Jones felt like an intruder, watching this tender scene between Aleister Crowley and his wife. Jones had suspected this for some time now. The truth was that, like Barkis, Jones preferred to believe in honour and integrity, instead of opening his mind to the deceit taking place all around him.

Despite the evil game Elspeth had played, Jones could not bring himself to hate her. She had given him friendship, support, and love when he needed it most; even if those emotions had been false, they had helped him.

She looked up at him, her face twisted in pain and remorse. 'I'm sorry for what I've done to you. The moments … the moments we shared were not false.'

'You are delirious,' Crowley said. He turned to Jones, face harsh in the lamplight. 'Her advances were part of my plan. She loves me and me alone. She is my wife.'

Jones could not stop looking at Elspeth, struck down and immobile. 'We must get her to safety. Barkis, too. Will you help me?'

Crowley remained silent. He stroked his wife's hair, teased out flecks of stone and dust.

'Please, do as he asks,' Elspeth begged him. 'This is no time for pride! I cannot move by myself.'

Jones extended a hand towards Crowley, and after a further moment of deliberation, his enemy took it and allowed Jones to help him to his feet.

Crowley looked wretched. 'The landslide got out of control. I didn't mean for it to happen like this.'

'Then how did you expect it to happen?' Jones asked, incredulous that Crowley was trying to defend his actions.

'I never wished for any physical harm to befall you. Barkis deserves to die, but I have encouraged your every endeavour! Do you really think your book would have seen publication without my help? In the long run, I need you. I have plans for you.'

'Keep them for when we have delivered Elspeth and Barkis to medical safety. I refuse to listen to any more of your madness.'

*

Jones sat alone on a boulder at Sty Head. The sun smiled warm and welcoming on the promised land of the mountaineer. Familiar hills surrounded him, old and faithful companions, each with stories and memories to tell; but all he could think about were the things that last night had taken from him.

He looked out over the snow-dashed flank of Great Gable, towards the Napes crags. Where the outline of Napes Needle ought to have jutted into the sky, nothing remained but an ugly brown scar and a scoop carved out of the cliffs behind it. Beneath the devastation, a long trail of debris stained the snow like a fountain of blood.

With his selfish act, Aleister Crowley had destroyed one of England's finest and best-loved rock climbs. It had been one of Jones' first ever climbs in Wastdale. He thought of all the future generations who would be deprived of the pleasure of ascending the Needle, the place where some said English climbing had been born eleven years ago.

His thoughts returned to the casualties: Elspeth, concussed and bruised but alive; and Barkis, leg injured by the shockwave of the explosion. After the difficult evacuation from the Napes, Tyson had driven the invalids out of Wastdale and to the nearest doctor.

The last thing that Elspeth said to him before the cart drove away was that she was sorry. Barkis had merely given a wry grin and advised him to be careful.

Crowley, of course, vanished as soon as they arrived at the hotel.

Jones wondered how he felt about Elspeth's betrayal, and realised he would need time to think. His initial reaction, beyond the shock, was that he felt desperately sorry for her. She had married a man who could grievously injure his own wife, then run away to save himself when she needed him the most.

Despite the impulse to travel with Elspeth and Barkis to the hospital, and prove himself the better man, Jones realised he simply had to take some time for himself to think things through and gain perspective on his life and all the things that had befallen him.

And so he would take up his ice axe and wander the hills, the truest friends he had ever enjoyed in his life.

PART TWO

THE GREAT WHITE VEIL

"SLEEP EVADED RACHEL THAT NIGHT"

CHAPTER ELEVEN

IN VINO VERITAS

12th of May, 1897

"MY DEAR MR JONES,

"It was so nice to hear your recent news. Everything is going well for you at last, or so it seems. What a relief it must be to know that the police are finally after Crowley! Your new job sounds exciting. I knew Eckenstein would try to get hold of those patents if the opportunity ever arose.

"On to the main purpose of my letter. This is a little awkward, & I have mentioned Peter as little as possible in the course of our correspondence out of respect for you, but I hope you will understand that things have now changed. On Monday evening, Peter asked me to marry him, & I agreed.

"I hope you do not mind if I open my heart to you, but you have always listened to my troubles. The fact is that I do not love him. I care a great deal for him; he is good and kind to me; I have not the slightest doubt that he loves me, and is that not enough? The sad fact is that my family is struggling. My father's illness has progressed & I am no longer able to pay for medical care, even though I have worked in the telegraph office for over a month. Peter is a man of good background, & he has the power to save my family.

"I know you will not judge me. I have spoken to nobody about this, especially not Peter. I hope you realise how important to me you are.

"Yours affectionately,

"Rachel M. Elliot."

*

Jones read his post with a rising sense of bleak inevitability. For months now he had resolved not to interfere with Rachel's affairs, but he simply could not imagine her choosing to marry any man she did not love. Her family's situation must be serious.

He had tried to harden himself against this day, tried to forget his feelings, make them fade. It had not worked. He sighed. Nothing could be done about it. The time for telling her how he felt had long passed, and now he had to take the news like a man, smile and wish her happiness.

A telegram had also arrived this morning; just another threatening message from Crowley. He screwed it up and tossed it into the waste paper basket. These wires had arrived at irregular intervals since the Napes Needle incident. Nothing ever came of them. In truth, Jones no longer let Crowley worry him too much. Ever since he had faced the man and stood firm, he found that he had a renewed confidence and cheerful attitude to life. Besides, he no longer had to suffer alone. The "Crowley case" had been made public and now everyone knew what a scoundrel he was.

Time to go to work. Jones drank the last of his tea, and left the house.

*

He enjoyed his daily walk to Eckenstein's shop on Charing Cross Road. A leisurely mile allowed just enough time to smoke his pipe and let his mind relax in preparation for the day of work ahead. His walk took him past the Greek Revival bulk of the British Museum, a place he liked to visit at weekends, along with half of the population of London, it seemed. After cutting down Bedford Avenue, he joined Charing Cross Road and walked the remaining quarter of a mile to the shop. The city hummed, clattered, and shouted with life all around him, a thousand vehicles all fighting for space in one relatively narrow thoroughfare. For once the bustle of life and industry cheered him up instead of making him pine for the wildness he loved away from town.

He had always liked this part of the city: decent taverns, plentiful bookshops, the Palace theatre. The disreputable district of Soho lay only a street away, but for the first time in as long as he could remember, he actually felt happy in London, his restlessness slaked.

No. 86, Charing Cross Road stood at the left end of a terrace of similar shops. Most of the floors above ground level were divided up into flats and offices. In addition to the shop itself, Eckenstein rented the first floor of No. 86, which he used as a residence and warehouse combined. From what Jones could see, Eckenstein actually slept there relatively infrequently.

Above the shop windows, the new sign made a bold statement, big black capitals against glossy white: "ECKENSTEIN ALPINE EQUIPMENT."

Unsurprisingly, Eckenstein had forgotten to put the "open" sign up in the window. Nevertheless, some customers had already wandered in and were browsing the displays of boots, clothing, knapsacks, assorted ironmongery, and racked ice axes of every description.

'Is that you, boy?' Eckenstein shouted from the back room. 'Get in here!'

Jones smiled. After checking that no customers needed assistance, he walked behind the counter and through the door into the little stock-room at the back.

As usual, Eckenstein wore a dirty white apron over his waistcoat and shirt, and sweated with hammer and tongs over a portable forge. Despite the concession of an open window the room felt like an oven. Eckenstein raised a hand to wipe the perspiration from his face, leaving a long smudge of soot.

'Ah, there you are. Hold this for me.'

Eckenstein thrust the tongs in Jones' direction. They held what appeared to be the front unit of a set of articulated ice claws. Jones took the tongs, and held them over the small anvil Eckenstein had installed in the stock-room.

Eckenstein grinned. His bearded face shone with sweat. 'I need a bit more beef for this. Hold steady now.'

He swung the hammer with both hands, pounding the front points of the claws. When he had finished, he instructed Jones to quench the piece in the water bucket.

'Tell me what you think.'

Jones held the claw close to his face. It steamed and sizzled, but despite the rough appearance of the metal, he could appreciate the modifications Eckenstein had made to the design. The twin front points, originally plain square-sectioned spurs projecting forward in line with the sole of the boot, were now flattened into chisel-like blades that curved downward at the end. The secondary points, which in the claws Jones owned simply pointed straight down, now swept forward at a significant angle.

'I see the benefits of the new front points, but what about these?' Jones touched the secondary points, wincing at the hot steel.

'If the climber drops his heels a little, they will engage with the ice and provide extra support. Takes away some of the strain.'

Despite his irritation at Eckenstein's tendency to ignore customers and focus on the engineering side of the business, Jones admired the work his boss produced.

'Ingenious. Have you checked it doesn't infringe anyone's patents?'

'Very funny.'

'I'm quite serious. Look at what happened to Holdstock—and besides, you don't want Crowley to come after you, do you?'

Eckenstein put the claw down. 'Jones, he is not going to come after me. Crowley is being hunted by the police now and has better things to do with his time. I'll wager he's languishing in Paris smoking his own weight in opium.'

'Possibly.'

Jones wasn't convinced. Crowley's actions in Wastdale were not those of a man easily dissuaded.

'Anyway,' Eckenstein continued, 'he and I go back years. I practically taught him every damn thing he knows. Why would he want to hurt me?'

'In fairness, you have bought control of the disputed patents. He won't like that.'

'I don't think he cares any more,' Eckenstein insisted. 'What did he do with the patents after he obtained them with his false name? Nothing! All he did was sell off a bit of surplus stock. I think our young friend is more interested in his inflated sense of self-importance.'

*

The shop remained busy all day, with a steady stream of customers in the morning and early afternoon. The cash register rang almost in time with the bell above the door. However, Jones noticed that a pattern in browsing and buying habits had begun to emerge. Many had clearly heard about the shop, either by word of mouth, through advertisements, or in the news, and had simply come to see what the fuss was all about. Climbers still tended to be of the educated or wealthy sort, and most English climbers lived in London.

He made many sales of ordinary items such as knapsacks, lip-salve, glacier glasses, alpenstocks, boot-nails and the like. He even sold a pair of ice claws, the fifth set he had managed to shift that week. In truth, Jones was surprised they had sold so many. The new ice climbing technique had received more attention recently, with notable ascents in Scotland being made by Raeburn and Collie, but the bulk of mountaineers preferred to stick to their tried and trusted methods.

The new ice axes could be a problem. They remained exotic items, priced so highly that only the elite would consider purchasing them. The ordinary man, off to the Alps for a spot of peak-bagging, would never dream of spending so much on a pair of radical tools when he could buy a traditional Swiss step-cutter for a few shillings at any outfitter. Consequently, Eckenstein worked tirelessly on the basic Holdstock design to simplify the manufacturing process and bring down the cost. A lot of work remained to be done before these tools could enter the mainstream.

At a little after four o'clock, Jones noticed another reporter snooping in the shop, looking at the rack of ice axes. Eckenstein had briefed him on how to identify and deal with reporters, but Eckenstein was currently out and Jones did not share his curmudgeonly view of the world; in his opinion, publicity could only be a good thing.

He approached the man with a friendly smile. The gentleman in question was short and stocky, about Jones' height in fact, and was dressed like almost everyone else in the City, with bowler hat and frock coat.

'Can I help you, sir?'

The man turned and offered his hand. 'Good day to you, Mr Jones is it? Alfred Varley, Observer. If it is convenient I have a few questions I should like to put to you.'

Jones looked around the shop. It was empty. 'By all means. Please follow me into the back room.'

Varley followed. As the door closed, he gave a short laugh, no doubt at the clutter of technical detritus that covered every available surface. Jones cleared a chair and offered it to Mr Varley.

'Do accept my apologies at the state of the office. My colleague, Mr Eckenstein, believes very strongly in working on his inventions until they are perfect.'

'I'm sure,' Mr Varley said, a little uneasily, as he sat down. He retrieved a notepad from his pocket. 'Would you object if I took notes?'

'Not at all.'

'I understand you are a mountaineer of some repute. It is also my understanding that Aleister Crowley is your sworn enemy. Would you agree?'

Jones felt the need for caution. 'That is an exaggeration. Crowley and I have our differences, both professionally and personally. As a climber, I have nothing but the greatest of respect for him.'

'Even though he assaulted you?'

'I was in the wrong place at the wrong time. Mr Varley, these facts are well known. Every national newspaper reported the proceedings of the Crowley case in great detail.'

'Quite, but I wished to hear it from you, since our little rag has not yet had the pleasure of an interview with your good self.' Varley grinned obsequiously.

'Then it is my wish that Crowley and I are not portrayed as arch-enemies. I find these comparisons between Crowley and Moriarty distasteful. This is not a Sherlock Holmes mystery.'

'I have heard rumours that you are rivals in love, also. There is talk of a girl.'

'There is no girl, I assure you.'

'Really? What about the woman Crowley asked to marry him two years ago? I've heard that the wedding may even have taken place in secret, before his little accident on the Matterhorn.'

Jones suddenly wished the conversation would end. He had done his best to protect Elspeth, but he knew that it could only be a matter of time before her role in the drama became known to the world.

'I know nothing of her.'

'No comment, right.' Varley jotted that down. 'What is your opinion on the Crowley case? Do you think he's a criminal genius?'

'I object to that label in the strongest possible terms! To look at the facts, Crowley has lost. The rights to the patents he fraudulently filed now lie with my employer, after a legitimate and transparent purchase.'

'Or so you claim. Why have you withheld information on the case?'

'Everything I wish to say on this matter has already been said in court,' Jones said sharply. 'I have nothing to add, not to you.'

'I've heard rumours about a witness who has yet to make a statement,' the reporter persisted, 'and when you throw the girl into the mix as well ...'

Jones stood up and opened the door. 'There is no witness and certainly no girl. You will excuse me, but I think it is time for you to leave.'

'One last question. Where do you think Crowley might be hiding?'

'I really have no idea. Try the Soho opium dens or the nearest mystic temple.'

'You don't think he has left the country?'

'No I do not. Crowley is not the kind of man to walk away from a fight he believes he can still win.'

*

Jones returned home that evening feeling down. The conversation with the reporter had unsettled him, causing that old sense of danger to resurface and disturb his contentment. As if in response to his renewed worries, his partially healed rib gave a twinge of pain.

When he reached his apartment in Russell Square, Jones discovered that the door was unlocked; moreover, he could see a glow through the frosted glass. He opened the door gently, trying to avoid the usual creak. A gas lamp in his study cut through the darkness of the hallway. He could hear someone pacing up and down.

No object to hand would serve as a weapon. Jones tensed himself and walked into the study to confront the intruder, fully expecting his rival to be waiting for him again.

Instead, Crowley's wife stood beside the book-case, flicking through a slim volume. She wore black once again, and a veil obscured her face. Two roses adorned her otherwise plain hat. She leaned heavily on a silver-capped cane.

Elspeth turned suddenly and closed the book with a snap.

'Oh! Mr Jones, I hope you will excuse me. I still have my key.'

Completely taken aback, he did not know how to respond to the intrusion. Although they had exchanged brief telegrams, they had not met since the incident in Wastdale. She had betrayed him, of that there could be no doubt, and yet Jones sensed in her a deep undercurrent of remorse, a wish to be a better person. In short, he did not know whether to regard her as a friend or an enemy. He certainly could not trust the wife of Aleister Crowley.

'I will thank you not to let yourself into my apartment in future, Elspeth. Is it a habit you learned from your husband? Oh, sit down for goodness' sake.'

She accepted the offered chair gratefully. 'I'm sorry, but I did not want to wait outside. It's dangerous for me to be here.'

She seemed agitated. Her face, never one of classical beauty, still possessed a stoic grace but betrayed a little more of her sufferings and worries than Jones remembered. Nevertheless, she seemed to be recovering well from her injuries.

'You are looking well.'

She gave a sad smile. 'That's a lie, but thank you. I can afford the best doctors. Besides, my injuries were not so bad. I'm so pleased to see you, Jones!'

'Really? Or is that Elspeth the actress speaking?'

'Please. I am trying to be ... better. I know I have hurt you a great deal, and not a day goes by when I don't hate myself and wish I could undo all the horrible things I have done.'

'Then why did you do them?'

'Because he is my husband! For the longest time I thought I was a widow. It is a terrible thing to go through.'

'Does that mean you are unable to think for yourself, to know the difference between right and wrong?'

'It's not that simple. You were there on the Needle. You heard the truth of the plot against Aleister.'

'I agree that your husband has been dealt a poor hand, but why the campaign of revenge? I don't understand.'

She looked ashamed. 'It all got out of control. Originally Aleister just wanted you to suffer some slight humiliation, in return for your part in his disgrace. The more he dug, the more he perceived you to be a threat. He—he wants you to be a worthy rival. The higher you climb, the further you shall fall, he said to me.'

'He is completely insane. You must see that by now.'

She paused for a long time, eyes never leaving his. 'Yes, I have come to realise that.'

'You could simply leave him.'

'It surely has not escaped your notice that Aleister has left me.'

Jones began to suspect that Elspeth had come here simply to beg forgiveness, but it was too close to the event, and the betrayal still stung. He felt angry at her weakness of character and willingness to be manipulated.

'I did not want to involve you with this. Why did you visit me? Now I shall have to lie if I am asked if I have seen you.' He paused. 'Or I could just hand you over to the police. I'm sure you can tell them where Crowley is skulking.'

'You could do that, it's true, but I don't think you will. I came here to help you, Jones! There is a new danger you know nothing about.'

'What do you mean?'

She closed her eyes for a moment, as if rallying her strength. 'I cannot tell you too much. Aleister has ways of knowing things.' Another lengthy pause. 'He wanted to hurt you where it would wound the most. That was what my role would be.'

'Clearly,' Jones said, unable to conceal his bitterness.

She looked even more ashamed.

'Since he has failed in his first attempt, he is going to try a new approach.' She reached across the desk and gripped his hand, her expression full of pain. 'Listen carefully. Rachel Elliot is in danger. I did not know of this scheme before, I swear.'

A stab of panic. 'What scheme?'

'I don't know the details, and I couldn't tell you even if I did. He will find out.'

'Please, Elspeth! I'm not afraid of him.'

She rose from her chair with some difficulty. 'I have told you this much out of love and respect for you, and out of friendship for a fellow woman I have never met. I've risked a great deal just to make this visit. This much I will gladly do, but no more.'

Jones felt helpless and confused by this new revelation. Was she telling the truth, or was she still loyal to her husband, sowing the seeds of some new trap? In the end, all that mattered was that his worst fear had been confirmed. Rachel could be in danger. Her disquieting letter had been cause enough for concern, but now he could no longer in good conscience delay action.

'Thank you for visiting me,' he said quietly. 'I appreciate your warning, even if it makes little sense.'

'And I apologise for the mystery,' she replied. 'I really must go.'

'Do you honestly think Crowley will know you have been here?'

'You may depend upon it,' Elspeth said grimly. 'I will suffer for this, and so will you.'

*

After she left, Jones went in search of Eckenstein to ask for advice. He knew better than to enquire at his lodgings, for the old sinner could rarely be found there. Instead, Jones began by checking the public houses and gin shops in the vicinity. If that failed, he would start looking in the Soho brothels and opium dens.

Darkness crept upon the city. The electric lamp-posts lining Charing Cross Road and Shaftesbury Avenue winked on one by one. The traffic had slackened considerably, but vehicles still rattled up and down; here a four-wheeler on a personal errand, there a lumbering omnibus, top-heavy and plastered with advertisements.

Jones dropped into the nearest pub. Local workers filled the public bar. Despite appearing to be a spacious establishment from the street, on the inside this proved to be an illusion, for the place had a cramped and mean atmosphere. Eckenstein often drank here, despite having been thrown out on at least two occasions.

Jones managed to attract the barman's attention. He looked down on Jones in much the same way that a gardener looks down on a slug.

'Yes, guv?'

'I'm looking for my friend.'

'In that case, don't mind me if I serve an actual customer.'

The barman was already moving away when Jones added, 'Have you seen Oscar Eckenstein?'

'You missed 'im,' the barman said, hesitating for a moment. 'Took off 'alf an hour ago, proper corned.'

Jones felt his spirits sink. He had no chance of finding a drunken Eckenstein in the depths of Soho. As he started to force a passage towards the door, the barman shouted out one more thing.

'Look out for that young fella with 'im: trouble and no mistake.'

'What young fellow?' Jones demanded, feeling uneasy, but the barman did not reply.

*

Jones always felt wary venturing into Soho after dark. As a Londoner, he knew that the degenerate reputation of the district was often exaggerated—a tool used by politicians and popular fiction authors for their own ends—yet it could not be denied that Soho had dangers.

He walked with confidence to avoid making himself a target. Trying to think like Eckenstein would after a few pints, he wondered which direction he should take. To this question there could only be one answer: deeper, particularly if Crowley accompanied him.

His mind worked over what the barman had told him. Eckenstein did not have many friends—he despised most people—and the only young fellow Eckenstein had ever formed a real bond with was Crowley. Jones wondered what new scheme might be afoot.

Two hours of searching the pubs and gin-shops of Soho yielded no clues. He finally ended up at an establishment on the corner of Great Pulteney Street, the Sun and 13 Cantons: a relatively modern addition to the area, but the architecture was gloomy and forbidding, a high-arched facade of red brick and mean, glowering windows. Despite its unwelcoming aspect, Jones had visited the place many times before in daylight and had found it to be decidedly better than most of the other drinking establishments in the vicinity.

Strangely for the hour, the pub proved to be almost deserted. He perched on a stool at the far left corner of the bar, glumly wondering whatever had possessed him to bother searching for Eckenstein anyway.

The barmaid sauntered over to him, polishing a glass with a towel. A cheerful young woman of maybe twenty-one, Jones had been on nodding terms with her for some weeks now.

'Good evening, Mr Jones. What can I do for you?'

'Evening, Harriet. I would like a pint of stout, please.'

She started pouring his pint. 'You look down in the dumps tonight, Jonesy. Missus kicked you out?'

Jones smiled. 'In a manner of speaking.'

'You'll be joining your friends in the back room, no doubt.'

'I beg your pardon?'

Harriet handed over his pint. 'Two gen'lemen in high spirits ordered drinks about an hour ago before retiring to the private room. One of them said to 'is mate that he expected you would be along soon. I hope I ain't said nothing amiss?'

Jones realised he must have turned white with surprise. 'Not at all. Would you mind pointing me in the direction of the private room?'

'Just through there, love,' Harriet said, pointing to a closed door left of the bar.

He picked up his pint and readied his nerves before closing his hand on the doorknob.

*

The private room seemed dark compared to the brightly lit main bar. Jones stood still while his eyes adjusted to the glow of two dirty old oil lamps turned down to their lowest setting. A fug of hashish spiced the air, and curtains pulled across the windows hid the activities within from onlookers in the street.

'The thing is … the thing is …' Jones heard Eckenstein slur, 'nobody else has ever really understood me.'

'I understand you,' Crowley replied in his slow, sibilant accent. 'You taught me everything I know.'

'That's what I said! Oh, who's that standing in the door?'

Jones turned up the nearest lamp to throw a bit more light on the scene. Eckenstein and Crowley sprawled on chairs in the far corner, each holding a pint glass in one hand and a pipe in the other.

'It's Jones!'

He approached, confused by this show of friendship. What precisely was going on here, he wondered: Crowley and Eckenstein settling their differences over a beer? Had Eckenstein forgotten everything the young scoundrel had done?

Jones took a seat beside Eckenstein. 'It took me quite a while to find you.'

Crowley smiled. 'No doubt you are unfamiliar with Soho. You don't strike me as being quite the type.'

'On the contrary, I know Soho quite well, although as you say I am not the sort to seek out depravity.'

Crowley's smiled broadened. 'But depravity is such good fun. Oscar understands, don't you my man?'

Eckenstein nodded fiercely, clearly far more drunk than his companion.

Jones took Crowley by the arm and led him to one side. 'What the hell are you doing?' he whispered.

'Showing my old friend a good time!'

'After everything you have done, he is no friend of yours.'

Crowley raised an eyebrow. 'I will thank you to unhand me,' he said coolly, shrugging his arm out of Jones' grip. 'We have been rivals for a long time, you and I. More recently we have crossed swords. I do not regret that in the least—we were never made to be allies—but in defending myself against my enemies I have also alienated my friends.'

'To be expected, given your methods.'

'The point is that I wish to make amends. I have no quarrel with Oscar. Now, if you will excuse me?'

Crowley returned to his seat and took a long draught of beer from his glass.

Jones didn't believe him. Crowley had to be up to something, ingratiating himself with Eckenstein to obtain some kind of hold on the business, perhaps. Crowley did nothing out of the goodness of his heart. The claim that he merely intended to catch up with an old friend did not sound plausible, particularly considering Elspeth's warning.

He sat down with them. The situation suddenly seemed ridiculous, enjoying a pint with his greatest enemy, and he stifled a giggle.

'What's the joke?' Eckenstein said loudly.

'Well, it's funny, isn't it? The three of us sitting here as if nothing had happened. Almost like the old days back at Wastdale Head, before the argument.'

Crowley smiled slightly. 'Heady days indeed. You would never just give up and admit I was the better climber.'

Jones considered that point. 'I don't believe you are the better climber.'

'You see? An unstoppable force meets an immovable object.'

'Which is which?' Eckenstein asked.

'I am the unstoppable force,' Crowley replied, his intense eyes studying Jones carefully.

'You don't fall off as much as Jones does, anyway,' Eckenstein said cheerfully. 'Therefore you must be better.'

Jones began to feel irritated. 'Why don't you employ him instead of me, then?'

'Perhaps I will.' Eckenstein downed the rest of his pint and belched.

'Alas, my labours are required in other fields, and anyway I'm a wanted criminal,' Crowley said. 'But thank you for the kind offer.'

'Any time. We're friends.'

'I am glad to hear that. Oscar, I want you to know that I bear no grudge against you. You're welcome to those patents; I don't have the time to invest in them, and don't need the money anyway.'

'That's very mag—magnan … magnanininimous of you,' Eckenstein managed to say. 'I insist you must be kinder to Jones in future though. He does try so very hard, despite his many faults.'

'I am still here, you know!' Jones said, outraged.

Crowley laughed. 'Stop being so tense. Enjoy yourself!'

'No, I've had enough of this. Eckenstein, it's time to leave.'

'Oh, don't be like that—'

'I insist.'

Jones grabbed Eckenstein by the arm and tried to heave him upright. The big man resisted, playfully at first, but when Jones tried to remove the chair from under him Eckenstein lashed out with his fist and punched Jones in the jaw. His face exploded in pain and he fell over in surprise. The floor dealt a second blow as he crashed to the ground.

He groaned and sat up, tenderly feeling his jaw, which had already begun to swell.

'What did you do that for?'

'You need to learn your place,' Eckenstein said sulkily.

Even Crowley looked surprised.

Jones picked himself up off the floor. 'To hell with both of you. I'm going home.'

He slammed the door behind him on the way out. He walked fast once outside in the street, not caring which way he went. His face hurt from Eckenstein's vicious blow, and his hip hurt from its encounter with the floor, but neither of those injuries stung as badly as the wound to his pride. Eckenstein could be an idiot when drunk—he knew that from experience—but he had never done anything as stupid as this before. His entire business plan was based on exploiting patents wrangled from Crowley. Jones simply did not believe the "no hard feelings" line.

Hearing a sound behind him, Jones turned to see Crowley hurrying after him. He tensed, ready to fight or run as the situation demanded.

'Wait a moment,' Crowley commanded as he drew near.

'What do you want?'

'Just a word. I suppose you knew I hadn't fled the country, didn't you?'

Jones studied his rival. Crowley stood a little taller than he, lean rather than muscular, pose confident.

'I know you haven't finished with us. You're up to something.'

Crowley spread his hands. 'I don't know why you would think that.'

'Keep away from Miss Elliot,' Jones demanded, then instantly regretted it. Would Crowley guess where he had got his information from?

A slow smile spread over the young man's face. 'Good evening to you, Jones.'

He turned to walk away.

'Stay away from her!' Jones shouted after him, feeling useless. 'I will tell the police where you are!'

'By the time you find a policeman,' Crowley called back, 'I will be gone. So long, Jones.'

CHAPTER TWELVE

THE DIRECT ROUTE

15th of May, 1897

"DEAREST RACHEL,

"I treasure our correspondence, but your recent letter filled me with dismay. I'm sure you have been anxious to read my reply, and I have struggled for some days with my conscience over what to send; I hope you don't mind me speaking candidly.

"You should not marry him. I understand why you feel you must do this, but you deserve so much more from your life. If you don't love him you will regret your decision in time. You thrive on adventure, that much I feel I know about you for sure; and to live a life that you do not want is not in your nature. Again, forgive me for speaking my mind, but I feel that I must.

"I wish to help you, but I feel we cannot continue to discuss this by letter, and I am reluctant to return to Cambridge. Might I suggest you try to attend the spring meet of the PMC in Fort William on the 24th? There we can talk freely, and perhaps have some adventures in the mountains.

"I will understand if you are unable to come, but I believe your future happiness may depend on the next few weeks. I am also convinced that Crowley still poses some danger to you and I will not be entirely at ease until I am satisfied that you are safe.

"Your devoted friend,

"O.G. Jones."

*

17th of May, 1897

"My dear Mr Jones,

"Thank you for your kind letter. I suppose in my previous communication I might have conveyed my feelings a little better, but as I am sure you will understand I was somewhat overwhelmed at the time. I am more sure of myself now & am quite certain that my decision to accept Peter's proposal is the correct one.

"When you meet him you will see what I mean. He is the most wonderful young man: generous, courteous, charismatic. I am sure you will like him immediately. Peter is a climber himself, & I am certain I shall not be deprived of an adventurous life if I wish it, although of course my first responsibility is to my father.

"That I do not love Peter, in the strict sense, is a mere detail in an otherwise happy arrangement.

"Nevertheless, I find myself tempted by the idea of a trip to Scotland. It will certainly be difficult to arrange. Peter is away on a business trip at present, so will be unable to look after my father. I ought to be able to call upon the assistance of my cousin. There is also the matter of whether Peter will consider such an excursion an impropriety.

"Be assured that I will be in touch to discuss details about Scotland, but in the meantime please do not distress yourself on my account!

"Your ever loving friend,

"Rachel M. Elliot."

*

The last time Jones had used a public telephone, he thought ruefully, he had been flirting with Elspeth and life had seemed a lot simpler. In the two months since that conversation his friendship with Elspeth had been destroyed, Simon Barkis had been disgraced and turned to the tactics of his enemy in desperation, and now Crowley threatened the woman Jones loved. Sometimes his problems seemed insurmountable.

One thing at a time, he ordered himself. Today he had to convince young George Abraham to cover his shifts at the shop while he went to Scotland.

'Who is speaking, please?'

'Abraham? It's me, Jones. Are you free next week?'

'Do you fancy a climb?'

'Actually I have a favour to ask. I need someone to cover my shifts at the shop while I go to Fort William for the PMC meet.'

Abraham laughed. 'My dear fellow, I have a shop to run myself.'

'Can't you get your brother to do it?'

'I suppose so.' Abraham thought for a moment. 'That Elspeth girl lives in London, doesn't she? We have been corresponding ever since she climbed Slanting Gully.'

Jones felt a sting to his pride. 'We climbed that route together.'

'Well, yes, but she did the hard bit first. Anyway I would like to visit her and have been trying to think of an excuse.'

In his eagerness for Abraham to agree to his request, Jones did not think to warn him about Elspeth.

'That's settled then. I'll need you from the 22nd until the 29th.'

A pause. 'How is Eckenstein?'

'You'll see. He went drinking with Crowley last week. We had words on the subject.'

Probably best not to mention the little scrap, Jones reasoned.

'Well, they always were friends. Where's Crowley now, not still causing trouble is he?'

'He's disappeared, thankfully. Eckenstein thinks he has gone to the Alps.'

'Where I should like to be,' Abraham said fervently. 'Summer is made for lying in the sun with pretty Swiss girls, drinking beer, and venturing into the mountains only when necessary to maintain the pretence of being a climber.'

Jones laughed. 'For you, maybe. If I get to go this year I have grand ambitions. If Holdstock and Barkis can do a severe north face then I certainly can.'

'Do you think that's what Crowley is up to?'

'Who knows? Look here, I must fly. I'll see you soon.'

'Enjoy Scotland, and Miss Elliot.'

Jones found himself blushing.

*

24th of May, 1897

Fort William. The weather outside felt warm and sunny, the sky a brilliant blue. High on Ben Nevis, far above the village, patches of old snow shimmered in the heat. A few clouds of midges, the advance guard of the onslaught that would arrive with the humid summer, hovered near the ruins of the old fort. Jones noticed very little of all this, as he was suffering from a bad case of hay fever and felt distinctly rotten. He made his way to the hotel as quickly as he was able, leaving his luggage in the yard to take care of itself.

Pollen tears blurred his vision. He approached the reception desk, but before he got there a group of unidentifiable figures cut him off, and soon he was surrounded by people calling greetings, patting him on the back, and heaping praise upon him. The change in his fortunes since joining the PMC—where his achievements were appreciated, not criticised—still surprised him.

Jones wiped his eyes. Somewhat restored, he was now able to make a little more sense of the situation. Raeburn, Bell and Oppenheimer all seemed to be speaking at once; in the background, towards the entrance to the lounge, Collie and Munro stood silently, puffing on their pipes.

'My friends, you will excuse me but I am rather the worse for hay fever today.'

'Very sorry to hear that,' Raeburn said quietly, although he did seem pleased to see him. 'I wanted to congratulate you on the outstanding work you have been doing for the club lately. The new equipment, your guidebook … do remind me to post you a copy of my notes on this winter's climbs for addition in the Journal.'

'I look forward to reading them. I believe congratulations are in order for your new route up the great ice wall on Ben Nevis.'

'Ach, it's merely a variation on the line yourself and Miss Mornshaw climbed on your last visit. The direct passage has yet to be opened up. Ice is still fat on the wall, so perhaps you will be making another attempt?'

Raeburn seemed eager, but Jones felt less enthusiastic. In addition to an old-fashioned long ice axe, he had brought his short twin axes but had not seriously expected to find a use for them so late in the season. His thoughts now turned to difficult new rock climbs and lazy days in the sun.

Collie strolled over and shook Jones' hand. He looked healthy, a little less gaunt than on their last meeting. Despite the heat he wore his deerstalker firmly rammed home over his ears.

'How are you, Jones? I'm pleased you could come after the uncertain noises you were making over the telephone last week.' He laughed. 'I hear there is a lady involved?'

Why did everyone seem to know every last detail of his love life, Jones wondered?

'A friend in need of some support.'

'Of course. I must echo Raeburn's comments. You are proving to be one of our greatest assets, as I knew you would be.'

Jones felt embarrassed at the praise. 'You give me too much credit.'

'Not at all, my friend. Oh, there is someone here who has been waiting for you. I believe you will find him on a bench in the green.'

Intrigued, Jones left the lobby, crossed the road, and wandered over the extensive green space in the centre of the town. Locals filled the garden, enjoying the warm and sunny weather, picnic rugs adding splashes of colour to the grass. A crowd of noisy schoolchildren on their lunch break ran past chasing a football. Jones found himself sneezing furiously again.

A solitary figure sat on the bench at the far side of the green, staring into the hills. He wore a light linen suit and hat. A cane rested on the bench to his right, and for a moment Jones entertained the wild thought that perhaps this stranger might be Crowley, before remembering that his rival never wore a hat.

As he approached, the figure turned away from his study of the mountain and rose with a little difficulty. Jones recognised his unfortunate friend Simon Barkis.

They shook hands. 'My dear friend, how good to see you!' Barkis exclaimed.

'And you. I feared after the unpleasantness you would vanish for good. How goes your recovery?'

Barkis smiled. His face, which had always been strikingly youthful, had aged over the weeks since their last meeting at the court hearing. His moustache even held a tinge of grey, and lines of worry creased his eyes. For a boy not long past twenty, the impression was saddening. Yet despite the marks of stress, his gaze held a sort of determined vigour, as if some new purpose in life animated him.

'My recovery is going well, but the scandal has ruined me. My family will never speak to me again.'

Jones sat down next to him. 'You should have contacted me. I can help you.'

A haunted look. 'To be honest old boy, I deserve everything that happened to me.'

'Nonsense. You are guilty of nothing worse than being dazzled by Holdstock's charisma and allowing him to think for you.'

Barkis smiled sadly. 'Holdstock has taken his punishment like a man. The public sees me as the villain of the story. Crowley is depicted as a tragic figure who has been forced to turn to crime by cruel circumstances.'

'I know, and it is all so terribly overblown, but you must realise that this will all be forgotten in a few months.'

'No, the cloud of dishonour will always hang about me. My reputation is ruined forever. I need a new start, some great act to define my life.'

They sat in silence for a while, watching the scene of happy activity all around: couples sitting in the sun, children playing, families walking along shadow-dappled avenues, the occasional bewildered tourist. Carriages clattered along the street, kicking up clouds of dust and the occasional spark from stones lying in the road.

Barkis sighed. 'I'm going to the Alps, you know. I want to revisit some of my old haunts, join up with Holdstock for some climbing now he's out of prison. I'm still not entirely recovered from my injuries, but I am determined to climb again. We have drawn up ambitious plans.'

'With Holdstock?'

He shrugged. 'He may be a villain, but he remains one of the best climbers in the world. He has a scheme afoot, and he wants me to take part. I am travelling out there within days.' Barkis suddenly broke off and slapped a palm against his forehead. 'I have quite forgotten! I met Miss Elliot at the station earlier. She asked about you.'

Jones' heart leapt. He had not heard from her in days. After a noncommittal wire indicating she might be able to come to Scotland, her communications had fallen silent. After all the preparation and excitement, the prospect of her being here, in Fort William, was exciting.

'What did you tell her?'

'I said that you would be staying at the Alexandra Hotel with the PMC. She asked me to convey the message to you that she would not be staying in Fort William, but out of a desire for greater privacy she has gone to Clachaig in Glen Coe.'

Jones had no particular desire to go back to Glen Coe when the party would be in Fort William. Besides, it would waste a whole day to get there.

'Is that the only reason she gave?'

'I'm afraid it is. Raeburn and Collie mentioned they would be paying a brief visit to Glen Coe also, so you would not be altogether away from the centre of things.'

Nevertheless, Jones felt disappointed.

'What about you? What are your plans?'

Barkis smiled. 'You shall see.'

*

After some discussion within the company, it was decided that Jones would travel together with Raeburn and the Professor to Glen Coe. His companions would remain there for a few days, with the goal of exploring the upper precipice of Bidean nam Bian, before returning to the main meet at the Alexandra Hotel. Jones felt a little annoyed that he would not be able to mingle with the ever-increasing numbers of the PMC, but he consoled himself with the prospect of seeing Rachel Elliot again.

He had never seen the journey to Clachaig in daylight before. The road seemed to mostly consist of potholes as it wound its way along the shores of Loch Linnhe, but conversation flowed freely in the carriage, returning constantly to the topic of mountaineering. Collie spoke enthusiastically about the coming Alpine season, and the vast potential that lay untapped in the mountains of Europe for the modern ice climber. Raeburn, by contrast, seemed content with his achievements of the past winter, and spoke at length about his exploits on the ice gullies of Aonach Dubh and Ben Nevis.

Jones felt grateful that his two closest friends in the PMC had gone out of their way to accompany him to Glen Coe when they could just as easily have stayed in Fort William with the bulk of the society.

At Ballachulish they negotiated the infrequent ferry service across Loch Leven and into the mountainous region beyond. Into the confines of Glen Coe itself, that wonderful secret place of waterfalls and roaring stags; although he had only been here once before, it felt like a homecoming. Jones loved this time of year in Scotland, when the mountains clung onto their winter plumage but the climber is rewarded with summer's embrace upon his return to the glen. These idyllic days promised all the mountain-lover could wish for: dry rock, long hours of daylight, warm sun, favourable snow conditions, and a settled barometer.

Soon they reached Clachaig. The rustic hotel, and its associated stables and outhouses, felt welcoming after the long journey. Jones looked forward to a seat in front of the fire with a glass of beer and a roast dinner. As they drew near the stables, he noticed no more than two or three horses, and only one carriage. The inn must be quiet.

Five hours remained before supper time at nine. After being shown to his room and unpacking his things, Jones decided to go in search of Miss Elliot.

*

He followed the dusty road from Clachaig to its terminus at a bridge over the River Coe. The river, calmed by a long spell of dry weather, whispered over the jumble of boulders that formed its bed. On the far bank, Rachel Elliot sat on a rock in the shade of a thorn tree, reading a book. Her attitude was studious but alert, attention flickering between the pages and the outstanding natural beauty all around.

Above and to the south, the terraces of the Aonach Dubh seemed to overhang, a confusion of sunlit bastions and dripping gullies. Beyond, further up the corrie, the pyramid of Stob Coire nam Bheith remained all but unexplored, and higher still, the snows of Bidean nam Bian gleamed in the sun. The Aonach Eagach formed a single continuous barrier on the other side of the glen. He felt like an ant surrounded by giants, or a primitive man in the presence of the gods.

The grandeur of the scenery was not lost on Miss Elliot who, Jones observed, had discarded her book and now silently contemplated the Aonach Eagach, shading her eyes with a hand. He watched her for a moment before announcing himself. She wore a plain and sensible woollen mountaineering gown with a high collar and long skirts, out of the bottom of which poked a pair of scuffed leather boots, dotted with clinker-nails. Her hat was small and fashionable, although it did not seem to be doing too good a job of keeping the sun out of her eyes. Curls of hair escaped from underneath.

She turned and noticed him, sitting up straight and giving a wave. Jones waved in return and climbed down the bank before hopping over the stepping-stones in the river.

'My dear Jones, I am so pleased to see you!'

Sparkling with happiness, she reached out and hugged him. Jones held her tightly, marvelling at the fortune of circumstances that had led them both here, to the most wonderful place in Britain. Despite all the dangers and the challenges, they had made it, they were here together, and only now did he feel content.

After a moment Rachel broke free from the embrace, holding him by the shoulders at arm's length, her expression radiant.

'I thought I would not be able to come. My cousin wavered but I have made sure she is at home where she belongs, with my father.'

'What about Merrick?' Jones wasn't sure he wanted to know, but at the same time he had started to feel an uncharitable resentment against this young man he had never met.

Rachel sat back down on her rock, shuffling up to make room for him. 'I mentioned your idea of an excursion to Scotland. He specifically forbade me to go.'

Jones was surprised. 'Why?'

'I do believe he is a little jealous of you,' she said with a laugh. 'You are my only regular correspondent, after all.'

That made him feel a little better. 'I'm glad you came regardless. Husbands—or future husbands—should not give their wives orders.'

'My father has the opposite opinion.'

Jones suddenly felt the need to change the subject. He still found that the idea of Rachel getting married at all made him feel depressed.

'Shall we go for a walk? There's plenty of time left before supper.'

'What a splendid idea.' She picked up her book and put it back in her knapsack.

Jones thought back to the last time they had gone for a walk together up Snowdon, not so long ago. How she had changed. From a bitter and disappointed woman who used sarcasm to insulate herself from the world, Rachel had opened up to him and shown a warm and kind side he had grown to love.

They crossed the river and climbed back up to the road. This track led for some miles to the hostelry at Kingshouse, then into the wilds of Glen Etive where a handful of people eked out their existence from trade coming up the loch from the sea. Before the railway came to Fort William, the long journey from Port Glasgow round the coast to Loch Etive had been the only way of reaching Clachaig.

'You haven't mentioned Crowley yet,' Rachel said after a while, with a hint of her old sarcasm. 'I'm so keen to hear why you think I'm in terrible danger from a boy I've never met.'

As they walked along the glen, Jones outlined the recent developments in the Crowley case, including his meeting with Eckenstein and Elspeth's warning. He also explained how the case had affected Simon Barkis: dishonoured, disowned, a broken man. Soon they passed beneath the north cliff of the Aonach Dubh, riven by the slot of Ossian's Cave. Jones suggested that they continued walking up the path into Coire an Lochan, the steep valley that led up to the heart of the Bidean range.

'I'm baffled why Crowley is bothering with us at all,' Rachel said when Jones had finished his account.

'Who knows? What concerns me is that he has not given up, and that you are in danger.'

'I don't think I am in danger. A cryptic warning from that Elspeth girl is hardly enough to concern me.'

Jones didn't like her tone of scorn. 'I believe her.'

She stopped and turned to face him. 'After everything she has done, why do you trust her?'

'Her husband has treated her callously. She has no loyalty for him.'

Rachel shook her head. 'You don't understand women. She is playing you and Crowley against each other and probably enjoying it.'

He didn't have the conviction to argue the point any further.

The path climbed steeply up the left bank of the burn coming down from the corrie. Although faint in places, shepherds had passed this way for centuries and their boots had worn a narrow trench in the turfy areas. Dust and small stones spilled from the eroded banks to either side of the track. Soon their boots were the colour of stone dust. They climbed on, breathing heavily from the exertion.

Jones had passed this way once before, on New Year's Day when they had climbed on Stob Coire an Lochan, but on that occasion the indefatigable Raeburn had carved a trench through the deep new snow that hid any sign of a path. Spring had transformed the landscape, and Jones could see the mountain's bones. Away to the right, the unexplored eastern cliffs of Aonach Dubh—an expanse of smooth slabs—dominated the skyline. Directly ahead the peak of Stob Coire an Lochan still held snow in the gullies, now old and brown with streaks of debris from the cliffs. Ravens circled far above.

'It is all quite beautiful,' Rachel said as they paused beneath the crags.

He still felt a little surly with her for slighting Elspeth, and felt the need to contradict her. 'I think it's wild and rugged, not beautiful. Lakeland is beautiful.'

'Peter would agree with you. I think you would get on well.'

'You should not marry him.' The words were out before Jones realised they had even crossed his mind.

Rachel smiled faintly. 'We have discussed this already in our letters. I thought I had explained my reasons.'

They kept going uphill. A grassy gully, down which a burn roared, split the crags of the Aonach Dubh in half. A square-cut tower stood alone to the left of the main mountain mass, perhaps two hundred and fifty feet in height. The front of this tower was a single unbroken wall of rock. It frowned in the evening shadow. Jones felt the lure of the inaccessible.

Rachel stopped and looked at him. 'I do believe you haven't heard a word I just said, Jones. This is important to me. Take your eyes off that crag!'

'Sorry,' he said with a sheepish grin. 'It is an awfully nice piece of rock.'

'I believe you were about to offer your opinion on why I should not marry Peter. I'm quite anxious to hear your reasons.'

Her lips were pursed together in that hard line, her eyes narrowed.

Jones realised that he could not win this argument. She had reason on her side: with a seriously ill father, the position of her family was tenuous. Peter Merrick represented safety. It all made so much sense, and in the face of such cold logic Jones felt lost. What could he offer her? His savings were meagre, and having abandoned a reasonable living as a teacher he now survived in the fledgling climbing equipment market. He often risked his life on a whim for no greater reward than fleeting satisfaction. Why would any woman ever want to marry him? The only real thing he could offer her was his love.

Jones summoned his courage. Now was the time to speak the truth and be honest with her.

'I have only one reason. I love you. Peter might be all those wonderful things, but he doesn't know you like I do—he has not been with you on the summit of Lliwedd, seen your wisdom and strength.' He suddenly felt foolish. 'Sorry for taking this long to spit it out, but there it is.'

She sat down on a nearby boulder. Her expression of annoyance did not change.

'Why do you say this now? Why place me in this position?'

'I can't sit back and watch you marry another man without telling you the truth.'

She sighed in exasperation. 'Jones, you are … impossible! I find your opinions ridiculous, your attitude to life irresponsible. And now you love me?'

Jones felt even more foolish. 'But we made such a good team when we worked together.'

'No we didn't. I need somebody who understands me, not someone who argues with me constantly.'

'How do you know Peter understands you? How well do you truly know him?'

She gave him a piteous look. 'I have spent more time with my husband-to-be than with you. You forget just how little you and I know each other, I think.'

Jones gazed up at the crag that had caught his attention a few minutes ago. Suddenly that direct line up the broad sweep of empty wall appealed even more strongly to his imagination.

'What do I have to do to convince you?'

'I have made up my mind. The problem does not lie with me.'

A problem. She saw his feelings as a problem.

He looked back up at the wall. 'I will be back in fifteen minutes or so. Wait for me.'

*

Jones leapt over the stream and struggled up the far bank, running over slabs streaming with water. The rejection hurt more than any physical wound. As with all troubles, the best cure was an encounter with the mountain.

Another minute of running brought him to the foot of the wall. He placed his hand on the cool rock and rested for a moment, taking deep breaths, steeling his nerves for the task ahead.

Such a tranquil place! Wild flowers grew in profusion at his feet. The air felt cool and still against his skin, and for a second or two he just existed there and let his heart beat in that calm place between the tension he had fled from and the danger above.

He looked up to gain some measure of the challenge he faced. The first part of the wall, perhaps fifty feet in height, was steep and obviously severe, the only visible faults a few thin cracks. Strange quartz markings flawed the stone. Further up, the angle seemed to steepen yet further before the final sting in the tail: an overhang right at the top. It seemed awfully far away.

Before he could reconsider his foolhardiness, Jones began to climb.

The route was steep and difficult right from the start. He found his nails skidding off tiny holds, but at least they were positive. Six feet above the ground, Jones reached his first irreversible move: a precarious shift of balance onto a little stone wedged into a crack. From now on, he was committed and could not back down. He wondered if Rachel watched him. His position now stable, Jones risked a glance back over his shoulder, and sure enough, she sat on a rock close to where he had left her, looking up at his position on the wall. The knowledge that she was watching gave him strength.

Upwards. Some more difficult moves gave access to a longer easier section. He resisted the temptation to let his guard down and move fast; with greater height the risk increased. Besides, if he fell now, he would bounce on the way down. He pushed all thoughts of falling out of his mind and concentrated. Just because the climbing was easier didn't mean his life was not at risk.

A ledge split the wall just under halfway up, and Jones reached this unexpected resting place with relief. It did not amount to very much—a sloping shelf maybe a yard in width, overgrown with grass and moss—but it was enough to permit a good rest and an opportunity to rally his courage. He wedged himself beneath the undercut back wall and rested in a squatting position, facing outward. Below, a hundred feet of rock swept down to the grass and scree at the bottom of the crag. It looked awfully steep, but he knew that the route onward would be worse.

Rachel had crossed the burn and was climbing the bank on the other side. She looked determined and angry.

'Jones, you must come down at once!'

'Hello,' he replied cheerfully. 'It's quite a sporting little climb.'

'It gets steeper. I think you should come down.'

He started up the second half of the wall. Immediately he could see that she was quite right. The rock here was plumb-vertical, featureless except for a system of cracks that offered the only way up. He made a few moves up from the ledge, locking his fingers into constrictions in the crack, but he could see that his boots would have trouble here. The worn clinkers slid on a tiny hold and with a shock Jones found himself back on the ledge, struggling for balance.

Rachel let out a cry. 'Come down! You will kill yourself for certain!'

Ignoring her warnings, he decided to remove his boots and proceed in stockinged feet, a tactic that sometimes worked when the holds got too tricky for nails. After tying the laces to his belt, he attacked the crack again.

It threw up a stiff barrier indeed, but at least without clumping boots to bother him he could focus on the climbing. It all seemed to rely on wedging toes into unlikely places and pulling on tiny finger-holds. After perhaps fifty or sixty feet he found a place where he could pause for a moment or two and savour his improbable position.

The situation thrilled him. In his years of climbing throughout Britain, he had never ventured into a place as forbidding and inaccessible as this. With a roped team, it would be impossible: no spikes or blocks to hitch the rope around, long blank sections between ledges. No safety. It could only be done by a bold man, and alone. Jones wondered if he would have been able to climb this route yesterday, and realised that the fresh wound of his rejection had given him the energy to do it.

He could feel the strain building in his fingers. Tiring but alive with the power of the climb, he pushed upwards. When he reached the final overhang, he considered avoiding it to the right where an easy ledge offered safety, but in a moment of supreme confidence decided against the easy way out. Through the steeps. Clinging to tiny holds above his head, Jones hoisted himself over the roof and relished the full measure of two hundred and fifty feet of air beneath his heels. Now he felt alive again!

The top of the crag, when he reached it, was an anti-climax: no soaring peak or victory cairn, just a flat piece of rock and some scree in the golden light of dusk. Nevertheless, success tasted good. He shouted his thanks into the sky.

He made a swift descent down a loose gully. Rachel waited at the bottom. She had been crying, but she stood her ground, not walking forward to meet him.

'What were you thinking of? Oh, I am so angry I could hit you!'

'I'm quite safe,' he insisted, although he felt a little ashamed when he saw how distressed she had become.

'Safe? You almost fell off and died! Imagine how I would feel if that happened right in front of me?'

'So you do care, then.'

This time she did slap him, hard. He staggered back in surprise, but said nothing: he deserved that.

'Of course I care,' she said more softly. 'I'm sorry, I did not mean to hurt you. You just make me so angry sometimes.'

'With good reason, perhaps.'

She smiled, and it was like the sun driving away a fleet of rainclouds. 'But I can never stay angry with you for long.'

CHAPTER THIRTEEN

ONLY A HILL

24th of May, 1897

A SUMMER EVENING at Clachaig. Jones sat by himself on the stump by the burn, gazing out across the glen, smoking his pipe. Behind him, the inn lay quiet, its seven occupants tucking into their supper around Mrs Macintyre's table. Muffled sounds drifted across the road from the stables, but silence soon returned, and Jones reflected.

As the sun sank, the light softened. Shadows lengthened on the spur of crag jutting down from Sgorr nam Fiannaidh. The Aonach Eagach's crest caught a golden ray for a few seconds before fading like a blown-out candle. Aonach Dubh, which bared its terraces head-on to the Clachaig and seduced all climbers who stayed there, had lost all definition in the last hour of daylight. Everywhere Jones looked, the landscape whispered legends of climbers who had gone before him, and promised a lifetime of adventure for all those who would discover this magical place in the centuries to come. The stories would never come to an end.

Midges started to come out with the cool evening, but the sky showed no sign of cloud, and the next day would be hot.

He thought about the proposed expedition for tomorrow: an ascent of the Church Door, the most imposing cliff so far discovered in the glen. Raeburn and Collie wished to include Jones and Rachel in the party. He felt a sudden flash of deja vu. In an instant he went four years back in time, and found himself sitting outside the Monte Rosa Hotel in Zermatt, drinking beer and planning mighty deeds in the high peaks above the village.

In many ways this felt like a summer's evening in the Alps. The peaks all around him had, through many adventures and hard-won climbs, attained the same stature in his mind as the Alpine mountains of his summer playground. That same quiet prevailed, the expectant silence of a tiny valley surrounded by legendary peaks, and the kernel of human dreams enclosed within it. Nothing could sum up the questing nature of man's spirit better.

What a true paradise—what a balm for a stressed soul! Why did mankind congregate in the foul wastelands of cities, feeding their greed and vanity, subjecting themselves and others to a life of iron and soot? There is

150

no misery in nature, only the majesty of God's green world. Jones did not consider himself a particularly religious man, but when faced with such timeless perfection he could not help but believe that some greater truth lay behind it all. A single moment in this realm of wonder was more valuable than a lifetime in the industrial world.

The light on the mountains began to burn orange, and Jones thought about how the Matterhorn glowed with its own inner beauty long after the valley was plunged into night.

Sitting on that tree stump in a dusk he would remember for the rest of his life, Jones felt like a more virtuous man, his pretensions and jealousies stripped away by the eternity of the mountains. This was why he lived this life: for these moments of truth when he sensed his part in the greater whole, and realised that mountaineering was a truly wonderful thing.

*

After extinguishing his pipe, Jones returned inside to join the others. The dining room at Clachaig was small, but quite sufficient for a country hotel of its size. Whitewashed plaster clad the stone walls, the thickness of which could be guessed by the sunken windows. In the centre of this homely room stood a long and very solid table. The bounty of the finest house in the glen was heaped in dishes upon the tablecloth: venison stew, baked potatoes, roast chicken, two jugs of beer, and a bottle of unlabelled whisky.

Miss Elliot sat at the head of the table, honoured as the only female guest in residence. To her left, Harold Raeburn attacked his stew with vigour, and to her right, Norman Collie sipped a dram with a contented smile. Mr and Mrs Macintyre, the middle-aged couple who owned and ran the hotel, sat opposite each other at the centre of the table. Their son and daughter sat nearby, both in their mid-twenties. They appeared to be the only servants currently in employment.

'It's a pleasant evening,' Jones remarked as he took his seat.

'A fine time of a day for a smoke,' Mr Macintyre confirmed, 'before the midgies get too bad.'

Raeburn looked up. 'Did I hear you say earlier that tomorrow would be a hot one, Mr Macintyre?'

'Aye, it will. Not a day to be climbing on the hills.' He particularly stressed the last sentence. Although Macintyre was a genial man, his generation thought of mountaineering in Scotland as extravagantly dangerous, bordering on madness. Mountaineers made up the bulk of his patrons, along with artists, composers, and dreamers, but nevertheless he always warned residents about the dangers of hill-scrambling.

Raeburn nodded, and turned to Collie. 'Some snow still remains in Great Gully. Should we take axes?'

'I think it would be prudent. Jones, what do you think?'

Jones did not hear him. His attention concentrated on Miss Elliot, who pushed food around her plate in a desultory fashion, staring out of the window with a far-off look upon her face. He wondered what she was thinking about. When she closed herself off, she could be so difficult to read. He dreaded a return to tight-lipped incommunicado and cutting sarcasm.

Their eyes met, and for a moment Jones felt that he saw a stranger in her. He wished they could talk in private. After he had come down from his climb, Rachel had insisted upon walking back alone.

'Jones?' Collie's smile seemed to be all too knowing. Jones wondered how much the wily old fox had guessed about his predicament.

'Sorry, I was miles away. Yes, I think we ought to take axes.'

Raeburn grunted in agreement. 'I for one am not inclined to leave the inn too early. Are we in accord, gentlemen?'

Rachel raised her eyebrow. 'Ladies and gentlemen, you mean.'

'Aye, of course.'

Silence for a while. The Professor sat back in his chair, folded his hands on his belly, and let out a satisfied sigh. 'I declare I cannot eat another morsel. Mrs Macintyre, I salute your achievement in preparing this feast. Your hospitality, as ever, does you great credit.'

'Hear, hear,' Raeburn added as he took a gulp of ale.

Mrs Macintyre, who was small but handsome in the way of Highland housewives, smiled and expressed her thanks. She and her family rose and cleared the table, leaving only the ale and whisky.

After their hosts had gone Raeburn sat back and smiled. 'This is true contentment: a balmy evening, good food and drink, the lonely inn, and the grand rocky hill that awaits us. Life is, I think, best appreciated in this way. Simple pleasures and simple challenges make a man's life complete.'

Collie murmured his agreement. He had closed his eyes and appeared to be enjoying a light doze while he smoked his pipe.

'How wonderful it would be to live forever in such a place,' Rachel said.

'I for one intend to live for as much of my life amongst mountains as I am able,' Jones declared. 'The summer has only just begun.'

Raeburn nodded approvingly. 'Where do you intend to spend the summer, then, Jones? Scotland?'

'It can only be the Alps. It is an exciting time for Alpine mountaineering.'

'Ach, this is the true country, not the Alps.'

Collie opened his eyes. 'I am inclined to agree with you both.'

152

'Be decisive, Professor! The Alps or Scotland?' Raeburn pressed.

He considered. 'For this summer … the Alps, but only because, as Jones says, this is an extraordinary time. There is much potential lying untapped, and if we do not take the opportunity then the continental climbers shall beat us to the mark.'

'Heaven forbid Europeans should be the first to climb routes on their own mountains,' Rachel said quietly.

'The Alps are almost an exclusive preserve of British mountaineers. It was a British team who first climbed the north face of the Matterhorn. Other ice-walls await exploration.'

'I have heard …' Rachel began, then stopped.

'Pray continue, Miss Elliot,' Collie insisted.

'Peter and I were speaking of this only last week. It is rumoured that a British effort on a mountain in the Bernese Oberland is being planned. I forget the name. It is not particularly high, but is said to have an impressive north face.'

Jones thought on her words. He had visited the Oberland region of Switzerland but done few of the peaks, instead concentrating on the centres of Zermatt and Chamonix. The Oberland contained some famous mountains and the biggest glacier in Europe, the Aletsch Glacier.

Opposite, Raeburn was frowning. 'I have also heard this rumour. I've seen a photograph of the face, and it is imposing.'

Collie seemed intrigued. 'This is all news to me! What is the name of this mountain?'

'It's called the Eiger,' Raeburn said. 'A man named Barrington made the first ascent in '58, if I recall the facts correctly. He went up the easy way, but in his account he noted the fierce aspect of the cliffs facing the village of Grindelwald.'

Jones knew little about this mountain, but he vaguely remembered having seen the cliff in question. He wondered if this mysterious scheme had anything to do with Barkis' hints at a major new Alpine endeavour.

'We must discover more about this effort.' Collie seemed animated by the promise of a bold new objective. 'Miss Elliot, what more do you know of the expedition?'

'It was a casual conversation. All I can remember with accuracy is that it is to be an independent trip, with no influence from the Alpine Club. I believe the team is going to be small, and they will climb in the same style as the Matterhorn north route last year.'

Jones found himself about to remark that Barkis had made mention of just such a project, but bit his tongue just in time. Perhaps Barkis wanted to keep his plans a secret.

'Peter is thinking of joining the expedition,' Rachel added.

Jones thought back to the letter Peter had sent him months ago, to which he had never penned a reply. In the letter, Peter had demonstrated inexperience, a stage all mountaineers go through, but not a quality expected of an aspirant north wall climber.

'I don't think he has the necessary experience to climb the north face of the Eiger,' Jones thought out loud. Instantly he knew Rachel would make him regret it.

'How would you know?' she said sharply. 'I cannot see what business it is of yours, anyway, unless you are jealous that he will climb the wall and you will not.'

Collie glanced between the two of them. 'My friends, mountains ought to bring us together, not divide us.'

Jones admired Collie's attitude, but sadly he knew all too well that mountains had the power to drive people apart, particularly when reputations or records were to be made.

*

Late the following morning, after breakfasting on smoked kippers and fresh bread, the four climbers departed from Clachaig. The time was a little before ten o'clock, but the sun had already been up for over five hours and Collie's thermometer read seventy-nine degrees at the inn.

Heat haze shimmered over the dusty road as they tramped towards Achnambeithach, the farmhouse at the foot of Coire Bheith. Jones found his flat cap—replaced after its loss on Ben Nevis—insufficient protection against the sun. His spectacles glared terribly and already the back of his neck burned. Combined with the hay fever, Jones felt quite irritable and looked forward to the cooler breeze of the upper cliff.

Collie wore the type of light flannel jacket currently fashionable for climbing in the Alps, no doubt infinitely cooler than the tweed Jones wore for all his mountain adventures. Rachel sheltered under a parasol and wide-brimmed hat, while Raeburn sweated in his shirtsleeves and waistcoat, jacket tied by its sleeves around his waist.

Coire Bheith proved to be an unending trudge. Jones had never been all the way into this corrie before, and despite the spectacular scenery the combination of endless steep grass and boulders was punishing. Happily, the path never took them far from the burn, which leapt from pool to pool in moss-fringed cascades, providing welcome refreshment.

At a flat alp above a gorge they paused to assess the ground ahead. Two peaks dominated the view: Stob Coire nam Bheith's pyramid, streaked with snow patches at the top, and left, dominating the upper coire, surrounded by the perennial snows, Bidean nam Bian itself.

The four of them leaned on their ice axes and gazed up at their goal. Two individual buttresses divided the cliff, split down the centre by a gully. The right-hand one, the square-cut Church Door, would suffer their attentions this afternoon. From this distance, it looked impregnable: a solid tower without weakness.

Raeburn squinted into the glare. 'Bidean nam Bian, my friends: the Pinnacle of the Mountains, in the old language.'

'Which is the Church Door?' Rachel said.

'That right-hand chunk of rock,' Raeburn replied, pointing with his axe. 'It has been prospected many times, mostly by Tough and Bell, but has always defeated them. This is my first visit to Bidean. I believe you have been here before, Collie?'

He nodded. 'In 1894. Another English team also failed on the route last year. It is going to be a tough nut to crack.'

A faint shepherds' track took them beneath the cliffs of Stob Coire nam Bheith. Collie informed them that these crags usually dripped with slime; the extensive drought had dried them right up. Following the burn, they crossed a field of boulders that clunked and rocked beneath their boots. Jones took the lead when they reached the snow.

It proved to be typical summer snow: rotten on the surface, firm beneath. Jones kicked steps and made progress more rapidly than on the loose rocks as they zig-zagged up the slope, aiming for the giant pinnacle of rock that guarded the entrance of the Central Gully. The slush sprayed up and made his trousers soggy, trickling cold water into his boots.

They paused for a rest at the foot of Central Gully. In the shade of the mountain, surrounded by masses of slowly melting snow and ice, this was a deliciously cool place and Jones took the opportunity to soak his neckerkerchief in anticipation of the hot work to come. Collie pointed up the step on the right side of the Pinnacle: a sort of cavernous chimney, jammed up with fallen blocks.

'That is the way. A scramble over those chockstones, and we shall be at the start of the route.'

Excited to be given another chance to attempt one of the last great climbing problems of Glen Coe, Collie took the lead and quickly vanished over the chockstone. Miss Elliot, of course, went last to protect her modesty. As her hat appeared over the lip of rock at the top Jones offered her a hand, which she refused.

The gully where they now found themselves was an imposing place. On either side, vast rock walls rose vertically for hundreds of feet. These walls and towers mostly hid in the shadow of the mountain, but sunlight glinted on the highest bastions. An obnoxious mixture of scree and banks of pock-marked, dirty snow filled the bed of the gully. Jones could not wait to get out of this hole and onto the sunny cliffs above.

Raeburn, ever the practical man, was already scanning the crags to their right, on the Church Door side of the gully. 'I see now why so many people have failed to climb the buttress!'

Jones could not help but agree. The cliff was a perfect confusion of rocks, with no single defined feature offering an obvious way up. Promising corners ended in overhangs, smooth and without holds; one chimney in particular, obvious at the bottom, vanished into the gloomy interior of the mountain, seemingly never to emerge.

'I vote we try the chimney route,' Rachel said with a nod towards the forbidding tunnel. Her words echoed strangely in the confined space.

Jones felt a strong aversion to the idea. 'What if we are unable to find a through passage? It might end in some desperate cave with no exit.'

Raeburn had already uncoiled the rope and was tying in with a bowline knot around his waist. Clearly in the mood to get straight on with the climb, he spoke little as he prepared and overhauled his equipment. Every inch of that hundred-foot line passed through his hands, allowing him to feel for damage in the fibres. He examined the soles of his boots, searching for gaps where nails might have been knocked out in the loose rocks further down the mountain; he took the length of thinner cord out of his knapsack, arranging it into neat bundles and tying it around his shoulders. His attitude was brisk, thorough, businesslike.

Jones realised that he had assumed Raeburn would pack two ropes. Raeburn had, after all, insisted on making all the preparations himself. Oh well, he told himself, one rope would do, and Collie always carried a spare rope if it came to it, although given its vintage Jones would not like to rely on it for much.

All remained silent as they weighed up the choices before them. 'Raeburn?' Collie inquired at length, 'What do you think?'

He blew through his moustache, and pointed to one side of a giant flake partially detached from the cliff. The gap formed a narrow crack, perhaps wide enough to admit a man. 'We go for the flake crack.'

*

The flake crack provided a sporting diversion. Once inside, it was not difficult to wriggle through to the top, although it would accommodate only one person at a time. Raeburn went first, Jones second, Collie third, under the gallant but mistaken belief that Miss Elliot might ask for assistance in the rear. From the ledge atop the flake, Jones observed the Professor squirming up through the gap, emerging with his cleanly washed and pressed flannel coat streaked with mud. When it came to Rachel's turn to ascend, she suffered a little difficulty on account of her skirts, but said nothing.

'Where next?' Jones said.

Raeburn did not immediately reply, instead focusing all of his efforts on finding the way. From the ledge, he set his boot on a nubbin of rock and gingerly transferred his weight onto it, stepping out over empty space. The nails skidded a quarter of an inch before biting, leaving a streak of stone dust. His left hand stretched upwards, fingers feeling for a secure hold. All three of his companions watched anxiously.

'I could use a good hitch,' he muttered. 'Jones, am I secure?'

Jones had been passing the rope around his waist in the manner that Elspeth had taught him, but he appreciated that Raeburn might be more comfortable with the old method of belaying. He looked up, and sure enough, a good spike promised a decent anchor. Looping the rope around it, he made it fast.

'You're safe, Raeburn,' he said quietly, 'but please do not fall off.'

'I think if anyone is likely to fall off, it's you,' Rachel teased him.

The Scot committed to his move, swinging out on the exposed traverse. It seemed that a corner had to be negotiated; more delicate steps into space. After tense minutes, Raeburn stepped onto a sort of steep rib that seemed to offer more security—or at least the illusion of it.

'I see no hitches here,' he called back. 'How much rope do I have?'

Jones checked his coils. 'A yard, perhaps two.' He did not think now was the best time to lecture Raeburn on the necessity of longer ropes on difficult routes.

'Then you ought to follow directly. Collie can secure us on the hitch at the ledge.'

Jones hoped Raeburn could find somewhere to stop and belay further up the rib. He had never particularly liked climbing with four people to a rope. It introduced problems exactly like this, when the length of rope between each man was reduced until it became difficult to reach the next available spike for making the team secure.

Nevertheless, Jones edged his way across the traverse. When he reached the rib, he found that the climbing eased considerably, but as Raeburn said there was nothing to hitch the rope around. Jones did his best by bracing his boots against a lip of rock and taking in the rope around his waist. When Collie reached his position, the older man grinned and attempted to brush a little of the mud from his coat.

'We seem to be going the right way. Some distance above here is where the fun starts!'

Something about Collie's jovial dismissal of the troubles ahead made Jones a little nervous. He took a moment to analyse his feelings. When had he started thinking so much about danger when on a climb? Jones had always prided his ability to push such thoughts out of his mind and concentrate on finding holds. He prized boldness above all other qualities.

Something had changed in him. He had noticed it creeping up on him gradually these past few months. What could it possibly be, he wondered?

Collie, veteran of expeditions to the Himalaya, discoverer of new cliffs and pioneer of virgin peaks, seemed happy with the prospect of climbing in such a large group towards rocks that had repulsed the most accomplished climbers in Britain many times. As Jones took in the rope to secure Rachel across the traverse, he shared a glance with his friend.

'What are your thoughts about the route ahead, Professor?'

'This is the strongest team to try their luck on the cliff. I'm confident. Raeburn is the man to smell out the way, I'm sure of it.'

'There are four of us on a rope, though,' Jones reminded him.

'It is of no account. We will not have to retreat.' Collie regarded him with a concerned frown. 'What's troubling you?'

Jones looked out across that exposed traverse. Rachel clung to the sheer rocks with easy grace, balancing on the tiny holds and stepping across as if there were no drop beneath her boots at all. Sensibly, she had left her parasol and axe at the foot of the climb, encumbered enough already by her skirts. Jones admired her poise on stiff ground that would make many experienced climbers tremble.

She looked up and smiled, clearly enjoying herself.

'I find that I have more on my mind, these days.' Jones smiled back to her.

'She is a fine woman, and likely more your equal than any other girl you will ever meet. I wish you every happiness.'

'It's not quite as simple as that. She is engaged to another man. I thought you knew?'

'That would explain her references to a man named Peter. Jones, I'm sorry.'

Rachel neared their position on the rib, and scrambled cat-like up to the stance. Collie shuffled up a little way to make room.

'That was quite an exciting bit of climbing,' she said breathlessly. 'Where next?'

Raeburn called down from above, urging them on.

*

Some time later, the four of them stood on a mossy ledge. It seemed to have been formed by two massive boulders which, having fallen from high on the mountain at some point in antiquity, now provided the only safe platform in the expanse of the Church Door. At the widest point, the ledge was about six feet across, providing ample space for four lost climbers.

'I think we ought to try a direct passage,' Raeburn said, eyeing the steep rocks above his head.

Jones felt doubtful that any climb straight up from their position would succeed. The rocks appeared quite vertical, with a baffling profusion of sloping edges. Moreover, there was no available hitch for the rope, and no security for a man to stand and belay with the rope around his waist. Any move upwards from the ledge would be very risky.

'It's a miracle we have found this ledge at all,' Collie said. 'On my previous attempt, we got lost beneath this point and were forced around.'

Rachel kicked a little at the moss covering the rocks. 'Has anyone thought of following the ledge to see where it leads?'

Jones decided to untie from the rope before progressing any further. His sense of unease with the situation had increased gradually throughout the ascent. When rock-climbing, the number of things that could go wrong increased with every extra person you put onto the rope: this was a proven fact. Besides, he did not fancy their chances if he took a fall on the ledge with no belay to hold him. At least if he went unroped, he would pull nobody else down with the fall.

Rachel frowned and touched his arm. 'What are you doing?'

'Exploring. I don't fancy going across there with a rope on, not without knowing if there is a hitch on the other side.'

He pointed to his left, across the ledge. From six feet wide, it gradually narrowed to a sloping shelf only a few inches across, overgrown with moss and lichen.

He set off. The first part was easy, but he felt thankful for the dry conditions. Upon crossing the narrowest section, he finally got a good view of what lay ahead.

Sloping slabs, that most feared enemy of the clinker-nailed sole, led to the foot of a chimney of sorts. He could not see into the chimney, but he could see enough to realise that the journey across to it would be exciting. A few shreds of vegetation clung into the crack at the top of the slab, some Alpine flowers and a tuft or two of grass, but the slab itself seemed perfectly smooth.

'What can you see?' Rachel called to him.

'A possible way ahead.' Then: 'You might all have to take off your boots!'

'Is there a spike for the rope?' Raeburn said.

Jones searched, and found a nubbin that the rope might fit around, but it would only offer security for one climber at most.

'Not really.'

A longer rope would enable the leader to reach the safety of that chimney, he thought, but again this was not the time to discuss it. As he removed his boots and tied the laces to his belt, Jones examined the moves across the slab, then looked down from the ledge: two hundred feet vertically down, at least, to the boulders of the gully.

Raeburn could cope with it, he knew; Collie would stroll across with a smile and a cheery wave; and Rachel … capable, certainly, but Jones wondered how his own nerves would stand up to it.

He set off across the ledge, at first easily, then with more care as the exposure mounted. The slabs proved to be not unduly difficult, but the hungry drop below would not permit a mistake. He reached the chimney, where he found enough room for a man to crouch, and jammed stones to hitch the rope around. It appeared, however, prodigiously steep. Once again Jones had doubts whether their entire party could be brought up here. Where would they all stand while the leader tried his luck in the chimney?

It was no use. To take a party of four along that perilous slab, with no safe ledge and no certain outcome above, was folly. They would have to climb back down. With Miss Elliot in the team, Jones did not feel bold today.

He marvelled at how the presence of the woman he loved could affect his climbing so completely. One day, the hurt of rejection fresh in his mind, he could abandon himself to fate and scale a smooth wall without the slightest concern; on the next, with Rachel exposed to some of the danger herself, he felt as timid as a novice.

Before he could communicate his concerns to the others, Raeburn had already appeared at his position, puffing cheerfully as he hitched the rope over the small and fragile-looking nub of rock on the wall above.

'Looks safe enough to me.' Raeburn balanced easily on the slab, very close to Jones, two fingers gripping an in-cut hold to keep him in balance. 'Not a lot of space to breathe, eh?'

'I am uneasy about this,' Jones admitted.

'Whatever for?' Raeburn peered up the chimney, which was jammed from top to bottom with a jumble of wedged rocks, some of considerable size.

'I think our rope is much too short to allow us all to climb the chimney. There isn't room enough for us all at the ledge. The last climbers will be forced to balance on that slab, in an exposed position, while the leader attempts the chimney.'

Raeburn frowned. 'You think it's too risky?'

'Yes, I do.' Good lord, Jones wondered, what has come over me?

'Climbing is a risky business! Either we go on, and suffer perhaps a little discomfort in the process, or go down and tell our friends that yet another party of the best climbers in Scotland have failed to climb the Church Door.'

There Raeburn had the answer: it was a matter of pride. Collie had failed; Hastings and Haskett-Smith had failed; Tough and Brown had failed; Green, Napier, and Bell had failed. In every case it had been a question of getting lost or poor weather. Today, with a strong party, dry rock, and the way ahead clear to see, Raeburn would take some persuading to give up.

Only one sensible course of action presented itself. 'I am going back down,' Jones said, 'and taking Miss Elliot with me. I think you and Collie ought to continue. You will have a far greater chance of success without us.'

Raeburn looked disappointed. 'Ach well, perhaps it's for the best. You don't seem yourself today, laddie.'

'It's just the disease that strikes us all down, sooner or later,' he said with a backward glance at the ledge where Miss Elliot and Collie stood chatting.

*

While Raeburn and Collie climbed upwards, no doubt to glory and immortality, Jones and Rachel climbed back down. They had taken the spare rope from Collie's pack—only fifty feet in length—and it stretched tight between them as they descended the confusing rocks beneath the platform. Rachel went first. They had not needed to discuss it; they both knew that, on this occasion, she was the better climber and more capable of making decisions.

Jones took up the rear, occupying the role of anchoring Rachel while she searched for the way down. Now that the retreat was in progress, he felt like a fool. He had allowed personal feelings to completely destroy his judgement as a climber: a fatal error, something he had berated others for in the past.

'I'm safe,' Miss Elliot called from below. 'You may climb when ready.'

Jones started to descend, feeling clumsy. He reached her position at the bottom of the rib, just before the traverse back to the top of the flake. She was not, Jones noted, remotely safe: poised delicately on a sloper, passing the rope over her shoulder, with no attachment to the mountain whatsoever.

They moved down a yard or two to a more secure stance. 'It's a good thing I didn't fall off on my way down,' he muttered in what he realised must be a surly tone of voice.

She arched an eyebrow. 'The rope isn't long enough to permit me to go anywhere else. What is the matter with you, Jones?'

'I'm not entirely on form.'

'I'll say! What made you want to come back down? Was it the sloping shelf? Honestly, it looked like nothing at all.'

Their eyes met, and Rachel's expression eased a little. Jones realised she was not angry with him, merely puzzled and a little annoyed at having to come back down.

'It surely cannot be held against me,' Jones said, 'that I was worried for your safety. You must have been able to see the consequences of taking such a large group across the shelf and up the chimney. You would have been left exposed on the slab while everyone else was further up. What if you had fallen off?'

She shrugged, but all traces of her earlier annoyance had gone. 'I had a rope on.'

'Have you ever taken a fall before?'

'No,' she said after a short pause.

'I have, many times, and it hurts.' Jones rested a hand on her shoulder. 'The force of falling even a short distance can break ribs. It takes only a minute or two of dangling in space to kill you by suffocation. I have seen climbers die that way, in the Alps.'

'So it was merely concern for my safety that held you back?'

He hesitated. 'The truth is that I find your presence distracting on a climb. I did not think it was a good idea to continue.'

'Wise decision,' she said with the briefest of smiles. 'Come, let us get down quickly so we can climb up the Great Gully and meet the others at the top.'

'So that they can gloat?'

'No, so that we can enjoy the view from the summit. Isn't that what all this ought to be about?'

"THE GULLY WAS AN IMPOSING PLACE"

CHAPTER FOURTEEN

THE EIGER DISASTER

28th of May, 1897

BACK IN LONDON after his holiday, Jones felt depressed. The contrast between the adventure of the mountains and the boredom of daily life seemed to have intensified over the last year. Non-climbing friends had likened his passion for mountaineering to a chemical dependence, and Jones thought the comparison apt: it only felt good when you were actually doing it, and the low after the high could be debilitating.

He had so many good memories from the trip. After the ascent of the Church Door and the triumphant return of their whole party to Fort William, they had spent a day exploring the wonders of Glen Nevis. A party of seventeen climbed under the guidance of Willie Naismith. Abilities ranged from the novice to the expert, and everyone found a partner to suit his abilities. Surrounded by the natural splendour of that fine glen, all unhappy thoughts fled and Jones found himself climbing without worry at his limit, engrossed in the rock beneath his hands and feet.

Now, back in the heat of London, all he could think about was how to escape again.

The overnight train had deposited them at King's Cross that morning. To his surprise, Rachel had elected to travel with him back to London; she wished to visit the shop, and also to say hello to George Abraham. Her mood had lifted after that magical evening watching the sun set on the summit of Bidean, just the four of them, and Jones ventured to think that their friendship might be repaired.

She made no further mention of Jones' feelings for her. He wondered if she needed time to think the matter over, or if she simply preferred to ignore it; a more likely choice given her imminent marriage.

Rachel insisted on hailing a cab to take them to Eckenstein's shop from Jones' apartment on Russell Square. Heavy traffic slowed the journey. Stuck in a jam on Gower Street, the reek of manure and coal smoke wafting through the cab, Jones could not help wondering why he had bothered to come back.

Finally they arrived at Eckenstein's shop. All looked exactly as it had been when Jones left a few days ago. The shop was still the smartest on the street, the window displays packed with bright ironmongery, waxed leather and coiled rope; heads still turned as passers-by remembered the Crowley nuisance and the connection between Britain's current favourite criminal genius and the shiny new shop on Charing Cross Road.

Miss Elliot nodded approvingly. She had changed out of her country wear, and now wore a flowing dress. In the stifling heat, Jones guessed that she must be far more comfortable than he was.

'Eckenstein Alpine Equipment,' Rachel read from the sign, linking her arm with his. 'And this is where you now work?'

'For my sins,' Jones said. 'Oscar Eckenstein is a good friend, but as an employer … well!'

'Hush now, let me form my own opinion.'

The shop door opened, and out stepped the giant man himself. Clad in a filthy apron, shirt-sleeves rolled up to reveal sunburnt forearms, a pair of welding goggles protruding from tangled hair, Eckenstein looked every inch the inventor he had always dreamed of being.

'Good to have you back, boy!' he shouted across the street. 'Young Abraham is a useless dolt. It'll be good to have you back here where you belong!'

*

The first thing Jones noticed when he entered the shop was how much stock had been sold while he had been away. The axe rack stood half empty, the rope supply was decimated, entire boxes of ice pitons gone. A good sign, he thought to himself as Rachel took in the busy interior of the shop.

The second thing he noticed was that every customer present seemed to be listening, rapt, to George Abraham, who held court behind the counter and spoke to the gathered crowd. Eckenstein had disappeared, no doubt into his cave at the back where the pounding of metal on metal had already resumed.

Leaving Rachel to look around, Jones fought through the throng and ducked behind the counter. Abraham told stories of daring deeds on the mountains of North Wales. Jones felt embarrassed to hear his own name mentioned more than once, and coughed to draw his friend's attention.

'Will you excuse me for one moment?' Abraham asked of his massed fans, and turned to face Jones. He had clearly not even noticed the intrusion, for his face lit up with delight.

'Jones, my dear fellow—I did not realise you would be back so soon! This job is monstrously good fun. Do you have a moment to talk?'

'If you're not too busy,' Jones said with a smile.

Abraham laughed. 'Just a little advertising. The customers like hearing stories about you.'

Jones led Abraham into the small office next to Eckenstein's workshop. He wondered why so much stock had gone over the last week. It must be the imminent summer Alpine season, he decided.

Abraham pushed a stack of folders to one side and sat on the desk. 'So how was your holiday? Tell me everything.'

'Later. What's been going on here? Has it been this busy all week?'

Abraham nodded. 'I've had to learn pretty fast, actually. Eckenstein hasn't really left the workshop much.'

'That doesn't surprise me. What's he been working on?'

'Some kind of prototype that needs to be rushed into production. We've had a couple of big orders.'

Jones felt a hint of suspicion. 'Who placed these orders?'

'I couldn't tell you, old boy—it has been perfectly manic and I've had a lot to take in.'

'Fair enough.' Jones couldn't help feeling a little angry at how Eckenstein had left Abraham to his own devices. 'I ought to go and see him.'

Suddenly he remembered the discussion at Clachaig about the British designs on the north face of the Eiger, and wondered if there could be some connection with this urgent order.

*

Jones entered the workshop quietly. Eckenstein drew himself up to his full height, removed his goggles, and wiped an arm across his sweating brow.

'Just in time. Come and look at this.'

Jones could not help being intrigued. He took a step forward and examined the item held in the jaws of a vice. Oval in shape, a bent and formed bar of iron, it looked rather like a section of chain. One segment looked like it should open outwards. Jones could not guess how it could have anything to do with climbing.

'A rather good discovery, this,' Eckenstein said proudly. 'Chap called Pelton patented it in '68. His company went bust years ago, and now the design is being licensed to me for a pittance. I'm making them by the dozen. The official name is the Pelton Ring but I'm trying to come up with something better.'

'Fine, but what does it do?'

Eckenstein rummaged around in the clutter on the bench, and fished out a finished and polished Pelton Ring. He clicked the gate open with a finger. 'It's for attaching to pitons, see? You bang your peg into the ice or rock, clip on this beauty, then clip the rope to the other end. Saves you tying a length of cord to run the rope through.'

'Ingenious,' Jones said. He took the Pelton Ring from Eckenstein. It felt heavy in his hand, but obviously quite strong. Strong enough to hold the weight of a falling climber, he wondered? Still, it had to be better than the dubious loops of knotted cord everybody used on the rare occasions pitons were placed.

'The rope runs more smoothly as well,' Eckenstein explained. 'Should enable longer ropes to be used on difficult pitches.'

Jones was tempted to give his report on the necessity of longer ropes then and there, but decided not to allow himself to be distracted.

'Look here, Abraham tells me he has been left in charge while I have been away. Big orders have been placed, apparently. Who placed them?'

Eckenstein shrugged evasively. 'The quartermaster for some expedition. Why?'

'I thought we agreed to thoroughly inspect the credentials of all customers, particularly for big orders? The Alpine Club still hates us.'

'We need the trade. Can't be too picky.'

His evasiveness made Jones suspicious. Eckenstein knew more than he was admitting, Jones could tell.

'It's not Barkis and Holdstock, is it? I understand they might want to keep their mission a secret ...'

'For heaven's sake, Jones! Why would it be them?'

Jones folded his arms. 'I want to know who placed the order. You are hiding something from me.'

'You forget yourself. I am your employer. It's my right to withhold things from you.'

'I'm also your friend, or had you forgotten that?'

'Crowley is my friend too!' Eckenstein snapped, then turned bright red.

Comprehension struck. Crowley had vanished — gone to the Alps, according to Eckenstein — and would doubtless be planning something. Restoring his friendship with Eckenstein before leaving had been a smart move; now he had a way to quickly get the equipment he needed.

'You took an order from Crowley!' Jones shouted, jabbing his finger at the bigger man. 'You idiot!'

'I will thank you not to address me in that tone,' Eckenstein said sulkily. 'I bear no grudge against Aleister. He's trying to put his past behind him and wanted some gear for a climb. I decided to help him out.'

'Even though he is a wanted criminal? What do you think the police are going to say when they find out?'

'They need never know. He used a false name and paid in cash over the counter.'

Of course he did, Jones thought; Crowley liked to use false names. Now they were in serious trouble. Whatever mischief Crowley got up to in the Alps, the company would be involved.

Jones sat down on a chair and cradled his head in his hands, groaning. 'I suppose it didn't occur to you that Barkis and Holdstock have also gone out to the Alps with ambitious plans? Have you heard of the north face of the Eiger?'

Eckenstein began to look worried. 'Nobody could climb that wall. Besides, Holdstock is in prison.'

'His sentence has been concluded,' Jones said patiently, 'and for good or ill he has made plans with Barkis. Crowley has made a perfect fool out of you.'

Eckenstein remained silent for a while, thinking things over, his expression becoming more worried with every second.

'It might be a coincidence,' he said eventually.

'You believe that if you want to. I think Crowley has gone out to the Alps to take revenge on the people who tried to kill him, and you have helped him to do it.'

*

When Jones walked back into the shop to ask George Abraham what he knew, the first person he saw, talking quietly with the lad in the far corner, a hand on his arm, was Elspeth Crowley.

She still walked with a stick. No longer dressed in black, Elspeth now wore a striped summer dress of pale blue and white. A straw hat, tied around with a red ribbon, perched on her black hair. Although the sun had done nothing to darken her pale complexion, she looked well.

Jones could not help liking Elspeth, but her presence here surely did not bode well. Last time they met, she had told him in pained tones how dangerous it was for her to be seen anywhere near him or his friends; and yet here she was, happily flirting with George Abraham in the shop where Jones worked! He recalled Abraham's interest in the girl and wondered how their friendship had developed in the past week.

He marched over. 'What are you doing here, Elspeth?'

Elspeth's eyes widened at the sight of him, but she composed herself quickly with all the skill of an actress. 'Mr Jones, how nice it is to see you. I thought you were still in Scotland.'

'Evidently.'

She glanced at Abraham, hand still laid protectively on his arm. 'George my dear, perhaps you would give us a moment alone?'

Abraham looked worried and a little embarrassed. Jones wondered what they had been talking about, and abruptly realised that George knew practically nothing of Elspeth's true story.

'Of course,' he said after a moment. 'I shall arrange a cup of tea for Miss Elliot.'

'That would be kind of you,' Jones said without taking his eyes from Elspeth.

When he had gone, Elspeth drew him out of the shop into the street. 'I do hope you are not jealous, Mr Jones, but when I heard you had run off to Scotland with Miss Elliot I took it to mean that your rejection was final.'

'Please, let us drop the pretence! I am sick of all the lies and schemes happening all around me!'

'There is no scheme,' Elspeth said, her face radiating innocence. 'I do believe George has developed an attachment for me.'

'And does he know that you are a married woman?'

'Of course not!'

'He is my friend, and I wish for you to leave him strictly alone. He deserves better than to get involved with someone like you.'

'Can you not understand that I am trying to put Aleister behind me? To start my life anew? I thought you might be my way into that life, but you have chosen differently.'

He studied her face carefully. Jones once thought he knew Elspeth well, but the events on the crags of Great Gable had proven she could lie convincingly. It had all been an elaborate deception.

'I do not believe you,' Jones said coldly.

She suddenly looked tired and unhappy. 'Then I suppose this is the final good-bye between us.'

Elspeth turned and walked away, towards the shade under the trees on the far side of the road. She still had a slight limp to her step.

'Tell me about the order Crowley placed with the shop on the 23rd of May!' Jones shouted after her. 'A major order. Enough gear for a major climb, perhaps. What is he planning?'

She paused mid-way across the street. 'I have nothing to do with my husband these days. He abandoned me, remember?'

She turned away from him. Jones wondered if he would ever see her again, and if he did, what the circumstances would be.

He felt angry with himself as he returned to the shop, powerless to stop whatever might be happening. He sensed that he could only comprehend the fringes of what was going on: a clue here, an ominous feeling there, all pointing to something sinister but not amounting to very much. Sometimes it made him feel like he was losing his grasp on reality.

Abraham had just finished serving a customer when Jones stepped through the door, and in a hurry he ducked under the hatch and strode over.

'Is anything wrong?' the boy said earnestly. 'Look, if it's about Elspeth and me, the understanding I had formed was that you had no interest in her. It's all very new, anyway.'

He put his hands on his friend's shoulders. 'You have done nothing wrong. I doubt you will listen, but I have to warn you that she is not to be trusted.'

Abraham frowned. 'I'll make my own mind up about that.'

'Now I want you to tell me about the large order placed on the 23rd of May. Get Eckenstein to cover the shop for ten minutes. This could be important, my boy.'

*

'Honestly, I don't remember the order.'

'Think,' Jones pressed. 'It's important. What happened on that day?'

'Well, Elspeth came to visit me.' Abraham hesitated. 'I don't remember much about what I did at work.'

The three of them squeezed into the office: Rachel and Jones on the little stools, Abraham on the desk. The sound of hammer on metal came through the thin wall from next door where Eckenstein worked.

'Surely you must remember something?' Rachel said. She cradled the accounts ledger in her arms, scanning through the records from the past week. 'The order is huge. Fifty-five pounds paid in cash over the counter!'

Abraham thought. 'I recall Eckenstein saying something about a quartermaster for an Alpine trip wanting a few bits and pieces. Now you come to mention it, the Times ran an article the other day about some plans for an ambitious British climb. I kept the page.'

Jones and Rachel waited while Abraham rummaged through a pile of paperwork for the article. They shared worried looks. He knew what she would be thinking: her betrothed had expressed an interest in joining this north face climb. He would be in danger if Crowley was involved.

'Here it is,' Abraham said at last, handing a scrap of newsprint to Jones.

He quickly read the article. Short on facts but stuffed with hyperbole, it was a typical journalist's interpretation of a dangerous mountaineering challenge. The writer clearly knew nothing about climbing. The north face of the Eiger, the author asserted, was "an unclimbed face of such obvious inaccessibility that only the deranged would contemplate an ascent." At the bottom it noted the names of the climbers, and the fact that they had made the first ascent of the Matterhorn's north face the previous year.

'My God,' Jones said. 'So it is them after all.'

'The quartermaster for the expedition must have placed the order,' Abraham guessed. 'I thought it remarkable that Barkis and Holdstock planned to climb together again, but never made the connection with the order placed last week. Isn't it exciting?'

Under any other circumstances, Jones would agree; indeed, he would do everything in his power to get himself on the expedition.

'Crowley placed that order under a false name,' Jones said.

Abraham laughed. 'Come now, I think I would realise if Aleister Crowley walked into the shop!'

'Not if the lovely Elspeth had you distracted,' Rachel said gently. She fired Jones a look that said, as clearly as if she had spoken the words, "I told you so."

'What has she got to do with all this?' Abraham demanded.

Jones decided to change the subject. He didn't think poor Abraham could cope with the news that Elspeth was married to Crowley. Moreover, he now felt a terrible sense of guilt building within him. After he had found Crowley and Eckenstein drinking together he ought to have informed the police, so they could catch him then and there; instead he had dithered, unwilling to get Eckenstein in trouble, and finally the adventure and romance of Scotland had swept the matter from his mind.

If anything happened to Barkis he would feel responsible. He had a moral duty to act.

'Our friends are in danger,' he said firmly to them both. 'We have to do something.'

Abraham shrugged. 'Take the information to the police. They're already working on trying to catch Crowley, aren't they?'

'But we have no direct link between Crowley's order and the planned Eiger climb. The evidence is circumstantial at best.'

Another thought occurred to Jones. Crowley was cunning; he knew that Jones viewed them as rivals, and that his pride would not permit any challenge to go ignored. He probably also realised that Eckenstein would tell Jones the truth about the order before very long. The only conclusion Jones could draw was that Crowley wanted him to know about it.

Rachel looked at him, worried. 'What if it's a trap?'

'I'm thinking the same thing. Crowley knows I will feel responsible and want to help Barkis, and he knows that I will want to prove myself against him.'

'Men and their petty rivalries,' she said with a roll of her eyes. 'I'm worried about Peter. He left for Europe some days ago on business, and I know how much he wants to get involved with a climb like this.'

'Get in touch with him and warn him, but don't mention Crowley's name. Eckenstein could end up in prison if we don't keep this to ourselves.'

'Are you going to go out to Grindelwald?' Abraham said. 'I think you should wait. The expedition has only just got there, and the weather seems to be bad. Nothing is going to happen for at least a week.'

Jones thought about it for only a second before realising he had no other choice but to go to the Alps. He would tell the police what he knew, of course, but he could not live with himself if anything happened that was within his power to prevent. If it proved to be a trap then he would deal with it. He had bested Crowley before.

'Yes, I will go out to the Alps to confront him,' Jones said eventually. 'This time, though, I will be prepared.'

*

Jones spent the weekend planning, worrying, and sending telegrams to everyone he could think of. The PMC had to be kept fully informed; as a committee member, it was his clear duty. Although Holdstock and Barkis held full club membership, they had chosen to organise their trip independently. Several members had spoken out against them in mountaineering publications. Some articles even went as far as to label them upstarts, conveniently forgetting that these men had been responsible for the birth of progressive climbing in the first place. National interest in the expedition increased when the Alpine Club added its disapproval to the mix.

Fortunately for Jones, this meant that newspapers had plenty to say on the subject, allowing him to keep track of what was going on out there.

Raeburn volunteered to drop his interests in Edinburgh and travel to the Alps at short notice, if necessary. Collie expressed more cautious enthusiasm, but Jones knew he could rely on them both. They were clearly interested in making a second attempt at the north face, should the first expedition fail, and Jones received many other telegrams from leading British climbers, all wanting to be involved in any future attempt to climb the wall.

He felt torn. All he really wanted to do was stand up to Crowley and protect his friends from danger, but the more he investigated the more he felt attracted to the idea of competing against Crowley. He did not doubt for a second that Crowley would want to climb the north face of the Eiger and claim the victory denied him the previous year on the Matterhorn. He would want to crush Barkis and Holdstock while doing so.

Research on the Eiger occupied much of his time. Not much had been written on the mountain. It was mentioned in a handful of the Alpine classics from his father's era, and in a few issues of the Alpine Journal. The Eiger, its summit at just a little over 13,000 feet above sea level, was the lowest of the trio of mountains above the village of Grindelwald, near Interlaken. Mountaineers climbed the nearby Mönch and Jungfrau more frequently due to their greater height. Jones had a basic knowledge of German, and understood the meaning of the names: Ogre, Monk, and Maiden.

At last, after a full day in the British Library, Jones came across a photograph of the Eiger's fearsome north wall. It had been taken, the caption claimed, in 1876 from a foothill called Lauberhorn. A walker stood on the cairn, lending scale to the vast scene beyond.

The photograph made Jones thoughtful for a long time.

It was the greatest ice wall he had ever seen, or heard rumours of, in the whole of the Alps. At over six thousand feet in height, the wall looked like the arched roof of a cathedral. It grew out of the meadows of the Alpiglen and towered over the valley, menacing the habitations beneath, cursing them to life in the eternal shadow of the mountain during the winter months. There were no obvious weaknesses in that huge fortress, no long couloirs to follow, no elegant ridges—just one huge sweep of ice and disintegrating cliffs. Looking at the photograph, Jones doubted it would be possible even for the very best climbers to navigate through to the summit.

*

On Sunday, the Times reported that Holdstock and Barkis had begun to carry supplies up to a bivouac a thousand feet above the foot of the cliffs. The world watched them through the telescopes at Kleine Scheidegg, the cluster of hotels at a high pass near the foot of the wall. Nobody seemed to think that the expedition would amount to very much. Despite their success the previous year on the Matterhorn, the public believed these men insane, even suicidal. The extraordinary interest given to this expedition originated not so much out of a will to see them succeed, but more from a morbid curiosity to see how they would die.

There could no longer be any doubt that Crowley's order and the Eiger climb were linked. The papers reported that the climbers used the very latest products from Eckenstein Alpine Equipment. Jones wondered how Crowley had masqueraded as a quartermaster without Barkis and Holdstock realising it was him. Somehow, Crowley had managed to keep his real name out of all this. So far, the only parties who knew the connection were Scotland Yard, and those within Jones' closest circle of acquaintance.

He heard from Rachel that day, and was profoundly glad to hear, for her sake, that Peter Merrick was not on the Eiger. He had found his way to Grindelwald, however, no doubt caught up in the sensation and wishing to observe events himself.

Jones got his equipment together, waited to hear from the police, and prayed nothing would go wrong.

At nine o'clock on Thursday the 3rd of June, Jones unlocked the front door of the shop. The weather had turned sultry, with the possibility of thunder. Apparently over the Alps high pressure reigned, blessing the Eiger with days of sunshine and calm skies. The ice on the wall, Jones knew, would be at its best.

No sign of Eckenstein. Still asleep, no doubt.

A customer entered the shop as Jones was resetting the cash register. He turned to see the smiling face, black bowler hat and short frame of Alfred Varley, the particularly tenacious reporter who had bothered him before.

Varley strode forward and offered his hand, smile fixed in place. 'Alfred Varley —'

'—Observer,' Jones finished for him, ignoring the outstretched hand. He remained behind the counter, keeping a barrier of authority between them.

Varley ignored the snub. 'I thought you might be able to give me a few words for the front page.'

'I thought your rag considers the Eiger endeavour foolish?'

'That is an interesting interpretation,' Varley said, jotting down a note in his pad, which had appeared as if from nowhere. 'Clearly you view it with greater importance, then.'

'I am in the business of supplying climbers with equipment.'

'Quite. Speaking of which, I gather your boss has made a pretty packet from Mr Holdstock and his chum. Are you sponsoring the expedition? What happens when they fail?'

'Those are not questions for me, sir. I have absolutely nothing to do with this order. I was in Scotland at the time, on holiday.'

'So you admit an order was made.'

Jones cursed himself. 'Yes, all right damn it, an order was made. I will say nothing further on that subject.'

'Fair enough,' Varley said with a slow smile. 'I would have thought, with the future of your job depending on the success of this climb, you would have expressed greater interest.' He turned to go.

'Wait!' Jones said, hating the man. 'What do you mean by that?'

'It's quite simple, Mr Jones. The Eiger expedition is almost exclusively equipped with items from this shop. Your company is already marked as having connections with shady goings-on. Crowley, for example. What do you think the press will do if the expedition fails because of your equipment?'

'You would not dare,' Jones said, knowing full well that they would.

'Surely you see it is in the public interest? Can't be having more gullible young men lured to their deaths by the promise of cheap glory, if only they buy the latest ice axe. Your company will be held to account for whatever happens on the Eiger, Mr Jones.'

'Holdstock and Barkis are the most accomplished alpinists in the world, hardly gullible young men.'

The argument was pointless, and after sparring for a little longer, Varley left. Finally Jones saw a piece of the puzzle he had been missing, another spring in the trap. Crowley, bitter that his business interests had been taken from him, had found the perfect way of destroying Eckenstein Equipment once and for all.

*

By Friday the 4th, the team had struck out from their advanced base at eight thousand feet. That first bivouac, a ledge scarcely big enough for the two men, poised in the midst of a vast crack system, captured the imagination of the public. Some brave journalist managed to take a photograph from a balloon, flown as close to the face as he dared; it was grainy and a trifle blurred, but detailed enough to show the drama of the situation. A huge amount of equipment, climbing gear, provisions and spare clothing, hung from pitons driven into the rock on either side of the ledge. It was a fitting base from which to launch the assault on the unknown realm above.

The climbers wasted a day when Holdstock chose the wrong line, bringing them up under a series of gigantic overhangs. They spent another day trying to find a way up to the right on steep ground; after that, they had been obliged to return to their bivouac to recover and stock up on food.

One last push. They achieved a thousand feet of severe climbing in a single day. Jones read the article and felt his spirits lift, hoping that his friends would make it.

Rock gave way to ice. Progress slowed, said the newspapers. At nine thousand feet, climbing barred by a huge roof fanged with icicles, they had been forced to bivouac in the most inhospitable place yet encountered. The article written by Varley in the Observer, heavy with sensationalism, described a miserable cave at risk from giant icicles falling from the overhang above. The description of this "Ice Trap", although intended to provoke excitement and dread in the ignorant public, made Jones' palms sweat. He could imagine the tension in that place, wondering when the next deadly spear would fall, if it would miss their resting-place again, or perhaps strike its mark. He prayed for their safety.

Then the storms came. Jones began to feel desperate and wanted to get to Grindelwald as soon as possible, but his contact in Scotland Yard, Inspector Warrington, forbade him to take any action until the police had decided what to do.

The Eiger, locals claimed, was the worst mountain in the Alps for storms. When the surrounding peaks basked in sunshine, the Eiger would often brood under its own storm cloud, lightning blasting the ridges, snow sweeping the north face. Now one of those vicious Eiger-storms came in fast, trapping Holdstock and Barkis in their refuge.

No news arrived for two days. Cloud obscured the cliff and made observation impossible. Jones hardly slept on Saturday night, consumed with worry and frustration at not being able to do anything to help.

Then, on the morning of Tuesday the 8th of June, he received two communications that would change his life.

*

Seven o'clock. Jones made his coffee strong, feeling tired from worry and lack of sleep. He wondered how long he would be able to cope with the stress, then told himself crossly that he was safe in London, nowhere near the terrible events happening in Switzerland at this moment.

Hearing the familiar thud of post landing on his doormat, he shambled into the hallway, coffee in hand. A few letters waited for him, and as he stooped to pick them up the doorbell rang, heralding a telegraph boy with a message. He collected his post and took it back to read over breakfast.

The first was from Rachel Elliot, dated June the 5th.

"My dearest Jones,

"I hardly know how to start this letter! I suppose, like me, you have been following the progress of our old employers on the Eiger & have prayed for their safety. It scarcely seems possible that Englishmen should be involved in such an endeavour, when only three years ago it would be seen as utterly beyond the realms of possibility. It is a symbol of the strange times in which we live.

"You cannot guess how relieved I am to hear that Peter is not up there now. You must hate to read his name, but surely you must understand my situation? This is difficult for me. Peter is my only chance for a happy life for my family. I feel I have had to justify this to you many times. You are dear to me beyond words, but you cannot give me what I need, and despite what my heart tells me I cannot harbour regrets.

"Peter is in Grindelwald, watching the drama on the wall himself. He has told me to come there with great haste & has said that we shall be married as soon as I arrive. I can hardly afford a holiday to Switzerland, but he has already paid for my train as far as Interlaken. I am leaving tomorrow, so I suppose by the time this letter is with you I shall already be on my way.

"You have been my dearest friend, my companion upon the mountain, my defender; now I must ask you to relinquish those duties to another.

"Yours affectionately,

"Rachel M. Elliot."

Jones read the letter again. He did not quite believe its contents. She was engaged, he had become used to that unhappy fact; but imminent marriage? It was tantamount to elopement, organised and paid-for. Despite the bleak message, her choice of words stirred hope within him. He felt sure that she loved him in return. It made the news of her elopement even more difficult to bear.

Hardly daring to hope that the telegram might contain better news, Jones tore it open.

"EIGER TEAM LOST BUT SEARCH UNDERWAY AND SECOND ATTEMPT BEING PLANNED STOP COME TO GRINDELWALD AT ONCE FROM COLLIE"

Lost? He wished Collie had been more specific. Frustrated by the brevity of the telegraph format, Jones screwed the paper into a ball and tossed it into the waste bin. He had to find out the truth. He needed a newspaper.

After dressing as quickly as he could, he stuffed a slice of toast between his teeth and left the flat at a run. Russell Square was still quiet; he would have to go further afield to find his newspaper. Finally, on Gower Street, he came across a bored-looking paperboy holding out a copy of the Times.

He thrust a penny into the boy's hand and took the newspaper. His heart was thumping. He had never felt so scared in his life.

Tuesday, 8th of June, 1897
THE TIMES
TWO LOST ON WALL OF DEATH
EIGER GLADIATORS PERISH AFTER EPIC STRUGGLE

WHO IS TO BLAME? ASKS PUBLIC

It can today be revealed that the Eiger, until recently a little-known mountain in the Bernese Oberland canton of Switzerland, has these past few days been witness to a tragic event …

Jones scanned onwards. Both men—his old employer, Thomas Holdstock, and his dear friend, Simon Barkis—had perished at their final bivouac in the Ice Trap. A few sad items, shredded ropes and bits of clothing, had been found in the melting snows at the foot of the wall.

Guilt cut through him like a knife. Why had he delayed? He should have ignored the police and gone to the Alps immediately, not waited for permission. He felt physically sick, a dull burning pain in his gut, when he thought of the wretched final hours those men must have endured: the cold, the hunger, the despair. God preserve all climbers from such a terrible fate.

All of his worst imaginings had come true. Rachel was about to marry a man she did not love, while at the same time hinting that she might have feelings for Jones. One of his closest friends had been killed by Aleister Crowley. The reputation of the company he had invested so much of his life in was shortly about to be destroyed by the vultures of the press. Jones also realised, with a sinking sense of inevitability, that Crowley would now climb the Eigerwand himself and claim the prize he had coveted for so long.

Jones could not sit back and wait for one more instant. He had been summoned to Switzerland by Aleister Crowley, and he no longer had any choice but to walk into the trap.

CHAPTER FIFTEEN

MERRICK

9th of June, 1897

RACHEL ELLIOT DID NOT sleep well that night. She adored the novelty of travel, but on this occasion circumstances had taken all of the joy out of the journey. She had been planning her wedding for weeks now. Peter had destroyed it all with his inexplicable summons. Surely, she thought for the hundredth time, the bride and her family should have the privilege of planning the wedding? This elopement ruined all her hopes for the day she had dreamed about. Her father would not be there to give her away. The whole business seemed almost shameful.

Already, she resented Peter's decision for a hurried wedding and wondered what she would say to him when they met. Although he had provided expenses, the sum did not extend to a servant's allowance and Rachel could not possibly travel alone. She hired a girl named Sarah Collins to accompany her across Europe.

After the mayhem of Paris, a place that reminded her all too readily of London, Bern had a welcoming atmosphere. Every stop on this journey seemed like an adventure in itself. Rachel had never travelled this far from England before, and despite her poor spirits she had made a promise to enjoy every moment, because in all likelihood it would never happen again. She would probably be a mother in a year or two, and that would be the end of climbing for her. What a depressing thought.

Hotel Bellevue, overlooking the river, provided an acceptable standard of accommodation and cheap dinners. She must have eaten something disagreeable, however, for nightmares disturbed her sleep that night. She woke early, gasping with thirst, and gulped down a cup of tepid water from the jug at her bedside table.

Dawn glow framed the curtains. She rose and crossed the room in her nightdress, eager to welcome the new day and get on with her journey. Throwing back the curtains, she saw, for the first time in her life, the Alps.

Mountains dominated the panorama. Beyond green foothills, a jagged background glowed white against the red band of dawn. Rachel gasped in delight. Never had she dreamed that the Alps would be so beautiful—or so big. She was used to the old beloved heights of Wales, and had thought them mighty, but Snowdon and Tryfaen hardly registered in comparison with these giants.

She could name not one single peak before her. Grabbing her Baedeker from the dressing table, she consulted the index and turned to page 135, where a map of Bern and a panoramic view folded out from the book.

"ALPENAUSSICHT AUS BERN". She understood no German, but the purpose of the panorama was plain enough and although she could not be standing on the spot where the drawing had been made, the view seemed identical. She returned to the window and held the picture up in front of her.

She identified the first big mountain on the left as the Wetterhorn, to its right the fine spires of Schreckhorn and Finsteraarhorn. Somehow these mountains did not command her attention as much as the next one. Although of an inferior height to many of its neighbours, it had a more imposing presence. The blunted pyramid of its north wall, facing Bern, seemed to frown. Rachel imagined it would always be in shadow.

Of course, she knew what it would be called even before she consulted her book. It was the Eiger.

Last night upon arriving in Bern she had heard the terrible news from Grindelwald: both young men dead on the mountain. It had shocked her terribly, having known both of them. Although she had not particularly liked either, the tragedy seemed immediate and personal. Once again she prayed that Peter did not have designs on the north face. He was, after all, a mountaineer of some accomplishment, despite Jones' dismissal of his skills.

Dear Jones. For a moment she allowed herself the guilty indulgence of wondering how he would have conducted affairs, had he been in Peter's position. He would have respected her wishes instead of arranging a shameful elopement.

A quiet knock sounded at the door. Rachel turned away from the window.

'Who is it?'

'Miss Collins, ma'am. It's seven o'clock and a wire has arrived for you.'

'Come in.'

The door opened, letting more light into the room. Sarah hovered in the doorway.

'A telegram has arrived for me, dear; wire is vulgar,' Rachel said. She still felt tired.

'Your telegram, ma'am.' Sarah waited obediently for her mistress to take it from her. 'From your young man, perhaps?'

'I doubt I'll be hearing from my young man until we get to Grindelwald. Would you have the goodness to find me something to drink? Coffee, perhaps? The kitchen must be open by now. Find yourself something as well.'

Rachel tried her best to smile as she took the envelope from the girl. Sarah had put up with Rachel's outbursts of frustration most patiently, and now she resolved to be kinder to her travelling companion. It was not Sarah's fault she was a cause of unwanted expense; after all, she had never visited a foreign land either, and had thanked Rachel profusely for engaging her services.

As Sarah left, Rachel wondered why she felt so reluctant to finally arrive in Grindelwald. In less than four hours of travel, by train, steamboat and finally train again, she would be with her beloved. She would also be right in the middle of all the drama and gawping that surrounded the north face of the Eiger.

The telegram lay untouched in her hands. Startled at her own forgetfulness, Rachel tore open the envelope.

"BEG YOU NOT TO COME TO GRINDELWALD SOMETHING TERRIBLE IS GOING TO HAPPEN FROM JONES"

*

'My name is Inspector Warrington of Scotland Yard. I will be telling you what to do from now on.'

Warrington, thin and faded, worn out from twenty years of chasing criminals in the streets of London, seemed to have been given fresh vitality by Jones' visit that morning. Their previous meetings to discuss the Crowley case had been frustrating affairs for both parties: Warrington never made any progress with his investigations, and Jones hardly ever had any new information to give to the detective. Jones considered their relationship an evil necessity. He disliked the air of cynicism and joylessness that the older man cloaked himself with. Nevertheless, Warrington had a reputation for tenacity, and would catch Crowley in the end.

Jones now gave Scotland Yard that chance. Nobody else had made the connection between Aleister Crowley and the Eiger north face expedition. Telling the police what he knew had been difficult, because it forced him to acknowledge withholding information about Crowley's relationship with Eckenstein; but now that he had come clean about it, he felt he had already gone some way to making amends for his own part in the disaster.

Unfortunately, Eckenstein would probably view what Jones was about to do as a betrayal. He had taken the news of Barkis' death badly.

'Why are you here?' Eckenstein demanded, standing by the door to his office, looming over the frail policeman.

'If you are going to do me the discourtesy of not offering me a chair,' Warrington replied mildly, 'then you had better remember that I have the power to destroy your business — or save it, if I choose.'

Eckenstein seemed taken aback by the threat, but did not move. Jones got up from his own chair and offered it to the Inspector. He stood by the door to watch out for customers and listen; the following conversation was for Eckenstein's benefit, and he decided to interrupt as little as possible. Eckenstein's guilty conscience would make him feel threatened and cornered by this policeman.

'Thank you,' Warrington said. 'I would ask for a cup of tea, but I doubt you can afford it, considering.'

Eckenstein took the bait. 'Considering what?'

'Sir, your business is doomed. The market you have chosen was dubious enough before this calamity, but now — well!'

'I would hardly call it a dubious market,' Eckenstein protested.

Warrington winked at Jones, taking an impish delight in leading Eckenstein by the nose.

'How many of the Queen's subjects do you think are involved in mountaineering of this kind? Thank heavens, hardly any. Make no mistake, when news spreads that those men died using experimental contraptions from your shop, nobody will buy from you again.'

Jones had more faith in the intelligence of their customers than the Inspector, but even he had to grudgingly admit that the theory was sound.

'All right, we're in trouble,' Eckenstein admitted.

'I think we can be more specific than that,' Warrington said in a colder voice. 'You, sir, are in trouble.'

Eckenstein looked frightened. 'I have done nothing wrong.'

'Really? Your accounts indicate the order was taken under a false name, which would theoretically make you innocent of any crime, but I have been informed that you sold this equipment to our friend as a willing accomplice.'

Eckenstein looked worried. Although unwilling to articulate his feelings, Jones could tell that his boss concealed a desperate guilt. He felt even more responsible than Jones, and for good reason; he had trusted Crowley, believed him, supplied him with equipment in the belief that it was to be used for an innocent purpose. Instead Crowley had used it to equip Barkis and Holdstock before sending them to their deaths.

Now he felt betrayed. 'Did you tell the police, Jones?'

'I had no choice!'

'Let us consider this calmly,' Warrington said in his reasonable tone. 'With hindsight, you made a bad decision. We all make mistakes. Consider yourself lucky that I am giving you a chance to atone for it.'

Eckenstein looked wretched. Jones felt profoundly sorry for him.

'Firstly, let us consider today's developments. We know that Barkis and Holdstock took an irrational route on the cliff. Experts widely believe they were fed misinformation.'

Warrington drew a folded newspaper from inside his coat and placed it on the table in front of him. The headline was ghastly: "THE ICE TRAP CLAIMS ITS VICTIMS", complete with a drawing of the snow-filled cave, fringed with icicles. With a finger, Warrington scanned down the column until he reached a particular paragraph.

'I quote, "The guides of Grindelwald offer a reward to the team who recovers their bodies. The mood in the town is that the Eigerwand has acquired a reputation as the last great prize of all the Alps: it has killed savagely, has the power to kill again, and this macabre fascination is drawing the best young mountaineers from all over Europe to Grindelwald."'

After a moment of silence, Eckenstein said, 'The fools are queuing up to die. Don't they understand that the craft of progressive climbing is still young? Some walls should be left to the next generation. If it defeated Holdstock and Barkis, nobody else will fare any better.'

Jones felt the same way. The accident had deeply shaken his conviction in progressive mountaineering. If even those two could die, the very best and boldest, then what hope did the rest of them have?

'I agree,' Warrington replied. 'There will be other attempts on the north face until it is either climbed or has killed enough people for the canton of Bern to put a ban on climbing it.'

'Frankly, I would support such a ban,' Eckenstein said. 'What are you hinting at?'

Warrington glanced at Jones. He took his cue. This was something he believed Eckenstein would respond to better if it came from the lips of a friend. It would still sound like treachery, but he might eventually realise that it was for his own good.

'We organise another expedition,' Jones said, 'a British expedition manned by the best climbers. Raeburn is keen, and although Collie disapproves he will help. Most of all, I want to go.'

'You must be insane.'

'Don't you see, this is our last chance? If we recover the bodies in a safe and orderly manner, our reputation might be saved. The safety advantages of the new equipment will be publicised. Scotland Yard will help us by putting pressure on the newspapers.'

Eckenstein considered this. He exhaled heavily. 'I admit that it would be almost impossible to mount a recovery operation in a place like that without the aid of ice-pitons, Pelton Rings and claws. Which is not to say,' he added with a stern look, 'that I think such a mission could be conducted safely. There are politics at work here.'

'Never mind about the politics,' Warrington cut in. 'That is my concern. Your concern is to repair the damage you have caused. I hope you realise that the future of your sport is at risk? Mountaineering in the Alps could be banned!'

'Rubbish. The Alpine economy is dependent on tourism.'

'Then unguided climbing could be banned, which I think it ought to be anyway. Are you aware that every single guide who has offered an opinion on the north face of the Eiger has condemned the endeavour as insanity?'

'Guides are all fools, and I refuse to put my name to your scheme.' Eckenstein drained his cup and rose. 'I demand you tell me the truth. You want us to catch Crowley for you: that is why you are here!'

'Of course I want Crowley. He is behind these deaths on the Eiger, and a great many other crimes besides, as you know better than anyone.'

Eckenstein's guilty look returned. 'I'm sure I don't know what you mean by that.'

'Come now, sir, you have been associating with young Crowley since at least 1893. I can easily bring charges against you if you defy me.'

Warrington's polite manner hid an undertone of menace, and Jones did not doubt for a moment that he would carry out his threats if either of them failed to comply.

Eckenstein glared, realising he had been trapped. 'Are you going to offer me some kind of a deal?'

'Give me Jones for a few weeks, and all the equipment and funds he needs. All you have to do is keep out of the way. In return, you get immunity from the law on this small matter, and our help in restoring the reputation of your business.'

Eckenstein pondered these words for a long time. He looked out of the window into the hot, weed-filled yard behind the shop.

Suddenly he laughed. 'Jones my boy, you have more guts than I ever credited you for. All right, I'll do it.'

Jones felt awful. It had been a necessary trap to weave, but it still amounted to a betrayal. It would work—he knew it would work—but he might never be able to look his friend in the eye after this.

Warrington smiled thinly and shook hands with Eckenstein. 'Splendid! We shall have this unpleasantness settled in no time at all. I personally promise to do all I can to protect your business once Crowley has been apprehended. Mr Jones, come with me please; we have details to discuss.'

After promising to keep in constant touch, Jones left for the police station with the Inspector. He felt an ache of foreboding settle deep inside him, both at the prospect of confronting Crowley once again and at the even more dangerous work that awaited him on the north face of the Eiger. For the first time, he realised that the crazy plan he had concocted with Warrington was actually going to be put into motion. In only a few days he would be on the most deadly mountain wall in the Alps: a place where all his skills, all his experience, and the best equipment available might not be enough to keep him alive.

*

In the summer of 1897, the Alpine resort of Grindelwald could still be described as quiet and obscure. Noted for its views of the two glaciers coming down out of the high Oberland, and the mountain walls dwarfing the chalets and hotels in the valley below, Grindelwald was principally known as a destination for tourists hoping to benefit from the healthful aspect and fresh mountain air. Mountaineers also visited. The town boasted a score of experienced guides, and decades ago it had been an important centre for the wave of enthusiasm that accompanied the initial exploration of the Alps.

By the closing decade of the century, however, the great years were long in the past. Grindelwald once again slumbered in obscurity, and mountaineers tended to be unoriginal in their aspirations, dwarfed by the reputations of their legendary forebears. The north face of the Eiger thrilled and horrified the tourists, along with the icy Fiescherwand and the rock walls of the Mettenberg, but nobody ever paid any more attention to them than that.

Nobody, that is, until Aleister Crowley dreamed up the incredible notion of climbing that wall, and seeded the possibility in the minds of Thomas Holdstock and Simon Barkis.

As Rachel walked through the main thoroughfare of the town with Sarah by her side, she sensed suppressed excitement. Activity surrounded every hotel: carriages queued in the road, porters struggled with suitcases, and groups of ladies chatted quietly to each other under their parasols. The fierce sun had driven many people indoors, however, and the shops seemed to be shut during the early part of the afternoon, much to Rachel's disappointment.

Pastoral beauty surrounded this miniature tourist metropolis on every side. Rough timber fences divided fields of extraordinary colour, lush greens dappled with yellow and scarlet flowers. Grain barns, raised on stilts to keep out mice, stood beside the torrents, which ran milky-white with glacier dust. Stands of pine sheltered marmots at play. It truly was an Eden of unparalleled beauty.

Their walk through the town finally took them back to the Bear Hotel. This grand building, five storeys of red brick, stood on a promontory overlooking the Lower Glacier and the mountains behind. Her betrothed, Peter Merrick, was somewhere in that hotel. Upon arrival, she had been informed by the receptionist that Peter was out on business, and would be back later. Truthfully, she had been disappointed not to find him waiting at the station platform for her arrival.

They sat down on a bench in the shade of a young poplar. Rachel angled her hat to protect her from the fierce sun which penetrated the leafy canopy above. The view from this position could not be grander: beyond the bulk of the hotel and the pastures behind it, huge mountain walls reared, laced with ice.

Sarah, who had not spoken much throughout their walk, perhaps overcome by the picturesque surroundings, now struck up a tentative conversation.

'If I may be so bold,' she began, 'oughtn't your young man be here to meet you?'

Despite the impertinent question, Rachel resisted the instinct to scold her servant. She felt a little lonely in this foreign land. Sarah's presence on the journey had been a comfort, and perhaps the question was meant as a gesture of friendship.

Rachel sighed and thought about how she would answer. In truth, of course, her forthcoming marriage to Peter had nothing to do with her own happiness, and therefore she could hardly complain if he did not consider it in his plans.

Sarah looked at her expectantly. She must be about eighteen, Rachel judged, and probably not very experienced; but she had a pleasant face and pretty eyes, and these things could take her far.

'You're quite right,' Rachel finally answered, with a laugh to show it did not bother her. 'Peter ought to have come to meet me. He's frightfully busy, of course.'

Sarah sat back on the bench and crossed her legs. 'What does he do, your Peter?'

'He works in insurance. How about you? Do you have a sweetheart?'

Sarah blushed and looked away. 'No. Well … perhaps.'

'Tell me about him,' Rachel said, but if Sarah responded she did not hear the answer, for at that moment Peter Merrick pushed through the revolving door at the front of the Bear Hotel and strode out into the square.

Rachel stood to get a better view. He looked healthy; in fact, very healthy indeed, bronzed and muscled, as if he had spent his European excursion doing hard labour in the sun instead of sitting behind a desk. His black hair was cropped closer than Rachel had seen it before, and he walked with a confident swagger. He wore the uniform of an Alpine climber: breeches, loose waistcoat, and a linen jacket whose tears and scuffs spoke of a hard campaign in the mountains. He wore a narrow-brimmed hat of the type she had seen some of the local guides wearing. His face glowed. Everything about him suggested a man at the peak of his physical powers, a god of the Alps.

Her first thought was that Peter had lied to her about the purpose of his excursion. He had obviously not been working in an office in Geneva.

He now leaned against one of the pillars at the front of the hotel, idly kicking the brickwork. A few of the men who had been passing through the square stopped to chat with him, and within moments a crowd of over a dozen had gathered. The meeting, she realised, must have been planned in advance.

Sarah had noticed the attention Rachel was paying to the group. 'Who's that over there? Do you know him?'

'That,' Rachel replied, 'is Peter Merrick. He has lied to me about his reason for being here.'

'Are you going to confront him?'

'I certainly am! You are to stay where you are.'

*

By the time Rachel reached the crowd, Peter had started to talk. The throng of men prevented her from getting any closer, and besides, she realised that it might be advantageous to listen and learn something about what had occupied Peter's time in the Alps.

Taking care not to be noticed, Rachel stood at the back of the crowd behind an elderly gentleman, who raised his hat to her. She was struck by his immense white beard and a face that looked like it had spent a hundred years squinting into the sun. Despite his extreme age, the man stood tall and without a stick.

'Thank you all for coming today,' Peter said in greeting to the crowd. He scanned the assembled guides with a solemn gaze. 'I have called you here to make an important announcement. You do not know me, so allow me to introduce myself: I am Peter Merrick of Cambridge, England, and the two men who died on the Eiger were my friends.'

A laugh sounded from the opposite side of the crowd to Rachel. 'So why do you call us here, Herr Merrick? Excuse my humble English, please, but are you here to blame us for the deaths of those fools? If you were their friend you could have stopped them. It is not our fault.'

'I am not looking for someone to blame, Herr Kaufmann,' Peter said. 'My friends took on the challenge of an unknown mountain face, and they can only blame themselves for what happened. My duty is to organise an expedition to recover the bodies and equipment. I cannot in good conscience enjoy your hospitality and not act.'

'You will die,' called out Kaufmann. 'You are a mere boy.'

Peter bristled at being called a boy. Despite her anger, Rachel smiled; she knew him well, and he was inclined to be sensitive on account of his boyish good looks.

'I have climbed more difficult routes than any man here.' Peter glared at them. 'I may be young, but I am more than capable. Jossi will vouch for my powers. Jossi!' he called.

A young guide stepped forward into the semicircle of yard where Peter Merrick held court—reluctantly, Rachel thought.

'It is true,' the guide confirmed. 'I accompanied the young Herr on a climb of the Fiescherwand last week. He is a better ice-man than I will ever be.'

'A better ice-man than even the great Jossi!' Peter shouted. 'I have climbed the Fiescherwand, and you all said that would never be done. Why not the Eigerwand too? Why put limits on what is possible?'

The elderly gentlemen standing next to Rachel now cleared his throat. Peter fell silent and every head in the crowd turned to face the old guide.

He shook his head scornfully. 'You are a fool. For fifty years I have watched the young immortals strutting off into the mountains with their brand-new ice axes and shiny boots. Sometimes their remains are found in the *gletscherschlucht*, their bones baked white, fine coats in rags, axes splintered. You will not live long, young man.'

A smile came to Peter's face. 'The esteemed Christian Almer! I welcome your advice, of course.'

'Then listen to me when I speak to you!' Almer snapped. 'I guided Barrington in '58 when we made the first ascent of the Eiger. Even by the easiest route from Wengen, it was a formidable peak then, as it is now. No good will come of these absurd variations on the north face. To climb there is to die.'

'I believe that nothing is impossible in the mountains.'

'Then you forget the first rule of climbing, which is to preserve life above all other considerations! What is it that your countryman Whymper wrote? Look well to each step, and from the beginning think what may be the end. Do you wish to die?'

'On the contrary, sir, my name will live forever.'

'I daresay it will, one way or another. Listen to me. No guide will accompany you, so you are doomed anyway. The last team went without a guide and they are dead.'

Peter smiled patiently. 'That is why I have called you here. Herr Almer, believe me when I say that one of your guides shall accompany me.'

Now the entire crowd started laughing, at first discreetly and then with open scorn at Peter's confidence. Rachel felt her heart ache. The man who faced the Grindelwald guides with a determined stare was not the man she had promised to marry, the kind and industrious Peter who worked hard for their future. He now seemed boastful and arrogant. Worse, he had lied throughout his entire time in the Alps—a trip Rachel now realised to be a selfish holiday, not an effort to gain promotion.

'Silence!'

Peter did not shout the word, but it was said with gravity. The laughing guides stopped at once.

'Here is my offer,' Peter said when he had their attention. 'I require the services of a first-rate guide for no less than five days. He must be willing to learn new climbing techniques and must own ice claws—*Steigeisen*—with forward-projecting points. If this is a problem, I can arrange for Herr Bhend to make some.'

A moment of silence, then a voice called out, 'What fee do you offer?'

'That is a point to be discussed later. You may rest assured, gentlemen, that I will pay the one who accompanies me very handsomely.'

Nobody volunteered, and the crowd began to disperse. Rachel pretended to drift away with the guides, but she ducked behind a tree a little way away and sat down on the bench beneath it. In the glare of a hotel window she could see Peter's reflected form, distorted in the glass, and as she had expected, one guide remained. Rachel could not see him distinctly, but he seemed to be a tall, barrel-chested man.

She had to listen carefully to hear their conversation.

'What is your name, sir?' Peter inquired.

'I am Ulrich Almer.' A thick, nasal voice.

'A pleasure to make your acquaintance, sir. Your deeds are celebrated almost as much as those of your father, Christian.'

'I do not wish to discuss my father,' Ulrich said harshly. 'I am my own man.'

'I understand that your father casts a long shadow. Do you have something to say to me?'

Ulrich seemed reluctant to mention why he had stayed behind when the others had left. Eventually, he said in a low voice, 'Tell me more about your planned climb.'

Peter kicked at a stone. It buzzed past Rachel's resting place. 'Why should I tell you anything?'

'Because my family is hungry, and work is not so good for a guide these days. I am not young. My great years are long in the past. Perhaps if I earn enough on one last climb I can live out my days escorting ladies over the Kleine Scheidegg. Perhaps my name also will live forever if we climb the Eigerwand.'

'If you wish to accompany me, then I would be happy to discuss rates. I offer one hundred and fifty francs.'

'Outrageous! I have earned more on the Matterhorn.'

The two men then proceeded to haggle tediously for some minutes, at the end of which period the sum had risen to two hundred and fifty francs. Rachel made a quick calculation: that amounted to over ten pounds, an obscene sum that Peter could not afford. Unless, she realised, his lies extended further than his summer plans.

Ulrich and Peter shook hands, and the guide departed, no doubt to visit the blacksmith to purchase the necessary equipment. Rachel jumped to her feet and rushed to confront him.

*

She caught him in the lobby of the hotel, a sunny hallway of wooden panels and mounted ibex heads. He leaned over the reception desk, chatting with the boy who manned it; he gave a carefree laugh at some shared joke.

She stood directly behind him. His ragged clothes, damaged by hard days on the mountain, were so at odds with the neat and respectable Peter she thought she knew that for a moment it seemed that a different man altogether stood before her.

'Peter!' she said sharply.

He turned. His eyes, which Rachel had always found so attractive, now widened in astonishment.

'Rachel! What are you doing here?'

She put a hand on each hip. 'You ought to know, *Herr* Merrick, unless the excitement of your great deeds has pushed me from your mind? You summoned me here so we could be married!'

He looked confused. 'I thought you were arriving tomorrow.'

'Did you need an extra day to hide your mountaineering costume and put on your morning coat and top hat? Do not take me for a fool!'

Now his expression became flinty. 'I do not care for your tone, madam. Control yourself.'

'How dare you speak to me like that!'

'I will speak to you in whatever fashion I choose.'

Peter took her arm, rather more firmly than she would have liked, and dragged her away from the bewildered receptionist.

'You listen to me. I am in the middle of something important here, and I can't have you making a mess of things.'

'You lied to me!'

'Only because I knew you would stop me if I told you the truth.'

'Then be honest with me now. What are you planning?'

'I assume you listened to my meeting with the guides?' He spoke with deep sarcasm, an emotion Rachel did not associate with him. 'I intend to climb the north face of the Eiger. I will be accompanied by one of the best guides in the canton. I shall succeed, and be hailed as a European hero, the greatest climber to have ever lived.'

Rachel didn't know how to respond. She realised that Peter was a man with many facets; why should it surprise her that he had chosen to hide some of those facets from her until now? After all, this was not a marriage of love. This union was for the security of her family and home.

'When are we to be married?' she said, no longer looking forward to the event, but dreading it.

'Since you are here, I suggest this evening. There is an English pastor staying in the hotel who has agreed to perform the ceremony.'

She felt a pang of disappointment. 'We are not going to be married in church?'

'My dear, the Swiss faith is Catholic; do you really want to be married in a Catholic ceremony? I doubt it would even be legal. I shall arrange for a discreet service this evening, before my departure for the Eigerwand.'

Peter left abruptly, leaving Rachel alone to cope with her feelings of abandonment, disappointment, and loss at everything she had hoped for her life.

CHAPTER SIXTEEN

REDEMPTION

9th of June, 1897

R ACHEL LOOKED AROUND for an escape, but could see no way out. It didn't look like much of a trap: just an ordinary private meeting room, identical to several others like it in the Bear Hotel. The old-fashioned wallpaper, whitewashed ceiling, and chandelier tinged with verdigris all felt so distant from the circumstances she had imagined for her wedding day. A table, laid with a white cloth, served as an altar. Someone had done their best to make it look colourful by placing a vase of flowers in the centre of the table, but the petals had wilted in the hot weather and she looked at the fading arrangement with a sense of dread. Everything felt wrong.

She wanted to look out of the window, enjoy a final glimpse of the world as a free woman. Her skirts rustled over the carpet as she walked. She tried not to think about her yellow dress, a disastrously bad colour for a willing bride. There had been no time to arrange anything better. She had expected at least a week in Grindelwald to prepare for the wedding and obtain a suitable outfit, but in the end Peter had instructed her to simply wear whatever she had with her. Thankfully only a few people would witness the ceremony.

Leaning on the windowsill, Rachel looked down to the courtyard below. Neither mountain nor glacier graced the view from the west wing of the hotel. Three storeys straight down to the yard, a pair of street Arabs played with sticks and a dog panted in a strip of shade.

A door creaked behind her, and Rachel turned to see the pastor enter the room, the Reverend Saxon. She had only spoken to the elderly gentleman once, an hour before. He had kindly agreed to perform the ceremony, being the only English clergyman in town.

'Have you seen Peter?' Rachel asked. She felt nervous and short of breath.

'Good afternoon, Miss Elliot. I believe Mr Merrick is looking for some witnesses for the marriage.'

The pastor said the words in the kindliest possible way, but there could be no escape from the implied criticism: that a wedding should be planned, a happy occasion, witnessed by the family and friends of the couple.

'How many witnesses are required?'

'By law, two.' The priest now sat on one of the chairs that had been left strewn about the room by the previous occupants. 'My dear, why don't you sit with me for a moment and compose yourself?'

She felt nervous and flushed. Perhaps his advice was sound. Rachel sat down; her corset creaked from the strain, but she had asked Sarah to lace it extra tightly for her wedding. Even if Peter didn't care about appearances, she did.

'You are very kind.'

'If you will excuse the impertinence, I feel bound by duty to express my concern. This is not the wedding you want, is it?'

Could she be read so easily? She had always tried to hide her feelings behind a mask of sarcasm and aloofness, a tactic that had protected her for all her adult life. Nobody had really seen through that shield except Jones, and his behaviour baffled her. Now, after a very trying few weeks, she felt that her defences were no longer sufficient.

'I had dreamed of something less austere,' she admitted. 'But he is fond of me, I am sure of it.'

'I hope so,' the elderly man murmured. 'Marriage without love is all too common, but is it worth it? The young do not think ahead and consider their old age.'

'Perhaps it is my place to marry without love.'

The door opened behind them, and Peter Merrick stepped into the room. He greeted them with a smile that seemed to encompass the world; indeed, he looked so different that Rachel began to believe that their quarrel had never happened. He wore his best morning suit, with starched collar and tie, and a low top hat that shone in the sunlight. He had shaved, too, and looked less wild. This was the Peter she knew.

She rose and greeted him with a smile. 'My dear—'

'We don't have much time for this,' Peter said, cutting her off. 'I have found some witnesses.'

His impatience offended her, and she felt her defiance return. 'Why do we not have more time?'

'I will discuss it with you later.' He turned his back to her and escorted the witnesses into the room.

The first witness was a local man, afflicted with cretinism, short and remarkably dirty. He shuffled into the room and began picking his nose. To her surprise, the second witness turned out to be none other than Professor Collie, and the sight of his familiar face made her feel unexpectedly weepy. What could he be doing here? He must have come for the Eiger, she decided. She rose to her feet, and the rush of blood to her head, released from her constricting clothing, made her feel faint.

After kissing her hand, Collie stepped back and studied her.

'Miss Elliot, this is a happy occasion.' His tone carried no conviction. 'It would be my pleasure to help in any way I can. When will the other guests be arriving, if you don't mind me asking? I have an appointment that cannot be missed in an hour.'

Rachel caught Peter's eye. He gave a tiny shrug, dismissing the question.

'There will be no other guests,' she said.

*

Once the meagre crowd had assembled — Peter and Rachel, the two witnesses standing behind them, and the pastor facing them in front — the Reverend Saxon began the ceremony.

'My friends, this is one of the more unusual marriages I have conducted in my years as a clergyman. It is my hope that the simple surroundings we find ourselves in may be compensated for by the love and commitment in the hearts of the betrothed.' He gave Rachel a long look. 'Before I begin, may I have the names of the witnesses?'

The cretin, who had been shifting about on his feet, said his name in a sullen Swiss accent. Professor Collie gave his name, title, and place of residence.

'And do either of you know of any reason why this marriage may not lawfully take place?'

Rachel looked over her shoulder at Professor Collie. Their eyes met, his expression grave, but he did not speak. Part of her wished he would stop the proceedings and save her from her fate, but he gave her a look that silently communicated the truth that she already knew, deep down: your destiny is in your own hands; I will do nothing to interfere. Perhaps she imagined it, but something in his expression also appealed to her conscience, and served as a reminder that another man loved her — a man who treated her as an equal, not a possession.

The Oberlander said nothing at all. He didn't care that these events would affect Rachel's happiness forever.

Did she truly have no choice? Was her fate signed and sealed already, as she believed, or could she change the future, even now, seconds away from the irrevocable moment? Perhaps Jones would burst into the room and sweep her away, take the responsibility away from her. She stared at the closed door, willing it to open, but it remained shut. She would have to make this decision for herself.

Reverend Saxon was speaking again, she now realised. The last seconds seemed to be slipping away much too quickly. Her mouth felt dry; her heart hammered in her chest; for a moment she thought she knew what it must feel like to be led to the gallows. This was all terribly, terribly wrong. How could she sacrifice her future happiness for the hope of security built on a foundation of lies?

'—and do you, Rachel Millicent Elliot, take this man, Peter Merrick, to be your lawful wedded husband—'

She breathed in for what felt like the last time. 'I refuse. I will not marry this man. I will not!'

To her right, Peter recoiled. He stared at her through the eyes of a stranger. For the first time in their courtship, Rachel understood that she did not know this man at all.

'Behave yourself,' he whispered. 'This is not the time for jokes.'

'I am not joking! I will not marry a beast such as you, who has lied to me and treated me this poorly! I do not love you—I never have. I … I love someone else.'

Why had she said that? She wasn't even sure it was true.

Peter's eyes narrowed, and the wildness returned. 'I knew it. Well, it does not matter. Reverend, continue the ceremony.'

Reverend Saxon looked relieved that he would not have to continue. 'Young man, the lady does not wish to marry you. I have to say that I think she has made a wise decision.'

'That is not your place to say,' Peter snapped. 'I have to marry today, before …'

'Before you climb the Eigerwand?' Rachel said. 'Why must you marry me before you leave?'

'My plans are far beyond your understanding,' he said, turning away from her. 'If this old fool won't marry us, I'll find someone else who will. Come.'

She backed away from him, wanting nothing more than to flee the room. Suddenly he frightened her. Peter may be younger than her by a couple of years, but this new, contemptuous aggression frightened her. Clearly he was not used to people defying him.

As if sensing her thoughts, Professor Collie stepped forward and offered her his arm. 'Miss Elliot, if I can be of any assistance at all, you need not ask.' He gave Peter Merrick a look of pure hatred. 'This boy is not worthy of you.'

She took his arm gladly. 'I would be grateful if you would escort me to my room.'

'You will do no such thing!' Peter shouted, moving to stand in front of the door.

The Professor regarded him calmly. 'There is no cause for raised voices. The lady has made her position plain. You would do well to take it like a man and withdraw.'

Peter froze for a moment, like a cornered animal. His eyes flickered between the Professor and Rachel, as if measuring up the forces arrayed against him. Between Collie's strength and Rachel's defiance, he must have decided that he was outclassed, for the fight suddenly went out of him. He sighed and slumped.

'Very well, but I will not forget this.'

He stood to one side. Collie nodded and led Rachel out of the room, keeping an eye on Peter as they passed, as if suspecting some act of treachery. Once in the corridor, he closed the door behind them, and they began to walk briskly away.

'I cannot thank you enough for rescuing me, Professor. I feel immeasurably better now that I am out of that room.'

'The credit must go entirely to you. I already knew you were a brave lady, but that took some courage. That young man—Mr Merrick? I feel I know him.' Collie frowned.

'He often climbs in Wales and Scotland. I daresay you might have met in passing at Pen-y-Gwryd.'

'Perhaps.' He frowned again. 'He is a bad sort. Jones, on the other hand …' He broke off and looked embarrassed.

Rachel laughed and squeezed his arm as they walked. 'You need not fear; he has already told me.'

'He may have his faults, but he is one of the best men I have ever known, and he adores you.'

'I know. Please, may we talk about something else?'

'Forgive me. Now is not the time.'

Indeed it was not the time. Rachel felt a world of uncertainty waiting for her. With her engagement broken, she no longer knew what the future would hold. Of only one thing she could be certain: she did not wish to remain here, to witness the gruesome spectacle that would soon take place on the Eigerwand.

*

'I would like to check in, please.'

The receptionist looked up from her ledger and smiled the careful yet warm smile that the Swiss employed to make their guests feel at home. 'Good morning, madam. May I take your name?'

'Miss Elspeth Mornshaw.'

Not for the first time, Elspeth felt guilty at using a false name. When she had first married Aleister Crowley and everything had been wonderful, it felt like a denial of their marriage on the rare occasions when it suited her to adopt the pretence of maidenhood. Later it became a necessity to protect herself. Now she did it through habit.

It crossed her mind that she was a very damaged individual. Normal women did not behave in this way, using false names, smoking in public, kissing in public restaurants. She felt ashamed of herself. Aleister's mistreatment had left scars.

The girl behind the desk reached up to take her key from its peg. 'You will be in room twelve, Fraulein Mornshaw. Have you stayed with us before?'

'Yes. I do not require a guided tour, thank you.'

Hopefully that had not sounded too sarcastic. She felt tired after her journey. Why in the modern age, she wondered, did it still take two logistically challenging days to reach the Alps? Normally she enjoyed travelling, but under the circumstances she wished she had been able to impart a sense of urgency to the sluggish timetable.

The receptionist's smile remained fixed in place. 'No problem, madam. Dinner is served between—'

Elspeth stopped listening. She impatiently waited for the girl to hand over the key.

'—and you have a letter.'

'What?'

'The young English gentleman staying in room seven left it for you last night.'

The girl handed over a plain white envelope. Elspeth examined it carefully: it appeared to be normal in every respect; it had no particular scent or discolouration; it seemed to contain only a folded sheet of paper. It displayed her name in neat capitals on the front. With her room key finally in hand, Elspeth turned away from the desk and addressed the porter who waited with her luggage.

'Room twelve,' she snapped, 'and be careful with that trunk.'

She ducked into one of the wood-panelled corridors leading away from the lobby. Only when certain she was not being observed did she open the letter.

"To my wife:

"I have not heard from you in some considerable time. Nevertheless, I know you well, and although you think you have changed for the better, I believe that you will follow the trail I have laid for you. Everyone is going to come here: Jones, Collie, Raeburn, probably Eckenstein, all the press of Europe, and as many gawkers and wastrels that can fit into the appalling little train up from Interlaken. The audience for my triumph is assembling.

"Although I have done things that have cost me your affections and your trust, I believe that you still love me and will help me. I need your help, Elspeth; I need your fearless heart, your strength as a climber, your devious mind. This is going to be the hardest struggle of my life.

"I have suffered some setbacks, but I believe that I can still both humiliate Jones and emerge as the better man. I deserve this so much, after all the wrong that has been done to me.

"You are to take the train up to Alpiglen without delay, and start the climb up to our first camp. I will place a lantern on the ledge to guide you. Bring all of your equipment and provisions enough for a five day assault. My plan is to raid the supplies of Barkis and Holdstock and use their provisions to help me get to the top.

"I do not trust my guide. I would prefer to climb with someone on whom I can thoroughly rely.

"Your husband,

"E. A. Crowley Esq."

Elspeth read the letter again to digest its contents, then tore it up before depositing the remains in a nearby ashtray. Had she really been manipulated so easily? Surely not; she had her own reasons for journeying to Switzerland. It had not been difficult to make the necessary deductions after reading about the Eiger disaster in the newspaper, and observing the movements of police at Eckenstein Alpine Equipment. The only difficult part of the whole business had been ditching that tedious boy George Abraham.

Perhaps Aleister had paid someone to follow her and report on her movements. She knew that her husband had formidable mental powers, but she did not like to credit the hypothesis that he could manipulate her so easily.

How dare he presume that she would feel well enough to attempt the most difficult and dangerous climb in the Alps? Still recovering from serious injuries, her strength was not at its best. She had only felt able to discard her cane a short while ago.

However, the letter touched her in precisely the way her husband had intended it to. Perhaps he really could control her emotions. Despite everything he had done to her, knowledge of his evil nature did not prevent her from still loving him—and then there was her confusion of real and pretended feelings for Jones, the result of her shameful part in the plan to ruin him. It all seemed so complicated. Once, in the first year of her marriage, it had been much simpler.

Aleister would be alone on the wall, accompanied only by an incompetent guide. He could die. The thought made her go cold. Damn him, she thought: he knows exactly which strings to pull to get what he wants. Perhaps she really was as weak as she feared.

'Miss Mornshaw, what an unexpected pleasure.'

She turned to confront the person who had spoken to her. Professor Collie stood there, regarding her with a polite smile from a distance of a few paces. The thin man looked a little strained, she thought; no wonder, if he was here for the Eiger like everybody else. Although tempted to dismiss him and leave to decide what she would do, she had always been rather fond of the Professor

'What brings you to Grindelwald? The Eiger, no doubt?'

She laughed. 'I must confess that my curiosity has got the better of me.'

'I hope you are not planning an attempt? Even the conqueress of the Slanting Gully might find her skills outclassed on that wall.'

'I am not planning anything,' she said a little sharply. 'I … had heard that Jones might be here.'

'He and Raeburn ought to be arriving today. We are mounting an expedition to recover the bodies. He also hopes to meet his young lady here, but …' He broke off suddenly and looked guilty.

Very interesting, Elspeth thought. She laid a hand on his arm and smiled at him. 'Dear Professor Collie, I can keep a secret. Besides, there is nothing between Jones and me. Nothing you say will upset me.'

'I ought not to say.' Collie looked uncomfortable, caught between indiscretion and politeness.

'Come now, you cannot tease me like this!'

'No, it is not my place.' He lifted his cap. 'Good morning to you.'

'Damn,' she muttered as he walked away. She had the feeling that he had been on the verge of telling her something important. Perhaps she would have to try a different approach.

Elspeth marched back to the front desk, adjusting her demeanour to appear as angry and flustered as possible. The girl she had spoken to minutes before looked up in surprise.

'Is everything to your satisfaction, madam?'

When in doubt, raise your voice.

'The key does not work! It will not turn in the lock! Really, I had expected better service from a hotel of such reputation.'

'My apologies. I will call for someone to assist you.'

'Can you not do it yourself, you silly girl?'

The receptionist hesitated. The lobby was empty except for the two of them, no porters or footmen in sight.

'Very well. If you would give me your key, madam, I shall see to it.'

Elspeth handed over the key and watched as the poor girl hurried off in the direction of the stairs. It would only take her a few minutes to realise she had been fooled. Elspeth ducked behind the desk and scanned the grid of pigeon-holes, looking for room 7: Aleister's room.

It contained an envelope. She took it and hid it in her purse before stepping back in front of the desk.

"To Peter Merrick,

"To say that I am upset would be an understatement. You have used me & treated me terribly. I feel as if I never knew you at all, as if you have been wearing a mask all these months. My father told me it was a mistake to marry after so short an engagement, & I suppose he must have been right, for you have proven yourself to be one of the worst men I have ever known.

"I wish to end our engagement, & indeed I hope we never meet again.

"Rachel M. Elliot."

Elspeth read the letter again, unable to fully digest its contents. Her husband had cheated on her using a false identity! Of course, she shouldn't be surprised. Aleister always did what he pleased. Elspeth may have confused feelings, but she felt no confusion where the duties of marriage were concerned—duties which Aleister had failed to honour. No doubt he would retort that she had not been entirely faithful either, but those instances had been ordered by Aleister himself, and if he used them as an excuse now then God help him, Elspeth thought savagely.

Her thoughts turned to the poor girl who had been ensnared and abandoned: Rachel Elliot. They had never been properly introduced, but had met in passing and had the acquaintance of Jones in common. Elspeth had once tried to warn Jones that a plot was afoot to ruin Rachel's reputation, but he had either not heeded the advice or had been unable to help her. She had never guessed the extent of the scheme.

She found Rachel Elliot's room easily enough: the only closed door in a corridor alive with maids in blue uniforms, scurrying to and fro changing bed linen, dusting, and sweeping. Although she wasn't supposed to be here, the servants did not bother Elspeth. She found a confident poise and determined stride sufficient to dissuade any attention.

A *"Bitte nicht stören"* sign hung under the doorknob. Elspeth hesitated for a moment, suddenly unsure of what to do next. Planning had never been her strong point. If she paused too long in front of a closed door, one of the maids would notice her and she would be questioned. Worse, she realised that a strange man was coming along the corridor in her direction. There could be no escape without getting past him.

She made her decision, and reached out to turn the knob. Predictably, it was locked. Should she knock?

Before she could do anything, the stranger reached her. He wore city clothing: knee-length overcoat, bowler hat, leather gloves. A greying moustache lent a certain distinction to his face, and with intelligent eyes the newcomer studied Elspeth, who must have appeared cornered and wary.

He smiled. 'You seem frightened. Are you here to see Miss Elliot? Do you mind if I ask your name?'

'Do you not offer yours in return?'

He raised his hat, revealing thinning hair.

'Inspector Warrington, Scotland Yard. Your accent … Edinburgh, I believe?' His smile became one of puzzlement. 'I think I can guess your name. How remarkable that you should end up here.'

He turned to the door and gave two sharp knocks, then said 'Warrington' when a male voice asked who was calling.

Elspeth felt her confusion grow. Whatever could be happening? Was this the detective who had hounded Aleister these past few months? Could Aleister possibly be in that room right now, perhaps begging Rachel's forgiveness? Horrible possibilities flashed through her mind. She did not want to be here.

She turned away, but achieved only a few steps before Warrington's order stopped her.

'Come back at once!'

She increased her pace, unwilling to attract attention but desperate to escape. A door opened behind her, followed by another shout from Warrington:

'Jones, fetch her back here!'

Elspeth broke into a run, no small feat in her restrictive clothing but something she had practiced in anticipation of situations like this. Heads turned; she crashed into a maid carrying a pile of laundry, which erupted about them both in a smothering cloud. Hands grabbed her from behind, and she fought like a cat to get free, snarling and clawing through the sheets that enveloped her.

'Elspeth! Elspeth, calm down; it's me, Jones.'

'Let go of me!'

He let go abruptly, and she tore the sheet away. Jones stood there, hands held uselessly at his sides, as if embarrassed at what he had done. He looked strong and healthy as ever, but his handsome face seemed to be shadowed by worry.

To her surprise she now felt safe, even though Jones was the one who had tried to capture her. She still felt something for him; quite what, she could not decide.

'I'm sorry,' he said awkwardly. 'I tried to protect you, but Warrington found out. Why are you here?'

'To see Rachel Elliot.'

The Inspector appeared and glared at the maid, who gathered up her sheets and hurried away. Warrington now smiled at Elspeth in an almost gentle fashion.

'I regret alarming you, but there is much we must discuss. Please … after you.'

His threatening undertone did not permit thoughts of disobedience. With Jones lightly holding her arm and the Inspector taking up the rear, Elspeth had no choice but to do as she was told.

*

Despite the advanced stage of the morning, curtains guarded every window and let in only chinks of light. A gas lamp hissed on a low setting. Rachel Elliot sat on the edge of her bed, still and silent, the centre of the grief in the room. Jones sat down next to her and took her hand. The sombre atmosphere made Elspeth think of bereavement, but nevertheless she felt an unexpected stab of jealousy at their closeness.

Warrington retired to the far side of the chamber and made himself comfortable, crossing his legs and jotting something down in his notebook.

Elspeth watched him, observed the glint of his eyes roving around the room. She wondered how she could remove this threat.

'Say what you have come to say,' Warrington ordered.

'I do not wish to say anything in front of you.'

'Then I shall call my constables in to arrest you, and we may discuss this matter at leisure with the Bernese Kriminalpolizei. Wouldn't you prefer a nice informal interview?'

Perhaps it made no difference, she wondered. Faced with the people she had conspired to hurt, she could no longer recall her motivations with any great clarity.

'Your husband is a criminal who has lied, bribed, and murdered,' Warrington continued in his reasonable tone. 'He has used you, broken you, and cast you aside. Think on that, then say your piece.'

She could hardly bear to look at Rachel. Their eyes met. Rachel's gaze conveyed sadness and confusion, but also a furious strength, a gathering of forces before the battle. Time to confess.

'Peter Merrick is already married to me.'

The words came out in a rush. She had planned to use a tone of regretful dignity, but stage fright had made her nervous. Rachel did not react. Jones, however, turned white and gripped her hand.

'That is impossible,' she said at length. 'You are married to Aleister Crowley.'

'My dear,' Jones began, 'we know how fond Crowley is of adopting alternative personalities.'

Now Rachel closed her eyes. 'I refuse to believe that.'

'This is my wedding ring,' Elspeth said, waving the gold band in front of the girl's face. 'We were married in Edinburgh in 1895. I also have a photograph of us on our wedding day.'

Warrington shifted in his chair. 'Give it to me, please. I shall require it as evidence.'

'Rachel needs to see it first.'

'I do not wish to see it!'

Jones was stroking her hand, trying to soothe her. 'Perhaps it's for the best.'

The photograph had resided in a silver locket for these past two and a half years. Elspeth carried it for many reasons: as a ghost of old happiness, a source of strength, a warning. The talisman helped to mediate her conflicting feelings when it came to Aleister, and always reminded her of the fact that whatever else might have happened, they were still married.

She lifted the chain from around her neck, opened the clasp, and handed the locket to Rachel.

'I'm sorry, truly I am,' she added, and meant it. Faced with the consequences of her actions, she felt overwhelmed with regret.

Rachel did not react for what seemed like a long time. She stared at the locket, closed the case, turned it over in her hands as if the smooth silver backing would tell her more than the photograph itself. Jones asked to look, and she gave it to him. He glanced at it for only an instant before handing it back to Elspeth.

'It explains everything,' he said.

Rachel shook her head, frowning. 'What have I ever done to hurt him? Why did he choose me?'

'To strike at Jones, through you,' Elspeth said. 'It's his way.'

'I hate him, and I hate you for helping him.'

Elspeth nodded and stepped away. 'I think I deserve that.'

Jones looked up at her, mistrust replaced with pity and perhaps the beginning of a new respect. He said nothing. Would he be considering how this news affected his plans? With Aleister already on the north face, and the law close behind him, this would not end well even if he survived the Eiger. Perhaps the time had come to cleanse her conscience.

'I want to help you,' Elspeth said impulsively. 'I know how Aleister's mind works.'

Inspector Warrington, who had been writing for some minutes, now snapped his notebook shut and rose from his chair.

'Give me the locket,' he instructed.

Jones glanced at Elspeth for permission, then handed it over. Warrington looked at it for a second and put it into his pocket.

'Superb.' He seemed pleased. 'That's another charge we can bring against the scoundrel. Mrs Crowley, how do you believe you can help us?'

'My husband's plan is to use the supplies left behind by Barkis and Holdstock, which is probably one reason why he sent them up there in the first place, to leave supplies for his own attempt. He likes to travel light. If he fails to reach the Ice Trap, he will not have enough gear or food to finish the climb.'

Jones looked disgusted. 'He is going to rifle through the bags of dead men!'

'He wants success, and this is his best way of obtaining it,' Elspeth pointed out. 'Your best chance to catch him is to get to the Ice Trap first. I can help you by delaying him.'

Inspector Warrington shook his head. 'What's to stop you helping Crowley instead of us?'

'I hate him! Can't you understand that? I hate him, and I hate myself for all the harm I have caused. I must do something to atone for it. Please, Inspector, let me help you.'

He looked surprised at this outburst. Elspeth had piled on the emotion in an attempt to manipulate him—it was so easy to do—but that did not make her desire for redemption any less genuine. She had failed to be a better person before. This time she would be strong.

'Very well,' the Inspector said at length, 'I shall give you protection in return, but I will break you if you betray us again. Jones, you can work out the fine points of the plan. I don't care how you do it, but I want you to give me Crowley.'

He left and closed the door behind him. The key turned with a click, and Elspeth realised they had been locked in. No doubt a constable would be standing guard in the corridor as well.

Elspeth looked at her husband's victims: the not-quite lovers, united in their determination to return their lives to the happiness they had once known. She thought back to the times she had shared with Jones, the difficult climbs, tobacco next to a fire, a kiss in a crowded restaurant. Then she remembered the affection with which he had spoken of Rachel. That was far more real than the deceitful connection she had cultivated with him. They deserved the chance of a happy life.

'I will accept Aleister's instruction to climb on the wall with him,' she said. 'I will join his team and pretend to be on his side, but I shall work for you. I shall prevent Aleister from making the first ascent of the north face of the Eiger.'

CHAPTER SEVENTEEN

ORDER OF BATTLE

11th of June, 1897

ELSPETH HEARD THE FALLING ROCK before she saw it. Silence gave way to an explosion from above, echoing around the vertical space locals called the Eigerwand. She stopped climbing and listened. Her ears strained to gather information about the approaching hazard.

More sound: a cacophony of crashes and bangs, confused by the echoes arriving from all sides, muffled by snow. The stone could be the size of a pebble and only a hundred feet above, or it could be a house-sized block falling from the summit. As the avalanche drew closer she could hear the buzzing, like a swarm of wasps. Given her exposed position on the lower cliffs, Elspeth could do little but cower against the wall and pray the rocks avoided her.

Suddenly it sounded more like an artillery barrage as the missiles exploded all around, spraying her with snow and chips of rock. A pebble struck the ledge near her face. It ricocheted like a bullet, and a fragment glanced the side of her forehead. Stunned for a moment, she fought to maintain balance. Any lapse of attention here would mean a long fall and a swift death.

The barrage ended, leaving the tang of sulphur and receding echoes. Aleister's voice called from far above, too late to make any difference:

'ROCKS BELOW!'

*

A hint of dawn helped her to find the route up to Aleister's camp. Hands, protected by fingerless gloves, caressed the rock above. Sometimes they touched snow, made hard and glassy by the sun, and she would swing an ice axe to hold fast and anchor herself. Sometimes she felt for the edges of the rock, searching for a good hold to pull up on—but she never dared pull too hard, for this lower cliff was a crumbling place, and as she climbed higher Elspeth felt a rising sense of commitment. She would not be able to come back down this way. Her boots found holds by contact, gripping the friable rock with their serrated edges, occasionally striking a spark as they skidded away. A lantern glinted out of the vast darkness above.

She had to fight to maintain focus. Anger battled with rising fear of what might lie ahead. She worried that she might lose her nerve if she thought too much about what she had committed herself to.

The route up to Aleister's camp seemed to be a wandering one. In the gloom, one frozen chimney looked very much like another, and on several occasions Elspeth found herself climbing into impossible terrain, and was forced to back down to the nearest ledge. She found her way by trial and error, until at last she could see the glow of the lantern on the roof of a cave a short distance above.

'Aleister!' she called. Although she had not shouted, her voice carried a long way in the silence.

No response. Perhaps they were climbing somewhere in the void above.

Just as she was about to call again, a rope came snaking down the slab and landed in a pile on the ledge beside her. She fumbled for the end in the snow, and tied it around her waist with freezing hands, hoping that someone reliable held the other end of the rope. The short climb up the slab proved to be a lot harder than expected, with powder snow coating all the holds, but perhaps she had simply stopped caring, knowing that the rope would catch her if she fell. She arrived at the bivouac ledge completely exhausted, hardly able to shoulder the weight of her rucksack.

Aleister reached out to grip her shoulder, preventing her from tumbling back over the edge. He urged her into the narrow cave, where they had to duck to avoid a roof that dripped with icicles. At first glance, the camp looked surprisingly empty. Two blankets lay folded side by side, with knapsacks as pillows. A few items of equipment occupied the remaining space on the ledge: a coiled rope, some pitons, a long axe for deep snow, and a pair of short axes for steep ice. A kettle simmered on a Primus burner. The spartan nature of Aleister's bivouac underlined his all-or-nothing strategy: climb fast, travel light, and use the provisions left behind by dead men. Well, Elspeth intended to upset that plan.

She could see little of him. The lantern's rays illuminated his smock and mittens, but did not penetrate far into his hood. Only those intense eyes glinted from within, watching her with curiosity.

'Thank you for coming. I'm glad you decided to help me.'

His humble words took her by surprise. She hadn't really thought ahead to this moment. Still confused by her feelings, but determined to make her husband pay for his treachery, she decided to act as Aleister would expect her to.

'I felt my duty was clear.'

He nodded. 'Indeed it is. I am glad we understand one another.'

At last, after their years of marriage, Elspeth felt she finally did understand him—but she didn't believe that he understood her.

Aleister turned away and started to coil the rope while Elspeth unpacked her belongings. No room had been left for her blanket. She wondered if they would be spending another night on this ledge, or if it was simply intended as a fall-back location in the event of a retreat.

'We plan to climb today,' Crowley said in response to her unspoken question. 'Almer is up there, checking the fixed ropes. It's lucky we found Holdstock's lower camp.'

Elspeth didn't think it made much of a camp. From this cramped ledge, the first Eiger expedition had led their sorties onto the upper cliff, navigating the complex ways above, trying to divine a route through the overhangs. They had died without gaining more than a thousand feet of ground, thanks to Aleister's cunning diversions. She wondered if he planned to follow their route, or if he knew of a safer way to reach the Ice Trap.

'So what is our plan?' she asked, not really believing he would tell her the truth.

He looked at her. 'We follow the fixed ropes. There is an alternative route, but I want to be sure of picking up every cache of food and gear Holdstock left behind. We won't survive if we can't scavenge for provisions. Do you understand that?'

'Death or glory. I see.'

'Precisely. I will risk everything I have to win this time. There's no point in it otherwise.'

Elspeth felt ill. How could he really believe that?

'What about me? What about the guide?'

'If I die, nothing matters anyway. All life is an illusion in the end.'

*

Jones felt tired and agitated. He had slept poorly last night, tormented by images of all the things that could go wrong. What right, he asked himself, did he have to put Elspeth in such danger? The girl had been consumed with remorse, hardly able to think clearly. He wondered where she was now.

He stepped out from the shade into the heat of the station platform. The arrivals board indicated that the first train from Interlaken would be here soon. A few people scattered about the station looked up at the sound of the approaching train: a man in a morning suit reading a newspaper; a young couple sitting on the bench, hand in hand; and a mountaineer, lean in build and ragged in clothing, sitting on his knapsack and gazing up at the Eiger.

The mountain seemed to glow today. Switzerland once again basked under clear skies and a hot sun. On the north walls of the giants, the spring snow would be growing crusty and rotten in places, while the deep freeze under the stars at night would build ice in the gullies. Jones wondered how long the good weather would last. The image of the Ice Trap, that deadly cave where Holdstock and Barkis had perished, haunted his thoughts and dreams.

The train squealed to a halt. Porters crowded the platform as the doors opened and the passengers disembarked. Jones scanned the crowd, wondering how many of the new arrivals had come for the Eigerwand: at least one, he thought as he saw Oscar Eckenstein swatting a porter out of the way and hefting a bag onto one shoulder.

'Be careful with that trunk!' he shouted back to a team of porters manhandling an enormous box out of the guard's cabin.

Finally he caught sight of Jones and began muscling through the crowd towards him. He stopped a few feet short and held out both hands in apology.

'I decided to come and see for myself what all the fuss is about,' Eckenstein said. 'I'm sorry I was angry with you. Will you let me help?'

'We'll have to talk to Inspector Warrington. He may not want you around.'

'Damn it, Jones, this is all my fault! I must do what I can. I've brought spare axes, waterproof ropes from Mr Beale, dozens of pitons and Pelton Rings.'

He seemed so contrite that, despite himself, Jones could not help but think better of his friend. Eckenstein could be so stubborn that sometimes it was easy to forget how helpful he could be when he felt like it.

Jones smiled. 'It's good to see you, anyway. Would you like a hand with the equipment?'

'No, best leave those idiots to it.' He looked back to the struggling porters. 'Keep it upright!' he shouted.

The porters did their best to load the box onto a waiting cart. Meanwhile, a crowd began to gather, among them several climbers. News would spread quickly that a case labelled "ECKENSTEIN ALPINE EQUIPMENT" had been delivered to the Bear Hotel. Within hours, everybody would know that Jones and his friends had designs on the north face of the Eiger.

'Perhaps I ought not to have stamped the company name on the box,' Eckenstein mused. 'I didn't think about trying to keep a low profile.'

'Makes no difference,' Jones said. 'News was bound to get out eventually.'

They walked in silence for a while. The town seemed busier today, swollen with a new supply of tourists, mountaineers, and adventure-seekers. A gang of children charged down the street, shouting and laughing; behind them rattled a line of hotel carriages, swollen with luggage, the horses snorting in the heat.

Jones could hear the clang of hammer against anvil. They turned a corner, and passed by the workshop of Herr Bhend, the blacksmith who manufactured everything from horseshoes to candlesticks, boot-nails to ice axes … and now, Jones noticed with alarm, ice claws. The front of the workshop was open for business, allowing passers-by to see inside. Bhend stood next to his anvil, holding a new claw up to the light, inspecting its points. The smith noticed that he was being observed, and smiled in welcome.

'Wie kann ich Ihnen helfen?'

Eckenstein had noticed the ice claw too, and seemed to be fighting a battle between his predisposition to be rude to strangers, and his respect for practical, scientific men.

'English,' he said abruptly, but stepped forward to introduce himself nevertheless.

'Ah, English! There are many from your country in Grindelwald this week. You would like me to make you an ice axe, sir?'

Jones followed Eckenstein into the workshop, which formed the ground floor of a prosperous house. It had a high gable like many buildings in Grindelwald, its shuttered windows flanked with colourful flower boxes. The workshop itself seemed dark in comparison with the sunlit street. A forge belched heat and sparks into the room.

Bhend wiped a sooty hand on his apron, and shook hands first with Eckenstein and then with Jones. They exchanged introductions.

'So, Herr Eckenstein, what can I help you with?'

'I'm actually an engineer myself. I could not help noticing that device you are working on. Would you mind explaining it to me?'

'These are my Steigeisen—or crampons, if you prefer French. I do not know the English word. The young English Herr has licensed the design to me. They allow you to climb up the ice, you see. Very useful for the brave climbers of today.' Bhend grinned proudly.

Eckenstein cursed. 'Crowley has been here! Crowley has actually been here peddling a design that I legally own to other manufacturers! I will beat some sense into the boy if I ever get my hands on him.'

This outburst seemed to confuse the blacksmith. 'My dear sirs, I do not understand. This design belongs to me now, and it is making me good money.'

'I wish you every success,' Eckenstein grunted, then turned to leave.

Once back out in the street, Jones turned on Eckenstein. 'Do you finally see what I have been trying to tell you all along? It is all part of a plan to destroy us. Crowley is already up there on the wall, after having told everyone he is doing it for the noble cause of recovering bodies. He has his blacksmith making equipment in his name. When people find out you've been making remarkably similar gear, and plan to finance and equip a second expedition, we shall be painted as the opportunists, not him!'

'All right, I need no more convincing,' Eckenstein said in a reasonable tone. 'To think that Crowley had the cheek to pass off my design as his own, after all I have been through to secure the patents!'

'Come now, it's not even the first time it has happened.'

'Our friend Crowley is a cunning little bastard, isn't he? You've got to admire how he has managed to trick everyone into thinking he is a noble hero.'

They continued walking, and soon arrived at the courtyard in front of the hotel. To Jones' delight, he noticed Raeburn and Collie sitting in the shade under a tree. They walked over directly to greet them. Everyone shook hands.

'How was your journey? Are the rooms to your satisfaction?'

Collie laughed. 'All is well, Jones. You look so anxious! Whatever is the matter with you? We are supposed to be on holiday.'

Eckenstein opened his mouth to say something stupid, Jones did not doubt, so he jabbed him in the ribs to keep him quiet for now. Raeburn knew a little about the Crowley story but Collie knew almost nothing. Jones dreaded having to tell the Professor the truth about why they were here. Their bargain with the police, and mission to capture Crowley, seemed shameful compared with Collie's noble ideals; he thought they would be climbing in the name of love, honour and duty.

To Jones' horror, he saw a familiar figure approach. Unlike Eckenstein's sensible approach to the hot climate, the newcomer sweated in his bowler hat and frock coat. Jones recognised the troublesome reporter, Alfred Varley. Had he followed them all the way from London?

'Mr Jones! Mr Eckenstein! One could hardly credit the coincidence. Here for the healthful mountain air, are we?' He smirked and pulled a notebook out of his pocket. 'And who else do we have here? May I have your names, gentlemen?'

Jones realised, unhappily, that he could not very well order Collie and Raeburn to remain silent. After obtaining their names, the reporter turned to address Collie, the member of the group with the highest social standing.

'Would you mind giving me a few lines for our little publication? The public is anxious for more news, sir.'

'Well,' Collie said, obviously flattered, 'perhaps I could provide a word or two.'

'Don't tell them anything,' Jones interrupted. 'This reporter is our enemy.'

Collie frowned. 'How can he possibly be against us? We have nothing to hide.'

'Is that so?' the reporter said with a chuckle. 'Explain to me your mission, if you please.'

'It is no secret. We intend to recover the bodies of our friends and return them to Grindelwald for a Christian funeral. I defy any man to find fault with that selfless ideal.'

Raeburn looked a little uncomfortable, and Eckenstein looked thoroughly ashamed.

Varley scribbled in his notebook, barely able to conceal his glee. The odious little pig must be loving this, Jones thought despondently.

'So,' Varley continued, 'you deny being opportunists whose sole mission is to climb the north face of the Eiger?'

'I would deny that accusation in the strongest possible terms. Who has said these things?'

'The evidence is hard to fault, Professor. Peter Merrick is the English hero who wishes to recover the bodies of his friends in the name of honour. The fact that you have come here after him and in secret, equipped with equipment obtained from fraudsters, is enough to convince me.'

Collie's mouth dropped open. He looked accusingly at Jones, who couldn't bring himself to meet the Professor's gaze.

'Well, well,' Varley said, putting his notebook back into his pocket, 'I see I have given you something to talk about. Good day, gentlemen. I'll be watching you through the telescopes once you're up there, and I think I speak for every British citizen when I say that I hope Merrick beats you.'

*

As the sun rose higher in the sky and still Ulrich Almer did not return from his reconnaissance, Elspeth began to suspect something had gone wrong. She had spoken little with her husband. Aleister, writing notes in his journal, ignored her presence on the ledge and indeed he might easily have forgotten

213

where he was; Elspeth remembered occasions during their marriage when he would drift away into his own world. Now he crouched in the farthest corner of the cave, scribbling in a rapid hand.

The dawn some hours earlier allowed Elspeth to see a little more of her surroundings. Perched far above the chalets of Alpiglen, their ledge commanded an eagle's eye view of the woods and meadows beneath. Grindelwald itself, larger than she had expected, sprawled beyond the forest; and beyond that, a gorge through the mountains led to Interlaken and Geneva. Closer to their position, the Wengernalp railway conveyed tourists to the pass of Kleine Scheidegg, famous for its views of the Oberland mountains. Its hotels would now be thronging with idlers and tourists, keen for closer views of the Eiger but not brave enough to climb on it themselves. Knowing that they were down there and she was up here gave her an intense thrill. Despite the dangers ahead, Elspeth knew this would be the adventure of her life.

She could see little of the wall above the ledge, but could feel a sense of vast space unlike anything else she had ever experienced. The mountain seemed to echo even when silent, which was rarely, for the sun had unleashed a relentless barrage of falling rocks and ice. Elspeth felt thankful for the roof of solid rock above their heads. More than once, avalanches thundered past nearby.

Glancing at the sun, she estimated the time to be nearly ten o'clock. Whatever could have happened to their guide? Climbing in the full heat of the day was not a sensible idea on a big cliff like this. Almer could be in serious trouble.

'What's the time?' she said aloud.

'Sixteen minutes past ten,' Crowley replied without looking up. 'To answer your next question, I do not know what has happened to Almer.'

'He must have been gone for hours. I thought he was just checking the ropes?'

Only now did Crowley deign to look at her. 'Thomas Holdstock fixed hundreds of feet of ropes, going in two different directions. Almer might have discovered damage that needed to be repaired, or perhaps he is investigating a different way. We must be patient.'

'I thought you wanted to reach the Ice Trap before Jones?'

'Jones and his clowns are still in Grindelwald. Trust me, a day spent checking for the correct way is an investment worth making.'

Elspeth stretched a little over the edge and tried to look up, beyond the roof of the cave. The sense of open space thrilled her, but she kept a firm hold of a piton ring, just in case. Above, she could see a line of cracks leading the way up a steep cliff, but no trace of their guide.

She considered the dilemma. On one hand, this delay could only help Jones' cause, and the longer they waited here the better; but on the other hand, she could not stand the idea of another human being suffering because of Crowley.

'I think we ought to climb up and help him.'

'I intend to stay here until the evening, then climb when the face has frozen again,' Crowley declared. 'If you wish to risk your life by going out there at this time of day, that is your own affair.'

His attitude infuriated her. She recalled previous arguments, usually over something trivial and domestic during their time in Edinburgh. He suffered from the delusion that his opinion could never be challenged. Perhaps it would do him good to be proven wrong.

Aware that she was not thinking calmly, but determined to do the right thing and help their guide, Elspeth picked up her sack and checked its contents: candle lantern, some salami and bread, flask of cold tea, spare pullover. She worked the frozen straps of her ice claws between her teeth to make them supple again, then tightened her laces and strapped the claws in place.

Crowley watched with amusement. After a moment, he handed her a knotted loop of rope with an attached Pelton Ring.

'You'll need this,' he said. 'Tie the loop around your waist. When you need to rest, clip the ring to one of the anchoring pitons for the fixed rope. Oh, and you had better take one of these hundred-foot lines in case you need to rope back down.'

She took the items without comment, stuffed the coil of rope into her sack and tied the loop around her waist as advised.

'Remember, this is the north face of the Eiger, not a dalliance on Ben Nevis with Jones.'

Without looking at him again, she took hold of the thick hawser leading up onto the wall, and began to climb.

*

The four climbers sat in silence as the cogwheel train ground uphill. They each sat a little apart, as if needing space for their thoughts and fears: Collie and Raeburn on the other side of the carriage, separated by an empty row of seats; Eckenstein just in front of Jones. The smoke from his pipe filled the compartment, but if it helped Eckenstein relax it had the opposite effect for everyone else.

'I ought to be coming with you,' Eckenstein observed after puffing away in silence for a while. 'It isn't right that I should be excluded.'

'In principle, my friend, I agree. I can think of no man I would rather have holding my rope. Inspector Warrington's word must be final, though.'

Eckenstein did not reply to that, and the others made no comment. The train continued slowly up the incline through the woods above the village. Jones pressed his nose to the window—he had deliberately chosen the left hand side of the carriage, to give the best view of the Eiger—but as yet could see nothing but the oppressive gloom of the pine forest. A marmot stood on its hind legs by the side of the track, watching the train go by.

Jones found his thoughts returning to his poor friend, Simon Barkis, who had died because of Crowley's schemes. Barkis' future had been bright: educated at Cambridge, one of the most naturally talented climbers of his generation, and a mind that was filled with love for all the beautiful things in the world. All that, gone. If Jones could do anything to help make up for the loss, he would consider his duty fulfilled.

He looked at the others. Raeburn scraped a file over the pick of one of his axes, honing the tip to a lethal point. The shaft, Jones noticed, no longer gleamed with new linseed oil: many adventures on the ice faces of Scotland had scuffed the wood. Collie stared out of the window to his right. That side of the carriage looked over the forest in the direction of Grindelwald, and Jones wondered what was going through the noble Professor's mind. He regretted the harsh words that had recently passed between them.

The train began to slow, and the conductor poked his head into the carriage to announce that the next stop would be Alpiglen.

Alpiglen consisted of a few ramshackle chalets and barns scattered throughout clearings in the forest. The train deposited them on the platform, and porters dumped their baggage in piles: depressingly large piles, Jones thought, as he considered the task of carrying all their gear and provisions up to the wall. Finally the train started to move again. A cold breeze blew down from the mountain, wafting away the steam from the engine, which drifted between the trees like morning mist.

Jones glanced up and down the platform. There was Raeburn, Professor Collie, and Eckenstein, over by the bags; and one other person standing apart, a slender figure wearing a cape and wide-brimmed hat. She—for it was obviously a woman—walked towards them, and as the steam cleared Jones recognised the graceful figure of Rachel Elliot. He had not been able to bring himself to say goodbye to her properly. In fact, they had spoken little since the failed wedding that had hurt her so much.

Collie caught his eye. He smiled and led the others away to divide the equipment into equal loads, leaving Jones and Rachel alone.

She stood a few paces away from him. The late afternoon sun, which had been hiding behind the clouds, now found a chink of blue sky and smiled down on the gloomy forest glade, transforming it to a fragrant alp of butterflies and flowers. Jones felt his spirits lift. The sunlight shone on Rachel's face, and he saw that her smile was one of genuine affection. Her eyes glittered with tears.

'I thought I was going to go home, but I found that I couldn't do it.'

'Why not?' Jones said.

'Because you are going to be fighting for me, up there, on the wall. How could I leave you alone?'

She took a step closer. He yearned to take her in his arms and tell her again that he loved her and would never stop fighting for her, but logic told him that this was not the time. Her place was in the valley, observing proceedings through the telescopes on the hotel balcony, not on the mountain wall they all feared.

She stepped into his embrace and rested her head against his chest. 'Let me help you. I'm frightened. I might never see you again.'

He had never seen her emotionally naked before, her mask completely abandoned. Her vulnerability surprised him. What had he been thinking? How could he have tried to slip away without seeing this wonderful person again?

Sometimes he wondered what all the struggle was for. Was he trying to beat Crowley in the name of justice, revenge, or simply to do the right thing? No: he did it for her. It had always been for her.

'Will you let me come with you?'

'Not on the wall,' Jones said firmly. 'Perhaps you can assist Eckenstein in running affairs at Kleine Scheidegg.'

'I want to be with you, not Eckenstein.'

He felt awkward. She may be saying the words he had wanted to hear for months now, but he was all too aware that only two days ago she had wanted to marry Peter Merrick, a man who, it turned out, did not even exist. She would naturally be confused. It was wrong to take advantage of her conflicted emotions.

She turned her face towards him. It would be so easy to forget about his misgivings and just …

'Stop being such a bloody gentleman and kiss her!' Eckenstein shouted from the other end of the platform.

Raeburn laughed, and Jones turned to see the three of them standing there watching him, all grinning. Collie looked particularly pleased, Jones noticed; he had always supported Jones in his pursuit of Miss Elliot.

Rachel stepped aside, her face a little flushed. The moment had slipped away, but their eyes met and for a moment Jones knew that the strength of his connection with this special woman would sustain him through the challenges ahead.

Above, the sun's last rays painted bands of gold over the cliffs of the Eiger. For one moment between day and night, the mountain smiled: dark fissures filled with light, snowfields gleamed, and a plume of spindrift danced over the summit like an elemental spirit.

A good omen? Jones hoped so.

CHAPTER EIGHTEEN

ÜBERHÄNGE

12th of June, 1897

THE OBSERVER

RACE FOR THE NORTH FACE

CONSTERNATION AS SECOND TEAM ESTABLISHES BASE CAMP

Today our man in Switzerland reports that a second team has begun its bid for the north face of the Eiger. This fearsome wall was the scene of a tragedy on the 5th or 6th of this month, when two men perished in the first attempt to climb what is certainly the most dangerous and foolhardy enterprise thus far imagined by mountain climbers.

A second expedition, led by P. Merrick and accompanied by his wife and a Swiss guide, was soon organised. Their noble intention, reported first in this newspaper, is to discover the fate of Holdstock's team, to recover their bodies, and learn what may be learned from the circumstances of their demise. Their effort has been generally applauded by the mountaineering community, although some stalwarts continue to condemn any climbing on the wall.

In direct competition with these heroes, the Progressive Mountaineering Club began to secretly plan their own effort. The fact that they kept their designs secret, and have chosen not to employ a guide, is proof enough of their dishonourable intentions. Sponsored by Eckenstein Alpine Equipment and obviously highly organised, it seems clear that the PMC may have been planning this expedition for weeks. The Progressive men, hungry for glory to give weight to their cause, have doggedly set their sights on the first ascent of the north face of the Eiger.

They care nothing for the noble objective of recovering the bodies of their dead comrades. Their only concern is cheap victory. I call for climbers to boycott the Progressive Mountaineering Club, and to join with us in our support of Peter Merrick, who climbs in the name of courage and humanity.

*

After hours of difficult climbing, and still no sign of the guide, Elspeth wondered if she had gone the wrong way. A profusion of vertical cliffs replaced the terraces and slabs of the lower wall, confounding her efforts to find the correct route. She had expected the fixed ropes to lead the way, but in reality sections of rope, pegged to the rock to protect the most difficult pitches, were interspersed by blank regions where only the odd scratch gave any indication that someone may have climbed that way before. The risk of getting trapped scared her, but failing to live up to her promises scared her even more.

Last night the blanket of darkness had protected her from the exposure of the wall. Now, alone and climbing increasingly serious ground, she began to feel unnerved. The cliffs grew steeper. Holds became smaller and coated with ice. She took her time and focused on the climbing. Angry thoughts of her husband melted away.

By the time she had climbed the cracked wall to a further ledge, the sun had sunk a little further in the sky, and shadows lengthened on the sunlit slab. The barrage of stonefall from above seemed to be more sporadic than it had been a few hours ago.

A faint cry reached her ears. So Almer was alive, somewhere up there, beyond the overhangs.

Where to go from the ledge? Features like this tended to accumulate snow, but a limestone roof a few feet above had protected it from avalanches. It would make a good bivouac place; she wondered if Holdstock and Barkis had stopped here. They had fixed a rope handrail along the length of the ledge. She grasped the rope and followed it right, but the ledge soon ended in a tremendous fissure, square-cut and glazed with old ice; it made her think of a tomb. The downdraft moaned in a crevice somewhere and blew flecks of dust into her eyes. She could not climb up that way, which left only one choice: to escape left, and find a way through the overhangs.

*

Jones found that he could not sleep. A cold breeze sneaked into the neck of his blanket, and the strange sounds of the wall invaded his dreams: bangs and rumbles, scrapes and slithers, the sigh of the wind and the crack of a distant glacier. He opened his eyes and looked down on a constellation of lights in the valley below. Although only a few miles away, Grindelwald might as well be on the moon; not a single person down there had ever been here before, and that fact alone made this mission worth it, no matter what else might happen. Exploring, pushing his body to the limits of endurance, were the things that made his life worth living.

He could not stop thinking about Rachel. He felt closer to her than ever before, but wished he had kissed her. Did they have a future together? Did she love him, as he believed, or had the turmoil and emotion of the past few days confused her? He had to come down from the north face alive, or he would never know.

The stars seemed to radiate cold. His scientific mind knew that a clear sky allowed heat to escape and a frost to form, but when he looked up he could imagine rays of ice penetrating the atmosphere from above. Mountains and stars always made a connection in his mind. Something about climbing, journeying into the strange and forbidden places of the world, suggested distant planets and the mechanics of the universe that would continue long after some cosmic accident had obliterated humanity. The timelessness of it all, the creak of the glacier as it marched through the aeons, watching the advance and fall of civilisations, spoke to the most basic part of his mind. Up here in the dark places, a man could touch eternity and see the futility of all human experience. Jones soaked in the perspective and let the mountain absorb him.

After a while, the need for warmth made him get up and move his limbs. They had selected a ledge fairly low on the cliff for their first bivouac, hidden in the maze of avalanche debris and shattered turrets of the lower face. Crowley, Elspeth and Almer would be at least a day's climbing above them yet. Careful not to wake the others, Jones moved to the edge of the platform and sat on a stone, swinging his legs over the abyss. He fired up the stove and packed a fistful of snow into the kettle.

Someone stirred behind him. Professor Collie, the rightmost of two caterpillar shapes on the ledge, sat upright to stretch and yawn.

'Can't sleep?' Collie whispered. He rose and stepped over to join him.

They warmed their hands over the simmering kettle.

'I have a lot to think about.'

Collie remained silent for a moment. Then: 'Have you considered the possibility that you may have over-reached yourself, my friend?'

'I know what I'm doing,' Jones insisted, but felt less than certain.

'Are you sure this is not about revenge?'

'Perhaps a little,' Jones admitted. 'Can you blame me for that?'

'I just wish we could be climbing for the sake of it, free from politics and trickery. Have you stopped to consider where we are? This is the greatest mountain wall in the Alps. Climbers spend their entire lives dreaming of such places. We are walking in the footsteps of history, and all you can think about is your feud with Crowley.'

Jones considered his response to that. Despite his friendship with Collie, their views on certain aspects of climbing differed greatly. Collie would never be a radical like Jones; his enthusiasm for the progressive ethos was cautious at best, and deep down he would always be of the old school, an explorer but not a rock-gymnast. Unlike Jones, he would never seek out the most difficult line on a mountain just for the sake of it.

'Why have you come with me?' Jones said finally. 'I know you don't agree with how this climb is being conducted.'

'To keep a watchful eye on you, dear boy!' Collie added tea to the kettle. 'Look here, we are not alike. Sometimes I think our bond is stronger because of it. We may be climbing on the Eiger for all the wrong reasons, but after all that, Crowley is the antagonist here, not us. Have you decided what you will do when we catch up with him, by the way?'

Jones had turned this point over in his mind many times. Warrington wanted him to bring Crowley down unharmed, but how would he accomplish that? Part of him was tempted to push Crowley to his death. He had never been a violent man, but if Elspeth helped him, perhaps he could find the strength to do it.

'Perhaps if cloud shrouded the mountain …' Jones mused.

'If bad weather comes in, we're in trouble anyway,' Collie said severely. 'Your thoughts are muddled with notions of revenge and victory, and to confuse matters further you are in love.'

Jones nodded, thankful for Collie's strong moral guidance. He took the kettle from his friend and poured a cup of tea through the strainer.

'If you feel it necessary, you are to take over leadership from me.'

'I think we can trust your judgement for now, but will you let me be your conscience? Come on, let's wake Raeburn so we can begin the climb.'

*

The sound of heavy machinery outside the window woke Rachel with a start. She lay still for a minute or two before opening her eyes, listening to the sounds of the world outside: the chug and hiss of a steam engine, breaking rocks, countless pickaxes. Closer, she could hear scurrying feet in the corridor and the ringing of servants' bells. Finally she opened her eyes and looked at the clock on the unfamiliar bedside table. Eight o'clock in the morning: time to wake up and face the day.

The facts of her situation came back to her. This was Kleine Scheidegg, the high pass beneath the Eiger, and she had come here with Oscar Eckenstein (a man she little knew and liked even less) to help manage Jones' expedition from ground level.

Images from her disastrous attempt at marriage kept running through her mind: Peter's sneer, her yellow dress, the dead flowers. Her hands shook when she remembered that she had nearly married Aleister Crowley. Instinct told her to run away, but for Jones' sake she fought to control her fears.

Dear Jones. When his face drifted into her thoughts, she felt both calm and excited, if such a combination were possible. She could finally admit that she had been suppressing thoughts about him for a long time. Now that she was free, she wanted to act on them. Was that too impulsive? Perhaps, but taking the sensible course had brought her nothing but sorrow.

Light flooded into the room. She must have drifted off again. A maid deposited a tea tray next to her bed.

'Good morning, ma'am.'

'Good morning,' Rachel replied sleepily. She focused on the girl's face, and realised it was her servant Sarah Collins. 'Good heavens—Sarah! I am sorry, I left Grindelwald in something of a rush …'

Rachel had completely forgotten about Sarah in her hurry to follow Jones.

'No matter, ma'am,' Sarah said. 'I caught the first train up this morning. It's a lovely day for your man to be climbing.'

'Oh, I hope so.' Then Rachel remembered her situation, and added, 'Not that I am involved with the gentleman, of course.'

Sarah looked confused. 'I was talking about Mr Merrick.'

Panic seized her, and she felt a powerful urge to vomit. She sat up in bed and closed her eyes. After concentrating and clearing her thoughts, the wave of nausea passed.

'Are you unwell?'

She opened her eyes again; Sarah looked concerned.

'I'm fine. Just … don't mention that man to me ever again. I can't bear to hear his name.'

She set out to explore her surroundings after breakfast. Two hotels occupied the Scheidegg: Bellevue, where she had found lodgings (and coincidentally the same name as the hotel she had visited in Bern), and the Hotel des Alpes, which offered newer and more luxurious accommodation. Her Baedeker guide mentioned only the Bellevue, and the train station that served Grindelwald and Wengen. Scaffolding obscured parts of the new railway line, which would eventually reach all the way to the summit of the Jungfrau. At present the cutting ended abruptly a few hundred yards up the hill amid a chaos of machinery and labourers.

She stepped out from under the balcony into the glare of the morning. Fair-weather clouds scurried across the sky, high above the level of the summits. For today at least, the weather would continue fine.

Reading on, her guidebook informed her that Kleine Scheidegg occupied a col at almost seven thousand feet, and had enjoyed recent popularity thanks to its fresh mountain air and splendid views, qualities which could be appreciated best from the top of the nearby Lauberhorn. Rachel noted a path winding its way up the green hillside between patches of snow. Perhaps she would make the ascent later, but for now she wanted to get a little higher so she could see the mountains, currently obscured behind Bellevue's five storeys of red brick.

Five minutes of walking brought her to a flat section in the path. Thanks to the altitude, the climb proved more strenuous than expected; she had never been this high before, and the thin air required quicker and deeper breaths. Almost seven thousand feet! Why, even Snowdon would only protrude a few yards above the rooftops of Grindelwald, all the way down there.

She turned to look at the view, and gasped.

The mountains of the Oberland that she had glimpsed from Bern now rose as precipitous walls to the south, dominating the sky: Eiger, Mönch, Jungfrau, Silberhorn. Rachel had never before felt so awed by anything. From Grindelwald the mountains loomed large, but as picturesque scenery; here they were like gods.

The Eigerwand was the biggest thing she had ever seen in her life. The overwhelming shadow of the wall devoured all individual features, made scale meaningless. It dominated the valley like a vast tombstone, or the biggest hawk in the world arched over its prey. In that moment Rachel lost all her pretensions as a climber. She knew, no matter how hard she may climb in the British mountains, that she would never belong in a place like that. The mountain would beat her out of sheer intimidation. No wonder people said that only the insane would climb it.

She scanned the cliffs, looking for any sign of movement. Where could Jones be? Perhaps she was even looking at him without realising. She remembered the telescopes on the hotel balcony, and hurried back down the path to get a closer look at the mountain.

The balcony hugged the east and south sides of the building, thronging with tourists of all nationalities and classes. Many leaned over the railings to take in the views, while others sat at the little round tables dotted here and there, eating breakfast and drinking coffee. Rachel elbowed her way through the crowd. The telescopes occupied a terrace free from tables a little distance away. The crowd seemed even denser there; no doubt everyone wanted a closer view of the drama on the wall. She made her way towards it.

'I wondered when you would drag yourself out of bed.'

Rachel turned, outraged. Oscar Eckenstein lounged at one of the tables near the telescope balcony. He wore a wide-brimmed hat and dark glasses, just like any tourist. Only the pungent smell of his pipe gave him away. An

English newspaper lay on the table, together with an untouched plate of bread and cheese.

'Sit down,' he instructed. 'Let's wait until the vultures lose interest in their prey.'

She took a chair opposite him, feeling sulky and disagreeable.

'All the telescopes are taken. We might have to wait hours.'

'Don't be silly. I've spoken to Herr Seiler.'

Rachel did not know who Herr Seiler was, but she had resolved to be helpful to Jones if she could not climb with him, and unfortunately that meant being helpful to Mr Eckenstein.

'What are we doing here?' She tried to sound less petulant this time.

'Watching the watchers.' Eckenstein nodded at the telescope on the right hand side of the balcony. 'Observe that fellow. He works for Reuters, name of Johnson. We can rely on him to be broadly sympathetic. The chap to his left is called Donders; he works for Tages-Anzeiger and his only concern is that the team with the Swiss guide gets to the top.'

Rachel observed the crowd more closely. Seven or eight men milled around the telescopes, with three actually operating them at any given time. All of them, she now realised, must be journalists. Tourists hovered at the balcony's edge, but she doubted they would get a chance to use the telescopes.

'Look at those twits,' Eckenstein commented, nodding in the direction of three men in mountaineering dress. 'Spineless, pathetic, fresh-faced twits.'

Rachel looked at the climbers Eckenstein had pointed out, but could see nothing wrong with them. They leaned over the railing, gazing at the Eiger with eager expressions, shading their eyes and scanning the wall. All three wore linen guide's jackets, climbing boots, and felt hats.

'What's wrong with them?'

'No sun burn, that's what! I saw those imbeciles in town yesterday. They're posers, here to lounge around on hotel balconies and pretend they're climbers. If they were real men they would be on a mountain by now.'

Although Rachel believed this to be unfair, she had to admit Eckenstein was probably right. She had seen a lot of men in Grindelwald wearing climbing dress who had obviously never been near a mountain before in their lives. Pretending to be a mountaineer must have become the new fashion. The public loved a good adventure story, and the north face of the Eiger certainly provided one.

Eckenstein poured her a cup of tea, then checked his pocket watch. 'Drink it quickly.'

'Why?'

She hardly had time to take a sip before a footman appeared to clear the balcony. The journalists protested but soon filed out of the way, hanging on in the margins to see what happened next.

The footman approached their table and bowed. Eckenstein scowled at him.

'Herr Eckenstein, you are welcome to use our telescopes at your leisure.'

Eckenstein waved him away without giving him a tip.

'Now everyone is watching the platform,' he grumbled when the footman had gone. 'You'd better use the telescopes first. Nobody knows who you are, but people are bound to be watching me.'

Rachel looked up and down the balcony. Nobody seemed to be paying any attention to them, but nevertheless she felt reluctant to step into full view. Why should they have to hide? They had done nothing wrong. Conscious that everyone would be looking, she stepped out onto the balcony and selected a telescope.

The footman showed her how to operate it. She had never used a telescope before, and found it surprisingly difficult to make it point at precisely the spot she desired.

'Which team are you interested in, miss?' the footman asked.

'Both.' She hesitated. 'Show me the lower climbers.'

He adjusted the telescope's controls, then stepped aside. Rachel peered through the eyepiece, and a section of cliff leapt into view.

A band of dirty ice, sandwiched between rocks, slashed the scene. At first, she could get no sense of scale, and could not determine the size of the feature; but then she noticed the climbers. A rope trailed from a tiny figure high up on the ice. Equipped with two short axes, he moved with a grace that only two climbers in the world possessed on steep ice: Jones and Raeburn. She wondered which of them it could be. Then he turned his head slightly, and Rachel could discern a quality of expression and glint of spectacles that made her heart race.

He seemed poised and in control. The rope hung from his waist down to the second man, wearing a deerstalker and smoking a pipe; that must be Collie, crouched in a niche to one side of the cascade, tied to pitons embedded in the ice. The rope led down beneath him out of the frame.

'The PMC team are going a different way,' the footman commented. 'I saw the fixed ropes yesterday, but they have chosen a gully below and left of them. I think they will soon overtake Merrick's team.'

Rachel drew in a sharp breath at the mention of his name, but the nausea did not return this time.

'Show me Merrick, please.'

The footman fiddled with the controls again. After a moment: 'I am sorry, miss, but I can only find the lady.'

She grabbed the telescope, eager for a view of her rival. She had no logical cause to dislike Elspeth—after all, she seemed to be on their side—but she could not suppress her hatred of the younger, braver, less conventional woman.

It took a moment to understand what the telescope now showed her. Elspeth seemed to be paralysed in an awkward position on a cliff face. Scrutiny of the scene revealed that she was anchored to a single piton, her boots balancing on tiny holds. The image shocked Rachel. She could imagine how frightening being cragfast in such a place would be.

Rachel twisted the dial, widening the view to show a larger portion of the face. Elspeth seemed to be trapped in the centre of a massive overhanging cliff. Over to the left, where Jones and his friends made steady progress, ice gullies slanted left and then back right around the bottom of the overhangs. Above all this, the Ice Trap nestled in a band of crag like a spider in the middle of its web.

She focused on the Ice Trap. The grave of Holdstock and Barkis looked fearsome: a column of blue ice led up to a cave, filled in with snow and guarded by icicles clinging to its roof. Above it, more vertical ice climbed a gully to emerge at an icefield in the centre of the north face. Rachel could not imagine a worse place to be trapped, yet that cave was the objective of both climbing teams.

She left the telescope and returned to her seat beside Eckenstein.

He pretended to study his newspaper. 'Well? What could you see?'

Rachel outlined her discoveries in a low voice, conscious that the reporters could not have gone far. Within moments they had jumped on the telescopes again, but Eckenstein did not seem to care that he had not seen events unfolding with his own eyes.

'Perhaps that half-witted Scottish girl will be of some use to us after all,' he mused. 'If what you say is true, she is successfully delaying Crowley while Jones bypasses the main difficulties. He's bound to overtake them.'

Rachel still felt uneasy. What if Jones came up against unexpected difficulties and Crowley got to the Ice Trap first? Strengthened by supplies and equipment left by the Holdstock expedition, there would be nothing to stop him from climbing the face and escaping.

'I wish there was something we could do to help.'

'We are responsible for fending off the press, monitoring the safety of our friends, and organising a relief expedition if necessary. What more do you want to do?'

'I feel so useless, watching in comfort while Jones is struggling for his life up there—and everyone thinks Crowley is the hero!'

Eckenstein shrugged. 'If Crowley climbs the Eigerwand, his crimes will be forgotten by the public. They will love him.'

'Only because they don't know the truth.'

Then an idea came to her. Perhaps there was a way she could help Jones, even from down here in the safety of the valley.

*

Elspeth took off her right mitten and chewed her knuckles to warm them a little. Her hands felt stiff after a night of clinging to the rock, supported only by a single piton driven into a crack above her head. She untied her waist loop from the piton now, and hung onto the iron ring for support while loosening the knot. It didn't want to come undone. She pulled harder, cursing her bad luck, but on second thoughts she felt glad it had held fast until now.

The previous day had not gone well. After her decision to take the left turn at the ledge, the terrain had become increasingly serious, blank walls capped with overhangs that dripped with ice. A perilous way existed between these dangers. She followed it because she had to; after traversing so far left, she no longer had the option of roping back down. The only way out was up, and as the holds became smaller and the exposure of the wall ate away at her calm, Elspeth found it increasingly difficult to fight back the fear.

Aleister must have known the dangers she would face, climbing alone. Perhaps this was merely another of his elaborate punishments for disobedience. During their marriage he had often exhibited casual sadism and a lack of empathy; why should she expect anything better from him on the north face of the Eiger?

Time to climb again. After forcing a morsel of food between her lips, chewing it with some snow to delay dehydration, she stretched her limbs and prepared herself for the ordeal ahead.

Then she heard a faint voice; just a muttered curse, in German, some distance above.

'Is that you, Almer?' she cried.

'*Ja! Hilfe mich!*'

She forced herself to climb. After a step left, the rope tied to the pitons led straight up. She found it difficult to grip the thick hawser, sheathed with ice after an overnight frost, and only the adhesion of her woollen mitts gave her any purchase at all. Looking up, a cornice of snow slumped over the top of the crag. Someone had cut a slot just big enough to admit a person.

By the time she reached the snow slope above the cornice, pocked by the impact of a thousand stones, she felt a little more like herself. This was climbing, after all—the passion of her life! She studied the snow for footprints, and followed the traces to the top of the slope, where another rock wall prevented her from climbing any higher. This cone of avalanche debris seemed to be poised in the exact centre of this portion of the face, a sanctuary amongst the overhangs. She kicked a stone off the edge, and it dropped straight down without hitting anything for hundreds of feet. Looking up, the terrain seemed even more inaccessible. Holdstock had certainly found no way up there.

'Hilfe!'

Almer sounded much closer now, perhaps just round the corner. The footprints stayed close to the upper edge of the snow, where water running down the rock had melted a deep crevasse. Almer must have clung to holds on the rock as he crabbed across the slope. Without the security of a fixed rope, Elspeth decided to do the same.

She found Almer sheltering in the crevasse around the corner, taking advantage of a bulge in the rock above to shelter from stonefall. He clutched an oilskin around his shoulders, but had not used a piton to secure himself. His lined face and hollow eyes told the story of the night he had spent in this eagle's nest; but unlike Elspeth, a woman in the first flush of her youth, Almer was an old man and less able to cope with such hardships. He coughed and clutched his arms to his chest as she approached.

'Do you have a little food?'

Elspeth rummaged in her pockets, and found her last crust of bread, which she gave to the guide. He wolfed it down without comment. After a moment he seemed to rally a little, perhaps cheered by the sensation of food in his belly. She hoped Aleister would bring some more food up with him. So far his prediction of finding provisions left behind by Holdstock had not come true.

'What are we going to do now?' she asked Almer.

'I should never have allowed us to split up,' Almer said with bitterness. 'Your husband should listen to the advice of his guide.'

'Perhaps, but he will be here shortly. Things will be easier when we are a roped team again.'

'There is certainly no way down from here.' Almer shuddered at the awesome exposure they could both feel.

She tried to calm him, although she felt far from calm herself. 'Please stay here and rest, Herr Almer. I will scout out the route ahead.'

Elspeth sat on the lip of the crevasse and tied her claws to her boots. Using an ice axe to steady herself, she followed the crevasse further around the base of the upper cliff to see where it might lead. Around another corner, and over a slight rise; from this vantage point she could see the way onward.

In the distance and still some way above their position, the Ice Trap glittered. A crown of icicles guarded the cave where food, rope and pitons could be found to fuel Crowley's push for the top. It also contained the frozen corpses of Thomas Holdstock and Simon Barkis. Elspeth dreaded looking into the eyes of those men she had known—and helped to kill.

Between the eagle's nest and the frozen pillar leading up to the cave, a band of ice traced a delicate path across the cliff face. Perhaps it clung to a ledge, but in Elspeth's judgement it looked exceedingly dangerous. In places holes gaped in the ice; in others it appeared to be in the process of falling down. Above and below this narrow strip, featureless rock forbade any prospect of an alternative way. They now had a choice: cross that tight-rope of ice, or starve to death.

Almer joined her at the snow arête.

'It will be very difficult. We should wait until darkness when it will be frozen in place.'

'Then we ought to stay here until Aleister catches up with us.'

As she spoke, a lump of ice the size of a writing desk broke free and crashed into the void.

*

'WATCH OUT!'

Jones flattened himself against the rock, trying to make himself as small a target as possible. He knew from experience not to look up. A pebble had struck him like a bullet an hour ago, destroying his spectacles and giving him a black eye.

Something exploded very close, showering him with debris. He opened his eyes to find a fresh crater in the snow to one side of the gully, surrounded by fragments of dirty ice.

'Another close one,' Collie exclaimed from behind him. 'This is more like Russian Roulette than climbing.'

'Stop dallying!' Raeburn shouted from his position in the lead. He sounded businesslike, as he always did when climbing, but the strain was starting to show.

The rope came tight. Jones began to climb. He could not see too well without his spectacles, and the awkward nature of the climbing in the gully slowed him down. Two hundred feet beneath, the ice had been thick and plentiful; here bare rubble showed through rotten snow, and chockstones dripping with water had to be overcome with combined tactics. To make matters worse, the gully channelled stonefall from above.

The *Überhänge* seemed to produce most of the falling rocks. It reared above them, an enormous overhanging cliff, the most difficult place on the mountain and a completely illogical route. If Crowley's misinformation hadn't sent Holdstock and Barkis that way, perhaps they would be alive now and none of this would be happening. Did Crowley think his greater climbing skill would allow him to pass that way where others had failed? Jones hoped Elspeth would be safe.

Collie reached his stance, grinning cheerfully. In the heat of late morning, he had removed his deerstalker and stripped down to his shirt. His knapsack groaned with clothing and food, and a jangling mixture of ropes, pitons, and Pelton Rings hung from his torso.

'I have seen Crowley,' he announced.

'What?'

'Up there—climbing along that band of ice.'

Jones fumbled in his pocket for his telescope, the only thing he could now use to focus at long distances. It took a moment to identify the feature Collie referred to: a little cone of snow poised in the centre of the *Überhänge*, at the top of a system of roofs. Left of the snow patch, a tiny figure stepped across a ribbon of ice, crabbing sideways in an exposed position. The rope trailed back to Elspeth, sitting in a crevasse in the snow. Jones smiled at the sight of her black hair escaping from under the brim of her hat. Another figure crouched next to her.

'They are higher than us,' Jones remarked.

'Higher, but look how far back they are! We shall get there first, I know we shall.'

Jones scanned left with his telescope. The path Crowley had chosen looked positively terrifying: it seemed to provide the only escape from the *Überhänge*, but it didn't look like it would last the hour. It was melting fast. The drips that fell all around them in the gully, and the chunks of ice that threatened their lives, fell from the leftmost extremity of Crowley's ice ribbon. It looked like it was held together with nothing more substantial than meltwater and air.

Raeburn jerked the rope angrily, reminding Jones to keep climbing. He pocketed the telescope and set to work, heartened by the fact that his team was making better progress than Crowley. Nevertheless, much work remained to be done, and Jones still had no clear idea what he would do when they got to the Ice Trap.

CHAPTER NINETEEN

CONSEQUENCES

13th of June, 1897

RACHEL ELLIOT SPENT Saturday lunchtime wondering why those three pretend-climbers seemed so familiar. By early afternoon she had remembered seeing them in Grindelwald several times. At four o'clock she realised that they hadn't left the terrace all day, and by the time the sun set over the Lauberhorn and the evening turned too cool to remain outside, she had convinced herself that the three climbers were policemen.

Should she tell Eckenstein about them? She considered it briefly before deciding to keep the matter to herself. If she was wrong and those men were nothing more than enthusiastic but lazy mountaineers, she would look hysterical; and even if she was right, and the police had sent spies to keep an eye on them, Eckenstein would restrict her movements. She decided to keep her suspicions to herself. If her plan was to work, she would need to be able to move about freely.

The sun had not yet risen from behind the Eiger when she woke on Sunday morning. Stepping out onto the balcony felt like walking into an ice-house, and she wondered how cold Jones must feel after another night on the wall. She couldn't see much of the mountain through the dawn glow.

Time to put her plan into action. After checking that no servants were watching, Rachel wrapped a cloak around her shoulders and slipped away.

Most of the visiting journalists stayed at Hotel des Alpes. Her plan depended on getting into the newer hotel unseen and making the rendezvous with Alfred Varley. She looked across the courtyard between the two hotels, wondering if she could cross unseen. A hundred windows overlooked this small patch of packed earth and grass, but most of the shutters were closed and she believed she had a good chance of getting across undetected.

Nerves gave her walk across the yard a hint of impatience. Running would attract attention, but she didn't want to linger. Halfway across, she realised that if someone had told her last year that in six months she would be dodging spies at a Swiss resort, she would have laughed in their face. What if nobody cared where she went? Perhaps those three men were indeed nothing more than posers and had no interest in her or Eckenstein. Her nerves had been under strain, after all, and she didn't belong to this world of mystery and subterfuge. She wanted security for her family, a decent man, an interesting life and the chance to travel. She didn't thrive on chaos like Elspeth did.

Then she noticed one of the spies watching her, from the only open window in the facade of the Bellevue, two storeys up. She could see only his face—vaguely handsome, a hint of a moustache, skin undamaged by the sun—but she had spent half of the previous day keeping an eye on him and his friends, and she recognised him instantly.

She broke into a run. In seconds she reached the front door of the Hotel des Alpes, and realised she had not thought this far ahead. A footman in hotel livery stepped out of the shadows to one side of the porch. He looked tired, and surprised to find a young woman rushing towards him at this hour of the morning.

'Guten Morgen, Fraulein …'

Time to improvise.

'Oh, you must help me, sir! He is after me!'

'Who is after you, madam? Are you a resident?'

'I—that is, my husband …' She trailed off, hoping she looked sufficiently distraught.

Now the guard just looked confused. He invited her into the hall and closed the door behind them.

The lobby of the Hotel des Alpes struck Rachel as being far grander and more modern than the Bellevue; it boasted electric lamps, an elevator, and even a telephone at the front desk.

'Please compose yourself, madam, and tell me how I may assist you.'

She leaned against a wall, making a show of steadying herself. 'I heard rumours that my husband may have been unfaithful, so when he disappeared last night I decided to investigate. I found him in the arms of another woman, and now he wishes to punish me for my disobedience!'

The guard did not reply to this, but frowned slightly.

'Why have you come here if you are not a resident?' he replied at length.

'To … to seek shelter from him, of course.'

'Forgive me, but I have seen variations on this pantomime many times. Usually it is the wife who is being unfaithful and has arranged some clandestine rendezvous at an unusual hour.'

Was she really so poor an actress? She had never really done this before; just how did Elspeth lie so convincingly? She tried to cry, but without much success. She imagined she looked ridiculously melodramatic.

'Please, you must help me!'

Someone knocked on the front door so hard it rattled on its hinges. Where could Varley be? He said he would be waiting in the lobby. She must pass on her information before the police caught her.

The footman shook his head. 'It is not our policy to get involved in these matters. I will thank you to leave the premises, madam.'

The elevator doors opened, and out stepped Alfred Varley. Rachel thought he looked hungover. He wore a crumpled shirt with open collar, and something in his eyes made him look at once exhausted and intoxicated. He must be celebrating his good fortune. The drama on the Eiger would be the making of his career.

'Hans! Hans, my boy,' Varley exclaimed, throwing an arm around the footman's shoulders. 'Why do you bother the lady? Has she not told you she is here to meet me?'

The guard looked embarrassed. 'Oh, I see. My apologies, Herr Varley.' He bowed and withdrew.

Varley chuckled after the retreating footman. 'God save the Swiss. So keen to satisfy their guests, so quick to turn a blind eye to any impropriety taking place under their roof, if the Herr pays of course.'

'We don't have much time,' Rachel said urgently. 'The police are after me!'

'You're not very good at this, are you?'

She kept an eye on the front door. The guard had opened it, but seemed to be arguing with at least two men in the courtyard outside; hopefully he would be able to stall them for a while longer. She grabbed the journalist's arm and pulled him out of view.

'Peter Merrick is not the noble hero you think he is. He is Aleister Crowley going under a false name.'

Varley stared at her for a moment, then laughed. 'What rubbish.'

'It's true! Ask Elspeth, the girl who is climbing with him.'

She felt guilty for bringing Elspeth into this, but Varley had injured her pride by pointing out yet another of Elspeth's qualities that Rachel lacked. No matter how hard she tried, she would always feel inferior to the brave girl who had such a hold over Jones.

Varley seemed to be having a hard time digesting this information. 'Are you trying to tell me that Crowley's mystery girl is here in Switzerland? What has she got to do with Peter Merrick?'

The arguing in the corridor got louder. Rachel became impatient. What if Warrington's men caught her before she could convince Varley of the truth? She pressed a letter into his hand, prepared earlier to explain everything. It contained no evidence; she had planned to steal the letter from Crowley to his wife, and use that as proof, but she had lost her nerve. Her statement would have to stand or fall by itself.

'Elspeth is Crowley's wife, and she has helped him to deceive us all! Don't you realise it makes sense? Crowley wanted to kill Barkis and Holdstock for what they did to him. He's been planning this for over six months.'

Varley stared at the letter in his hand. No doubt he could sense his triumph crashing down around him. If his hero turned out to be a fraud, he would be finished—unless he could think of a way to play this to his advantage.

Footsteps sounded in the hall. A shouted command in German made Rachel jump, and she gripped Varley's arm, imploring him with her eyes to believe her.

'Don't tell them you have the letter. All I ask is that you publish the truth. It's the right thing to do, Mr Varley.'

Inspector Warrington charged around the corner, face twisted with rage. Two of the pretend-climbers followed close behind. They stopped in front of the guilty pair, caught exchanging secret information; for a moment nobody spoke, and the Swiss plainclothes officers seemed to fill the corridor.

Inspector Warrington took a step forward. 'Miss Elliot, what is the meaning of this?'

His gentle voice made Rachel even more afraid. She had never met a more threatening man in her life.

'This is a private matter. I have done nothing wrong.'

'You are interfering with my investigation.' He nodded at one of his henchmen. 'Arrest her.'

Now Varley came back to life. 'Wait a moment, Inspector Warrington. I'm pretty sure you aren't allowed to do that outside your jurisdiction.'

Rachel glanced between the two men. Did they know each other? Their body language seemed tense; of course, it was a tense situation, but she sensed something else passing between them. They had dealt with each other in the past, she was sure of it.

'This is none of your business,' Warrington replied to the journalist. 'I can assure you that I am acting with the full cooperation of the Bernese authorities in hunting down a notorious criminal. That is all I have to say.'

A crafty smile spread over Varley's face. 'So it is true. You're after Crowley.'

'I will make no further comment, and I warn you that this woman is not to be trusted. Anything that she has said to you is most probably a lie.'

Varley looked at her as one of the Swiss officers took her by the arm. She couldn't read much in his bloodshot eyes, but as the police led her away under arrest, Varley gave her a wink and patted the shirt pocket where he had secreted the letter. So he believed her! If he had corresponded with Warrington on the Crowley case, the Inspector's presence must have been just enough to make Varley believe Rachel's claims. Her plan had not turned out so disastrously after all; she may not be as experienced in deception as Elspeth, but she had done her bit and the world would know the truth about Peter Merrick.

The police led her past the protesting guard and out into the courtyard. What would happen to her now?

'Where are you taking me?' she asked as they marched back towards Bellevue.

'You will be confined to your hotel room until my investigation is concluded.' Suddenly he stopped and turned to look at her. 'You are like a child, lashing out against the thing that hurts you with no thought for the consequences of your actions.'

'I am trying to help Jones! I thought you were on his side?'

A thin smile. 'Let me clear up that little misunderstanding. I am here to catch Crowley. That is my only concern, and I will do whatever I must to attain that goal. If helping Jones is in my interests, then that is well and good; but if locking you up and preventing you from talking to the press is what I need to do, then believe me, I will do it.'

*

When Crowley arrived at the eagle's nest, he expressed no concern that his wife had spent the night trapped on a vertical cliff, or that the night in the open had seriously weakened their guide. He demanded a report on the supplies each of them carried—no food at all, and only a little fuel—then climbed up onto the snow ridge to spy out the route ahead.

'Herr Merrick,' Almer began after sharing a look with Elspeth, 'we must rest here for the day. It is too hot. Only at night will the ice be safe to cross.'

At first, Crowley did not seem to hear him. His hooded head scanned back and forth across the ice bridge, taking in the gaps, the dripping icicles, the crack of breaking ice. Then he turned to look at his companions. Those intense eyes had not lost their obsessive quality, but now Elspeth saw an emotion that dislodged old memories from a time when she had not feared her husband: excitement.

'It looks fun, wouldn't you say? If we wait for nightfall, Jones and his rats will get ahead of us. We climb now.'

'Young man, you would do well to listen to your guide. If we climb now, we die. Alpinism is not a race.'

The excitement in Crowley's eyes turned to irritation. He climbed back down from the snow ridge and approached the older man, who stood tall and proud for the first time that morning. Elspeth sensed that he had recovered his faculties. Almer may never have done a route like this before, but he had been climbing on these mountains for thirty years and seemed to be well aware of his advantage of experience.

Crowley balanced easily on the snow slope, held by his front points, taunting the guide with his lack of concern for the exposure.

'Look at you. So old. A symbol of the past, when mountaineers were weaklings who needed to employ criminals like you to get to the top by the easiest route.'

Almer's expression hardened. 'And look at you, so young and ignorant. I have met a thousand like you, who think you are better than your elders, who fail to understand the old laws of climbing. I know how to deal with your kind.'

Crowley laughed. 'The only reason I employed you at all was to give my ascent some credibility in the eyes of the world.'

'Never in all my years as a guide—!'

Crowley slammed an axe into the ice next to Almer's head. 'Wasted years! Guides are cockroaches who have destroyed the spirit of progress and adventure in mountaineering. You are the worst species of Alpine parasite, you and all your kind!'

He spat in the guide's face, and Almer recoiled. Elspeth realised that this outburst had not been part of the plan. For all Crowley's intelligence and foresight, he had never been much good at controlling his emotions—and that was the tragedy of his vision. He had destroyed everything he believed in with his desire for revenge, blasted the progressive movement back into the ground before it had a chance to grow.

Almer looked crushed. He swung his knapsack onto one shoulder and climbed out of the crevasse.

'Very well. If I am not required, I will leave.'

Crowley turned away and started to sort through his climbing gear. 'There is no descent from here. The only escape is up.'

Almer said nothing to that, but the look he gave Elspeth compounded the sense of guilt that she carried with her, a feeling that grew with every minute she spent in her husband's company.

'I refuse to cross that ice ribbon until nightfall,' Almer persisted.

'Then you can wait here and cross in the dark, by yourself and with no rope. Elspeth is coming with me.'

She hesitated. How could she best serve Jones? The onward path frightened her in its current condition, but it would be time-consuming to tackle it as a roped team. Alone, her husband would certainly reach the Ice Trap first.

'Of course, Aleister,' she replied, and the look of disappointment in the old guide's eyes wounded her.

*

Conditions on the Eigerwand remained calm and warm, but wispy clouds, far above the level of the summits, signalled change. Jones had not been paying attention to the weather. Back in the lead again, he had an icy slab to negotiate and a two thousand foot drop to ignore. He placed his palms on the smooth rock at shoulder-height and crabbed across the traverse. Without the plating of ice under his claw points, the pitch would be impossible. He wondered if they would be able to get back down this way.

At the far side, he kicked out a platform in the snow and hammered a piton in, then set to work sorting out the unruly rope.

'Climb when ready!'

'Climbing now!'

Jones took in the rope as Raeburn levitated across the traverse. The Scot balanced on nothing but a few inches of dripping ice, slotting his claw points into the holes made by Jones on his crossing. Looking down, the lower snowfields reflected sunlight, but Jones realised that the glare that had troubled him earlier in the day no longer burned so harshly. He looked up at the sun.

Cloud! Surely the sky had been clear only a moment ago? When he thought about it, he could not be absolutely certain when he had last looked at the sky. Time flew by quickly when climbing.

Raeburn reached the stance, breathing heavily but buoyed up by a joyful smile. He had followed Collie's example and removed his tweed jacket, now folded under the hood of his rucksack. Shirt torn by an ice axe, waistcoat stained with the grey mud that oozed from the rock, he looked more like a vagabond than a mountaineer.

Raeburn brought Collie across the pitch while Jones worried about the weather, about what might happen if the ice melted, and about how they were going to get down. On the descent, they would have Crowley in tow, not to mention the bodies of Holdstock and Barkis, if they succeeded in recovering them. It would be serious work.

Collie joined them on the small ledge and clipped himself to the anchor point with a Pelton Ring. 'Heavy weather is on its way,' he remarked. 'In ten hours at most, this place will be a whirlpool of snow and rocks.'

'Are you sure?'

'As eggs is eggs. I have seen this weather pattern many times in the Alps, and it always results in a storm.'

The three friends shared glum looks. To have come so far, only to have their success threatened by bad weather, came as a bitter blow. Raeburn, Jones knew, still had hopes of making the first ascent of the wall, and although that had never been their objective, those hopes had now been dashed.

Could they risk it? Nobody had ever survived a storm on a major Alpine wall. While they had the advantage of superior equipment over the master alpinists of the previous decade, that equipment had not saved Holdstock or Barkis. They had died despite finding shelter.

Jones looked up. Although the steepness of the wall foreshortened the view, he could make out some of the principle features: to their right, the water-streaked walls of the *Überhänge*, and two or three hundred feet straight above, the Ice Trap at the top of its guardian icefall. Beyond that, all features merged into each other, a frowning precipice that blocked out the view of the summit far above. No human had ever been up there.

'I think we can get to the Ice Trap within an hour or two,' Jones said, hoping he sounded confident. 'Crowley will either climb into it to find shelter from the storm, or climb back down to the waiting policemen. Either way, we will have won.'

Raeburn did not look convinced. 'Except that we will be stuck in the Ice Trap. Why do you think the newspapers gave it that lurid name?'

They all knew what nobody quite dared to say: that if they tried to sit out a storm on this face, they would very likely all die. Other than a sweater, tweed jacket, balaclava helmet and mittens, they had no severe weather gear. Climbing equipment and food had been the priority when packing the knapsacks.

Collie put a hand on Jones' shoulder and looked into his eyes. 'My friend, we must think about when to retreat. This mission is not worth our lives.'

'Of course it isn't.' He looked up again. The Ice Trap looked so close, and they were still ahead of Crowley. 'If the weather has deteriorated by the time we get to the foot of the frozen pillar, we'll go back down.'

*

'Almer can go in the rear. He's supposed to be the experienced one, after all.'

Elspeth wondered why her husband was so determined to punish Ulrich Almer. It wasn't his fault that a guide had started the avalanche on the Matterhorn, or that Crowley's early experiences in the Alps had been ruined by incompetent guides. Something seemed to have changed in her husband. His thirst for revenge had become indiscriminate.

She took Crowley's arm and led him to one side. 'If you put Almer in the rear, he'll endanger us all. Look at him! He won't cope on that traverse without help.'

'Putting him in the middle of the rope would certainly be a humiliation for such an accomplished guide. All right, I'll do it.'

They roped up. If Almer felt dishonoured by his position on the rope, he did not complain. Crowley went first. Fuelled by unshakeable confidence, he danced across the ice and soon arrived at a belay where a stalagmite of rock formed an anchor.

Almer shuffled across the traverse while Elspeth paid out the rope. The ribbon of ice and dirty snow varied in height between about five and twelve feet. In places snow had piled up in fissures and provided a more secure platform, while in others water running down the rock had damaged the ice. Debris crumbled and fell from these points, making the pathway less secure with every collapse.

Where Crowley had climbed with confidence, Almer hesitated. He didn't dare kick in his front points and let those little iron spikes keep him safe. In such a stressful situation he reverted to the methods he knew best, and clung to the lip of the crevasse while he chopped out steps with an ice axe to increase his security.

An hour passed. The guide had covered less than a hundred feet of ground while the ice dripped and stones dropped out of the sky like cannonballs. Cutting steps despite Crowley's protests, Almer gained ground slowly but safely; until, that is, he reached a place where the ice had broken completely away, leaving a yard of bare rock.

'Wedge your claw points in the crack and step across,' Crowley shouted. 'It's easy.'

'*Nein*, I cannot!'

Almer clung to the near side of the breach, unable to move either forward or back. Knowing perfectly well that Crowley would do nothing to help him, Elspeth untied herself from the anchor, knocked out the piton, and began climbing towards the guide. She coiled the rope around her shoulders as she climbed. If she fell now they would all die: there was too much slack in the rope, but Almer was in no condition to be thinking about belaying her.

She copied her husband's climbing style, using small, precise movements and hooking her axes instead of smashing them into the ice with force. She did not allow herself to look down and see the stupefying gulf beneath her feet.

Soon she reached the terrified guide. He clutched at the rock, clawed boots scrambling for purchase, entire body shaking. The fear of falling gripped him. Elspeth had learned how to master that fear—all climbers had to—but she knew what the terror felt like, and sometimes it could not be avoided despite one's best efforts to hold it back.

The look of panic in his eyes frightened her. *'Hilfe! Hilfe!'* he cried over and over again.

She looked around for a crack she could sink a piton into—there, to the left—not much, but it would do. While holding on with her right hand, she fumbled at the spaghetti of equipment dangling from her waist and selected two pegs at random, both battered and bent from previous use. In went the pitons, hammered home with blows from her axe. After tying herself to the first, she turned to Almer.

'I'm going to secure you. Pass me your end of the rope.'

He shook his head. *'Ich kann nicht bewegen!'*

She took a step towards him, keeping the line tight between her and the piton. It flexed in the crack; she did not dare put her full bodyweight onto it. Now that she could reach Almer, she leaned into the rock to settle her centre of gravity, and rummaged through the tangle of ropes between them until she found the end coming from Almer's waist loop. Now she tied the rope to the second piton.

'There. You're safe.'

His expression told her he was not convinced. Meanwhile, Crowley had begun tugging on the rope.

'We must keep moving! Give the old cove a kick if he is being stubborn.'

Another jerk on the rope caused Almer to lose his grip, and he stumbled off the ice, claws scraping gouges in the rock. He came to rest in an ungainly position a foot or so below the ledge, in a dank scoop where he fought to maintain balance. Both of his axes fell into the void. Elspeth tensed herself. In this position, she could not belay Almer with the rope around her waist, as she had done when she caught Jones' huge fall on Nevis. If Almer fell, the only thing that could save him was a sliver of forged iron wedged in a crack.

He looked up, and their eyes met. Despite Almer's years of experience as a mountain guide, when faced with death he became just like everyone else: an animal fighting for its last few breaths, all dignity gone. Elspeth could see no trace of humanity in that staring face. In that moment, looking into the eyes of a doomed man, she realised that the intangible rewards of mountaineering could never be worth the price that so many climbers paid.

Then the stone came out of the sky. It passed by Elspeth's left shoulder, missed it by an inch, and hit the waiting target of Almer's head. His body jerked back against the straining ropes. When the spray of blood had cleared, Elspeth found herself unable to look away from the stoved-in skull that had been an expressive human face, fighting and alive, only a second before. Jets of blood spurted up from the dying man, painting red streaks over the ice at Elspeth's feet. With a final gurgle, Almer sagged back.

She found herself paralysed with horror. Only slowly did she begin to hear Crowley's shouts.

'Elspeth, cut him free. We have to get out of here.'

'He could still be alive!' she replied, but after another look at the raw meat that had once been a face, she knew he was dead.

'If you don't cut him free, the piton will pull and you will die. Come to your senses!'

Focus returned. The piton that supported the guide's hanging corpse had pulled halfway out of the crack already. If it came out, the coils of loose rope between the hanging body and Elspeth would come tight, dragging her off the ledge in seconds. Her own piton could not withstand such a force.

At the other end of the ledge, Crowley took the line connecting him with Almer, and sliced through it with his knife. Now it was up to her.

It went against her instincts to cut away the body of a comrade and give him to the mountain without ceremony. On this occasion, however, her husband was right. She swung an axe at the rope. It took only the slightest effort to sever the tensioned strands, and with a sound like a pistol shot the body was gone.

She watched as Almer fell, loose-limbed like a doll. He bounced, each time becoming less human, more a destroyed thing of broken bone and flesh. Only when the body had passed out of sight did Elspeth feel able to look away from the awful fate that could claim anyone who dared climb on the Eigerwand.

Soon she joined Crowley at his stance. She felt numb as she passed the coils of rope and bundle of pitons to him. He did not speak to her, but for all his cruelty, Elspeth could detect a sympathetic emotion trying to break through his defences: shock, or perhaps the realisation that careless actions had consequences he did not intend.

So he was still human after all. She wanted to hug him, but could not bring herself to do it.

*

Jones felt the first spot of rain land on his forehead as he reached the frozen pillar at the foot of the Ice Trap. The time had come to make a decision. Could they go back down from here? He doubted it; after the traverse, the climbing had become looser, steeper, harder. Going back down would be a nightmare. It did not amount to much of a choice, but soon the skies would release hell on them.

He hammered a piton into the boss of ice that flowed from the base of the pillar, like fat coils of cooling lava. Then he brought his friends up to the position. Raeburn climbed with vigour, Collie less enthusiastically. He felt a pang of conscience. These men had followed him here. Anything that befell them would be his fault.

Jones shook himself to avoid such morbid thoughts. They took a moment to rest and eat a little food. Nobody spoke as they watched the sleety rain, each wondering if this signalled the start of the storm. Collie put his jacket back on.

'I suppose it's time to head back down, then,' he said, cheerfully enough.

Jones noticed Raeburn trying to catch his eye. Was his Scottish friend thinking along the same lines? The notion of retreat, so close to their objective, went against the grain. Less than a hundred feet of steep ice lay between them and their goal, the Ice Trap, where they could say some prayers over the bodies of their friends; and besides, Crowley couldn't be far behind. If they meekly went down now, he would plunder the stores and head for the top, storm or no storm.

'I think we should wait for a while longer,' Jones said.

Collie frowned. 'Jones, you said I should be your conscience. Please listen to me. We agreed to retreat if the weather got any worse.' He looked at Raeburn. 'What do you think?'

'I agree with Jones. The laddie may be a fool at times, but he knows his duty. What will become of the lady and the guide if Crowley keeps climbing through the storm?'

'If we remain, we could all die,' Collie said in a firmer voice. 'Do you not see that, Raeburn? You are not still thinking about climbing through to the top, are you?'

Raeburn looked a little guilty. 'I admit I have dreamed about being the one to make the first ascent, but I think we all realise that is impossible now. There is, however, the question of duty that remains.'

A gust of wind shook the ledge, accompanied by a flurry of sleet. Now the precipitation no longer seemed light and gentle, but a threat to survival. Jones listened to his companions argue: Collie's famous prudence on one side, an appeal to their greater duty on the other. Suddenly he realised that there could be no turning back. In the past he had tried to suppress the prideful side to his character, the impetuous Only Genuine Jones, but that very quality had driven him to success and established his reputation. Who would he be without his boldness, his instincts, and his ambition?

He would not give up. For months now Jones had chased his rival, always failing to stop him doing more damage. This would be the last chance. If he failed, everything would come crashing down, and Crowley would rise above it all, reborn as the hero of the Eigerwand. Peter Merrick would be remembered as the man who fought for the spirit of progressive mountaineering while at the same time crushing it forever with the weight of his bitterness.

The world Jones loved, of climbing with dear friends in beautiful places, of adventure and challenge without fear of judgement, would come to an end. Everything he cared about depended on this decision.

'Gentlemen, I intend to continue. I must insist that you go back down before the weather becomes too heavy.'

Collie looked at him in astonishment. 'My dear friend, I could not possibly leave you alone up here. We move as a team or not at all.'

'The Professor is quite right,' Raeburn said. 'I won't give up yet.'

Even though Collie thought him a fool, and Raeburn probably cared more for his own life above honour than he dared admit, Jones felt a fierce affection for these comrades who had accompanied him to the most inhospitable place in Europe.

He looked up at the frozen pillar. It would be a tough challenge, as steep as the toughest pitch on the Great Wall of Ben Nevis, but at high altitude and with bad weather setting in, not to mention their heavy packs. A reunion with old friends awaited them at the top of the frozen pillar—and a confrontation with an enemy, if all went to plan.

*

Death had transformed the face of Simon Barkis. In life he had been strikingly handsome, boyish despite the moustache. Now Jones looked on the face of an old man. Eyes stared up at the icicles clinging to the roof of the cave, snow stuck to the ragged stubble on his chin, and although decomposition had not yet begun Jones could already see the shadow of a skull, angular through his wasted features. Only the head and shoulders remained above the drifted snow.

Jones took off his hat and bowed his head. He spent a moment remembering the good times they had enjoyed together: climbing on sun-washed rock, a quiet pint after work, plans for the future of mountaineering.

These moments of friendship would continue to enrich his life for as long as he could remember them. What had Barkis thought about in the final moments before he died? Jones tried to put himself in that position, trapped in this fearful place with the storm getting worse every hour, trying to think of ways to escape.

Soon he might find himself in the same predicament. Outside the cave, rain slashed through a blanket of mist. Drips fell from the hanging swords of ice twenty feet above his head, a constant warning that they might fall at any moment.

Jones heard the thud of ice axes behind him, and turned to see Collie climb up onto the rubble-strewn slab at the entrance of the cave.

'This is a grim sort of place, isn't it?'

Collie had a point. From below, the Ice Trap looked deeper and safer than it really was. In reality, it offered poor shelter. A sloping floor, covered with rubble, drifted snow, and discarded tin cans, extended some ten feet back. The roof was too high to provide much protection against avalanches, and in any case those icicles presented a constant threat from which no corner of the cave offered safety.

Worse still, Jones could see no way out. The walls overhung and ran with water. Unless it got much colder and an ice pillar formed in the cave, there could be no way to climb out from here. Only by roping back down the frozen pillar could they escape.

While Collie busied himself setting up an anchor to bring Raeburn up the pillar, Jones looked around. Next to the remains of Simon Barkis, an arm protruded from the snow, clutching a tin mug with a white hand. Jones dug a little to uncover the body of his former employer, the man who had arguably started the whole feud in the first place. Unlike his climbing partner, Thomas Holdstock looked at peace, as if he had accepted justice in his last moments of life.

What a terrible way to die: inspired by the prospect of another historic north wall ascent, the eyes of the world on them, only to be cut down in the most brutal way possible. Jones wondered if Crowley felt good about his revenge.

All three climbers now stood at the top of the slab, heads bowed in prayer as they thought about the life and death of these men they had known and the lessons that could be learned from their end. Outside, the wind screamed and rain beat against the rocks, and one by one the three friends came to terms with the possibility that they might share this grave with Holdstock and Barkis. If they could help Elspeth and prevent Crowley from fulfilling his plan, their deaths would be worth something.

From below, at the foot of the frozen pillar, a shout cut through the growing roar of the storm. The words did not carry into the cave, but there could be no mistaking the tone of rage from someone who had been beaten at a very important race.

Aleister and Elspeth Crowley had caught up with them.

"JONES TOOK OFF HIS HAT AND BOWED HIS HEAD"

CHAPTER TWENTY

THE ICE TRAP

14th of June, 1897

RACHEL FINISHED READING the front page of the Observer. Varley's article both relieved and disgusted her; it told the truth about Peter Merrick, but hyperbole and morbid speculation tainted every line. At least Varley had done the right thing and told the truth.

Once again she had to remind herself that she had done this to help the man she loved, not as revenge against Crowley. Since Warrington had locked her up in her hotel room she had found plenty of opportunities to think, and had come to the conclusion that she had behaved stupidly from the beginning. In the desperate search for security, she had almost chained herself to a confidence trickster, a criminal, possibly a madman. The memory of it made her flush with shame. Perhaps she deserved to be here.

She lay back on her bed and stared at the ceiling, an inconsequential novel abandoned on the sheets beside her. Despite Warrington's stern words, her imprisonment was civilised enough, with three meals a day and all the reading and writing material she could wish for. Everything she cared about, however, was fighting for life on the north face.

She looked up at the sound of a knock on the door. Surely not time for lunch yet?

The door swung open just enough to admit a large figure, then closed again. The twilight of her room could not compete with the lamps in the corridor outside, and until he spoke, Rachel could not discern the identity of her visitor.

'Miss Elliot, are you awake?'

Oscar Eckenstein. She sat upright and smoothed down her dress.

'Mr Eckenstein, is it proper for you to invite yourself into my room unannounced?'

He perched on the dressing table chair, looking tired and crumpled. 'Don't be childish. I have used up just about every ounce of my influence with Herr Seiler to arrange this meeting.'

Stop being such a girl, she scolded herself. Eckenstein unsettled her, with his surly manners yet powerful presence. If it had been Jones she wouldn't have minded.

'I'm sorry. I appreciate everything you have done for me.'

'Good. Now listen quickly. Jones is in big trouble, but we think he has reached the Ice Trap.'

Her hands clenched. 'What do you mean, you *think* he has reached it? Can you not see?'

'We can't see anything through the cloud. Haven't you looked out of your window this morning?'

'It faces north, away from the Eiger, so I don't see the use.'

Nevertheless, his words worried her. She stood, stretched to relieve cramped muscles, and opened the curtains. Ragged low cloud brushed the tops of the Oberland foothills, and the landscape had a rain-washed look to it; quite a contrast to the summer sunshine of the past week. How could she not have been aware of this change? She liked to think she had a connection with Jones, and would sense when he was in danger. Perhaps she had been too self-absorbed to feel anything.

She turned back to Eckenstein. 'How can we help them?'

'We can do nothing unless the weather clears. The outcome is down to fate now, if you believe that nonsense.'

Eckenstein sounded resigned. That worried her. Rachel wasn't ready to give up yet; she would not give up until she saw Jones' corpse with her own eyes.

'Tell me more. I want to know everything.'

'Well, there isn't much to tell. When I last saw our friends, they were climbing up the slabs beneath the *Eisturm*—forgive me, the frozen pillar; all the guides call it the *Eisturm*. The storm had already begun at that point, but I have no doubt that Jones and his friends made it to the Ice Trap.'

The Ice Trap! Rachel felt a chill pass over her at the memory of seeing it through the telescope, and her prayer that Jones would not be forced to take shelter there. It had killed Barkis and Holdstock. Why would Jones and his team fare any better?

'Perhaps they decided to climb back down.'

'Ha! Are we talking about the same Jones here?'

She took his meaning. While Jones could be remarkably lazy about things he did not consider important, he also had a stubborn side and did not give up on ideas that captured his imagination or his sense of duty. Panic rose within her at the thought that he might die, for the first time an immediate possibility in her mind.

'What will happen now?' she whispered.

'They will spend a few days singing songs and playing cards, then climb back down when the snow clears.'

'Don't treat me like a child!'

'Then don't ask stupid questions! Good God, do you think I'm not worried sick myself? He is my best friend!'

'Then can you not at least be honest with me?'

He stood up. 'I'm sure you can imagine what will happen just as vividly as I can. I have to go now. The housemaid who is currently entertaining your policeman guard will not be able to keep him occupied forever, pretty as she is.'

She felt desolate, abandoned. 'Thank you for telling me the news, even if it is awful to hear.'

Eckenstein hesitated at the door, and his expression softened for a moment as he looked back on her. 'Look here, you may think I'm grumpy and selfish—I don't care much for what others think of me—but I will never stop fighting for Jones. He is the best of us all.'

*

Elspeth doubted she could survive another night without shelter. After the elation of realising that she had helped Jones to reach the Ice Trap first, thoughts turned to what would happen next. As expected, her husband did not spare a thought for the possibility of retreat; instead, he had flown into a rage, striking the cascade at the foot of the Ice Trap with an axe, as if attempting to sever it and imprison his rivals in the tomb above. The storm would trap them soon enough without Crowley's help.

She leaned back against the rope which anchored her to the ice. Crowley's selected route climbed slabs into a narrowing funnel that echoed with the groans and cries of the mountain. They could see little in the gloom. Occasionally, the gulf above spat rocks and ice down at them, but debris tended to bounce down the sluice of muddy water in the centre of the gully. For safety, they stuck close to the left edge, where the ice had survived the thaw a little better. Rain soaked through every layer of clothing, chilling her skin.

She had not warmed up since the miserable night spent huddling together on a ledge the size of a bookshelf. Would they find shelter tonight? Elspeth hoped so, but realistically she doubted any shelter could be found in this ominous trough into which they now climbed. She wondered if her husband had any idea of what to do next.

'CLIMB!'

The order jolted her into action: hack piton from the ice, hang with others at hip, unclip Pelton Ring, retrieve axes, climb. The motions of climbing using the progressive equipment had become as instinctive in this place as the laws of avoiding stonefall. Bits of grit and slushy water rained down on her face as she hacked into the ice. Breathing heavily, fighting the breathlessness of altitude, she climbed up to her husband's position.

Aleister's forlorn figure hunched at the belay, smock drooping with the weight of water it had soaked up. His face, once mesmerising and seductive, now just looked exhausted. A patchy boy's beard grew over his chin. Elspeth found that he no longer intimidated her.

'Where will we spend the night?' she demanded.

'I imagine there will be a ledge somewhere,' he said, gesturing into the void above their heads.

The vague response irritated her. 'What do we do if the storm gets worse? Have you given any thought to that at all?'

'It's just a little rain. We are above Jones, and now that Almer is dead we have enough supplies. We cannot give up!'

'I don't care!' she screamed. 'You have no idea where you are going, the ice is in a terrible condition, and we are climbing into a stone chute. We have to go down.'

He grabbed her shoulder and twisted her to face him. The sudden movement unbalanced them both, but the piton held. 'Again you are disobedient. You are my wife and you will obey me.'

Once she would have obeyed without thought, but now she glared back at him. 'I am not here to follow your orders without question.'

'Then why are you climbing with me?'

She could feel her heart pounding with apprehension, or perhaps with the growing courage that would help her beat the monster who had controlled her for so long.

'I climb for Jones!' she shouted in his ear. 'He sent me to delay your attempt so you would be denied Holdstock's supplies. For once in my life, I am doing the right thing.'

Crowley released her. His eyes widened with genuine shock. Had he really never expected his mistreated wife to lash out at him one day? He was seeing his plans collapse all around him, and for the first time since meeting Aleister two years ago Elspeth saw fear in his eyes.

'I don't need your help,' he said in a low voice, barely audible over the noise of the storm.

Once again he looked up into the tumult of foaming water, falling debris, and melting ice. Would these dangers be enough to make Aleister doubt his abilities? Confidence had made him the best climber in the world, and if that confidence was shaken he would fail.

'You do need me,' Elspeth said. 'You cannot survive alone.'

He said nothing for a long time. They gazed upwards together, in the direction of the summit: an incalculable distance through hardships never before faced in the history of mountaineering. Elspeth suddenly felt very small and out of her depth. She had done great things as a climber, but none of them had prepared her for this. The new age of climbing seemed a hundred years away now, a story whispered in safe places far from the roar of avalanches and the crash of disintegrating ice.

Crowley looked away from the realm above. 'We will climb on. I have survived before, and I will survive again.'

Despite the bold words, Elspeth sensed another change in her husband, a diminishing of his stature. The Eiger was changing him from a young immortal into something far more vulnerable: an adult.

*

After twenty four hours in the Ice Trap, Jones knew that they had to escape. The atmosphere of fear and recriminations ate away at his nerves. His two living companions now agreed that climbing up into this place had been a bad move; his two dead ones judged in silence. The sloping floor of the cave, criss-crossed by cracks and strewn with gravel, did not lend itself to any position of ease, and forced the prisoners to adopt half-crouching, half-lying postures.

The snow at the back of the cave melted with the thaw, revealing ghastly artefacts as it receded. The two corpses slumped, sodden and stinking, over piles of gear. Jones caught Raeburn eyeing this treasure trove from time to time, and wondered if he still thought about going for the top. Perhaps he was just hungry. The supplies they carried had not fared well in the damp atmosphere. Soon they would have to rifle through the bags of the dead men and look for something edible, something canned perhaps.

He could not decide on the appropriate manner to honour his friends. How did one bury a man on a mountain? Would it be like a burial at sea, the bodies committed to the void, or should they raise a cairn over the remains? The first solution did not sit right with him, and they did not have enough stones for the second.

Thoughts tumbled through his head, disordered and frightened, rotten with guilt. Meanwhile water trickled through the cave, saturating everything they owned.

'We have to get out of here,' Raeburn said towards the end of that first day. 'The ice pillar won't take much more running water before it comes down.'

Nobody spoke for a while. Jones sat a little way apart from his companions, on a flat stone overlooking the entrance of the cave. Until Raeburn's observation nobody had spoken for hours. The sound of human speech jolted him out of his depression. He stood and peered over the edge, holding on to the rope handrail they had fastened around the inside of the cave.

A waterfall ran down the ice pillar. He could see water flowing behind the ice as well as in front, moving in slug-like bubbles against the rock. Part of it broke away with a crash and fell to the screes below.

'My God, you're right!'

Collie got up unsteadily. His deerstalker hat now clung limply to his head, flaps tied down to warm his ears. He looked old and haggard.

'It's not much of a choice,' he said. 'Go and die down there in the dark, or fade away in here.'

Jones forced a smile. As the youngest of the party, as well as the appointed leader, he believed the duty fell to him to keep up morale. 'Come now, it isn't that bad. We still have fuel to melt snow. There's fight in us yet.'

Raeburn watched him with the expression of a man who believed he had been misled.

'You are supposed to be our leader, Jones,' he said quietly. 'So lead us.'

Jones looked over the edge again. He felt nervous about this decision. Collie had summed up the situation exactly: if they roped down the pillar and tried to retreat, they would be exposed to the full force of the storm, and would almost certainly not survive for long. Besides, it would soon be dark. On the other hand, if they stayed, they would still die eventually.

They had all cursed Crowley's name for leading them into this trap, but perhaps that was not fair. In the end Jones had made the decision.

He felt scared, but put on a brave face for the others. 'Death on the cliff face, with an ice axe in my hand and the wind in my hair, or just sitting around waiting for it? I know which I would choose.'

Collie looked at the corpses hunched up in the back of the cave. 'Those two chose to stay. Look at what happened to them.'

Raeburn still watched Jones. 'I think we should have turned back the moment the weather changed.'

'What about your little speech on duty?' Collie demanded.

'Aye well, perhaps I was wrong. I think Jones was definitely wrong.'

Jones turned his back on them, hands shaking as he flaked out the main rope. It lay in coils in the mud, soaked and heavy, probably weakened from all the abuse it had suffered. He remembered Eckenstein lecturing him on the dangers of using wet rope, but now was not the time to think about vague risks.

'We'll have to leave this rope fixed in place. If we use it doubled up, it won't reach the bottom.'

Raeburn broke off from arguing with Collie. 'Pardon?'

'The pillar,' Jones said patiently, although he felt nothing but panic. 'It's about seventy feet high, is it not?'

'Approximately. Are you going to go first, oh brave leader?'

He ignored that remark, instead wondering what to use as an anchor. A nest of pitons at the back of the cave, tied together with frayed cord, seemed to be the best solution. To reach them he had to crouch in the slush beside Barkis' corpse. He stretched, pathetically frightened of touching it. A hand brushed against damp tweed, and he sprang back as if it had burnt him.

Jones sacrificed three Pelton Rings and a yard of rope to make the anchor safe. Finally satisfied with it, he dragged the coils back to the edge of the cave and threw them over. They hit the ice with a wet slap.

The next move would require nerve. After passing the rope under his buttocks, over his chest, and around his shoulders, he leaned back against it until taut. Water squeezed out of the fibres, but it held. While controlling the rope with his right hand, he stepped carefully back towards the edge, not daring to look down. Claws bit into the saturated ice. The rope crushed his ribs like a python, hurting his old injury. After taking several more steps down into the waterfall, he looked back up at the fringe of icicles guarding the mouth of the cave. Water streaming from the icicles splashed on his face.

Then the largest of them fell.

It dropped towards him like a spear thrown by an angry god. He lurched out of the way just as the mass of ice passed him, and for a moment he saw his own terrified expression mirrored in the surface, an inch from his nose. Then the impact came up through the pillar and blasted him away into space. A rumbling explosion engulfed him as he swung on the end of the rope, and he realised that where solid ice had been only seconds before, now nothing remained but slime and blackness.

Great Scott, the pillar has collapsed with me on it!

He took a moment just to breathe, glad to be alive. Looking down, the waterfall continued through fifty feet of air to fall on a jumble of smashed ice and rock. Worse, the collapse had severed his rope some distance above ground level. There could be no way down; what about back up? He swung in space, held there by the friction of rope around his body.

The pillar had broken off at about the level of his neck. Raw ice, bleeding water, seemed to offer a way back to the cave, but it no longer had any support from below. Would it take his weight?

An axe placed as high as possible seemed to stick fast. After winding the dead end of the rope several times around his leg to secure it, he hauled on the shaft of the axe, realising that if the next move failed he would not be able to save himself.

Quickly, now! He unclipped the safety loop from around his waist and passed it over the head of the axe, then back to his waist where he clipped it back onto its Pelton Ring. Now he could rest on the tension from the axe. He adjusted the descent rope that twisted around his body, taking in the slack.

He hammered a piton as high as possible, taking care not to hit it too hard. The remains of the pillar shook and twisted with every movement he made.

Finally he could get his claw points to engage and take away some of the excruciating strain. He put his weight back on his feet, until the left one sheared through the ice and left him hanging again; more caution, Jones!

Ten minutes later, he lay exhausted in the mud with the faces of his friends looking down on him. Fiery liquid scalded his throat. Never before had a tot of whisky been more welcome.

'There is no way down,' he gasped. 'We stay here.'

*

Tuesday's dawn brought a merciless frost. A third night with no shelter left Elspeth marvelling at the resilience of the human body. She had slept for no more than minutes at a time for days now, and on many occasions she found herself talking to an imaginary third member of their team, sharing her fears with him, only to come to her senses and realise that they were alone. Reality and dreaming intertwined.

She found the pain in her feet more difficult to cope with than the hallucinations. At first she had followed the golden rule of all long mountain excursions, which was to change your socks often and keep your feet dry; but that task quickly became impossible, and she had resorted to tightly lacing up her boots and ignoring the pain.

The rain passed overnight, and for an hour so did the clouds. Everything froze as the stars twinkled in the heavens, hard and cruel. A glaze of ice coated rocks that the previous day had run with water. The patter-patter, drip-drip of the storm gave way to silence as the frost locked the wall tightly up again.

Then the cloud returned, and with it came the snow.

'Wake up, Aleister,' she muttered, shaking the slumping form of her husband, inert on the ledge beside her.

Shadows rimmed his eyes. 'Let me sleep.'

'If you sleep, you'll die. It's getting much colder—and it's snowing. We cannot stay in this gully.'

He came to slowly, as if surfacing from a great depth. 'Yes, we should climb on.'

For once, Elspeth agreed with him. This bivouac, hacked from ice at one side of the gully they had been attempting to crawl up for the last day, would become unsafe if it snowed heavily. Avalanches—huge avalanches—would sweep through here from the upper face.

While she attempted to make a brew with their unreliable Primus, Crowley sorted the gear. The ropes, piled up on the ledge and used to insulate their bodies from the ice, had now frozen into a useless mass. He hacked at it with an axe for a while before throwing the implement down in the snow.

'If only we had access to the stores in the Ice Trap! Ropes, pitons, Pelton Rings, food …' He turned to look at her. 'How much food do we have left?'

'Enough.' Enough for what, she wondered?

'But only one second-rate rope, now that we've lost this one. Damn Jones, damn him to Hell.'

'We could go back down. Talk to him.'

The ghost of a smile. 'I don't think he would wish to talk to me.'

'You would kill us both out of pride?'

'This has always been about pride. Come on, let us get out of this infernal gully.'

*

Two full days of imprisonment had passed: two days in their cell that stank of death and the fear of death. As the rain turned to snow, blowing through the entrance between the icicles with every blast of wind, Jones huddled against the rock and tried not to think. The men no longer spoke much. It seemed that every conceivable subject of conversation had been exhausted long ago.

He often caught himself gazing at the wasted features of Simon Barkis. The thaw had not been kind to his face, drawing the skin tightly over the skull, sinking the eyes back into their sockets. Now snow had started to blow over the bodies again, providing them with some measure of dignity.

The icicles no longer creaked and fell down. Instead they grew by the hour, fed by the fresh snow in the unknown regions above the Ice Trap. Water ran over their surface; not the streams of the previous day, but a slow, regenerating trickle, adding layer on layer of ice.

Jones stood, hating his frailty. He climbed up to the ledge where the dead men lay. He needed to eat; time to break the taboo and pick through the stores for some food. Raeburn looked up with interest when he saw Jones move, but Collie remained motionless, head bowed to his lap.

Raeburn crawled up to join him. 'I don't want to feel guilty doing this. These men would have wanted us to make use of their provisions.'

Jones lifted Barkis' arm away from the knapsack where it rested. 'I agree. There is a difference between Crowley's intention of looting the corpses, and our need to help us survive. Isn't there?'

'A moral difference, aye.'

The drawstring proved stiff to open with frozen fingers. He delved into the sack while Raeburn busied himself trying to lift Holdstock's corpse away from the baggage beneath. His hand brushed something hard and angular—a piton, perhaps—and probed past to touch the soft wool of a sweater. That would help keep Collie warm a little while longer. He needed it the most.

'I've found a tin!' Raeburn cried.

Surprised at his own excitement, Jones pulled the sweater out of the bag. They compared trophies: an old jumper and a dented tin of jam. Not much, but it might make their imprisonment a little easier to bear.

He rummaged around in the bag. It produced a length of Manila rope, two pieces of bacon wrapped in brown paper that had survived tolerably well thanks to the cold, and several tins of beans. Raeburn discovered another sweater, a rotten loaf of bread, and an empty paraffin can. Underneath the knapsacks, a wealth of Pelton Rings and pitons lay amongst the remains of several ropes too damaged by frost and water to be of any use.

They looked at their treasures with a renewed sense of hope.

'It won't keep us alive for long, but it's something,' Raeburn said.

Jones felt thoughtful. 'They died before they could finish the last of their food. What killed them?'

'The cold.' Raeburn rattled the empty paraffin can. 'They ran out of fuel, and look at how poorly equipped they were for cold weather. They didn't even have mittens.'

'They never expected to have to sit out a storm. Travel light and all that. Holdstock was Mummery's pupil, and he always advocated a light pack.'

'He's dead too. Perhaps he was wrong.'

The best climbers of the age were all dead, or about to die. The new age of climbing would never dawn.

They woke Collie, who accepted the pullover gratefully, and together they warmed a can of beans over the stove.

'What has it all been for?' Raeburn said between mouthfuls. 'I believed in it more strongly than anyone, I think. The notion that climbing had no limits, I mean.'

'A failed experiment,' Collie replied as he ate. 'We have proven beyond any reasonable doubt that there are places where climbers cannot go. I allowed myself to be distracted by the enthusiasm of it all, but I stand by my earlier convictions. Our traditions and rules exist for good reasons.'

Such pessimism, Jones thought sadly. So much had been achieved, so many stern walls conquered by brave men and women. A world of exploration and possibility awaited; but if their deaths frightened people away from the steeper routes, it would all mean nothing. They would just be three fools who had taken on something too difficult for them. He wanted to inspire people to explore the world and not feel constrained by tradition, but instead he would become a symbol of stupidity. Eckenstein Alpine Equipment, whose reputation depended on the outcome of this expedition, would fail; Eckenstein himself would never be allowed to sell climbing gear again. The new-fangled gear would be blamed by the public.

It was all over, this grand experiment. Mountaineers would go back to being dragged up the Matterhorn's normal route by surly guides, the ice claw and short axe would be forgotten, and the north faces of the Alps would remain unexplored.

'If only we could get down safely, provide them with a little hope,' he thought out loud.

Raeburn, he noticed, was eyeing the icicles that continued to lengthen at the mouth of the cave.

'Perhaps if that icicle grows by another few feet, and maybe joins up with a few of its neighbours, we might just have a chance.'

*

Elspeth had been performing mental arithmetic to stay awake during that second night of frost, but her husband seemed determined to sleep. Their new bivouac, a miserable hole dug in powder snow high up the wall of the gully, seemed to provide even poorer shelter than the open slopes. It collected debris from powder slides as they swept the cliffs: unthreatening sloughs imitating the avalanches that thundered down the bed of the gully two hundred feet below.

They had failed to find a way out. Overhanging cliffs guarded the top, slopes of unstable powder snow prevented any way out at the sides, and if they split up they would lose each other in the mist. They had spent the day blundering about, blind and exhausted, hungry and at times only partly conscious. Aleister still refused to consider the possibility of going back down.

She looked sideways at him. Slumped forwards, straining against the rope securing him to the wall, he remained insensible. Snow covered his canvas smock, stuck to his eyebrows and beard. What would she do if he died? Neither of them could survive alone.

'Aleister,' she said, shaking his shoulder. 'Aleister, wake up!'

He flopped lifelessly, like a puppet. She felt a stab of alarm.

'Wake up! Wake up, damn you!'

At length he stirred. 'I am sleepy. Leave me alone.'

He sounded like a child, his voice slurred—giving up the fight. How remarkable, Elspeth thought, that she should prove to have more strength in her than the most driven man she had ever known.

'If I think you are sleeping again, I will hit you. Do you understand me?'

'Make him go away. I don't like how he watches me.'

She felt uneasy. At night, the wall howled and groaned, cracked and shifted; an eerie place of dangers both real and imaginary.

'Who is watching you?'

'Almer.'

'Almer is dead. You killed him.'

He shuddered, drawing his arms around his body, ice-crusted mittens gripping his sleeves. Elspeth wondered if he would recover some measure of sense in the morning. After a while she realised he had slumped forward again, so she hit him hard, and felt a little better.

*

The third day in the Ice Trap dawned foggy and still. Jones shifted, dislodging the snow that had settled on his shoulders and hat overnight. Puzzled by the complete lack of sound, it took him some moments to realise that the wind no longer blustered outside. The storm was over!

Instead, freezing mist enveloped the wall, coating everything in fog crystals. The world sparkled. Gemstone-encrusted statues of Raeburn and Collie slumped against the wall. Most importantly, the ice from above had formed a thick pillar that all but connected with the floor of the cave. Could it be climbed? Would it support three people?

'Wake up!' he shouted. 'We have a way out!'

Slowly, the others came back to life. Collie could do little until he had eaten some hot food, but Raeburn seemed excited by this new development, and crouched with Jones near the entrance of the cave, examining the structure.

'It's a hanging pillar,' Raeburn observed, his voice numbed from the cold. 'We will have to be very careful.'

'Can you lead it? It might be beyond my present powers.'

Raeburn looked doubtful. 'Maybe. We don't know what lies above, either.'

'There is a chimney that continues for some hundred and twenty feet,' Collie remarked in between mouthfuls of beans, 'and after that, an icefield. I saw it through the telescope from the hotel.'

'That settles it,' Jones said. He felt hope stir within him, an emotion he had not expected to be acquainted with again.

It did not take long to pack up their things. They decided to leave a great deal of equipment behind, taking just what they would need to get them safely off the mountain: their warm clothes, a little food, some ironmongery, and their least damaged rope. Jones felt weak from three days of sitting in freezing conditions without enough to eat and precious little sleep. He hardly felt up for a day of hard climbing at the limit of his powers. Professor Collie had fared even worse.

Nevertheless, this would be their only chance, and as Raeburn gingerly tapped the pick of his axe into a depression in the ice, Jones prayed that the pillar would hold.

CHAPTER TWENTY-ONE

PERDURABO

16th of June, 1897

W HEN RACHEL SAW the foot sticking out from under a rock, she thought her heart would stop. They had been searching the screes at the foot of the north face for over an hour now. Eckenstein took the lead, sweating in shirtsleeves and braces, poking and prodding amongst the rubble with his long ice axe. Inspector Warrington and their guide, Almer the Elder, took a higher line on the mountainside, roped together. If the Inspector saw any indignity in being tugged along on a short rope by a man twenty years his senior, he did not complain.

Rachel searched alone, trapped in her own private world of horror and worry. After three days locked in her hotel room with little news of the outside world, she had begged Warrington to release her, and eventually he had agreed. What further damage could she do, he had said, now that everyone was surely dead? All that remained was to find evidence of what had happened.

She stared at the severed limb. Its boot, still strapped to the frame of an ice claw, was partially crushed; stone dust tinged the skin grey. She could not bring herself to step towards it. Instead, she emitted a strangled cry.

Eckenstein came bounding over. 'What is it?'

She pointed at the foot, and he crouched over it, shielding his eyes from the sun as he examined the relic. Warrington and Almer made their way over.

'Swiss boot-nails,' Eckenstein remarked after a moment.

'Everyone uses Swiss nails,' Rachel said shakily.

'The claw isn't one of mine, anyway. Made by that fellow Bhend, I expect.'

Not Jones, then. Rachel found herself able to breathe again, and she gulped down lungfuls of mountain air, feeling faint from the heat. She took a tentative step towards Eckenstein and the discovery.

'Stay back,' he warned. 'This is not a sight for your eyes. Go back to the path. Warrington and I will look for more … parts.'

A cry rang out from the others. Warrington stooped over something, then stood up abruptly, removing his hat. This time Eckenstein could not prevent her, and together they ran up the sliding piles of scree towards the site.

The two men stood over an object partly buried by dust and gravel: a tattered sack of tweed, suggestive of angular forms beneath, hardly recognisable as the human being it had once been. With a stab of shock Rachel saw part of a flattened skull protruding to one side of the remains. Wispy hair stirred in the wind.

'So this is what has become of my son,' Christian Almer said in an anguished whisper.

Nobody spoke. Words seemed inadequate to express the horror of the discovery. Rachel felt her hopes for Jones fade.

'I will go down and organise a bigger search party,' Warrington said at length. 'Herr Almer, you have my deepest regret that your son has died as a result of this foolishness.'

'It was his job. It is a risk we guides run with every climb.'

'Nevertheless, I am sure we will discover that Crowley was responsible.' Now he looked at Rachel, his shrewd features softening for a moment. 'This does not mean that Jones is down here too. He could still be up there, perhaps even alive.'

'Please don't. I know what the chances are.'

Warrington looked at her for a moment longer, then shook his head. 'Such a senseless waste.'

The implied criticism wounded her. She knew all about Warrington's views on mountaineering, and now that the sport had produced a tragedy on such a scale, perhaps his opinion would gain momentum with the public. In the wake of the 1865 Matterhorn disaster, the Queen had wanted to ban climbing outright. It could happen.

Eckenstein let out an explosive sigh. 'Right then. Warrington, go down and fetch your policemen. Herr Almer, perhaps you had better accompany the gentleman in case he gets lost.'

Warrington did not smile at the attack. 'I am quite capable of retracing my steps, thank you.'

'Nevertheless, you are a complete idiot when it comes to mountains, and we wouldn't want you to lose the path, would we? Miss Elliot, you shall accompany them. I will stay here and see what else I can discover.'

'Let me stay,' Rachel said on impulse. 'Perhaps Jones and the others are climbing back down. I want to be here to meet them.'

In her heart she knew that she waited for a dead man, who had once loved her; but she could not bring herself to leave until she knew for certain.

Eckenstein looked at her oddly. 'Very well. Inspector, would you be so good as to send a blanket and some food back up with your men, just in case Miss Elliot decides to stop for the night?'

'The young lady has courage,' Warrington said after a long pause. 'I would not want to stay in this ghastly place for a moment longer than necessary. Good day to you.'

He glanced up at the Eigerwand. It still glowered down at them, pale under its new coating of snow and ice; but for the first time in days the sun pierced through and burned away the last of the mist clinging to the mountain.

*

Jones planted an axe in the soft powder on the other side of the snow ridge, and slumped against it, exhausted. Never in his life had he felt so drained. Were it not for the new hope that escape had fired in each of them, he would happily give up now and drift into unconsciousness. Only Rachel's face remained clear in his mind. All other things from his life before the Eiger — the taste of food, or how it felt to be warm and dry — faded into a jumble of vague impressions.

The Eiger would change each of them drastically. Collie would likely never climb a difficult route again. Raeburn, he suspected, might take perverse delight in pushing his limits further than ever, once the fear had been forgotten. His lead up the hanging pillar had been the most tense moment of each of their lives, both possibilities co-existing for fifteen frightening minutes: collapse, and the dashing of all hopes, or success, and the slender chance of life. Raeburn had cried for joy as he squirmed his way up the ice-choked slot beyond.

Jones wondered what had become of Crowley and Elspeth. Had they gone for the top and died in an avalanche, or perhaps found some safe place to sit out the worst of it? Could they even now be dusting themselves off and thinking about making a second attempt? Surely Elspeth would do her best to sabotage Crowley's effort. Perhaps the race was still on.

Just as these thoughts passed through his confused brain, he saw something move in the vast bowl of white on the other side of the ridge.

The arête where he now rested seemed to be a natural division between two regions of the face: a steep icefield behind him, and a snow-filled combe just ahead. The combe, he realised, continued from the ice gully passing below and right of the Ice Trap. That must be the route Crowley had selected, but no escape from the bowl seemed obvious, now that the cloud was gone. If Crowley and Elspeth had come up that way in the storm, they would surely be dead. Such places attracted huge avalanches.

Yet again, a speck of movement. Without his spectacles, he could not see the cause of it.

He felt a tug on their precious rope, damaged by water and frost but all they had left. He remembered the others waiting for him, and after taking a turn around the shaft of his ice axe, he brought them up to the stance on the snow ridge. Even the action of belaying exhausted him and he had to stop every few seconds to draw deep, ragged breaths.

Collie appeared beside him, a macabre figure of crusted ice. He grinned.

'You look clapped out, dear boy.'

'I don't know how we're going to get down.'

'The important thing is that we are out of that cave.'

They no longer spoke of Holdstock and Barkis. The storm finally buried them with snow, blown through the entrance. The mountain had taken them for its own.

Jones pointed into the snowy combe. 'Your eyes are better than mine, Professor. Tell me what you see.'

'A great deal of snow. Hold on, there is something else … I cannot quite make it out.'

'I suppose we'll see when we get there. That gully is our way down.'

*

Elspeth hit Aleister again. She had endured almost two days sitting in this miserable scrape in the ice, fighting to keep her husband alive, hoping for some change in either the weather or his condition. Now that the weather seemed to be finally improving, she no longer knew what to do. She doubted she had the strength left to go either up or down.

Snow piled up around her shoulders. It melted slowly, trickling through the carapace of ice that had formed over her jacket, through the saturated wool, down to her undergarments and chilled body beneath. All sensation had vanished from her feet a long time ago. Useless lumps clad in expensive boots and ice claws swung at the end of each leg. Her hands nearly suffered the same fate, but she took her mittens off to chew her knuckles through the fingerless gloves she wore beneath, and in this way kept some circulation going. After a while she had rammed Aleister's hands into her armpits to keep them warm, and spent a lot of time hugging the insensible man, trying to give some warmth to his fading body.

Why did she fight to save him? Sometimes clarity cut through her delusions, and she remembered all the pain he had caused her, the people he had plotted to destroy. She tried to convince herself that she was keeping him alive for selfish reasons, that all chance of her own survival died with him if he succumbed to the cold. However, the truth was that despite her own crimes, her natural instincts craved the preservation of life. She could not let anyone else die.

She could see every detail of the valley from her vantage point at almost ten thousand feet. Away to the left, the detritus of industry surrounded Kleine Scheidegg's hotels. Straight down, beyond the snows, the chalets of Alpiglen lurked in the mountain's shadow. In a few hours night would fall, and she would look down on the field of stars winking back to life, one by one, in the sleeping world below. She wondered if this was what death would be like: an awareness that existed in this place for the rest of time, as her body melted into the mountain and her spirit became part of the creaking and groaning of the Eiger. She could no longer tell where her body ended and the ice began.

Then she saw the wraiths approach.

Three ragged ghosts waded through the snow towards her, thrusting ice axes into the pack to secure themselves. The man in front raised a hand in greeting. She tried to return the gesture, but found that she could not move her arm.

Time passed. Now the figures stood in front of her, and through the haunted expressions and ice-plated clothes she recognised something from a former life. If they had names, she could not remember them.

'Elspeth? Good God, are you alive?'

'I'm frozen.'

'It's all right,' the second wraith said, 'we can get you down—and you too, Crowley—I can see you squirming there.'

With effort, she turned her head to look at her husband. He looked dead, a stiff corpse buried in the ice; then a limb convulsed, and snow fell from his hood. He looked up at the newcomers with a face ruined by frost.

'Can you stand?' Jones said. She recognised him now.

'I'll try.'

He helped her up. After several attempts, she found herself standing unsteadily in the snow, not yet trusting her sense of balance. Her body resisted being pulled back from its comfortable slide towards death. She no longer felt numbed and at peace; fire coursed through her body as limbs unfolded and ice cracked away from her skin. The sense of cold came back to her. Were it not for a swig of tea from Raeburn's flask, she would have collapsed and probably never risen again.

So, she could stand, and move her arms. Perhaps there was some hope.

While the others attended to her husband, Jones stepped forward and hugged her. He smelled of tobacco and old sweat, but it was Jones, the man who had made her want to become a better person. She hugged him back, and they stood there on the Eigerwand draped in ropes and clanking with metalwork, glad beyond words that they had found each other again.

'Do you remember our climb on Ben Nevis?' Jones said in her ear. 'Each of us caked in snow, just like this.'

She tried to smile. 'No warm observatory to take refuge in this time.'

He pointed down the gully, towards the sunlit fields far below. 'Less than a day's climbing to warmth and safety. Do you have a usable rope?'

'It's not much good. Our main rope froze.'

'Ours too. All right. Elspeth, we can do this together. We can get down.'

She found herself believing in him, the handsome man with the gaunt smile. Had he not been spoken for she could so easily love him. She would never love her own husband again. Aleister squatted in the snow, tapping the side of his face where his cheek had frozen and turned black.

'You should leave me here,' he said awkwardly, unable to correctly form words.

They all turned to look at him in surprise. Aleister Crowley stared back at them, his once striking face a mess: blackened skin, bleeding lips, beard a lump of ice. Only his penetrating gaze reminded them of the person he had been before. Elspeth wondered if the Eiger had beaten the arrogance and cruelty out of him. Did he still think himself immortal? The Eiger had done its best to kill him—just like the avalanche on the Matterhorn—but it had failed. Aleister Crowley endured. She hoped her husband would at least learn some humility from the experience.

'We can all get down,' Jones repeated firmly. 'Now is not the time for misplaced heroics, especially not from you.'

'I'm sorry,' he whispered.

'Save your apology for when we get down. Raeburn, you and I will rope up with Crowley to keep him out of mischief. Professor, would you be kind enough to attend to the lady?'

Collie bowed. 'Madam Crowley, I am once again your servant.'

Elspeth caught the eye of her rescuer, and Jones smiled back at her, confident and happy again at last. He had won.

*

Sleep evaded Rachel that night. She bedded down on the flattest patch of gravel she could find, with a stone for a pillow and a blanket tucked under her against the cold ground. Part of her believed she didn't deserve to find any rest when the others had suffered so much.

The mountain watched her lie there. A pointed wedge blocking out half the stars, it glowed in the moonlight. Occasionally she heard the cliff shift and move: a rattle of stones here, the groan of ice there. Sometimes she thought she saw a candle's flame dancing high above, but could not be certain. Each time she sat upright and tried to get a better look at it, the phantom light vanished.

Day came, and with it dozens of Swiss policemen with their long poles and marker flags. They had recovered the remains of Ulrich Almer and taken him back down to the village for burial; now they searched for more corpses. Five people remained unaccounted for.

This would be remembered as one of the worst disasters in the history of Alpinism. The total losses stood at eight, including Holdstock and Barkis; never before had so many of the best and most beloved climbers died in such a grisly manner. Rachel wondered if mountaineering as they knew it could survive. She predicted a long silence falling over the Alps, as climbers grew too timid to try anything but the easiest routes. The general public would once again form the impression that to climb was to tempt death. A century of progress would be wasted, and the man Rachel loved would be dead.

She sat on a rock next to a stream, alone with her memories of a man she now felt certain would not come back to her. The sound of the torrent—endless, unchanging—helped to remind her that everything was transient, and that in time she would forget this moment. A tuft of Edelweiss, poking between two rocks, brightened the desolation. She realised then that the mountain was not an ogre, but rather a function of the natural rhythms and laws of the universe: at most a symbol of human futility, or perhaps a canvas onto which the brave and stupid painted their own dreams. The Eiger, when stripped of human baggage, meant nothing and would continue to mean nothing until the glaciers advanced once again and ground the mighty peak to a smear of gravel. The men who had died to conquer the north face would be forgotten, just as every human memory and emotion would in time be forgotten. She looked up at the sky and marvelled at the glorious futility of it all.

The sound of Eckenstein's approach jolted her out of introspection. He advanced up the scree path, hands in pockets, eyes to the ground: a dejected man.

'Sleep well?' he inquired.

'Not in the least. You?'

He sat down on the rock next to her. 'I searched through the night but found no further traces. Perhaps there is hope yet.'

Rachel looked back up at the Eiger, the thing that would outlast them all. 'I don't think so. I think they are all dead.'

She wondered why she was unable to cry for him.

Eckenstein put an arm around her shoulder and drew her into a tentative hug. It lasted only for a second before he released her.

'I'm sorry Jones got involved in this.'

'Me too.' Rachel felt touched by Eckenstein's attempt to comfort her, however clumsily. 'I think it is what he was born to do, though.'

'Anyway,' Eckenstein said after a moment, stepping away, 'I must find Warrington. I gather he is keen to get back to England—as am I, truth be told. I have never been so eager to leave the Alps in my life.'

*

The first sign of movement on the Eigerwand came in the form of an avalanche of stones, away towards the snow patch below the wet bivouac cave. Rachel looked up eagerly, as she always did when the cliff made any sound. A tongue of dirty brown stained the snow. Nothing else moved, so she returned to her sorrowful contemplation of the flowers near her feet.

She heard another sound, this time more like the clatter of metalwork. She stood and gazed up at the mountain, shading her eyes with a hand. Something moved! There, on the scree just beneath the snow, something moved …

'Eckenstein!' she shouted. 'Eckenstein, someone is up there!'

Heads turned amongst the search party. Eckenstein stood with Warrington and one of the Swiss officers some distance away.

'It's just an avalanche,' he shouted back.

She looked up again, not willing to doubt her new hope. Figures walked through the heat haze that rose from the rocks … or perhaps she had imagined them; now she couldn't find them again. Stones shifted with a rattling echo.

'Ahoy there!' came a faint cry from above. 'Ahoy!'

Her heart raced. Without thinking, she picked up her axe and started to run. The stones slid beneath her boots, trying to drag her back down the mountain. At times she had to crawl on her hands and knees, and soon little craglets started appearing here and there, requiring the use of hands for assistance.

She paused to breathe. Five ghostly figures staggered towards her, dressed in rags, bearded and gaunt. They had survived!

Behind her, she could hear shouts as the Swiss police made preparations for the arrest of Aleister Crowley.

In moments Rachel stood face to face with the survivors. To her shock, she could hardly recognise them. Collie, always a thin man, now looked like a skeleton; Raeburn stood tall but had a haunted look in his eyes; and dear Jones … he had lost his spectacles and cap, and a bruise darkened one eye, but the confident expression was the one she knew and loved. He had the look of a man who had learned a valuable lesson about himself and gained back his self-respect.

He stepped forward towards her, festooned with bits of rope and the shredded remains of a tweed jacket, blunted claws still attached to his boots. She dropped her axe and ran to him, then hugged this wild man of the mountain so tightly that he winced in pain. He felt thinner than she remembered.

'Are you injured?'

'Just my rib. My God, I never thought I would see you again. Are you real?'

Rachel took his face in her hands, ignoring the grime and the stubble that still had bits of ice clinging to it. She stood on her toes and kissed him. After a moment of surprise he kissed her back, and as they relaxed into the embrace her only thought was that she would never let him go again.

Eventually they broke apart and stood close together, Rachel holding both of his hands. They smiled the disbelieving smiles of two people who had found each other against the greatest odds imaginable.

She wondered if she should tell him that she loved him. He didn't say anything himself, perhaps too full of emotion to give words to how he felt, so instead they just looked at each other and enjoyed the moment. There would be plenty of time for talking later. For now she just felt overwhelmingly glad that he had come back alive.

Awareness of the world gradually returned, and she realised that the others were watching her, all of them smiling. Crowley and his wife sat on a rock some way apart. Elspeth looked pleased for them both but also wistful, as if she still felt something for Jones. Crowley just looked utterly defeated, slumped against his wife like a man who waited for death. He didn't show his face.

Warrington and Eckenstein now appeared with a cohort of policemen.

'Which of you is Aleister Crowley?' Inspector Warrington demanded, out of breath from the climb.

Crowley raised his head with great effort. Rachel gasped at his appearance. Now the ugliness of his character would be visible for all to see, instead of hiding behind his charm and good looks. He would be forever marked as a monster. She felt sick when she imagined being married to him.

'I am Crowley,' he rasped.

Warrington nodded to two of the Swiss officers, who moved forward with handcuffs. Eckenstein stopped them. He looked horrified at the condition of his old friend.

'I don't think they will be necessary, Inspector. Look at him. He needs medical treatment.'

Warrington stepped around Eckenstein. 'Keep out of this. He is my prisoner. Damn it, I've chased the blackguard for long enough.'

'Might I be permitted to speak?'

Everyone turned to look at Crowley. He stared up at them with his destroyed face.

'Do not judge me,' he continued, breathing with difficulty between words. 'I did what my will dictated. Jones did the same. He won this time, but I have endured. I always endure.'

Jones looked at him with pity. 'You're wrong. You may be alive, but you're powerless now. You cannot threaten us any more.' Now he stepped towards Inspector Warrington. 'I insist that your first priority must be a doctor for Crowley and Elspeth. It's a miracle they are still alive.'

Warrington looked at Jones for a long moment, taking in his appearance, the evidence of the torment they had all survived. Finally he said, 'Very well. It goes against my instincts to show any mercy to this creature, but I think it is evident that he has suffered enough for the time being—as have you all. You have my gratitude for your services to justice.'

'Services to justice? Inspector, all we have done is rescue our comrades. If you believe for one moment that my priority during the storm was to deliver Crowley to you, then you are a fool. Preserving life was the only consideration.'

Warrington smiled stiffly. 'Yes, well. That may be so, but the result is all that matters.' He nodded at the Swiss police. 'Take him to the physician, and the girl too. They are both under arrest.'

Elspeth struggled to her feet. Her compact frame, previously bursting with energy and youth, now seemed a little deflated; nevertheless, she did not appear to be severely injured. A sprig of black hair escaped from one side of her hood.

'I thought you promised to protect me if I helped you?' she demanded.

The Inspector looked down on her with distaste. 'Ah, was there some sort of agreement?'

'You damn well know there was—!'

Jones stepped between them, his ragged appearance contrasting with Warrington's freshly pressed clothing and trimmed moustache. It was like a beggar standing up to a City gent, Rachel thought: a fitting metaphor for the egalitarianism of the mountains, a principle that Warrington's kind failed to understand. In that moment she felt a fierce love for all the good that came out of climbing. What else could bring people of all classes together on such equal terms? In the real world climbers might be divided by the walls of class just as surely as everyone else, but when they shared a rope all differences vanished and they were judged by their true human qualities.

'I distinctly remember an agreement,' Jones said quietly. 'You will protect Elspeth, or I will never let this matter lie. Ever.'

Warrington paused for a moment, no doubt considering his options. As a Detective Inspector, he could easily have Jones imprisoned and put out of harm's way, but was it worth it just to break his promise to Elspeth? In the end his resolve faltered and he took a step back.

'It doesn't matter. I will need to question Elspeth anyway, but you have my word that she will be free to go after making her statement.'

The police departed with the Crowley couple. Aleister shuffled along with head bowed, but Elspeth glanced back at the group: a regretful look, Rachel thought, or maybe a last plea for forgiveness. Despite her jealousy, Rachel felt sorry for the girl.

Now Jones beckoned to them all—his two Eiger comrades, Rachel, and Eckenstein—and they sat on the flat rocks on top of a craglet, looking down to the green meadows below. Rachel sat very close to Jones and linked her arm in his.

Collie gave a drawn-out sigh, as if finally allowing himself to relax after the hardships behind them. 'So that is the end of that. I intend to sell my ice claws and go back to pottering around in the Cuillin until I am old. I'm sure twenty more ascents of Pinnacle Ridge will reward.'

Jones nodded. 'After that experience, I can hardly blame you. Besides, sunshine and good company on Skye sound heavenly. Rachel will come with us, won't you?'

'I think we had better keep away from mountains for a while.'

He gave a mischievous smile in reply to that. 'But why? I can no more keep away from mountains than I can keep away from you. Mountains are in my blood.'

'Provided your blood stays where it belongs and not spilt all over the mountains, I will have no complaints.'

He laughed. Then: 'What about you, Raeburn?'

Raeburn drained his flask of tea and leaned back against the rock. 'It's the Himalaya for me. Another look at Nanga Parbat, perhaps. This isn't the end for the progressive school.'

Eckenstein slapped his thigh with a palm, and laughed loudly. 'A customer! One customer; perhaps just enough to keep my business going for a little while longer. I thought this Eiger nonsense would be the end of me.'

'It was very nearly the end for us all,' Jones reminded him. 'I intend to hand in my notice right away, incidentally.'

'Oh.' Eckenstein looked crestfallen. 'Of course. I suppose you'll be wanting a more dependable career if you are to start a family.'

Rachel blushed and gripped Jones' arm even tighter. He didn't look at her, but responded by squeezing her hand. She knew in that moment that the Eiger had changed him. Always Jones had pushed himself, sought out danger for the joy and prestige of it, but for the first time in his life, he had someone else to think about instead of just himself. She didn't want to be a burden to him or diminish his reputation. If she could share his life, maybe moderate his wildness a little, she would be happy. Perhaps love would make the Only Genuine Jones open his eyes and understand that the greatest joy of all had nothing to do with mountains.

Above them, the Eiger smiled in sunshine, a thing of beauty once again.

THE END

Many a little hand
Glanced like a touch of sunshine on the rocks ;
Many a light foot shone like a jewel set
In the dark crags.

TENNYSON, 1850.

JOIN THE CONVERSATION

If you have enjoyed this book, check out the author's website at **www.alexroddie.com.** Alex keeps a regular blog where he discusses the world of Jones and his contemporaries, from the slums of Victorian London to the snow-clad heights of Scotland, and everywhere in between!

Alex can also be found on Facebook at **https://www.facebook.com/ alexroddiewriter**, or on Twitter **@alex_roddie**. The hashtag **#TheOnly GenuineJones** is also used for discussion about this book. Look for his author page on Amazon where his other work can be found, including the novella *Crowley's Rival*, a prequel to this story.

Lastly, if you want to support the hard work of this author, please tell your friends about this book and consider writing a review for Amazon. They really do make a difference!

Please turn the page for historical notes on how the imaginary world of this story differs from true events.

HISTORICAL NOTES

This is very much a 'what if' story. All events taking place after the 24th of July, 1896, are imaginary and based purely on speculation.

In reality, the north face of the Matterhorn was not climbed until 1931. The north face of the Eiger was climbed in 1938 after several failed attempts, some of which ended in tragedy. Both of these climbs were years ahead of their time and had a profound impact on subsequent developments. In my story I have made slight changes to the Eiger's topography; although many of the features described have counterparts in reality, others (notably the Ice Trap) do not exist on the real mountain. Accepted names for features on the Eigerwand, including the White Spider, the Hinterstoisser Traverse, and the Swallow's Nest, date from a period after 1897 so were not used. The high point reached by Jones, above the Ice Trap, corresponds roughly with the bottom of the Second Icefield.

For more information on the Eiger, including a detailed account of the 1936 disaster which partially inspired some events in *The Only Genuine Jones*, Heinrich Harrer's classic book *The White Spider* is highly recommended.

Many of the British climbs featuring in the story were not climbed in reality until much later. These climbs include S.C. Gully, Slanting Gully, the Orion Face, Nirvana Wall, and the Church Door Buttress. Most of them, however, were objects of speculation for the pioneers and I believe they may have been climbed much earlier if equipment and techniques had allowed.

The revolutionary climbing technique of using crampons with front points and short ice axes with curved picks did not achieve popularity until the late 1960s, although there are hints some climbers may have experimented with the method long before this point. Similarly, other climbing hardware mentioned was not in reality used until the 1920s at the earliest. In fact, Oscar Eckenstein was a key figure in the early development of modern crampons; his 1908 design is substantially similar to the "ice claw" featured in this story, although front points were not added until 1929. Eckenstein also invented the first widely used short ice axe.

Although some young climbers had begun to complain about the conservatism of their elders by the mid-1890s, in reality climbers were always an eccentric and ambitious bunch compared to the majority of

Britons. I have exaggerated the divide between the two schools of mountaineering thought for the purposes of my narrative, as I believe the introduction of such radical equipment and techniques would have polarised the climbing community. However, the phenomenon of the "new mountaineer" certainly existed, albeit in a less dramatic manner, and was characterised by the deeds of men like A.F. Mummery, O.G. Jones, and Aleister Crowley. Guideless climbing, and ascents of severe routes for the sake of difficulty alone, were two of the developments that emerged during the 1890s.

O.G. Jones worked on two guidebooks during his lifetime: *Rock-Climbing in the English Lake District*, and *Rock-Climbing in North Wales*. In my fictional history he published the first in 1896 and the second in 1897; in real life he published his Lakeland guidebook at the end of 1897 and was still working on his Welsh book at the time of his death in 1899. He was elected to the Alpine Club in 1892. He remained Physics Master at the City of London School all his life, a position he fulfilled with great ability and enthusiasm. Although a friendly man and a keen climber, his penchant for self-publicity, exaggeration and lack of caution made him several enemies. His feud with Aleister Crowley is based on true events although I have increased the scale of the argument.

I've also used artistic license with the character of Aleister Crowley. Although without doubt an odd young man in the mid-1890s and an astounding solo climber, he wasn't really quite as wicked or talented as I have portrayed him here. Nevertheless, I don't think any of the situations I have placed Crowley in are entirely out of character for the man who said that "do what thou wilt shall be the whole of the Law."

The characters of Thomas Holdstock, Simon Barkis, Elspeth Mornshaw, and Rachel Elliot are entirely fictional.

ACKNOWLEDGEMENTS

I would like to thank the following people for their support, assistance, and advice over the years it has taken to complete this project.

Firstly, my partner Hannah. I met her when I was struggling to finish the first draft of this book, and over the next two years she provided much more than encouragement. She read my work with a critical eye and helped me avoid falling prey to procrastination. I could not have written this without her support.

When I first met Susan Fletcher I was a little intimidated by the idea of a real author being so normal and approachable, but we soon became friends and she has been the best mentor a fledgling writer could wish for. She has guided my steps, provided recommendations and introductions, and most importantly of all, believed in my work.

My brother James has always been an excellent critic, but he also deserves the double honour of also being the best mountaineer I've ever climbed with. He's fearless and bold, yet also thinks like me and is willing to throw the guidebook away. When I cannot climb an obstacle, James is sure to overcome it. The lessons I have learned from climbing with James have found their way into this story.

My parents Ian and Anita have supported me at every stage of this journey, and their belief in my work has sustained me through many difficult moments.

My editor, Clare Danek, deserves special thanks for her meticulous proofreading and correction of the manuscript.

Jamie Bankhead and Isi Oakley both helped shape my time in Scotland by showing me what the Highlands have to offer and making me a better and safer climber. This was often a painful experience but you both deserve a lot of credit for your patience!

A number of people helped out by reading drafts in various stages of completion and providing feedback. Others provided guidance in other areas but you all contributed towards the final result, and I couldn't have done it without you. Special thanks go to Paul Blanchard, Erik Brunskill, Jamie Hageman, Chris Highcock, Dawn Hollis, Glyn Hughes of the Alpine Club Library in London, Mike Lates, Nicholas Livesey, Andrew Moore,

Rachael Murphy, Mike Peacock, Lauren Richardson, Gordon Stainforth, Toby Stainton, Darren Tuffs, Clint Warren, and the staff of the Bibliothèque Communale in Zermatt.

Finally I must also thank my friends and former colleagues at the Clachaig Inn. 2008 to 2011 were brilliant years that helped form this story. *'Check on!'*

BIBLIOGRAPHY

I hope I have inspired the reader to learn more about the history of mountaineering. In this bibliography I have included some of the titles I have found useful, and I believe they will be of interest to anyone wishing to study the subject further.

Baedeker, K. (1891), *Switzerland and the adjacent portions of Italy, Savoy, and the Tyrol: Handbook for Travellers*. Karl Baedeker.

Crocket, K. & Richardson, S. (2009), *Ben Nevis: Britain's Highest Mountain* (2nd. ed.) Scottish Mountaineering Trust.

Dent, C.T. et al (1892), *The Badminton Library of Sports and Pastimes: Mountaineering*. Longmans, Green & Co.

Hankinson, A. (2004), *The Mountain Men*. Mara Books.

Hankinson, A. (2005), *The First Tigers*. Mara Books.

Harrer, H. (2005), *The White Spider*. Harper Perennial.

Hutchinson, R. (2006), *Aleister Crowley: The Beast Demystified*. Mainstream Publishing.

Rébuffat, G. (1963), *On Snow and Rock*. Nicholas Kaye.

Rey, G. (1946), *The Matterhorn*. Basil Blackwell.

Thompson, S. (2010), *Unjustifiable Risk? The Story of British Climbing*. Cicerone.

Waller, M. (2007), *A Lakeland Climbing Pioneer: John Wilson Robinson of Whinfell Hall*. Bookcase.

Whymper, E. (1897), *A Guide to Zermatt and the Matterhorn*. John Murray.

Young, G.W. (1933), *On High Hills: Memories of the Alps*. Methuen & Co.

CPSIA information can be obtained at www.ICGtesting.com
Printed in the USA
BVOW032243200213

313841BV00001B/56/P